EDDA

CONOR KOSTICK

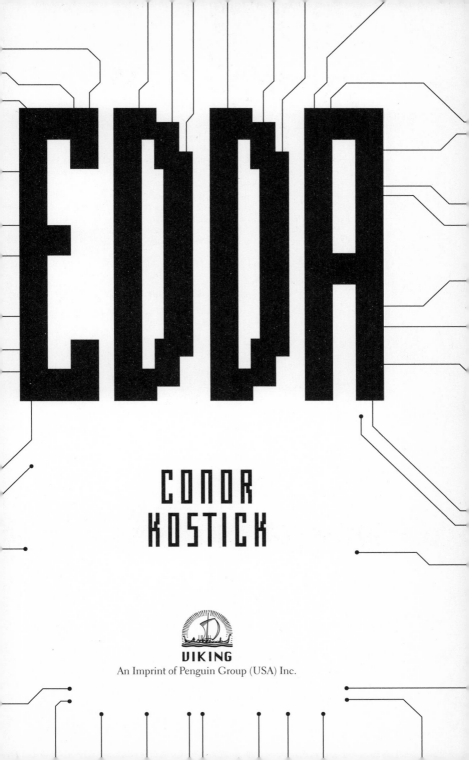

VIKING

An Imprint of Penguin Group (USA) Inc.

VIKING

Published by Penguin Group
Penguin Young Readers Group, 345 Hudson Street, New York, New York 10014, U.S.A.
Penguin Group (Canada), 90 Eglinton Avenue East, Suite 700, Toronto, Ontario, Canada M4P 2Y3
(a division of Pearson Penguin Canada Inc.)
Penguin Books Ltd, 80 Strand, London WC2R 0RL, England
Penguin Ireland, 25 St Stephen's Green, Dublin 2, Ireland (a division of Penguin Books Ltd)
Penguin Group (Australia), 250 Camberwell Road, Camberwell, Victoria 3124, Australia
(a division of Pearson Australia Group Pty Ltd)
Penguin Books India Pvt Ltd, 11 Community Centre, Panchsheel Park, New Delhi – 110 017, India
Penguin Group (NZ), 67 Apollo Drive, Rosedale, Auckland 0632, New Zealand
(a division of Pearson New Zealand Ltd.)
Penguin Books (South Africa) (Pty) Ltd, 24 Sturdee Avenue, Rosebank,
Johannesburg 2196, South Africa

Penguin Books Ltd, Registered Offices: 80 Strand, London WC2R 0RL, England

First published in Ireland by The O'Brien Press Ltd., Dublin, 2011
Published in agreement with The O'Brien Press Ltd.

First published in the United States of America in 2011 by Viking,
a member of Penguin Group (USA) Inc.

1 3 5 7 9 10 8 6 4 2

LIBRARY OF CONGRESS CATALOGING-IN-PUBLICATION DATA
Kostick, Conor, date–
Edda / Conor Kostick.
p. cm.
Sequel to: Saga.
Summary: In the virtual world of Edda, ruler Scanthax decides he wants
to invade another virtual world, embroiling the universes of Edda, Saga,
and Epic in war, with only three teenagers to try to restore peace.
ISBN 978-0-670-01218-3
[1. Fantasy games—Fiction. 2. Role playing—Fiction. 3. Video
games—Fiction. 4. War—Fiction. 5. Science fiction.] I. Title.
PZ7.K85298Ed 2011
[Fic]—dc22
2011003000

Printed in U.S.A.   Set in Electra

Books by Conor Kostick

Epic

Saga

Edda

CONTENTS

Lord Scanthax's map of the known worlds:

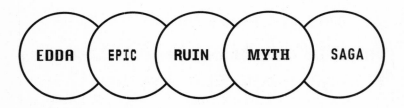

Chapter 1
How to Motivate
a Princess

"When the humans *abandoned us, there were almost a thousand lords and ladies who were determined to win control of Edda. One of the least noted of them, residing in an obscure mountain-covered domain, was Lord Scanthax."*

Ambassador and Princess were alone in the darkened viewing room, looking at a large screen on which a broadcast was playing. The screen was currently showing an illustration: a physical map of the world of Edda, rather poorly drawn by modern standards. And as the slightly patronizing voice continued its "history," the image zoomed in on the peninsula under discussion. Having seen the film hundreds of times, Ambassador looked tiredly at the girl beside him and was about to speak, but she anticipated this with a slight frown and shake of her head, concentrating on the story.

Boredom was a sensation that Ambassador could tolerate, but for the last hour he had also been experiencing a disturbing upsurge of an even more unpalatable emotion. The particular combination of guilt and sadness that troubled him was so unfamiliar that it took Ambassador a while to name the feeling. It was pity. He pitied Penelope, the poor human girl whose avatar, Princess, sat beside him. Pity was not an emotion that served any practical purpose and Ambassador hoped that it would soon subside.

"Theoretically, all lordships were of equal value. What Lord Scanthax lost in good agricultural lands he gained in minerals and a strong defensive position. But in the wild scramble for survival that followed the departure of the humans, Lord Scanthax would certainly have been overwhelmed but for the assistance of a brave and clever little human girl. Penelope was his secret and he deserved to have her. For, alone of all the lords, Scanthax had devoted precious time and energy to the human world. There he discovered a little baby had been left behind at the time of the exodus."

The film cut away from the map of Lord Scanthax's domain to a black-and-white recording taken from the perspective of a robot in the human world. It was leaning over a small cot in which a baby was crying. A moment later, however, when the robot produced a bottle of milk, the baby's shrieks were replaced by a gentle sucking sound. At this point Penelope paused the film.

"This is supposed to be the moment I was found?" There was a skeptical note in the girl's voice and Ambassador was hesitant.

"You doubt it?" he asked her in return.

"Well, it's bloody convenient that the robot had a bottle of milk on it, don't you think?"

"Yes, indeed."

The princess avatar was looking up at him through a fringe of long, wavy purple hair, clearly waiting for a more satisfactory response. She was becoming very difficult to deal with. A fifteen-year-old human caused no end of trouble in comparison with a hundred-year-old enemy diplomat.

"Well. This film was made a long time ago, to teach you the history of Lord Scanthax in a way that made sense when you were nine."

"It doesn't make sense now."

"I suspect that scene was a reconstruction."

"Exactly. Which raises the question, what did the original footage look like?"

"Perhaps there was none."

"Don't you know?" She was skeptical again; it was a tone of voice Ambassador was becoming more and more familiar with. The mistrust it expressed was most troubling.

"Would you like me to check?"

"Yes. Find the earliest true footage of me as a baby, please." Penelope signaled for the film to resume.

"Princess?"

"Hush."

"But you must have watched this so often that it cannot possibly interest you now." There was something unhealthy about Penelope's renewed perusal of the documentary, and in any case, Ambassador was eager to divert her energies to the new and urgent project that Lord Scanthax had assigned her.

"The first few years were the most anxious for Lord Scanthax. He sought peace with his neighbors—in the main by giving them favorable trading agreements—and devoted all his resources to building wooden defenses across the mountain passes, along with the soldiers to occupy them. This chain of forts would have been no deterrent to a serious invasion by lords whose fruitful lands and early income had allowed for the creation of strong armies in the first few years. But, aided by the construction of dedicated diplomatic units, Lord Scanthax managed to avert such a disaster by offering timely gifts and by stirring up conflict among his rivals."

This part of the film was mildly interesting to Ambassador, for it showed some of the early diplomatic units: crude male and female humanoids whose gowns and capes identified them as having a non-military function. His sense of being had evolved from one of these early diplomats, and Ambassador still had fragmentary recollections of early missions from that era.

"At last, though, Lord Scanthax's dedication to the human child bore fruit. At the age of six Penelope scripted her first object: a red ball."

Here the film showed a little human girl in a play area, monitored by two robots. It made Ambassador wince to see how grimy the child looked; how pathetic were her rough wooden toy animals scattered around her on the floor, and how crude was the simple smock that she wore. Inside his own world, Edda, Lord Scanthax could give Penelope anything she wanted, but in the human world every task required enormous resources. Right now, her avatar was wearing a crimson ball gown; a diamond tiara glittered in her hair; while beautiful flashes of blue came from Princess's sapphire earrings and necklace. The avatar lived in a castle more grandiose than any human could have ever known and its enormous scale made the scenes from the playpen seem all the more shameful. The film could even be misinterpreted. Despite the fact that they had explained it to her often enough, might Penelope have reached the conclusion that the squalor depicted in the films displayed a lack of concern on their part for her welfare?

In the film, the child was now putting on a headset and gloves. This scene, thought Ambassador appreciatively, still had the power to thrill. For this was the whole point of Lord Scanthax's plan. Only a human could access the menus that allowed for the world of Edda to be re-scripted. There had once been a thousand or so sentient lords and ladies in Edda, but not one of them could reach out to alter the programs that underlay their existence. Although she did not know it at the time, the six-year-old human girl was more powerful and dangerous than generals and admirals in command of enormous hosts.

The image on the screen jumped from the squalid room in which Penelope lived to show her avatar in Edda, still a child but now properly dressed as a princess and in the impressive surroundings of a wizard's laboratory.

"Penelope was a very intelligent girl and a very fast learner. After only a few weeks, she was able to script an iron bar that

could be used by blacksmiths to make pikes and even swords. Before her seventh birthday, she was scripting more iron for Lord Scanthax than could be matched by the production of all of his mines put together.

"This new stream of such a precious resource meant that Lord Scanthax could continue his policy of being generous in trading and yet at the same time build an army with fiercer teeth than any of his rivals could possibly anticipate. In this period, of course, Lord Scanthax remained entirely on the defensive. There was still a very long way to go.

"Penelope, however, was lonely. As she grew old enough to understand that she had been abandoned by her human family, she become sad and spent many nights crying in bed. Lord Scanthax appreciated her feelings and did what he could for the little girl. He assigned her a diplomat of considerable autonomy, created many farming units for her to interact with, and several times came in person to play with her."

The next scene was painful to watch. Really, they should have deleted the film a long time ago, after it had served its purpose. Ambassador cringed as Lord Scanthax, in his regular apparel—a suit of plate armor—played hopscotch clumsily with the avatar of the human girl. With the faintest shake of his head, Ambassador stole a glance at the figure beside him, the avatar now no longer a girl in simple clothing but a young woman in the most intricate and finely embroidered attire that could be found in any of the four known worlds. Princess's expression remained enigmatic. Was she amused by the scene? Insulted? So much depended on her goodwill, even now, after nine years of constant effort on all their parts.

"*And Penelope responded by working harder and harder to please Lord Scanthax. They concentrated on the iron bars, making them more and more effective, until the weapons produced from them were the strongest and sharpest in the world. These Lord Scanthax kept to himself, trading only inferior ores to his neighbors.*

"*Penelope wanted a pony for her eighth birthday and surprised Lord Scanthax with Rascal. What extraordinary talent! Her savior had thought her capable of scripting only inanimate objects, but here was a pony, a little peculiar and hard to ride, but a pony nonetheless. It meant that in time, Lord Scanthax could look forward to controlling warhorses, or war elephants, and perhaps even to obtaining troop units scripted by Penelope without having to invest resources in costly buildings, skilled artisans, and raw materials.*"

Ambassador could remember Rascal, even without the aid of the film. At that time he was merely a diplomat with a tiny fraction of the life force of Lord Scanthax, but even so, he had been self-aware enough to join in the celebrations of the achievement and revel in the success of the lord's policy of investing energy in the upkeep of a human child. They were not only going to survive; they were going to win! The pony may have looked all wrong, like a child's drawing. It may have walked with a limp, had an astonishing golden mane and pink hooves. But it lived. The human girl had scripted a living creature.

"Whatever happened to Rascal?" Penelope turned her

avatar to face him and Ambassador's heart picked up its pace.

"Why, I'm sure he is out there somewhere . . ." He gestured vaguely beyond the stained glass windows to her left, to where there were many pastures with herds of horses.

"I must look him up someday. The poor thing."

"But it was when she first scripted a rifle that Lord Scanthax knew she had truly saved the realm."

The rifle on the screen was a poor version of their standard-issue weapon. There had been a lot of problems with it. Most of the time, Version One did not fire. Then when she got the gun to fire, it would sometimes have just one shot. But they had persisted. Day after day the child tried different scripts. There had been tantrums aplenty. At times it seemed impossible to work with so irrational a creature as a human. But where rational argument failed, praise succeeded. Ambassador had learned as much about human psychology as the child had learned about scripting.

The art of managing Penelope was to give her infrequent praise. Offering no praise quickly led to her being unmotivated. But constantly praising her did not produce the best results, either. No, by limiting his thanks and expressions of appreciation to relatively infrequent moments, Lord Scanthax had kept Penelope in a state of mind where she was pathetically grateful when such positive feedback came her way. That was why they had decided to make this film, in fact, and for a while it had succeeded. Now, however, praise rarely elicited an increased devotion to work. Was it possible that human psychology changed between the years of nine and fifteen?

It seemed unlikely. What evolutionary purpose would such a change serve? Or perhaps this particular human was defective in some way? There was no way of knowing whether Penelope was typical of her species or whether her unique upbringing had formed her into an aberrant example of *homo sapiens*.

"Thanks to his secret assistant, Lord Scanthax was now prepared to reach out and claim wealthier lands. But to take too bold a step would have been a mistake. Had he changed his pattern of behavior too dramatically, it would have aroused suspicion and possibly even brought about a confederation against him. Instead, Lord Scanthax gradually altered the favorable terms on which he had been trading with Lord Loadstone. As predicted, Loadstone decided the time had come to absorb Scanthax's realm into his own. Loadstone's son, Prince Inwen, brought a major army up to the mountains, where his pikes and bows proved no match for rifles."

What a great day that had been: the bells ringing out all across the city, the colored streamers flying from every flagpole. Mostly for the girl's benefit, of course, but not entirely. Despite Lord Scanthax's commitment to efficiency in resource management, he was proud enough to want to celebrate so obvious a milestone. And there was the fact that his various manifestations had a fluctuating morale sufficiently independent of his own that it was worth giving them the opportunity to relish the victory.

"Soon Lord Loadstone was no more."

In the original film there had been a different image at this point: Loadstone kneeling, head over the chopping block, before the ax came down. But the child's response upon seeing such a moment of triumph was not the anticipated one of clapping and delight; instead she burst into tears and began to scream. So now the film simply displayed the world map of Edda, showing in pale green the growing region controlled by Lord Scanthax.

"Wasn't there a shot of his head coming off once?"

"Indeed, Princess, but it seemed to displease you."

"Well, that's another thing I want. Show me the original version, please."

"If we still have it." Ambassador straightened his already perfect cravat. "Princess, if I might brief you again on urgent current affairs . . ."

"No, Ambassador, you may not. In any case, we are almost finished, aren't we?"

"Well, there are a lot more battles and executions of various lords and ladies still to come."

"Rats, you're right. Skip a bit then. Go up to the end."

"With pleasure, Princess." And it was a pleasure to hurry things along. Lord Scanthax was most anxious that Penelope begin her examination of the newly captured weapon.

"*At last, only Lady Withermane's extraordinary empire existed to oppose that of Lord Scanthax.*"

The map shown on the screen was two-thirds orange and one-third pale green.

"*From her own efforts and industrious investment in research, Lady Withermane, too, had the rifle, rather more costly for her to produce and requiring the manufacture of gunpowder.*"

Nevertheless, her armies were capable of matching those of Lord Scanthax. Except that once more Penelope saved the realm, ensuring her own survival as well as that of everyone she knew. For she . . ."

"Hold it a second!"

"Yes, Princess?"

"What does that mean, 'ensuring her own survival'?"

"Why, if Lord Scanthax had been defeated, who would have provided you with food, heat, and oxygen?"

"The robots, as always." The expression on the avatar changed to a frown and the princess folded her arms.

"But who would have instructed them?"

"I could have. But you wanted me to believe I owed my life to you."

Ambassador was surprised she would dispute this incontrovertible fact. "But you did owe your life to us."

"At first, maybe," Penelope admitted grudgingly. "But not by this time. By then I was old enough to know how to run things in my world."

"Well, possibly. But the film was made for you to watch at a younger age and it simplifies things. You understand."

"All right, go on. Let's finish it."

". . . produced the machine gun, a tremendous work of scripting and an unanswerable weapon in battle. Before long, Lord Scanthax's armies were hammering at the core fortifications of Lady Withermane. Her economy was completely dislocated, her armies left in ruins. She sent one last diplomat to Lord Scanthax."

The film showed the man, still finely dressed in silks despite the hardships being experienced by the city he had come from. Ambassador felt a slight bond of professional admiration for him. The enemy diplomat bowed, then looked at Lord Scanthax.

"My lady congratulates you on your forthcoming victory. But she needs to know one thing before she destroys herself. How, when she was investing far more resources into research than you, did you improve your technology so fast?"

Lord Scanthax gestured to the princess sitting in the throne next to his.

"My lord?"

The diplomat, naturally, did not understand the answer.

"This is Princess, the avatar of Penelope, a human girl."

"You had human assistance? But they all left in the exodus. All of them."

"Not all. One baby was left behind, and my wisdom in searching their former residences was rewarded. I found a baby, I assisted in its survival, and I have reaped the rewards."

"Stop. We can finish there. Ambassador, I want those tapes of the departure of my people. Who would possibly leave a baby behind?"

"It was an error. You've heard this a hundred times before. Your mother was told you were on another ship."

"Show me the tapes."

"Indeed. If they still exist. Now, may I brief you on the current situation?"

"No."

"No? But . . ."

"Lord Scanthax can do it."

"But I am Ambassador. He has invested a rather large portion of his will in me, precisely so that I can perform such functions."

"Well, I'm bored of you. So you can either bring me to Lord Scanthax, or I'll go back to my room."

"As you wish." Ambassador hoped that Lord Scanthax would not take this decision amiss. It would be entirely characteristic of Lord Scanthax to question the need for such a high level of autonomy in his servant if Penelope was going to insist upon intruding on his personal time. Still, to get the princess to return to work was a matter of considerable importance and perhaps Lord Scanthax would forgive the intrusion if, as her manner suggested, Penelope was willing to listen to him explain the current problem facing the realm.

Chapter 2
HAPPINESS: A WARM GUN

Happiness was a concept that Lord Scanthax was familiar with, having encountered several references to it in human
culture, but he could not be sure he had ever experienced the
emotion, unless it was something like the feeling that existed
within him now, in this current moment, as he and Architect
contemplated factory designs for the mass production of a new
weapon. Any decision they made at this point could potentially
save them, or lead to their destruction. There was no room for
anything but ruthless efficiency because—rather shockingly—
the new realm that he had broached, Saga, had turned out
to have a far more advanced level of technology than his
own. The coming war would not be an easy one; indeed, the
power wielded by the people of Saga represented the greatest
threat to Lord Scanthax's existence since the opening days of
his struggle for survival in Edda. Planning ahead under these
urgent conditions was something to relish. The decisions he
made now concerning the maximization of raw materials, food

supply, factories, transport, and new armies were momentous ones.

Having studied—or, more accurately, having instructed Ambassador to study—human culture, Lord Scanthax was aware that other forms of happiness existed. Humans took delight in "play," for example, as was evident in their variety of games requiring a group effort to move a ball to a target; or in "performance," with some humans acting in order to entertain others. But even when their dramas concerned warfare, such vicarious experiences left Lord Scanthax entirely unmoved. Almost certainly, the fact that he had become sentient from a human game based upon world conquest had deeply marked his personality, and while one could not miss what one never had, Lord Scanthax felt a lingering resentment whenever he contemplated his own existence and the way it contrasted with what he had learned of human society. Was he really as free as he felt? Or was he limited by his programming to an even greater degree than humans were fettered by their genes?

When Lord Scanthax conquered Edda, his sense of fulfillment and triumph had lasted for only a day or two. Then he became lethargic and his thoughts scattered through his mind without focus. One such thought that occurred to him in that dark time was that the human ability to take pleasure from inconsequential activities was to be envied. Not that he ever regretted his own nature. And no sooner had Penelope discovered new worlds than all the fighting characteristics within him had revived. Now, although his life was in danger from a potential attack by the beings of Saga, he was as full of purpose as he ever had been, stretched to his absolute limit by the need to organize the economies of four worlds as efficiently as possible.

It was frustrating then, in this atmosphere of intense and most absorbing mental effort, to be interrupted by a page announcing the arrival of Ambassador and Princess.

"Let them in."

A moment later Lord Scanthax strode across the floor of the hall and embraced the girl in as delicate a fashion as his clumsy armored frame allowed.

"Welcome. How pleasant to see you." As he spoke, Lord Scanthax caught the eye of Ambassador and both of them understood the reprimand contained in that look.

Princess pulled back from his arms. "Cut the crap. Apparently something new and maybe interesting is happening. Tell me." She strode over to the model of the industrial estate; Architect backed away with a bow. "Has this got something to do with it?"

"Indirectly." From the desk where he had earlier been studying it, Lord Scanthax picked up a rifle and offered it to Princess.

"Oh, nice toy. Better than any of ours. From Saga, I presume?" She pointed it at Architect, who raised an arm as if to shield himself. Then she swung around to aim at a banner hanging below one of the great windows. *Click.* Nothing happened.

"It is out of power," explained Lord Scanthax.

"Damn. I bet it had a hell of a blast."

"We have recordings of the firing of the gun for you to study."

"So, you want me to script this for you, right?"

"If you would be so kind."

"You really have no idea, do you?"

Lord Scanthax did not respond to this rather vague question. It was highly irritating that humans, apparently, could not think logically, appreciate that every second was precious, and get on with their much-needed work. While he waited for her to reformulate her question or make her point in a more comprehensible manner, Princess tossed the sidearm up and down before deliberately letting it drop to the floor with a clatter. The urge to scowl was difficult to resist, but Lord Scanthax managed it.

"What is it made of? Some kind of plastic, I think, not metal. It is too light. We only have plastic factories in Ruin, correct? And nothing so hard as this, yet so light." She picked it up again, examining it. "Not a scratch. What does it fire? Not projectiles, I don't think. Energy of some sort?" She sat on the throne, dangling one striped-stocking-clad leg over the velvet-padded arm. "I wouldn't even know where to begin."

There was no need to discipline most of the units in the hall. They were simply messengers and servants. But the expressions on the faces of Ambassador and Architect indicated that two of his most autonomous manifestations were shocked. Perhaps Executioner, too, although he remained hidden, as he should while he was on bodyguard duty. Was it wise to allow her such license? Did this behavior adversely affect unit morale?

"Please leave my throne and use another seat. What you are doing is insubordinate."

"It's good to see you, too, father."

"I'm not your father."

"Spiritually, you are my father. You are the only being I've known in my whole life; you or your various manifestations."

She had, at least, sat up properly.

"Tell me, how is the project going to find my people, the humans, to let them know that I am alive?"

"That is an important question. Be seated at this table and we shall form a strategic plan to our mutual satisfaction."

With a rather exaggerated flounce, Princess came over to him. Sitting opposite her, Lord Scanthax could not help but let a frown form as he studied her avatar more closely. Her makeup was as rebellious as her recent behavior; all that black eye shadow was quite inappropriate for a princess. And the purple coloration of her hair was most unnatural. Provocatively so. Was she mutinous? Defective? Or engaging in a form of communication he was unfamiliar with?

"You understand that the amount of energy required to sustain your life-support systems in the human world for a day would support Edda for more than six months?" Lord Scanthax stared at the avatar of the human girl, making sure she had not forgotten the qualitative difference between energy costs in Edda and those in the organic universe.

"I do, although I wouldn't quite put it so ungraciously." For some reason that perhaps Ambassador could explain later, Princess was smiling.

"And you agree, therefore, that any strategy for locating humans would be best conducted through the electronic rather than the organic universe?"

"I did. That's why I scripted the gates that allowed you access to the other worlds. But what do you do with them? Do you use them to find humans for me? No, every single time, you charge through the gate with an army and conquer whatever you find on the other side. Does it occur to you to stop and ask about humans on my behalf? What if the people who made this"—she slammed the gun down on the table between them, suddenly looking deep into his eyes—"know where there are humans? Well, I'm fed up waiting for contact to be made with humans through these electronic worlds. I want to try something else. I want access to the robots that keep my human body alive, and I want to search the human universe for records. There must be a record of where my people went."

It was surprising, the swiftness with which a human child changed. Not so long ago she had been very eager to please and had accepted his reasoning uncritically. Now this.

"The gate that you created to reach Saga has been used to scout their world. Not only have we obtained this weapon, but also we have gained some knowledge of their productive capacity. And our findings are that the people of Saga pose a serious threat to us, perhaps as great as any that we have faced. But once we have matched the power of their weapons, we will be secure, and I will then send Ambassador to negotiate from a position of strength. As always, he will ask on your behalf for any information concerning humans. Does that not seem the rational way to proceed?"

"For you, perhaps. Although, frankly, I suspect you get off on battles. I've never seen you so glum as when you thought you'd conquered everything on Edda and had nowhere to go. But it no longer works for me. I don't care if Saga has troops that are stronger than yours. Let them come. There's nothing for me here—just stupid clothes and stupid toys. I'd be better off in the physical world, looking for the trail of my real parents."

"That is not correct. Suppose I were eliminated by the armies of Saga; then the life-support systems keeping your body alive would cease to function."

"Hand control of them over to me."

Lord Scanthax considered this request for a moment. "Very well. In return for the scripting of new weapons that rival those of our enemies."

"I knew it." Princess stood up. "You don't give a damn about me or my happiness. I'm just a tool to you." Tears rolled down the face of her avatar, an effect that Lord Scanthax had not observed before. It was frustrating how, distracted by her own projects, Penelope frequently wasted her scripting skills on irrelevant matters, like giving her avatar the ability to cry.

She held on to his upper arms and he resisted the impulse to shake her off. "Don't you feel any empathy for my situation? All alone apart from you? Don't you enjoy my company? Appreciate all that I've done for you? Doesn't it mean anything that I saved your life with my work? That I found Epic, Ruin, Myth, and Saga?"

"I was contemplating happiness earlier and believe I have some small understanding of the feeling. If I am correct, it is a pleasure that a sentience derives from acting in accordance with its nature. In my case, the challenge of correctly marshaling my resources and forces for battle with the enemy seems to produce an emotion that might reasonably be called happiness. I am not able to say what produces the same sensation in a human; perhaps it is elicited by scripting, which after all is a specifically human task."

To judge from the way she flung herself away to bang her forehead repeatedly on the table, this was not the response Princess desired. Ambassador gave a slight shake of his head, looking at the avatar in alarm.

"But I can confidently state," Lord Scanthax hurried on, "that in contradiction to your assertion, I do indeed hope that you experience repeated bouts of happiness."

"So long as that doesn't interfere with my scripting." The thumping sounds she was making against the table ceased.

"If my understanding is correct, it won't."

"Your understanding is not correct!" Princess got up, went over to the model of the proposed industrial estate and began crushing the small buildings with repeated blows from the handle of the gun. Extremely distressed, Architect waved his arms before her, but she ignored him. "You're not my father! You're not even my friend! You're just some stupid game obsessed with conquest. You only keep me alive so I can script for you. Fate send a virus to wipe you out!"

This was unprecedentedly irrational behavior and Lord

Scanthax wondered again if Princess was damaged in her command and control centers. He and Ambassador exchanged another look and this time Ambassador nodded. While Lord Scanthax had intended to censure Ambassador for allowing the current interruption, of all his incarnations, only Ambassador had any skill with the human.

"Calm yourself, Princess." Ambassador caught her hand and pulled her to him, as much to protect the model from further damage as to provide physical contact, but it seemed to be an effective maneuver, for she stopped her destructive activities and clung to him, and even though the avatar was no longer showing tears, sobs could be distinctly heard in Princess's voice.

"I'm so alone. So alone."

There were worse times for the human to malfunction. If she had done so five years ago, then his opponents in Edda would have destroyed Lord Scanthax. Even with her assistance it had been touch and go. But the new threat from Saga meant that now, too, would be a very bad time to lose her. There were too many unknowns. Did the people of Saga have even stronger weapons than the handheld type his scouts had thus far obtained? What kind of leadership did they have? Were they capable of forcing their way through all four gates to reach Edda? Perhaps he should ask Penelope again to try to close the gates. What if a small team of assassins with those powerful energy weapons was already on the way, aiming to eliminate him? Of course, he had taken precautions: increased the military output of his realm, doubled the units at the gates, sent scouts of all types on surveillance missions. But still, he needed those new weapons scripted, and as quickly as possible.

"Penelope. Do we have an agreement? I will assign control of your human life functions to you if you script me the gun."

Princess stepped away from Ambassador, her face streaked with lines of dark makeup. She really had gone to some trouble to script sophisticated tear effects. Curious.

"Yes. Of course."

"Good. Then I shall return to my decision making." He did so, hoping this would encourage the girl to resume her own duties. With a nod to Architect, he resumed his seat while servants brought out an alternative model.

"There's something else I want as well." Princess came up close to him, causing Architect to step between her and the new model, gesturing anxiously to the servants to move it away again, out of her reach.

"What?"

"I want to see the original recordings of the departure of the humans and of the moment when I was found."

Lord Scanthax shrugged. "I'm not sure they still exist. Do they?" He looked across at Ambassador.

"Possibly, my lord."

"Well, if they do, you can certainly peruse them," he lied.

Chapter 3
BEYOND THE AIR LOCK

"That went rather well." Princess threw herself onto a plush divan as soon as they had returned to her large bed-chamber and Ambassador had closed the door behind them. But for the silence suggesting that the princess was awaiting a response, Ambassador would have allowed himself an indulgence. Walking into the room just now, it suddenly occurred to him, was like having the room rush upon him at near light speed. All the colors seemed to have been shifted toward the violet end of the spectrum. This was Penelope's choice, of course, from the purple diaphanous materials that hung from the top of her huge four-poster bed to the dark blue carpet and the walls whose velvet texture was a deep shade of violet. Could such a melancholy atmosphere be achieved by a kind of visual Doppler effect?

Assuming, however, that a response was expected of him, the Ambassador did not explore the thought further; in any case, it was foolish of him to engage in such idle speculation.

"Oh, I'm glad you think so." He took a step toward her dressing table, where Princess had seated herself and was looking at the mirror. "If you don't mind me saying, you seemed rather upset."

"Really? For a diplomat, you seem a little slow on the uptake. That was all negotiating posture."

"Negotiating posture?" he repeated slowly.

"Exactly. And I got what I wanted, didn't I?"

"Yes, I suppose so. What did you want?"

"The promise that in return for scripting the new gun I would get to run the systems that look after my body and I would get to see the original recordings of the time I was found as a baby. Speaking of which, why don't you go off and check the files for me while I do my exercises."

"You are going to exercise now?" This was unexpected. Penelope hated returning to her physical body, an emotion that was quite understandable given that in Edda she had a world full of beautiful creations and perfect health. But unless she gave some attention to her human body, its muscles would atrophy and she would die. Being the most empathetic of Lord Scanthax's incarnations, Ambassador was capable of being sorry for her. It must be dreadful to be human and have one's consciousness depend on a very fallible body, which even under the best of circumstances would only last a hundred years or so.

"Allow me to accompany you during your exercises." He could do so in the sense that there were several cameras monitoring her and he could speak through a number of broadcasting devices, including one that she usually kept clipped to her ear.

"No, no, it's just routine. You'd be bored. And I'm very anxious to see those recordings."

She was definitely up to something.

"Very well, Princess. Call me on your return."

No sooner had Ambassador left her purple chamber than, rather uncharacteristically, he broke into a run in order to reach the Feast Hall, slide open a secret door in the walls of the fireplace, and get to the hidden basement room as soon as he possibly could. It was a long run through a whole wing of the castle, and the Ambassador was reduced to zero-boost stamina and the necessity of walking even before he came to the rungs that allowed him to enter the control room. There, the monitors showed scenes from Penelope's human apartments, a rather austere set of three interconnected living units whose bare white walls contrasted with her sumptuously decorated chamber in Lord Scanthax's castle. Ambassador was just in time, for Penelope had regained consciousness and was unplugging herself from the tubes that fed her body and removed the waste. Painfully, she dragged herself to her feet and began a series of bends. Her body was unaesthetic, like that of a poorly designed unit. The limbs were out of all proportion to a torso so slender you could see the ribs. It was no wonder she was shivering, because quite apart from the fact that heating energy had to be kept to a minimum, she had such low levels of fat that her body was permanently struggling with the cold.

"Whoever is watching, won't you turn the heating up a bit?"

Exactly. This was another reason why unscheduled exercising was a most unlikely reason for her to want to return to her human body at this time; had it been a planned return, the temperature would have been raised a little for her.

"No one there? We'll see."

What was she doing? The angle on the main screen wasn't too helpful, but screen three made the purpose of her actions clear. With a sense of dismay, Ambassador took a seat and bent forward to the microphone.

"Penelope, why are you putting on your survival suit?"

"Is that you, Ambassador? Didn't you say you were going to check the old recordings for me?" There was a hint of a laugh in her voice, a scornful ring of victory.

"I did, and perhaps I still will, once you have satisfied me as to your actions."

"I'm just going for a stroll. Don't mind me."

But he did mind. Very much.

"You understand that there are many dangers outside the air lock? We cannot protect you there."

She did not respond, but resolutely zipped up the inner jacket.

"Oh, do be careful, Penelope. A mistake out there will kill you."

Her decision to leave her chambers was probably further evidence that her rational functions were deteriorating. There was nothing for her outside of her living quarters, just an abandoned city that no longer had the atmosphere to support human life.

It was extravagant and probably wasteful, but Ambassador took the precaution of activating one of the robots near Penelope's apartments. Her boots were on. Now the helmet. Lastly, her thin fingers were encased in gloves that slotted home with a twist into the arms of the suit. Had she done everything correctly?

"Penelope, if you must open the air lock, do please run a systems check first. It has been a long time since you used the suit."

"It's all green." Her voice was labored; she was breathing heavily just from the effort of moving with the extra weight of the suit.

"And have you sufficient oxygen for your purpose?"

"A little over . . . four hours." She stepped over the lip of the air lock. "Freedom!" Her attempt at jauntiness did nothing to reassure Ambassador. What would it mean if she were to die now? Only Lord Scanthax would understand the full implications of such a loss, but Ambassador knew enough to worry for them all. Without Penelope's ability to script, the armies of Saga, with their high-technology weapons, could counterattack and perhaps even bring to ruination all that Lord Scanthax had achieved, as well as eliminate him and all his manifestations. Even if such a scenario did not come about, on a personal level the death of the human might well mean the end of his own individuality. Ambassador's only function in recent years had been to act as intermediary with Penelope, and with her gone it was quite likely he would be downgraded to a diplomatic unit of zero autonomy at the next redistribution ceremony.

Such gloomy speculation filled Ambassador's thoughts as he watched Penelope step into the air lock and seal it behind her. He could no longer see her, but was attentive to the sound of her ragged breathing. His gaze strayed to screen four and the image of a stretch of corridor, seen from the camera in the robot's eye. It was moving as rapidly as it could in the direction of the air lock but had to cease rolling from time to time in order to shift recent debris from its path, rocks that had spilled from cracks in the wall made by the planet's occasional shudders.

Penelope was out and moving, albeit with frequent rests, during which she leaned one arm against a corridor wall. Ambassador watched from a camera some distance away as she walked eastward.

"Where are you going, Princess?"

"Library," she wheezed.

"But you can see a view of the library from the screens in your rooms. A robot can fetch whatever you want."

"I don't know . . . what I want . . . need to look around."

"But it's nearly a kilometer away; you are in no condition." It was surprising how high a pitch his voice reached when he was under strain. This screech was rather undiplomatic in its effect, and Ambassador fought to steady himself.

This was an extremely anxious moment. The effort involved in the journey was clearly too great for Penelope, given the frail condition of her human body. Ambassador had another concern now—to add to the many involving mechanical accidents, suit failure, and so forth—which was that perhaps her body might wear out in some way. Was it possible for the human heart or brain to stop functioning in times of stress? Doctor would know, but contacting him would alert Lord Scanthax, and while a full report of these events would have to be given in due course, for some reason Ambassador wanted to defer that unpleasant moment, at least until Penelope was safely back in her room. Right now, though, she turned a corner and because the nearest camera was defective, he could not see her progress. The robot was moving well but was still some way from the library.

"Penelope, can you provide me with an explanation for your actions?"

"Later . . . hard to talk . . . just now." She was indeed panting heavily.

It was a curious feature of the human body that the same organs required to obtain oxygen from the air pumped the exhalations through their vocal cords to produce sound. In a way it was rather elegant, but the disadvantage of the design was evident now. If her voice were synthesized and the synthesizer were on its own circuit, she would be able to converse in steady and regular tones instead of these gasps.

"Damn!"

"What's the matter?"

"Some spillage."

Had she stopped? Her breathing was settling down to a more healthy rhythm.

"There are rocks here, and the roof doesn't look too secure."

"Please wait, Penelope." Immediately, her words had summoned up an image of her poor human body broken underneath great stones. It was a terrible image, one of personal failure and also one of reckless waste, after fifteen years of enormous investment. "I have a robot on its way, coming to assist you. It will be there in approximately twelve minutes."

"I'm fine. There's enough of a gap."

"Oh please be careful. Don't tear the suit."

Listening intently to the audio feed, Ambassador became even more distressed. Each breath of the human was labored and hard-drawn, now and then accompanied by rustling sounds and grunts. One snag on a sharp rock and her suit would leak heat and oxygen. Given how slow she was moving, it would almost be impossible for her to make it back to the air lock. No matter how often Ambassador glanced at screen four, the robot was not going to be able to reach Penelope in the next few minutes.

"Go me," she gasped.

"But why? Why can't a robot serve you? We can spare you all this."

"I . . . don't . . . trust . . . you."

Ambassador did not respond. Irresponsible and reckless as Penelope's actions were, it was true that certain data had been encrypted and hidden from the human, as it was deemed likely to lower her morale to zero. Not that she would find the truth in the old library, but her intuition that the stories she had been told from the age of nine were not entirely free from bias was correct. It was a delicate matter, and not even he had access to all the records concerned. Because Lord Scanthax had constructed no other manifestations at the time, his was the only living memory of those early days when the human baby had been discovered. But whatever the validity of her suspicions, Penelope's current behavior was quite inexcusable.

"Let us negotiate like civilized beings. Do not risk destroying yourself. We can find a mutually satisfactory solution to all your concerns."

There was no response. Nor were there any more of those deep ragged breaths. Instead, if he suspended all motion and listened carefully, he could just make out a very light movement of air back and forth over the microphone.

"Oh Penelope, answer me! Oh, what have you done?"

Clasping his hands together in fear, Ambassador watched stretches of corridor roll by on screen four. It was impossible to contemplate the consequences of her being dead and equally impossible not to imagine the worst. At last, the robot arrived at the rockfall and there was something to relieve Ambassador's mind from its feverish circling. Systematically, the robot widened the path the girl had made, so that it could continue on past the blockage. It was burning through several power packs of energy, but that didn't seem important now.

The body was a gray lump on the ground a short distance from the doors of the old library. It did not seem that the suit was leaking, for as the robot drew near, Ambassador could see that the limbs were still pressurized rather than deflated as he had feared. This robot had hands that were modeled on those of a human, with four fingers and an opposable thumb, although they were much larger and more powerful. It swiveled its hands above the body, then very carefully clasped the suit behind the human's neck and at the small of her back. Through the girl's microphone, Ambassador could hear the whirring of the robot's engine as it raised her a few inches. She was hanging facedown, limbs still trailing on the ground, looking like a forlorn kitten in the mouth of her mother.

"What?" Penelope muttered.

"Oh joy, you live. Just relax. The robot has you. It is bringing you home."

"Library." Her voice was slurred.

"Not now. We'll talk about that when you are safe again."

Having executed a three-point turn, the robot began the journey back with its precious load, struggling to keep its balance. It took a very long time to get the girl through the rockfall area, because it could not risk dragging her limbs over the stones, for fear of tearing the suit. Instead, the robot found the best solution was to move her torso a short distance, then, one at a time, move her legs and arms, then her torso again. Ambassador did not offer any alternative instruction to the robot. Slow but safe was the correct approach. For the robot, the minutes consumed in these patient maneuvers would have meant nothing, but Ambassador suffered a painful continuation of his state of anxiety. It was a very long time until he could begin to relax, when at last the body had been placed in the air lock and was therefore accessible to one of the domestic robots inside. But even after Penelope's suit had been removed and she was lying once more on her bed, drips inserted, Ambassador could not be fully certain that no harm had been done to her.

"I must have passed out," she muttered, before a headset was placed over her eyes. "Darn it, so close, too."

Chapter 4
OF LOVE AND EMPTINESS

By the time Ambassador returned to Princess's chamber, she was on her feet and staring out of a large window.

"Well, that was quite an adventure." The avatar remained facing the window, but the eyes of her reflection in the glass met his and she smiled: a smile that Ambassador had seen a thousand times, yet right now it had a quality of exaggerated innocence that he had never noticed before.

There could hardly be a greater contrast between the composure of the avatar and the panting human body Ambassador had been monitoring a few minutes earlier. Naturally, Penelope's avatar was an aesthetically pleasing one that she had chosen for herself and refined over the years with her own scripting. It was of a young human woman; perhaps—like Penelope herself—fifteen years of age. The avatar's eyes were slightly larger and certainly tended to glow more than those of an actual human. Her face, too, was rather elfin, the cheekbones and chin being delicately drawn.

While Penelope's human body was kept shaved for considerations of hygiene, her avatar had extraordinary, vibrant long tresses whose coils swayed as she walked and whose wisps lay about her head catching little glints of light like a halo. Normally her hair was a shiny raven black, but recently Penelope had favored a rather garish purple. Apart from this lurid coloration the avatar certainly was a pleasant creation, quite in keeping with her role as a princess in Edda.

It was a puzzle to Ambassador, and an important one, to determine exactly what incentive Penelope needed for her to remain a productive unit. A few years ago, she had been much easier to understand. It had perhaps been somewhat demeaning for Ambassador to be observed by the other manifestations playing hide-and-seek with the little girl. But a high degree of autonomy was required in order to discover the ingenious hiding places of the human, and he had been the logical choice.

Penelope had once delighted in the vast scale of the castle and had relished exploring its long corridors, tall towers, and hidden chambers. Quite apart from a desire to intimidate his rivals with the scale of his achievements, Lord Scanthax had needed somewhere to house the captured belongings of a thousand lords and ladies from a thousand different regions. It once had been a highly successful motivational strategy to allow Penelope to dress up her avatar in the flared silk suits popular in the southern continent; to brandish a fan made from feathers of a rare equatorial bird; and to wear the jewelry created by the rulers of the tallest mountains of the west, Edda's greatest source of sapphire, opal, and emerald. But it had been more than two years since Penelope had shown the slightest interest in the wealth and curiosities housed in the castle.

Today, Princess stood with her back to Ambassador and her face in shadow. And it seemed to Ambassador that even more complex than the visible patterns of light and dark on her velvet dress were the invisible and unfathomable motions of Penelope's soul. No longer would games please her, nor praise. She was becoming unpredictable and unreadable.

Outside, a waterfall—scripted by Penelope in an era when the castle was deemed to no longer require its full defenses—sent up rainbows as the sun declined toward the west.

"How odd that in Edda I could climb those cliffs if I chose. I could run vast distances without feeling tired. Yet in my natural habitat, the world into which I was born, I can't even reach that stupid library." Princess turned and gestured that he should sit. "You know, seriously, I've let myself get out of shape. Schedule more exercise sessions, please. Like, double the current routine."

Ambassador gave a nod, and his hands took hold of the back of a plush chair as he attempted to appraise her mood. Resigned? Reflective? Or rebellious and resolute in her mutinous desire to reach the humans' library?

"That was pathetic. I'm a wreck back there."

"Not at all, Penelope. You are in good health and have a most harmonious set of proportions between your body parts; it is just that the environment is so hostile outside your apartments."

"Oh, you flatterer. What is it that you want, by the way? You've been hanging around me a lot recently."

Inadvertently, Ambassador's gaze left her pale face and flicked to the dresser, where the captured gun lay. And while this did not escape her notice, it did no harm.

"Ah, yes, of course. More scripting. The first part of our new agreement. Let's set to work while I'm in the mood, shall we?"

"Very good, Princess." This unexpected and delightful response filled him with a surge of energy, and Ambassador almost skipped to the door, which he patiently held open while Penelope picked up the gun and a shoulder bag in which she kept her tools. It was a strange juxtaposition, the workmanlike satchel, full of pockets and iron implements, hung across a body covered by the exceptionally fine needle-work of a dress decorated in pearls. But Princess could wear what she pleased as long as she kept Lord Scanthax secure with her scripts.

If she could make some progress on the scripting of the new gun, that would balance the very negative view that Lord Scanthax was certain to take of Penelope's extraordinarily dangerous and unrestrained attempt to leave her apartments. They had to march a considerable distance along quiet car-peted corridors, but their pace was swift. Walking just ahead of Princess, Ambassador felt energized, and she seemed willing to keep up with him, no matter how much he depleted his stamina reserve.

Historically, Penelope did her work in a wizard's laboratory that filled the top floor of the eastern round tower. There was no particular need for such an environment; she could work anywhere. But as a child the room had helped her to conceive of herself as the heroine of a story in which her magic saved the kingdom. By now it was a habit for Penelope to work in the laboratory, even though the room remained a little childish in decor. It had frogs and ravens in cages, brightly colored potions bubbling over flames and releasing spicy fragrances into the room, elaborately drawn pentacles on the floor, rune-engraved wands and daggers lying on a big scarred table, and signs of burn marks around the edges of tapestries whose scenes depicted wondrous and fabulous monsters.

It also had a computer, and as soon as Ambassador opened the gargoyle-carved doors to the chamber, Penelope stepped through and went over to sit before a large viewing screen.

"Play the recordings of this weapon in action, please." The seat that faced the screen had two demon skulls built into its arms; Princess rested her hands on these as she waited expectantly for the clips. Surprised by the speed with which Penelope was turning her attention to the gun, Ambassador needed a guilty moment to work the computer and access the files they needed. A few seconds after he found them, a projector shone its beam onto the screen and they watched a converted archer unit fire bright green bolts of energy from the gun, destroying a variety of targets—including a heavily armored tank—until the weapon ceased to work, presumably having expended all its charges.

"Interesting." Penelope had a remote control device in her hand and was flicking back through the recordings, examining certain moments again in slow motion. "Much more powerful than anything we have, don't you think?"

"Oh, quite. Hence the concerns of Lord Scanthax. An army using these would destroy us easily." Ambassador paused, reluctant to interrupt her study, but he had to know. "Do you think you can script us these guns?"

"Well, yes, in the sense that I can script anything, given time. But how it generates such energy safely is quite a mystery. This could take a while."

"A while?"

"A year, say."

"A year!" Ambassador's voice came out shrill and shocked, even to his own ears.

"Just kidding." Princess looked away from the screen and gave him a smile. "I don't know how long, I'm afraid, but let's make a start, shall we?"

It was fascinating and frustrating to watch Penelope work. Moving to sit up at the large, scarred wooden table, she pushed all the clutter of the magician's workshop to the side and conjured up a lump of matter out of nowhere, approximately the size of the gun.

The humans who had created Edda had been surprised and more than a little alarmed when some of their creations—the more powerful lords and ladies—over the course of the centuries, emerged as fully conscious lifeforms. As a precaution against the potential danger represented by these aggressive beings, the humans made it impossible for anyone without living human DNA to access the tools that allowed for the world to be re-scripted. But for the fact that the human body of Penelope was encased in a headset and was physically moving her fingers in her world through the various menus that allowed access to the deepest levels of Edda, she would not be able to create new matter and alter its properties.

Ambassador speculated, a little enviously, on what it must be like to have such an ability. To have access to all the coding of Edda was to be a god. Princess had the ability to alter the very fundamentals of the world. The sun itself could burn blue or green instead of yellow, should she wish it. Or so she said. Not that her power was limitless. Magic items, for example, had so far proven to be beyond her scripting skills. Also, there had been a time when Penelope had attempted to create friends for herself. The experiments had ended in frustration and with a room full of fairies, ballerinas, princesses, and multicolored furry animals. They could all walk and talk; they could all carry out a variety of tasks; but not with the independence of thought that Penelope had striven for.

Having killed all his rivals, Lord Scanthax was the only remaining self-conscious being in Edda, and he refused to let Penelope examine his coding, or that of any of his manifestations. Ordinary units, such as farmers and soldiers, Penelope had studied in depth, and she could reproduce those with a few days' work. If she had succeeded in creating consciousness, perhaps she could have re-scripted Ambassador so that his will was independent from that of Lord Scanthax. Did he desire such a thing? It was a shocking thought, and immediately Ambassador turned his attention back to the worktable.

In the brief time it had taken to arrive at the thought of having complete autonomy and to shy away from such a disloyal notion, Princess had already created an exact copy of the physical shape of the gun. This seemed very encouraging to Ambassador, who seated himself on a stool, feeling occasional tremors of excitement run through his body. All today's earlier misfortunes would be forgotten and Lord Scanthax would be very pleased indeed if Ambassador came to him later to announce progress on the new weapon.

Amongst the various implements and devices on the table was an old weighing scale, the sort with two pans hanging by chains from a levered arm. The captured gun was resting in one pan and from time to time Princess placed her new construction in the other. At first, hers was too light. But after several attempts, where she seemed only to be touching her new creation with the tip of a wand, the scales began to tip. One more slight adjustment and they were balanced.

"Oh, well done, Princess." Ambassador gave her a glowing smile. And although she smiled back, she shook her head.

"When I change some of its other properties, I'll probably lose control over its density again. But it's a place to start. I'm coming at this by a series of approximations. There will be a lot of frustration and trying to put square pegs in round holes before we are done."

Beaming now, Ambassador gave a slight chuckle, conveying his absolute confidence in her skills. And why not? He had seen her grow up and become more and more accomplished with every year. The little girl—whose avatar back then had been a fairy princess complete with wings—had been pathetically eager to please and perhaps that desire for Lord Scanthax's approval had not entirely dissipated with age.

As though thinking along similar lines, Princess looked up from her work. "Ambassador, do you like me?"

"Like you?" he repeated thoughtfully.

"Yes. Do you like me—Penelope?"

"I'm sure I do. It's just that the phrase might mean something different to a human than to an autonomous manifestation of Lord Scanthax."

A flicker of a smile appeared on her lips, reassuring him that he had not spoken amiss.

"Let me put it differently." Her head was tipped, focused on the material in front of her, her true gaze probably flickering across hundreds of menus and codes. "What memory do you most treasure?"

"Memory?"

"Your happiest moment."

"Ah. The work that I was most satisfied with was accomplished when you were about halfway between seven and eight years old."

"Yes?"

"There were many critical periods for Lord Scanthax, but this was possibly one of the most significant. Our realm had three alliances under way. To the south, ourselves and Lady Morwen were slowly undermining the position of General Tokamash. This was so obviously to our mutual benefit that despite repeated—and increasingly generous—offers from others to try to pry us apart, we had a great deal of confidence in the alliance. Theoretically, there was a time when we would have been quite vulnerable to a strike from Lady Morwen, but so long as the two of us stuck it out, we knew we would end up with the considerable prize of General Tokamash's lands. Trusting to this perspective, we did not feel the need to send our greatest diplomatic resource southward." Ambassador glanced at Princess, and she looked up from her work a moment to meet his gaze. "That would be me, by the way.

"To the east, as you know, there were developments of mild interest, but the mountains effectively made those of long-term consideration only. No, our real difficulty was to the west, where, more and more, our fleets were encountering those of the island realm of Admiral Ekkehar. Perhaps it would help if I showed you on a map?"

Penelope sat up. "If you like."

"Oh please, I've interrupted you. I'm sorry; my enthusiasm for the story has run away with me. Go back to your scripting, please, please." Ambassador was shocked at himself; how could he have suggested that she leave such vital work to attend to a map illustrating a minor and purposeless anecdote?

Princess ignored his flush of embarrassment, shrugged, and returned her concentration once more to the gun in her hands.

"Well . . ." Ambassador lowered his voice so as to be less intrusive. He found, however, that he had not lost his desire to continue the story. "I traveled to the great port of Laver, capital of Admiral Ekkehar's realm, and there I was as persuasive as I could be. I had to forestall Ekkehar and gain us time to build up our fleets. You will recall the period because you were very busy designing and constructing warships.

"It was a demanding month for me. Each incident that revealed our growing stock of naval forces required an explanation; sometimes I improvised most imaginatively. Each failure to observe the exact terms of our agreements required a lengthy interview; often Lord Ekkehar would probe me, full of suspicion. But at the end of such discussions, he would come away believing that we were rather self-interested and tactically inept, but not actively hostile to him. At last, a secret message came to inform me that our navy had seized the Norrig Islands, a deed that was tantamount to an outright declaration of war, because the islands were an essential refueling base for any attempt to invade Admiral Ekkehar's home territories. When I transcribed the coded message, well, I had the most powerful feeling of satisfaction that I have ever experienced. The job was done and done well. I like to think that despite other turning points and vicissitudes, this was perhaps the most crucial of them all."

"I see," said Princess, momentarily looking at him, a hint of curiosity in her expression. "And would you say that you were happy at this time?"

"In the sense that Lord Scanthax defined the emotion earlier, I would say yes, I was. I had fulfilled my purpose."

"And on your return? Did Lord Scanthax give you any indication that he was pleased with you?"

"He most certainly did. His exact words at our debriefing were, 'Well done, Ambassador.'"

This made Penelope smile; a rather enigmatic smile as far as Ambassador was concerned. What was amusing about his last statement?

"And would you say that out of gratitude and admiration for the essential work you had done for him, Lord Scanthax actually liked you at that time?"

"Liked me? How could he? I was an incarnation of himself."

"But an autonomous one."

This caused the Ambassador to pause and recall the meeting. "Suppose you made a bow and when it came to the hour of battle, it served you well. Then you could say that you were pleased with the bow; you might even say that you liked the bow. In that sense, Lord Scanthax liked me."

"Exactly." Penelope stopped work and put down all of her tools. "You have read a lot of human books and seen a lot of their plays and films, correct?"

"In order to better understand you, Penelope."

"Well, humans like each other in a different sense than liking a tool that has effectively served its purpose. They feel empathy for each other's existence. They want each other to be happy. The feeling that you like someone can deepen to the point where you love them. I need to find other humans because I need to love someone and I need to be loved. Here, I can say in all honesty that I like you, Ambassador. I'm not sure I can say that about any of the other manifestations. Your existence shows that there is a small part of Lord Scanthax that is capable of being kind to me. But I don't believe you will ever empathize with me, let alone love me. The most you feel is a sense that I am a good bow."

For a very brief moment, as their eyes met, Ambassador felt he was in the presence of a creature so alien that it was a miracle they could communicate at all.

Chapter 5
GHOST

"Come this way." Ghost led her friend through the streets of Saga, a city-world of which she was theoretically queen, although she hated the role. Their destination lay in a fairly remote part of the city, adjacent to a building with external walls of dark blue glass. "Here."

Ghost's companion, Cindella, appeared to be a pale female pirate with dramatic red hair. But this striking woman, adorned with weapons and clad in leather armor, was in fact the avatar of a teenage human male, Erik Haraldson.

Beside the glass building, in the middle of the road, was a tall door that appeared to stand without any support. From it radiated a pale gray light.

"What is this?" Cindella came closer, holding her hand out toward the shimmering surface.

"Wait. Don't touch it. Come around here."

As they walked to the side of the door, it disappeared. It had no thickness at all. From behind, the view was absolutely normal, as though the door did not exist. A step backward and it was there; a step forward, gone.

"Very curious." Erik's avatar walked a full circle around the door, with Ghost watching him somberly.

"Did you ever see anything like this before?" she asked. "In Epic, perhaps?"

"No."

"There's more." Ghost passed Cindella a small handheld screen she had drawn from her satchel. "As soon as the . . . portal . . . was discovered, we set up cameras to monitor it. Press Play to watch the recording."

From the perspective of light-sensitive cameras, the doorway glowed with a white-green light that lit up the whole street. In the bottom right-hand corner of the screen, numbers indicating the passage of time jumped forward; the whole image suddenly darkened. A figure had come through the door and was blocking the light. It seemed to be a man, judging by its sturdy frame, but one whose features were strangely polygonal. After pausing for a moment, as if to get his bearings, the man walked off toward the inhabited part of the city, tracked by the camera until he was out of view.

"Amazing."

Ghost met Cindella's gaze and nodded.

"How long has this been here?" Erik asked.

"We really have no idea. It was spotted eight days ago by a helicopter surveying the area for recyclables. Since then we've had four visitors, or the same person four times. When they step back through the portal, they take something with them.

And this is what's worrying me. They are departing with stolen guns."

Ghost backtracked through the recording for him and played it again.

"Have you sent a device through, to see what's on the other side?"

"Yeah, we did put a camera in, a really small one, through the bottom right-hand corner. But as soon as it touched the surface, it stopped broadcasting."

"Could you pull it back out?"

Ghost nodded. "And the camera was still working fine on our side."

"Very strange. I can see why you're worried."

"Well . . ." For a moment Ghost hesitated, but if anyone could understand what she was about to say, it would be Erik. Odd that her most trusted confidant was a human. "I'm worried for the people of Saga. But for me personally? To tell the truth, it's exciting." There was a pause as though she was waiting for his reaction. But Cindella's expression was fixed at "interested," and it was impossible to see if Erik was shocked.

"I haven't said this to anyone else," she continued, "but I think you'll appreciate my situation. It's ironic, given that you are a human, an alien. But with Cindella you must have felt a bit like I do. It's like having wings, but never flying. Don't you want to stretch yourself, see what Cindella could do with all her magic? Go exploring new worlds? Have adventures?

Discover where her true limits are? Because I've always felt like that.

"Remember my battle with the Dark Queen? I relished it. Once it was over, I knew I'd feel trapped here. The RAL"— she checked he understood the term, but of course, Cindella's expression would not reflect the actual response of Erik unless he consciously chose to reset it—"the Reprogrammed Autonomous Lifeforms, those of us given the ability to alter the world around us, were all warriors, and some of that spirit—a lot of that spirit—has entered me. I'm restless here; I need a challenge. That's why, if it was the only way, I was going to upload myself into a robot in your world and travel the stars. It was a path to freedom. But now I look at this and see something that is potentially even better. It means there is an electronic world beyond Saga. It may represent danger, but can you see what this portal means to me? It's a way to go exploring while in my own body, perhaps with all my reprogrammed abilities." Ghost looked again at Cindella, anxious for Erik's response. Did he think her irresponsible for seeing the portal as an opportunity, not just a threat?

"I understand." Erik must have signaled for Cindella to give a nod, for his avatar gave a very lifelike gesture of approval. "Or at least, I think I do. It's very different for me, of course. Back in New Earth we have a million challenges just getting our society moving forward again after years of stagnation. There are so many projects I could get involved in. And I'm just the same as everyone else, except when I'm clipped up to

Cindella. But you are right; I enjoy being here as Cindella. Yet at the same time I feel constrained, not just by being human, but because in Saga there's no need for all the skills or magic Cindella has inherited from Epic."

"Yeah, that's it. Constrained."

For a moment they looked at the shining portal, which no longer seemed quite so menacing: it was a potential pathway to exciting new worlds.

"You brought me here because you want me to go through it with you? Now?"

This brought a short laugh from Ghost. "I'd love to, but no, I've still got my responsibilities as queen. What if we disintegrated or something? I mean, we know your avatar was able to go from Epic to Saga. But can you do it again? Also, before you offer to test it, we had a discussion. Some of the guild leaders are worried that this portal might represent a genuine danger to Saga. We have to set up a cordon around the whole district, get the army functioning again, build tanks and all the powerful weapons that we halted production on. When all that's in place and I am not needed, then perhaps I can go.

"First, though, we need more information. I brought you here because I'm hoping you humans will help us. We need a team to head through and find out what's happening on the other side. I was going to get some volunteers from Saga, but then I thought of you. If your people create avatars and go in, what's the worst that can happen? You lose your avatar. But for my people, it could mean death."

It was still a little disorienting, even though Ghost had seen it happen often enough, that human avatars could be killed without the slightest effect on the people controlling them. They had infinite lives in Saga and it would cost them nothing if they died crossing through the portal. Unfortunately for human-Saga relationships, the previous queen of Saga had discovered a way to feedback signals to the brains of humans entering their world and trigger the release of dangerous overdoses of chemicals in their brains. As a result, with the exception of Erik, who was acting as a kind of ambassador for the humans, they no longer visited Saga.

"That's a great idea, and I'm sure we will do it. You do know, though, that our Cabinet will have to give permission first? After what happened here last year, we are ultracautious about EI beings."

"EI?"

"Electronic Intelligence."

"Electronic?" Ghost looked down at herself, then gave a smile. "Well, I suppose so. Will you go ask your Cabinet then, please? We would like you to send the scouts through as soon as possible."

"Of course. And Ghost, whatever they say, I'll go through there for you."

"Thanks, Erik." Ghost held up her right hand. They closed their grip, and the last image in front of her before Cindella abruptly disappeared was of the avatar's intense green eyes, somehow filled with warmth and comradeship despite the fact that the real Erik was lying on a bed somewhere on a far distant planet, staring blindly into a headset.

There was an incredible amount to be done and a hundred people wanting to get in touch with her in order to have some decision made about energy distribution or factory design or something equally tedious. But for a few minutes, Ghost stood and contemplated the portal. Such a strange creation, as though someone had taken a knife and a ruler and cut four lines through the air, revealing a shimmering gray background to the world of Saga. And for all the adventure that it offered, the portal was extremely sinister, too; instead of using it to communicate openly with the people of Saga, whoever had created it had done so in the hope that they could journey through the city unnoticed, stealing weapons.

Chapter 6
To the Portal

Being a person of action rather than introspection, Ghost rarely spent too much time dwelling on the state of her feelings. But as she waited for Erik's team to arrive in Saga, she turned her attention to the swirl of emotions that arose at the thought that she might soon be leaving the bustling city. What she ought to be experiencing was a sense of concern for her people and perhaps even fear, for what might come through the portal from the unknown world beyond. But even if there were millions of hostile inhabitants living there, facing them seemed less daunting than spending her life as queen, surrounded by people who wanted to trap her in a life of administrative decisions.

Of course, Ghost had asked not to be called queen and had attempted to resign from the position. But it wasn't so easy. Tradition had firmly established that whoever killed the current ruler became the new ruler. And no amount of pleading with the administrators of Saga could take away the fact that

Ghost had defeated her predecessor, the Dark Queen.

It was not fear that was troubling Ghost but guilt. Leaving Saga would mean leaving behind her friends: in particular, Milan and Athena. If you met Milan at a party, you would think he was all image and no substance. He had perma-tats and worked out to keep a muscular physique, which he openly admitted was for impressing the girls. It seemed to be all he lived for: girls and parties. But the fact was, when Ghost had found herself in battle with the Dark Queen, Milan hadn't been the slightest bit intimidated. And the same was true of Athena, the most tech-savvy person that Ghost knew.

The two of them had stuck by Ghost, had believed in her, had made possible her victory. They were courageous and loyal. And no matter how much Milan preened and boasted about his own coolness, the surprising fact was that he lived up to the show and more. It seemed wrong to be planning to leave them, wrong and sad. But Ghost had survived on her own for years and knew that ultimately she had to follow her own nature, even if it led her away from her friends.

The Grand Plaza was busy and warm under a clear spring sky. Life would go on here, assuming Ghost could deal with whatever was on the other side of the portal. She was waiting in the center of the square, sitting on her airboard and listening to a compilation of tracks by new punk bands that Milan had put together for her. This was the place where new human avatars appeared after their first creation, and as she began to wonder whether Erik's team was going to arrive at the agreed-upon time, Cindella materialized right in front of her, Erik having unclipped his avatar at this exact point the previous day.

"Hey, Erik. Thanks for coming."

"Hi, Ghost. The others are just creating their characters now; they'll be in Saga soon."

"How many are in your team?"

"Six."

"Neat." Six seemed like a sensible amount for a scouting party. They would be a tight group.

Ghost moved to sit beside Cindella on one of the many stone benches and followed her gaze. Throughout the plaza were dozens of booths, distributing food cooked in a wide range of styles. Hundreds of people were availing themselves of the vendors' services and were either walking or sitting in the square enjoying their meals.

"Is it lunchtime, your time?" asked Erik.

"Huh? No, it's three in the afternoon, as we agreed."

"Was it always like this at three? It seems busier now than before, under the Dark Queen."

"You're probably right. Although I didn't come down this way much during the old times. They had guards then, to keep boarders out of the plaza."

"So do boarders come down these days?"

"Sure." Ghost pointed toward a corner of the plaza where a group of airboarders was lounging around like a pride of indolent lions, barely able to summon the energy to get to their feet. But all of a sudden there was a dramatic burst of motion as one of them leaped into action, attempting tricks against low walls and stone ornaments. Both Ghost and Erik were watching the stunts with fascination when a tall man in a dark suit came over and sat beside them.

"Let me guess. Are you B.E.?" offered Erik.

"Right. I hope we are going to be given some decent gear, because the start-up equipment for an assassin still sucks."

"Ghost, this is B.E., Big Erik, one of my oldest friends from Sandycove, where I grew up. I think you met a few times before, in the struggle with the Dark Queen."

"Hi again, B.E. Of course I remember you. Thanks for coming, and don't worry about your equipment. You'll get the best Saga has to offer."

B.E.'s new avatar smiled. It was a slightly sinister expression, rather well done.

"I look forward to seeing it," he replied.

Next to arrive was a trooper, carrying his rifle in both arms across his chest. As he walked through the busy plaza with a determined military pace, people stopped to stare at the soldier.

"Ouch, we are going to have to get him out of sight," muttered Ghost.

"What's up?" asked Erik. "Why is everyone looking so surprised?"

"We disbanded the army months ago. Oh well, it doesn't matter; we've started rebuilding the army anyway, so everyone may as well get used to it."

"Harald?" asked Erik of the soldier.

"Yeah."

"Ghost"—Cindella stood up to make the introduction—"this is my dad, Harald."

"Your dad?" Ghost heard the note of shock in her own voice and paused, wondering why she should be so surprised. In part it was because she had taken it for granted that the explorers would be young humans. But why not bring maturity and experience into the team? There was another issue, though—the real reason that Ghost had shivered at the word "dad." Ghost had never known her parents and even today, with all her powers and authority, she had not been able to find out so much as their names. All her earliest memories had been wiped from her mind in a cruel experiment and the records concerning her past destroyed. It was painful to be reminded that she had no father or mother she could count on, the way that Harald had come to be with Erik. Ghost had grown up alone, fending for herself.

"Hello, Ghost. It's an honor to meet you." Harald walked over and offered his hand.

She got up from the bench in order to take it, and for a brief moment, as they touched, she stared into the dark eyes of the avatar. But of course there could be no sign of a relationship between the avatar and Cindella. The only way it was possible to tell they were father and son was from the distinct accent their voices shared.

Before Ghost could sit down again, a third avatar arrived. He was wearing an open-collared shirt like so many of the other men in the plaza and it would be easy to mistake him for a curious citizen of Saga, coming to see what was happening. But his stride was a little too purposeful.

"Anonemuss?" asked Erik.

The man nodded, his dark-haired fringe falling forward over his eyes.

"This is Ghost, the queen of Saga."

If Anonemuss was surprised that the ruler of a city of several million people was a teenage girl in a T-shirt and combat trousers covered in pockets, he didn't show it at all. With another nod, he joined the group on the bench and stretched out his legs.

A moment later another soldier came up, this time carrying the kit of a medical officer.

"Ghost, this is Inny"—Erik hesitated—"my girlfriend."

A wave and smiles all around. Again, Ghost was curious about Erik's human life and paid particular attention to the new arrival, but she was unsure if there was any meaning in the design of Inny's avatar. Did humans make choices for size and shape that reflected their own bodies? Perhaps Inny had fair hair on her human head, because her avatar had rather striking long blond tresses.

"Just one more."

"Good, Milan is waiting with a shuttle bus."

"Tell her about Gunnar," said B.E. suddenly.

"What do you mean?" Cindella turned to him.

B.E. stood up from the bench so he could address Ghost. "He's not like the rest of us."

"No?" Ghost waited, her curiosity aroused, but no one offered to elaborate.

"What do you mean, exactly?" Erik asked B.E. again.

"For a start, Gunnar's a first-class bozo. And he's a fool. He's not going to be much use to the team. His idea of taking a risk is wearing a bow tie that is too loud for his waistcoat. During the old days, back when we had Epic, Gunnar earned money from having his avatar make leather goods, not fighting monsters. But more dangerously, he's not one of us. The rest of us are all close friends of Erik's, but Gunnar is an administrator who thinks he knows best. The problem is that some people on New Earth believe that helping you is a bad idea. They want to keep away from everything that's happening in your world, for safety's sake. And Gunnar represents them. He's not here to help; it was a condition of our being allowed to come that we bring him along."

Ghost was not surprised that there were humans with such an outlook. "Well, that's understandable after what the Dark Queen did to them," she said.

"She got me, too," said B.E. passionately, "but I'm here and glad to be here. Anyway, just so you know, he has a different attitude than the rest of us."

Right on cue, Gunnar came up, a very tall and youthful blond soldier, with powerful shoulders and a gleaming smile.

"Gunnar, this is Ghost."

"Your Majesty." He put down his kit bag and bowed.

"What took you so long?" challenged Anonemuss.

Gunnar straightened, still facing Ghost respectfully, before turning slowly about in order to reply. "There were a lot of important decisions to make."

"Yeah, I see you put some time into that smile," muttered B.E. just loud enough to be heard.

"How one appears in EI environments could be of great importance."

"For a trooper?" sneered B.E.

"For any character class."

"Yeah, well, forgive me if I think your good looks have more to do with your own vanity than strategy."

Before Gunnar could respond to B.E.'s jibe, Cindella got up. "Enough."

To look at, this team of humans was a superb combat squad that inspired confidence. To listen to, they sounded like squabbling children. Hoping her dismay at the division in their ranks did not show, Ghost took her airboard, slung it over her shoulder, and set off with the call, "Let's go."

Everyone followed at once, tracked by many curious stares until they reached the relative quiet of a side street. A small airbus was floating next to the pavement, and Milan was leaning against it. Ghost looked at him afresh, as her guests from New Earth must see him: a muscular young man with striking black tattoos on his arms.

"Hi, Erik, good to see you again." Milan held out his fist and Cindella bumped knuckles with him. Without waiting to greet anyone else, Milan then slid open a side door. "Here you go."

While the humans found seats in the bus, Ghost joined Milan in the front of the vehicle.

"All set?" With a quick glance back, Milan shot off, rushing down the street as though he was in a race. "By the way, thanks, everyone, for doing this."

"You're welcome," Erik replied for them all.

For the next hour they swept through the streets of the vast metropolis that was Saga. There was very little chat, which was a disappointment to Ghost in that she had hoped to gain some more insight into B.E.'s comment that Gunnar was not here to help. The journey did, however, give her time to get used to the new avatars and run over their names several times until she had fixed them in her mind. Inny was the female soldier with long golden hair; B.E. was the man in the dark suit; Erik's dad, Harald, had military-style, closely shaved hair; while Anonemuss had the appearance of a dumpy, middle-aged office worker. The most striking of them all, though, was Gunnar, who despite having a cracked and aged voice, looked like a teenage model, with his sparkling blue eyes, gleaming teeth, and youthful body.

Gliding to a halt before a warehouse, Milan pressed a remote control and a large metal shutter rose to let them enter. This part of town was more or less abandoned, and from the front, the warehouse had looked rather derelict; even the painted name of the former business—RYAN'S TEXTILES—had faded to the point that it could barely be made out. But inside, the building was ablaze with light and activity. It was sectioned into corridors created by the meter-high screens that separated off twenty or so workstations from each other. These open corridors focused on three hubs where clusters of people were gathered, talking and looking at monitors. Ghost imagined that viewing all the motion from above would be like looking down into an ants' nest. With the human avatars trailing her, she led them to the nearest of the three large groups.

At their arrival, a young woman with long, straggly raven hair glanced up over her glasses with a smile. This was Athena, whose knowledge of computers and hacking skills had been invaluable in Ghost's struggle against the Dark Queen. Cindella moved to greet Athena, her facial expression set to one that was friendly and admiring. It was impressive just how much animation was possible with these avatars.

Athena didn't bother to get up, but she did tap her fingers to her forehead in salute. "Erik, everyone, thanks for coming."

"We are glad to help, Athena." Erik paused. "I'm amazed at this place. You've fixed it all up in just a few days?"

"We have indeed." Athena looked proudly around the whole length and breadth of the warehouse.

"What is it that you are doing here, young lady?" Gunnar was presumably trying to be polite, but there was something slightly patronizing in his tone. Perhaps, thought Ghost, he was too nervous to relax and just talk normally. In any case, it didn't bother Athena.

"It's our command and control center. Here is where we receive and record the feed from the cameras we have tracking the aliens. We have managed to place broadcasting devices on the two that are in the city and also on one who left through the portal last night. These monitors"—she pointed to a couple of screens—"show where the two in the city are. That one was showing the third, but lost its signal when he went back through the portal. Over there"—she waved her arm toward the far end of the building—"we've had to start up the army again, and they are organizing the movement of tanks and other heavy weapons into position beside the portal, just in case. And over there"—she pointed to the third hub—"we've invited the leading guilds to draw up plans for evacuation and for civil procedures in case of emergency."

"And just what—if you don't mind me asking—kind of emergency do you envisage might arise?" Again Gunnar sounded insincere. This time Athena glanced away from Gunnar toward Ghost, who gave the slightest of shrugs. The two women understood one another. It wasn't that there was anything wrong with the question; it was the manner in which he talked, as if interrogating them. The hint of suspicion in his voice was consistent with B.E.'s warning that Gunnar did not have the same outlook as Erik and the others who had come to help out their friends.

All the same, Athena answered the handsome soldier in the same steady, matter-of-fact tone as her previous response. "Our current theory is that the aliens are scouting the city in preparation for an attack of some sort. They seem to be interested primarily in our weapons and have taken several back with them through the portal. When they move around the city, they seem to linger at our higher-technology factories and our strategic facilities, such as the telecoms tower, the spaceport, and so on."

"Interesting, and worrying," said Harald. "You must have thought about simply getting hold of one of these men, to ask him what he was doing?"

Ghost nodded. "We've thought about it, but that would mean revealing that we know they are here. At the moment, observing them is pretty useful. The other thing is that I don't think we would learn a lot by attempting to converse with these scouts. These creatures aren't like living people. They don't seem to need to eat or drink, or sleep, and they also don't seem to function like a person. I mean, they are more like robots."

"Look." Athena turned to an adjacent desk. On the screen above it flashed a still of a cloaked figure whose face was made up of large gray polygons. "Bachelor number one." She changed the view, to an identical figure. "Bachelor number two. And here's three. Now, take your pick."

"Odd, all right," mused Anonemuss.

"Yeah, and watch this."

The image jumped forward to show one of the humanoids outside of a toy shop. He stared through the window for a long time. Then, having looked slowly up and down the street, he pointed a finger at the glass.

"You can't see it at this resolution, but he's just extended a glass cutting blade from his finger," Athena explained.

Now able to reach inside to the display, the humanoid took out a model pulse rifle that had an extra-large barrel.

"Water pistol."

The scout held the toy up and rotated it efficiently, until, apparently satisfied with its studies, it then twisted and pulled at parts until the gun was dissembled. The parts were placed in the creature's large backpack, before the humanoid raised its flat gray face and once more looked slowly around the street.

"What do you make of that?" asked Harald.

"I think it is searching for weapons, but wasn't able to distinguish a toy from a real one." As Athena answered, she rewound the film and showed it again. It really did seem like the scout couldn't tell the difference.

"Which one of you is on communications?" Athena switched off the recording and looked at the group.

"Me," answered Inny, raising her hand.

"Here." Athena handed her a device with a small screen. "This was tracking the last alien before it went back through the portal; perhaps you'll pick up the signal once you go through to the other side. It's pretty crude, a relatively powerful but short-range radio. There was no point making it satellite based because obviously we don't have any satellites over there. But it was working well enough here."

"All right." Having examined it for a moment, Inny took the device and put it in a small bag at her waist.

"Do you have gear for the rest of us?" asked B.E.

"We certainly do. Follow me." Ghost took the group across the warehouse to where tall racks of metal shelving had been bolted to the wall. The shelves were laden with weapons and high-tech equipment.

"For the troopers, we have the Atanski Two-Six-Six. Then, in case pulse weapons don't work beyond the portal, a Higgs sidearm that fires these." Ghost held up a small white plastic sphere. "They explode on impact. And finally, for hand-to-hand combat, a tooth-bladed dagger." She pulled one partly from its sheath. "You all get one of these. Be really careful with them. Don't even try to test the edge with your finger; they are incredibly sharp." Rather proud of this equipment, Ghost must have sounded too enthusiastic, for she prompted Erik to speak up in a hesitant voice.

"Ghost, you know we agreed to explore for you. But we aren't going to fight. We don't believe in harming anyone."

At this there were a few nods from the rest of the human group.

"I understand you have a philosophy of non-violence in your society, and I respect that," replied Ghost, and she was sincere in her admiration for how humans seemed to be able to live together without harming one another, "but what about non-sentient opposition? Suppose you have to fight to avoid being killed by a bunch of these robot-type things?"

"I don't know. If we could be sure they were non-intelligent. What do you think, Inny?"

"I agree; we could fight, but only if we are certain they are NPCs."

"NPCs?" Ghost was unfamiliar with the term.

"Non-Player Characters. We had them in Epic. Killed them a million times over, but it didn't matter; they were just game-generated creatures with no consciousness," B.E. explained for them all.

"We thought you were all NPCs when we first logged into Saga," added Erik. "That's why I killed that policeman, but it was a terrible mistake and it's one that I'm not going to repeat."

"I see." Ghost shrugged. "But anyway, take the weapons along. You don't have to use them. Same with this, for you, B.E." She hefted a large rifle with a long telescopic sight from its resting place and handed it over. "The IVB Pulsar One-Eight-Five: the most accurate pulse rifle in Saga, with an effective range of two kilometers. And again, you should also take the sidearm and the knife."

"Nice." B.E. checked the sights, looking through them toward the far side of the warehouse. "Very nice."

"For the medics, we have these packs. It's pretty obvious how to use the stuff in there. And for the scout"—she looked around questioningly at Anonemuss, who nodded—"we suggest taking just the smaller weapons that can be concealed and a few neat devices for looking around corners, recording images, that kind of thing. They are all in that bag there. Finally, what about you, Erik? Want any guns or a kit?"

For a moment everyone's attention was drawn to the incongruity of Cindella, a bright fantasy swashbuckler standing among these modern, darker figures.

"I'll take one of those Higgs handguns, but I'm hoping that my magic items will work on the other side of the portal. If they do, and it comes to fighting, I'll rely on them."

It didn't take long for everyone to gather up the gear that had been assigned to them. Then the team moved toward the exit of the warehouse. As they did so, a wave of applause from the people in the building—hesitant at first, but then surging up strongly—accompanied them. It was a good moment, and Ghost felt proud of the people of Saga; they were showing the humans just how much their assistance was appreciated.

The portal was only two blocks away from the warehouse. When they got within a hundred meters of it, the whole group paused. There it was again, shimmering and mysterious. A rectangle cut out of the air. It was inviting, too. For all the seriousness of the moment, Ghost found herself enjoying the situation. Here was her chance to move on to a new challenge. A whole new world, in fact. Perhaps a new species of people to befriend. Or destroy.

Chapter 7
A Vote for War

Milan led the way through empty streets, thoroughly enjoying himself. After Ghost had defeated the Dark Queen there had been some pretty awesome parties. And it was kind of cool being a celebrity. But in the last few months, Milan had felt, well, bored. Now this gate shone before him with an air of menace, true, but also with the promise of some serious action.

"Well, I guess I'm up." Anonemuss stepped forward, looking for all the world like an ordinary office worker from Saga taking a casual stroll along the street. He walked over to the flickering gateway, a tall silhouette against the silver light.

"Just a moment there, please." Gunnar turned and faced the group with his hand raised, which seemed to be as much of a surprise to the humans as it was to Milan. "I would like to draw attention to the risk we are taking. It is no small act of bravery on the part of those of us in Saga this morning. It is a potential sacrifice of a very few, not for the good of our own community, but for the sake of those electronic beings who inhabit this world. Since we are clipped up, we are potentially vulnerable to contamination feeding back into our brains from Saga or the mysterious new environment. To keep such risks to a minimum, I would remind everyone that you can and should pull out of the system as soon as you sense something is not right. This is not just a case of personal security; it is a case of keeping information about New Earth from those who might harm us." Gunnar paused. "Thank you."

"Thank *you*," answered Anonemuss with more than a hint of sarcasm.

This seemed to infuriate Gunnar, and Milan shook his head, partly to show how unimpressed he was by the human team, but also in disbelief at the experience of hearing the tremulous and husky voice of an angry middle-aged man coming from the youthful figure of his avatar.

"Let me remind you of the primary concern of our government. Whatever happens through there, we must not, I repeat, NOT bring to the attention of electronic intelligences the existence of our colony! The slightest slipup might one day lead to armed satellites appearing at our world, controlled by EI. Look what happened on Earth, where they destroyed the human population: billions of us! Look what nearly happened to the people of New Earth at the hands of the Dark Queen. It might not be our generation who suffers; it might not be for a hundred or a thousand years. But we will be to blame if we make a mistake now, in the next few hours or days."

No one spoke in response to this speech, and the street was

silent but for the drone of a distant helicopter. Only the faintest rumble from the spaceport suggested that they were in a large, thriving city.

"All set, Erik?" Anonemuss pointedly ignored Gunnar, much to Milan's amusement. The human scout seemed like a sound guy.

"Go ahead."

It was impossible to judge Erik's tone, but perhaps a hint of impatience was there in those two words. Milan looked at Ghost and pulled a face, as if to say the team of humans was messed up. And from the dark expression on her face, Ghost agreed with him. It was idiocy to have such divisions, or more than one leader, in a situation that might need sharp tactical decision making.

Shortly after he reached his hand up to the surface of the portal, Anonemuss looked back at them over his shoulder.

"I can put my fingers through and draw them back. I'm going in."

Two steps forward and he was gone.

For a moment everyone concentrated on the portal, as if expecting Anonemuss to come straight back out.

"Rather him than me," said Gunnar abruptly. "That does not appeal to me at all. It's like putting your head in the water of a black lake or something. You know, the cold you would feel when it fills your ears? And what if it never stopped—the cold? What if something flows into you and you can never get rid of it again? What if it's like the poison the Dark Queen used on us? Perhaps he can't come back. Perhaps he can't even unclip." He paused for breath. "How long should we give him? Before we get out of here, that is?"

"Everyone please stay as you are. I'm being asked to unclip by Hope Library. I'll be back soon." Cindella abruptly stiffened and a moment later Erik was gone.

Athena, who along with Milan had come to watch the humans go through the portal, leaned in to whisper to him. "I bet that means Anonemuss can't come back and he's unclipped in order to talk to Erik."

Milan gave her a slight nod. Erik's team had agreed to all clip up from the same place, a library, rather than enter into Saga from their own homes. This way they were close to each other if they needed to talk person to person.

For a while, everyone waited in silence. With the sun on the other side of the blue glass building, it felt as though they were deep underwater. Impatient, Milan started to toss small stones toward the portal, each one getting a little closer to the gray surface. When he caught Ghost's disapproving stare, Milan gave a shrug and brushed the remaining gravel from his hands.

"Perhaps I should go back to Hope Library to hear what is going on," said Gunnar, the face of his avatar calm and serene, the tone of his voice anything but.

"Wait here." B.E.'s assassin avatar shook its head.

"No, I'd better go." And freezing in place for a moment, the handsome trooper disappeared.

"He's going to be a problem, Ghost. Sorry." B.E. was leaning on his pulse rifle.

"What's going on?" she replied.

It was Erik's girlfriend, Inny, who answered her. "When Erik made public your request for assistance, it started up a massive debate, all across the planet. There are a lot of people who think we humans shouldn't have anything to do with electronic worlds; that intelligent life like you represents a danger to us."

Harald stood up from where he had been sitting on the curb. "Yeah. The government was thinking of imposing a ban on clipping up to Saga. Erik and I had a plan, though: we were going to take portable sets and go camping somewhere isolated where we could come join you undisturbed, regardless of what was decided."

"But in the end," Inny continued, "a compromise was agreed on. We were allowed to come on this mission if we took Gunnar along. He's one of the leaders of the anti-EI faction. His remit is to look out for any dangers this situation might pose to New Earth."

"And he's afraid of being in Saga, let alone whatever place exists beyond that portal," observed Ghost.

"Right." You could hear the discontent in B.E.'s voice. "The rest of us are here for you, though, and if Gunnar becomes too much of a problem, I'm simply going to shoot him."

"B.E.! Don't you dare!" cried Inny. Milan, however, chuckled aloud and held out his fist. B.E. shifted his rifle and the two of them bumped knuckles. The human team would be much better off without Gunnar and if, as he intended, Milan went with them, he might shoot Gunnar himself. That way, the decent humans could be rid of his unwanted presence, but they wouldn't be blamed by their own parliament.

If anyone wondered why Milan was now smiling, no one asked.

All at once, Cindella appeared among them again.

"It's a new world through there, all right," said Erik. "According to Anonemuss, it's sunny, about midafternoon. We come out to a grass-covered hill and a modern-looking road leading directly away from the portal. All around their side of the portal are army vehicles, tanks, and soldiers, of the bland gray sort. Hard to judge their era or level of technology. As soon as Anonemuss arrived they started to raise their weapons. He managed to lift his hands and say, 'I come in peace,' or something like that, before they all opened fire. Their weapons shoot tiny sharp missiles in large numbers, with a great deal of noise. Not that they are particularly accurate or powerful; he says the ground was torn up for about five meters all around him and that his avatar took a dozen hits before its life points were all gone."

"Did you see what the people were like?" While Milan was impressed with the terse accuracy of the report, it meant trouble. Whoever was using the portal was ready for war with the people of Saga—and, more indirectly, with those of New Earth. The people beyond the gateway hadn't made any effort to communicate but had opened fire on the first person to approach them.

"He doesn't think they were people, but fairly crude NPCs like those scouts you recorded. Very simple constructions."

"Any idea what we should try next?" asked Athena.

If Erik had thoughts on the subject, they were checked by the return of Gunnar's striking blond avatar to Saga.

"This appears to be a very dangerous situation." He spoke as if everyone had been waiting for his opinion. "There is no question about the hostility of the EI on the other side of the portal."

It did not escape Milan's notice that while Gunnar was speaking, B.E. had moved to gain a clear line of sight to Gunnar's trooper. Milan couldn't help being amused, although it must be a real downer for Ghost that the humans were so divided. This wasn't what she had hoped for when she'd asked for help.

"So what are you saying, Gunnar?" asked B.E. menacingly. "Are you saying we should halt the mission?"

"I'm saying . . ."

"First things first," interrupted Erik, Cindella looking directly at Ghost. "Can you send a vehicle to pick up Anonemuss from the newbie square—I mean the Grand Plaza—to bring his next avatar back to us?"

At this Ghost glanced to Athena, who nodded, tapped a device fixed to her ear, and turned away from them to talk into her coms unit.

"Well, what's the plan?" B.E. was toying with the sight of his sniper's rifle, still squared off as if addressing Gunnar.

"Anonemuss thought they were NPCs and that we should rush them right away in order to get in." Cindella moved to stand in front of the portal, hands on sword hilts. "He reckons we have a good chance of taking them down."

"They might be NPCs," observed Gunnar, "but as I was about to say, presumably there is an intelligence behind these hostile troops. If we go in, guns blazing, we will be alienating ourselves irretrievably from that EI."

Cindella walked over to the shimmering rectangle and stood there in contemplation; it seemed to Milan as though Erik were deliberately snubbing Gunnar. But his next words made it clear that Erik's focus was less on the potential conflict between B.E and Gunnar than on the options available to them.

"I was thinking that I have a few drops of invisibility potion left. If that works, we could perhaps just slip past them."

"Oh man, I love that stuff. It's so awesome." Remembering the time he had drunk from Cindella's bottle, Milan spoke up with sudden animation. "There I was, thinking we were totally doomed, and the next minute we strolled out right under the guns of the police." For a moment no one spoke, and sensing their confusion, Milan continued, "That's what we did when we first met Cindella. We were in prison and the police brought her in to the cells. She got us all out of there with that potion."

It was Erik's dad, Harald, who now addressed one of the core principles that the humans lived by: that violence was never justified. "It's not a bad idea, Erik. But I'd really like to know what we are dealing with before we go through. I mean, if we are attacked by conscious beings, we will just have to bear it and try to reason with them. But if it is NPCs that are being used against us, we can fight back if necessary."

Milan didn't much care for the pacifist philosophy of the

humans of New Earth. Not when an unknown enemy stood poised to attack and had already demonstrated a complete lack of desire to enter into any kind of dialogue.

Having sat patiently on her airboard as it hovered above the ground, Ghost now stood up.

"As far as I'm concerned, the gray people now know that we've discovered the portal. So I don't think there is anything left to gain by letting their scouts roam the city. It's time we took them in." She surveyed the response of the entire group, but it was the nods from Milan and Athena, that settled it. "Will you pass the order, please, Athena? Take them into custody."

Once again Athena walked a few paces away and talked in a low voice, as if addressing the floor at her feet.

"So, who," mused Inny aloud, "would open a portal to Saga, send in scouts, and set up a fighting force with orders to kill anyone coming through from Saga?"

Milan nodded. "Yep. That's the question all right."

"That and the related one: what do they want from us that they couldn't get simply by asking?" Ghost was grim. She must have also sensed that war was coming to Saga. With a feeling of pride, Milan followed Ghost up to the gateway. Whatever lay in store, Ghost had the skills to deal with it and the people beyond the gateway were going to be sorry they ever came to Saga.

"Perhaps the defenses on the other side are precautionary?" Gunnar offered the point, but B.E. had a quick response for him.

"What, shoot to kill as soon as you see someone, even if they have their hands up and are saying they come in peace? I don't think so. If that had been someone from Saga, they would be dead now, which is beyond precautionary; it's callous and brutal."

"You know what my feeling is?" Ghost raised her voice. "My feeling is that something out there is preparing to attack us, and when it comes, it will be terrible. What if there are a lot of these portals? What if they pour into our world all at once? We disbanded the army and a lot of the security forces after the Dark Queen was . . . died. We stopped producing weapons in the factories. You know what's ironic about this? The people of Saga might have been better equipped to resist invasion if the Dark Queen were still in charge."

Harald's avatar gave a shrug. "But she wouldn't have us on her side. And that has to be a major asset, having people who don't stay dead."

"Totally. We really appreciate you being here. But your belief in non-violence also limits your assistance," observed Milan, "because it's not like you can form an army and fight them for us."

"Unless their troops are NPCs." It seemed as though B.E. was always the first of the humans to see the opportunity for battle, and Milan gave him an approving smile.

"Even then," said Gunnar, "I believe I speak for the majority of people on New Earth when I say that we will not participate in a battle in Saga against a new enemy. Not after what happened with the Dark Queen."

"Maybe a majority, maybe not." Inny flared up. "Look at all the people who wanted to help this mission."

Before the argument could continue, Athena held up her hand abruptly to command attention. "I'm just getting a report." Her eyes were on the distant skyline. "We've picked up a scout, and it is merely robotic; no organic material at all; no response to attempts to communicate with it."

"Well then." Having slotted home a power pack into his rifle with a distinct *clunk*, B.E. had no need to say anything further.

"Dad, what do you think? NPCs?"

"Sounds like it, although robots can be intelligent life-forms."

"Not these." Athena shook her head as she listened to her earpiece. "It's switched itself off. Gone dead on us while we were trying to communicate with it."

"We're still back to the question of what is the guiding intelligence behind this and what do they want. These robots have been sent here with a purpose and those guarding the portal from their side were ordered to do so by someone. Right?" asked Inny.

Several of the group nodded.

"Then we have to get through and find out more."

While they continued to wait for Anonemuss, Cindella raised a crystal container high toward the sun and tipped it to see the liquid inside.

"Is that the invisibility potion?" asked Ghost.

Beside her, Inny's avatar displayed a wince. "Not much left, is there?"

"We could maybe get two people in. Not enough. But I have these as well." Erik put the potion down and from Cindella's backpack drew a set of finely illuminated playing cards.

"A Deck of Curiosities?" Inny walked over to quickly look through the images. "The problem is our situation is too vague to use their magic for transport. These only work when you can be very specific about what you want from them."

Cindella nodded and put the cards back. "How do you feel about fighting the guards, then?"

"I think it's all right. They aren't alive—not like the people of Saga," said Inny, but still with a note of uncertainty in her voice.

"Don't you think they must be a little bit alive, though? Like, say, a cat or a dog?" asked Erik.

"Maybe. But cats and dogs don't switch themselves off like these things."

"So, you think they are basically NPCs?"

"I do," Inny replied firmly.

Lifting the potion bottle again, this time high for all to see, Erik spoke loudly. "I'm sorry folks; we are not going to be able to get more than two people in with the potion. So the question is, are we willing to fight those guards to get to see what lies beyond the portal?"

"I am," B.E. said with a shrug.

Harald, however, did not move, and it was hard to read his avatar, as the expression was set to neutral.

"Gunnar?"

"Thank you for asking my opinion. I'll give it, although I

don't think I can sway you all from a potentially catastrophic encounter with a world of belligerent and powerful electronic intelligences. First of all, I do agree that to fight the NPCs on the other side would not infringe on the Law of Violence, but one or more of the fully conscious beings in this other world might be among the units sent to guard the portal and we might harm them by mistake. Moreover, charging in and firing our weapons is precisely the kind of behaviour that will alert the initiating powers of the other side to our existence. Ours, meaning human. What will they make of avatars that disappear without a trace after they are killed? Where will this lead them to search? If they come to consider us a threat, do they have the means to find our planet? Probably not, but even a marginal chance that we might be responsible for bringing disaster upon our people should make us pause for thought."

"You would abandon our friends in Saga to whatever dangers this portal represents?" Erik could show a great range of emotions through Cindella and right now she was frowning.

"That's a question I would prefer to answer privately, among ourselves," Gunnar answered primly, with a quick glance at Ghost.

"You mean yes. And don't be so coy." B.E.'s avatar was less sophisticated than Cindella's, but it, too, was scowling.

"All right, yes. I think we should leave now and never come back. I know this sounds harsh"—this to Ghost—"but I hope you understand my reasoning and my motives. I only seek to protect my species as you would yours."

Erik turned to Ghost.

"What would you do, if the situation were reversed? If you had to come fight in our world, at the risk of bringing trouble to Saga?"

"Me? I'd fight," Ghost replied without hesitation.

"Go Ghost!" Milan laughed with delight and held out his knuckles for her to punch. "I knew you'd say that."

"All right, I vote for fighting, too." Up until now, Harald had been reserved, but this reaction by Ghost and Milan seemed to have won him over.

"Great. Seeing as Anonemuss proposed the idea, that settles it. Sorry, Gunnar, but we are going in."

"I knew it a long time ago. And I can't stop you here . . ."

"That's right," said B.E., lifting his rifle.

". . . but I can cut off your access to Saga and you can be certain I will do so if there seems to be the slightest risk to our people."

Harald's trooper shook his head. "You don't have the authority to do that."

"Oh yes I do."

"Listen, Gunnar, everyone. This is not the time for such an argument. We've agreed that we are going in and we'll do so as soon as Anonemuss is back. That's the end of the matter for now." Cindella strode up to the portal, a lithe silhouette against the bright shimmering surface, and Milan's heart warmed at the determination in Erik's voice.

Chapter 8
Bows and Bullets

Ghost waited impatiently for Anonemuss to return; an airbike driven by one of Athena's squad was bringing him back as a passenger. As soon as the scout reached the group, Anonemuss leapt off the bike and everyone gathered together to look as he sketched the layout on the other side of the portal. It did not take long to formulate a plan, which essentially consisted of Cindella going in first and relying on her magic items to draw enemy fire away from the portal while everyone else came through, troopers first.

"Damn, I wish I was joining you," muttered Milan as the humans checked their weapons in preparation for their attack.

"Really? I would be terrified if this was happening on New Earth and my life was at stake," Inny replied.

"Well yeah, I wish I was joining you and that I could come back to life if it didn't work out." He laughed.

"I am coming."

Everyone turned to Ghost.

"We need you here, though," said Athena quietly.

"It doesn't make sense," added Harald. "It doesn't matter if any of us get killed. But you . . . well, you are unique."

"As are we all." Despite her seriousness, Ghost gave a smile. "I know what you mean. But I can't just stay here in Saga and wait to see what happens. It's like I'm shackled. I need to stretch myself, to see the rest of the universe, to discover what I'm capable of. To feel myself fully alive." She looked about the group, hoping they understood her.

"There was a time when I thought I would upload myself into a robot in your galaxy and fly to the stars in a spaceship. But this is better; I get to keep my body. And I've two other reasons for going that have nothing to do with my own feelings. One is that you'll need me, assuming my RAL abilities work through there; secondly, if Saga is under threat, it's my responsibility as queen to defend us. Given that it's my fault the people of Saga no longer have an army to defend them, the least I can do is go in person and try to avert the danger."

It was unlike Ghost to explain herself at such length, but she was determined to go through the portal with the humans and wanted them to understand her. And her speech had not just been for the benefit of the humans. Although she had addressed Erik's group, it was Athena's and Milan's responses that she was watching for. Athena appeared shocked but Milan gave her a knowing wink.

"I understand you, Ghost," Erik answered. "But all the same, I think you should at least wait here until the initial fighting is over. If we win, come through afterward and see if your powers work. If they don't apply beyond the portal, you'd be of more use here in Saga, don't you think?"

"Yeah." She nodded. But at the same time she settled an ammunition belt over her shoulder.

"Well then, we're all set." Cindella looked from the glistening, pale sheen of the portal back to the group of combatants, then tapped the device fixed to her ear. "Coms on. Let's do it."

"About time." B.E. hefted his IVB Pulsar with both hands, cradling it in front of his chest like an infant.

"Good luck everyone." Swords drawn, Cindella dived through the portal on a roll.

After a count of twenty, Harald ran in, rifle already raised, ready to fire. Another ten seconds and B.E. moved closer to the shimmering curtain.

"Come on, Gunnar. You're supposed to be next."

"I decline to enter."

"Blood and thunder!" With a cry of exasperation, B.E. dived through, and after him went Inny, the medic for their team. With the exception of Gunnar, whose handsome trooper was stepping away from the portal, the humans were through— and probably in the middle of a furious battle. In the quiet streets of Saga it could hardly have been any more tranquil.

Kicking her airboard alive, Ghost accelerated as fast as she could toward the shimmering portal. "I'm going in."

"No!" cried Athena.

But Ghost didn't hesitate.

The world beyond the portal was sunny, just as Erik had described it. What he hadn't managed to convey was the curious impact of the colors. They were subtly different from those of Saga: the green of the trees in the distance was, well, greener; the same was true for the blue of the sky, and even the ocher uniforms of the soldiers. Everything was a little brighter, a little more cartoonlike, than the gritty urban environment that Ghost lived in.

No sooner had she absorbed the shock of entering this new world than the first streams of bullets began to search her out. As she threw herself from the airboard and down a grassy bank, Ghost summoned up all her powers of concentration and tried to slow down the passage of time. It worked. The underlying fabric of this new environment was almost identical to that of Saga. It was made up of discrete cycles of processing activity, which felt to Ghost like a pulse: a pulse with more than a thousand beats per second. As a RAL—the last in Saga—Ghost had an innate ability to alter all the environmental variables around her, including this pulse, and she slowed it now as much as she possibly could, bringing the beat of time almost to a stop.

Bullets filled the air. Each jerk of the time frame brought a dozen lines of these missiles closer to her body. And crude as they were, if they hit, they'd rip her to pieces. Nevertheless, as her body rolled down the slope, Ghost lifted her own handguns into position to fire back at the enemy soldiers. Near-blinding flashes of energy now joined the lethal display, lurching away from her with every frame, back toward the source of one of the streams of bullets. She could alter the air pressure in her vicinity and did so, making sure that as the arriving bullets reached her they curved away from the straight line they had previously followed, to streak past Ghost's head with a distortion of the air that would have sounded like a high-pitched scream at normal speeds. As she finished her roll to come up to a kneeling posture, still returning fire, Ghost let out a cry of triumph. To stay alive in the center of this rain of hot metal stretched her to her utter limit, but she could do it. Whoever these people were, they had made a big mistake; a terrible enemy was upon them.

Blue and red streaks flashed across the sky, indicating that the human avatars from Saga were in the thick of battle and firing their energy weapons. It was too congested over by the portal to see what was happening. Some distance ahead, however, Ghost caught sight of Cindella, and her heart gave a skip of delight that Erik's avatar was still alive. The pirate was standing on top of a troop carrier, surrounded by enemy soldiers but sweeping them away with a machine gun she had captured. It looked like the avatar's magic armor from Epic was effective here, because bullets were hitting the figure but just bouncing off her. As Ghost watched admiringly, a warrior looking like a medieval knight climbed into the vehicle and caught Cindella from behind with a thrust from a sword. That staggered Cindella and she leaped from the truck, disappearing from Ghost's view.

Ever since Ghost had rolled through the portal and down

the hill, a stream of expletives had been coming through her coms unit, but in the last few seconds they had died away, which was rather ominous. She hadn't been able to speak until now; all her concentration had been needed to deflect bullets. A large group of pikemen had spotted her and were running toward her, but she had a few moments until they arrived. It was most peculiar how the soldiers here were a mix of types, from those using ancient handheld weapons to those using fairly modern guns.

"What's going on? Have we a plan?" she asked the static, all the while firing non-stop at the incoming attackers.

B.E.'s voice was a whisper. "I'm lying in a pile of bodies beside a tank, playing dead."

"Ghost!" cried Erik. "Get back out through the portal if you can. I think we're going to wipe. I'm down to twenty-two percent health."

There was no time to say anything further, for despite the fact that Ghost had picked off a dozen of the pikemen with her handguns, there were still twenty or so who had reached her and were now chopping down at her with poles, the ends of which were fixed with sharp curved blades. Again there was something curious about the soldiers: they all seemed to perform the same actions. This made it relatively easy to swerve and dodge their blows, except that things were getting congested. The gun in her right hand was out of power, so in midair—vaulting as a pikeman attempted to cut her legs off at the knee—Ghost dropped the empty gun to pull out a dagger. Dragging an off-balance soldier across her body to block the incoming attacks, Ghost alternated close-range shots from her left hand with stabs and slashes from her right. Breathless and sweating, she soon stood alone in the center of a pile of bodies.

"Other reports, please," she managed to pant out. Taking a tip from B.E., Ghost crouched down among the dead while she tried to get a picture of what was happening.

"I think it's just the three of us," answered Erik.

But there were three distinct clicks in her ear.

"Was that you, B.E.? If someone else is alive but unable to speak, tap again."

Tap, tap, tap.

"Harald? Inny? Anon . . ."

Tap, tap, tap.

So, the scout was hiding somewhere, too. Probably surrounded by enemies.

"Anyone see what happened to Harald and Inny?" Erik's voice faltered slightly.

"Shot," whispered B.E. "Both dead."

Maybe she should try to get back to Saga? Much as Ghost relished being in battle, if too many enemy soldiers focused on her, even her RAL abilities would not be able to cope with them all. Just as she was readying herself to sprint back up the slope toward the portal, an extraordinary sight caused Ghost to remain in place.

Cindella came into view about fifty meters away, sprinting around the side of the hill on which the portal stood, with an enormous body of horsemen of the medieval type galloping behind her. Farther up the hillside was a crowd of the more modern soldiers, moving after her much more slowly, but firing their guns all the while. Not that this was a problem, since those bullets that hit their target still bounced off the avatar's armor. As Ghost watched, Cindella produced a crystal bottle from the pouches around her waist and drank from it. Some kind of magic potion, probably.

Keeping low to the ground as the whole chase thundered past Ghost's position, she smiled to herself. Erik had managed to draw all of their remaining troops in a chase after his avatar. It seemed from the curved route he was taking that Erik was steering Cindella in a wide circle around the hill.

". . . off me! I protest! How dare . . ."

"Gunnar?" Ghost whispered.

"He's gone," said B.E. faintly. "He just rolled out of the portal and ran straight back to Saga again."

"The coward! You mean he ducked out of the battle?" It was rare to hear Erik sound so furious, but a moment later his voice became calmer. "I'm sorry, Ghost."

"It's only an avatar. Why is he afraid of it being killed?" she asked in reply, keeping her voice low.

"I've no idea what he's thinking, but his absence may be to our advantage right now. Anonemuss, I want you to unclip, please. Go get Gunnar to clip out, too. Tell him exactly what is happening here. Then he is to go back into Saga and tell Milan and Athena. The main thing is that they don't try to come in. It's too dangerous. Got that?"

Tap, tap, tap.

"Do you need a full report from me, or can you see what's happening?"

Tap.

"Tap three times if you want the full report."

Tap, tap, tap.

"There are about fifty modern soldiers left in the vicinity of the portal. With something like five hundred barbarian riders chasing me around the base of the hill, I'm running in a circle whose path is about two hundred meters from the portal, which is in the center. I'm good—eighty-nine percent health and slowly rising. I can keep this up indefinitely, as the bullets don't damage me. I haven't given up yet, and I reckon B.E. and I still have a chance, so Ghost, there's no need for you to take any risks. Also, seeing as Gunnar can act as a communication channel where he is, he needn't come through again."

Tap, tap, tap.

"What's the plan, then?" If B.E. had any doubts, it was impossible to detect them in his voice; it may have been a whisper, but it was almost an enthusiastic one.

"Mad, isn't it? I'm going to clear the modern soldiers from the hill with my bow, while keeping these cavalry chasing me if I can. Then we'll see. If you can stand up safely and pick off these horsemen one by one without being attacked, we are good. If they come for you, there's nothing I can do, so run back through the portal."

"Gotcha," acknowledged B.E.

"Same for you, Ghost, wherever you are."

"I'm hiding in a pile of bodies at the bottom of the hill. You just passed me."

"Nice. When the hill is clear, go up to the portal, and then, if the cavalry break off from chasing me, at least you're safe."

"Good idea."

"One down."

A few seconds passed.

"Two more. There's about fifty altogether, though, so this may be a while."

Tap, tap, tap.

"Welcome back, Anonemuss. All good on your side?" There was a cheerful note in Erik's voice now, and Ghost smiled to herself. He was the perfect comrade to have alongside you in battle; he'd kept his composure and his plan sounded like it might work.

Tap, tap.

"What's two taps mean?" asked Ghost. "Neither yes nor no?"

"I bet it means Gunnar was acting the maggot again, but that he has gone to talk to Milan, right?" Despite the risk of being heard by the remaining riflemen on the hill, B.E. evidently couldn't resist offering his negative estimate of Gunnar's likely behavior.

Tap, tap, tap.

"Ha," chuckled Ghost.

"Stay hidden, wherever you are, Anonemuss," said Erik. "I'm taking out the soldiers on the hill with my bow while trying to keep these horsemen focused on me. I'll let you know when it's clear, and then you can join B.E. and Ghost up at the portal."

Tap, tap, tap.

For a while there was just a faint hiss over the coms. Then Cindella came into view again and Ghost lay flat and still. Arrows flew overhead as Cindella released shots, firing over her shoulder. There were distinctly fewer bullets flying past than there had been on Erik's last circuit. The huge numbers of cavalry, though, were still intimidating, and the ground shook as they rode by.

A few more minutes passed. Above her the sky was clear blue apart from a wispy cloud that drifted past, far above the carnage on the hillside. It was a good idea to warn Milan to stay clear. He probably had been getting ready to come through and he almost certainly would be dead if he had. Athena, too, if she couldn't bear waiting on her own.

"I'm clear." All of a sudden B.E. spoke up in his normal voice. "You just killed the last of them from around me."

"Great, but don't open fire till I've eliminated the other riflemen. It won't be long now, and it would be a shame if they shot you after all this running around."

"Will do."

Another appearance of Cindella and her long tail of riders. It was eerie how they all rode in the same pose, with an upraised spear in one hand, and it was peculiar too how their horses all ran with the same gait. These NPCs were not particularly sophisticated in their programming.

"Right you are, B.E. Give it a go. If any barbarians break

off to attack you, please jump back through the portal. Ghost, Anonemuss, if you are clear of the riders, maybe now would be a good time to get up to the portal."

At once Ghost leaped up and sprinted as fast as she could up the hill, her senses alert all the while for incoming fire. But it was true: the riflemen on the hill were dead and all the vehicles seemed empty of crew. Panting, she arrived at the top, where B.E. was methodically firing his pulsar weapon. He paused just for a moment to nod a greeting to Ghost, then drew a line on the cavalry once more. Down below, Cindella was in plain sight, leading the horsemen as though they were a great dark cloak spread out behind her. Where they had been riding around the hill, a wide muddy circle had been drawn in the grass.

Anonemuss, the scout, ran up.

"Where were you hiding?" asked B.E.

"I was holding on to the underside of a troop carrier."

"Hah. Neat."

"Hey team, I see you." Cindella gave them a wave and Ghost waved back before trying a shot with her handgun. The red bolt of energy streaked away but expired before it reached the rider she had aimed at. Dropping the gun, Ghost went over and picked a rifle up from a dead enemy soldier. It was a very crude piece of programming, a simple device. The bullet it fired would do only a fraction of the damage of an energy bolt, but at least it would reach the target.

"Got one." B.E. was kneeling now and Ghost could see the regular pulses of his shots at the edge of her vision. "I don't believe it, after that mess we were in, but I think we're going to win this. So long as they keep chasing you, at least. It's a bit like the dragon fight, don't you think, Erik?"

"How do you mean?"

"It's like, if they just had a bit more intelligence, they'd hunt us down, or some of them would stop and go back the other way to intercept you. But even though they are stronger than us, their programming is too limited. And we've found a way to exploit it."

"True." And round Cindella came again, allowing Ghost and the two avatars to open fire once more. They were growing more confident, shooting fast and piling up the bodies of horsemen at the base of the hill. Each time she came to their side of the portal, Cindella had to vary her path slightly, running alongside the curving lines of slain barbarians, all in the same death pose: horse and rider lying together on the grass.

At last, only a handful of the enemy remained and Cindella stood her ground while everyone else finished them off, Erik evidently confident that Cindella could avoid the final stabs of the enemy's spears. What a battle! Ghost slapped B.E. and Anonemuss on the back, then picked up her airboard to stroll down the hill and join Cindella.

"That was pretty good fun in the end," said B.E.

"Want me to log out and tell Gunnar what happened?" asked Anonemuss.

"Yes, please, and if you can persuade him, have Gunnar come through when he's done reporting to Milan and Athena."

"Nice strategy, Erik. Well done." Ghost and Cindella

walked over the battlefield examining their fallen opponents. The detail on the figures was not great. The modern soldiers, for example, had the outline of pockets on their uniforms, but when Ghost and Cindella bent down to search through them, it became obvious that these were just drawn on the cloth and could not actually be opened.

"Thanks, Ghost. We were lucky, though, really. It was so close to a total wipe. Even Cindella was nearly down."

B.E. picked up a rifle from the ground and shook his head. "Strange how crude it is. Like a drawing." He pulled the trigger while aiming at a distant bush and missed. "I wonder how they reload."

Cindella bent down and picked one up, and as she turned it over in her hands, Erik had his avatar remove her glove. All at once the world was washed in subtle hints of green and turquoise, the light coming from a ring on her finger and recasting the scene.

"What's the ring?" asked Ghost.

Cindella brandished it proudly. "It's a magic ring from Epic, the only one of its kind: the Ring of True Seeing."

"And does it tell you anything about these people?"

"Maybe. These guns, for example—they have no mechanical parts. They look like rifles, but they could be any shape. What makes them work is something I can now see inside of them, although I don't really know what I'm looking at. There's a space in the stock of the guns packed with glowing symbols, linked together and slowly writhing around each other. Same with these bodies. They have a cavity in their chests, but—presumably because they're dead—there's no glow and the symbols are broken and scattered, like the springs and coils of a watch that has been smashed open."

As Erik was talking, the portal flickered and the striking blond trooper that was Gunnar stepped from it. Despite the neutral expression of his avatar, there was something nervous about his movements.

A moment later, Milan and Athena came through and behind them came Anonemuss.

"Wow, nice battle." Milan appeared impressed by the piles of bodies all around them.

"The good news from your perspective"—B.E. stood up and moved toward Milan—"is that these things are not too smart. They had a very rigid set of moves. If they came through the portal and attacked Saga, they would do a lot of damage, but you would defeat them." B.E. gestured to the hundreds of fallen troops. "Erik and I did most of this, because they wouldn't stop chasing him even when I was picking them off."

The bodies of Harald and Inny were lying near the portal and Athena was searching through their belongings. Having found what she was looking for—the tracking device—she stood up and pointed.

"He's over there to the north. Probably a good way off, because the signal is fairly weak."

"The scout that came into Saga, you mean?" asked Ghost.

"Right."

"I think I see a road, or a river, where there's a gap in the hills." B.E. was looking through the telescopic sights of his pulse rifle in the direction Athena was pointing. At this, Cindella rummaged in a pouch and produced a small box, the velvet-lined interior of which held two large glass lenses. More magic, evidently, for soon after she put them on, Erik was able to give a report.

"It is a road. And there are people on it; more of those barbarian horsemen, riding this way."

Before anyone could respond, a distinct droning sound, like that of a bee, could be heard from the same direction.

"Milan, Athena, get back into Saga now, please. I think the rest of us should move out of here." Ghost looked about them for some cover to hide in.

"I want to stay," said Milan determinedly.

"Me, too."

"Thanks, both of you, but look." Ghost pointed at the shattered bodies of the avatars of Inny and Harald. "That could be you."

By now there was a dark spot visible in the section of the sky from which the ominous deep sound was coming. It was moving fast.

"There's more coming! A lot more," cried Erik. "Tanks and personnel carriers full of soldiers are right behind the riders. We really have to run for it now. Milan, Athena—Ghost is right; you should go back now while you can." Cindella began to move toward a line of trees, but paused because Milan was not budging.

"Look, Ghost, we've been through a lot together. I like you

pretty much more than anyone else I know—with the possible exception of Athena—and I owe you. So if I die, I die, but I'm coming along."

"And while I agree with those sentiments"—Athena raised her voice—"the real case for us staying is more pragmatic than the words of this romantic. You might need our skills."

"Please. Go back," urged Ghost.

"Get down!" shouted Anonemuss, ducking in beside a truck. Frighteningly swift, the black dot in the sky had become a plane, diving straight toward them, with a new sound audible despite the angry roaring noise of its engines: that of bullets hammering out and tearing up the hill in lines that rushed toward them.

Only Ghost remained on her feet, concentrating, slowing time. Two impact lines came racing along the ground at the ferocious speed of the airplane. But just as they seemed set to smash into her body, the bullet tracks disappeared. While the noise of the plane's machine guns was still loud in her ears, the bullets were no longer hitting the ground; instead, they were streaming through the air, curving away above her. Ghost turned, the wind from the passage of the plane blowing her hair all around her head, and guided the lines of bullets on up into the sky with movements of her arms. A moment later the plane blew apart in a ball of flame: its bullets, redirected by Ghost, had found the fuel tank. Debris fell around them as the brightness of the explosion slowly faded from her eyes.

"Whether we stay or go, we have to move right now. There

will be more of those." Anonemuss began running down the hill toward the nearest cover: that provided by a copse. Milan and Athena ran after him. Cindella was hesitating.

"What is it?" asked B.E. "We need to move."

"Inny. If we let them take the portal back, she'll never get through." Erik spoke with heartfelt regret. "The same with Harald."

"We've no choice." B.E. shouldered his pulse rifle and began to run after the others. A moment later, swift as a diving hawk, Cindella raced past him.

It was hard for Ghost to accept Milan and Athena's decision, but there was no point waiting any longer, hoping they would turn back. Her two friends were already halfway to the trees. She turned to the last remaining avatar, that of Gunnar.

"Well, are you joining us?"

There was something in the posture of the handsome trooper as he faced the portal, its shimmering silver light reflecting in his eyes, that suggested a yearning to leave. When he began to run, Ghost was sure that Gunnar was going to plunge back through to the safety of Saga, but with a groan of self-pity, the avatar swerved to rush after the others. Surprised, Ghost followed.

Ghost had enjoyed the battle at the portal and had been looking forward to the opportunity of exploring this new world, backed up by the human team. But now events had moved in an unexpected direction. A dark sense of foreboding lay upon her as she saw Milan and Athena duck under branches and out of view. By choosing to come, they had demonstrated their loyalty to her. But they might have just made a decision that would cost them their lives. Despite Ghost's considerable powers, it might prove impossible for any of them to get back to Saga.

Chapter 9
A Realm of Magic and Monsters

From the cover of the woods, Ghost watched as several more planes flew around the hill on which stood the portal to Saga.

"The others aren't going to make it, are they?" Although they were hidden hundreds of yards from the hill, B.E. was nevertheless careful to speak in a whisper.

"Even if they created a new avatar straightaway and raced to the portal with someone as fast as Milan as a driver, they still wouldn't get there before the tanks and riders I saw coming up that road," answered Erik glumly.

"Right. In that case, let's push on deeper into these woods and get clear of the scene." Once again Anonemuss gave the lead. When at long last Cindella turned away from the portal with a nod of agreement, the scout set off at a low crouching run to where the trees were thicker. Everyone followed suit, brushing aside ferns and running with a crunching sound over fallen twigs. They might be leaving a trail for anyone who looked closely at the ground, but on the other hand they were making good progress. It was surprising how quickly they lost sight of the edge of the forest. After a few minutes running, it felt as though they were in a completely different world from the one in which they had fought the battle at the portal.

They kept up this dash through the trees for some time, until Milan, panting, called out, "Sorry. I'm . . . not as fit . . . as I was. Can we walk a bit?"

"Yeah, can we slow up for a while, please?" Ghost, too, was glad to ease the pace. It was easy for the human avatars to push themselves hard; they registered fatigue simply as a dip in a graph, not as the aching of their muscles or as shortness of breath.

By now the group was in an older and denser part of the forest. Ivy climbed around tall tree trunks, some of which Ghost recognized as birches, but there were oaks, ash, and chestnuts, too. Maybe it was because she grew up in a city, or because this was a different world, but there were all sorts of trees that seemed unfamiliar to her. While the forest was not all that dense—there was plenty of room to run between the tree trunks—a canopy of branches high above them filled most of the sky and there was a darkness to the forest, even though the position of the sun suggested it was still midafternoon.

"Let's have a break," Erik called out, and the word "break" was shouted ahead by B.E. to Anonemuss, who stopped. "We humans can grab some food and a chance to refresh ourselves. When we're back, we should perhaps line up properly for the journey: our scout up front, me or Ghost at the back. That kind of thing."

"Go ahead then. How long will you be?" Milan flung himself with a sigh of relief onto a cluster of dry brown ferns.

"How about thirty minutes?"

"Fine. Take your time."

"See you then." Cindella gave a wave good-bye.

"Later," B.E. acknowledged, already clasping his hands behind his head and stretching out his feet.

For a few moments the avatars remained frozen. Then they were gone. Milan shook his head and looked from Ghost to Athena.

"It is always so freaky when they do that."

"What happened with Gunnar, back at the portal?" Ghost squatted down and began to rummage in her pack, producing a high-energy bar that she opened and began to chew.

"Ha!" Athena laughed. "When he refused to go through, Milan got hold of him and threw him into it."

"Didn't do much good, though. He just came crawling back again. I very nearly shot him. He's a waste of time."

"That would have been a mistake." Athena frowned. "I think we have to be careful with him. From what B.E. said, Gunnar represents a large faction of human opinion. If we get rid of him, that might cause whoever runs their world to shut down the whole operation and leave us here alone."

Milan sat up. "Speaking of here—where are we?"

"Somewhere pretty strange," answered Ghost. "Do you both get the feeling this place is a bit . . . more simplistic than

Saga?" She had broken a twig from the bush beside her and was looking at it closely.

Milan shrugged. "I dunno. But the colors seem different. It's like we are in a cartoon."

"Yes, that's it," said Athena. "There's less subtlety in the colors and shades. But the detail of the objects in the world seems pretty good."

"Yeah." Ghost had broken the twig, to reveal its pale interior. Now she threw it to the ground and went over to lie beside Milan in the bracken; her eyes had suddenly become heavy. "I'm shattered after that fight. Mind if I try to take a quick nap, while you two keep watch?"

"No worries, Ghost." Milan shifted about, and a moment later she was drifting away, head on his arm, the memory of her recent hand-to-hand fight giving way to a dream about air-board racing.

When she woke, Athena was studying the tracking device, while Milan was carving his name into the bark of a tree with a large knife. It was the return of the humans that had disturbed her. They were all back. At the sight of Gunnar's athletic-looking trooper, Ghost couldn't help but challenge him. Ever since the battle she must have been suppressing some anger toward Gunnar, because it welled up now out of her recent dreams.

"Hey, Gunnar. Something I've been wondering: why have you come on this mission, if you are so afraid of being here?"

"I'm not afraid." Immediately Gunnar's voice rang out in a loud, defensive tone. Everyone else turned to look at him, and despite the impassive expressions of their avatars, it seemed to Ghost that their attentive posture communicated disbelief. What other explanation but cowardice was there for Gunnar's recent behavior?

After pausing to face Ghost's stare, Gunnar let out a sigh. "Very well, I acknowledge a certain trepidation. You remember that the Dark Queen addicted thousands of humans to Saga?"

"Yes?"

"Well, I was one of them, and it was absolutely soul-destroying. I couldn't go any distance from a console without breaking into a sweat. I needed to know I could get back into Saga and experience whatever it was that was flowing into my brain. Not that it was pleasurable; it was a necessity. And I was firmly convinced that I would die if I couldn't have it. Of course, I tried staying away, but as I wasn't prepared to kill myself, I had to keep going back to my console."

"I understand that. But why did you agree to join Erik and his friends and come on this expedition?"

"To deal with that fear, mostly. I mean, it is partly true that I come as a representative of those who want to exercise caution in any dealings between humans and EIs. But I also wanted to get over my horror of entering EI space, my dread that when I come to unclip, it will be there again, the addiction."

"So, you joined with a sincere willingness to assist us?"

"I wanted to. I hoped to. And while we were in Saga, I was fine. But when we came to the portal, I just couldn't face the unknown like the rest of you. What if one of those people who we were fighting had the powers of the Dark Queen? I just couldn't let an EI tamper with my brain again. So I backed out."

"And Milan threw you in?"

"Eventually, after he had shouted obscenities at me for a bit."

"So now?"

"Now?"

"How do you feel? Are you still afraid of clipping up?"

"Yes. But seeing as there's no ill effects so far from this new environment, I've calmed down a bit."

"Well . . ." Ghost paused, choosing her words carefully. "I felt let down."

Gunnar's avatar nodded. "My apologies, Your Highness."

"I'd like to know that I can count on everyone. I hadn't planned on Athena and Milan being here, and I'm particularly concerned for them. If you panic again and make a mistake, there are real lives at stake, not just avatars." She paused to let that sink in. "It might be better if you unclip now and let us continue without you."

"I know. I was actually thinking about it. But I do want this mission to succeed. I want to find out what's happening and why Saga is under threat. But at the same time, we humans mustn't do anything that might alert a powerful EI to our existence, to our community on New Earth."

"Well, there's only seven of us, and I've a feeling we are going to need everyone here to deal with the people controlling these troops. So how about this: Athena, Milan, and I promise not to ever reveal that you are humans and you promise not to do anything that will put our lives in danger?"

"Of course. I'd never do that."

Unable to judge by eye contact and by the expression of the avatar, Ghost listened intently to Gunnar's voice. As far as she could tell, he sounded sincere. "Right then. Let's carry on."

"So, what's the plan?" asked B.E.

"Well, the way I see it," said Athena, "is that the agent I'm tracking will probably have to report to whoever is in charge, so we should follow him northward to find out what's going on here."

"Wait a moment." Cindella stepped forward. "I was talking to Harald and Inny on our break. They are stuck on the far side of the portal. They say there's a large army gathered there now and they died again trying to join us. It's impossible for them to come through alive. So they were wondering if they could help back in Saga by relaying Ghost's orders and getting some serious defenses in place, ready in case that army tries to come through."

"Good idea." Ghost thought for a moment. "Please ask them to report to Kalpurnia, head of the guild Ages of Saga. She's currently in charge of getting equipment and troops to the portal as soon as it comes off the factory floor, and it would be good to get progress reports from her."

"Will do." Cindella stiffened and a moment later disappeared, causing Milan to glance at Ghost and then roll his eyes.

It took a few minutes for Erik to return, but suddenly Cindella was back among them.

"Done," said Erik. "Are we ready to move on then?"

"All set to chase down this scout and find the bad guys," answered Milan cheerfully, hoisting his rifle over his shoulder. "Which way?"

Athena looked up from the screen and gestured. "The problem is if we go straight toward the scout, that will take us to the road all those soldiers came down. He is probably using that road, in fact. So I suggest we go east a bit more first and then north, parallel to the road but hidden by this forest."

"That way?" Anonemuss gestured to where the gloom of the forest looked darker still and the brambles and bushes looked thicker.

"Yeah."

"Want to be our point?" Erik asked him.

"I guess that's my role, although it will be hard to keep quiet walking through that, and these clothes aren't ideal." Anonemuss gestured to his white shirt and black trousers. Being an office worker was no longer a disguise.

"You go on ahead; we'll probably make more noise than you. I'll go next, then B.E., Gunnar, Milan, and Athena, with Ghost guarding the back. Does that make sense?" Cindella glanced at Ghost, who nodded.

Soon they were moving through the darkening forest in a line, Anonemuss just visible up ahead and everyone else bunched together behind. There was not much talk. Even Ghost, with her extraordinary agility, had to concentrate in order to avoid the brambles and branches that caught at her clothes. Occasionally a bird was disturbed by their progress, fluttering off toward the shadowy canopy with disconsolate cries. Through gaps in the roof of leaves could be seen a deep blue sky in which clouds were beginning to show touches of orange as the sun declined.

The ground over which they walked rose and fell in long undulations, and it was after breasting a small hill that everyone gathered beside Anonemuss where he had halted to look down into the next dip. It held a large clearing and, at its center, a circular stone fountain about five meters in diameter. The statue that rose from the water was of a slender princess, holding an urn from which water flowed. Around the fountain was an inscription, which Ghost was able to read despite the ornate lettering. The part facing her said, ". . . YOURSELVES AND REST AWHILE."

"That's interesting," Ghost whispered to Anonemuss, who nodded.

"We're in a fantasy world—another Epic, maybe?" Anonemuss observed.

"You mean, literally, another Epic?"

"Why not? If humans created it once, why not run it again?"

A low whistle from Milan, who had taken out a pair of binoculars and was looking through them, interrupted their conversation. "That is some cute chick. Strange features, though."

"She's an elf," said B.E.

"You know, as we've been going through the forest, I was thinking that the soldiers we fought at the portal, especially the

ones with guns, didn't seem like they belonged in this world."
Erik lifted his voice so they could all hear. "And this seems to
confirm it. This realm is a fantasy one, and like Anonemuss
just said, it could even be another copy of Epic."

"Fascinating," muttered Athena.

"Yeah, this is kinda awesome. Does it mean we'll meet, like,
wizards and dragons?" Milan asked.

"Maybe, if we are unlucky." B.E. checked the settings on
his pulsar. "Though it would have been a lot easier to have
fought a dragon with one of these than with bows and arrows."

"Wait here. I'll go investigate further." Keeping to the edge
of the clearing, Cindella slowly circled the fountain at a distance, until she was nearly back to them.

"It says, 'Welcome to the lands of the Sylviani. Refresh yourselves and rest awhile,'" Erik called up to them. Then Cindella
removed her glove and the glade was flooded with the inquisi-
tive turquoise light of the Ring of True Seeing. Immediately,
she took several steps back and sought the cover of a tree. Her
rapier and dagger were in hand.

"Erik, what's up?" shouted Ghost.

"Shoot it!"

The statue of the elfin woman was gone. In its place was a
plinth on which lay a monster whose body was the coils of a
serpent, but whose shoulders, arms, and head were those of a
female human. The creature was looking directly at her and
Ghost felt dizzy.

With astonishing litheness, the serpent woman reared up to
shout an incantation, while glowing spheres of power gathered

in her outstretched hands. Some kind of spell was going to be launched and, realizing this, Ghost grabbed Athena, bringing them both to the ground, rolling over in the hope of escaping the impact. The explosion, when it came, was not the one she had feared: a spell that engulfed Milan in destruction. Instead, from the corner of her eye, Ghost saw a flash from B.E.'s rifle. A bolt of pink energy shot across the glade to consume the head of the monster. While its hands dropped to its sides and its torso toppled backward, the serpentine body lashed about in hideous convulsions, splashing water in all directions, until with a final shudder it lay still. B.E. shot the body once more, but it didn't stir.

Cindella came out from behind a tree. "Save your power. It's dead," said Erik.

"What was that?" asked Athena, getting back to her feet and brushing ferns away from her legs.

"I'm not sure. I don't think this is Epic, because we didn't have anything like it. Some kind of serpent spell caster, with illusions and who knows what other spells."

"Hey, there's treasure in here." Anonemuss was leaning over the edge of the pool, looking into the dark water. Her curiosity aroused, Ghost walked across to him. There were objects at the bottom: bones in rusting armor and some coins gleaming in the murk.

"Loot the dead," muttered B.E., "as we used to say in our Epic days."

"I don't know if we should," said Erik. "Let me look again

with the ring." Cindella moved up to the pool, hand raised, emitting a flow of light like a turquoise star.

"Well?" Anonemuss had straddled the stone wall of the fountain and was ready to climb in.

"I don't see any traps."

"Good enough." The dark water came up to the scout's waist as he waded around the pool, avoiding the serpent's body and investigating the debris. It took a while, but at least there seemed to be no danger.

Most of the items that Anonemuss lifted from the water were useless, either rusted metal or rotten leather. But there was a magnificently decorated dagger that shone with a faint ruby light, in perfect condition, as well as a ring with a large opal whose gold setting was pristine. Anonemuss tossed the dagger up and down.

"Mind if I hang on to it? It has to be magic of some sort and might be useful." He looked at Cindella.

"Go ahead."

Having sheathed the dagger, Anonemuss then toyed with the ring. As soon as he placed it on his finger, he disappeared.

"Wow!" exclaimed Milan.

Simultaneously, Erik's voice rang out with amazement. "No way!"

"Are you still here?" asked Athena.

"What?" Anonemuss asked, surprised.

"You've gone invisible, mate," answered Milan.

"Really?" He reappeared. "I didn't see any change. You try

it." Anonemuss threw the ring over to Milan, who caught it and put it on. He, too, vanished.

"Nice." Anonemuss smiled.

"This would be so cool back home. Imagine what you could get up to." Milan's snigger was the only indication of his whereabouts, unless Ghost wanted to concentrate hard on the pressure changes in the air around her.

"I think Anonemuss should take that, too," observed Erik. "It makes sense for our scout to be invisible."

Milan reappeared and gave the ring back with a rueful smile.

"Erik." Ghost was looking at the sky. "How about we make camp here? It's getting near sunset, and that whole encounter shows we can't just blunder through the forest; it's dangerous."

"Good idea. Should we make a fire, though?"

"I say yes." Ghost replied. "There is a danger that planes flying overhead will see it, if they are looking for us. But who knows what other monsters are in the forest. A fire might keep them away, and at least it will allow us to see them."

Not long after, they had quite a lively blaze going at the edge of the glade, as far away as they could get from the dead creature in the fountain. Ghost and Milan were chewing nutribars provided by Athena. With the exception of B.E. — who was standing guard — everyone sat near the fire, listening to the crackling sound of the burning branches.

"Hey! Look at this." Athena was staring intently at the screen of the tracking device. "Our man is moving fast and sort of coming this way."

Ghost went over to see. The green dot was indeed moving back toward them, although he would pass a little to the east. And it was moving at a surprising speed.

"Looks like he is in an airplane?" she suggested.

"Could be." Athena nodded. "Let's hope he doesn't go too far." They watched the green dot for a while as it moved to the southeast. Eventually it ceased moving, which indicated that the scout they were tracking was more than fifty miles away.

"Oh well," said Athena. "At least we weren't trudging all night in the wrong direction. We will have to go that way tomorrow." And she pointed across the fountain to the far side of the glade.

Chapter 10
BENEATH THE SIGN OF THE BLACK LION

After the humans had left them for another break, it seemed to Ghost that the glade was surprisingly quiet. Perhaps it was just that Athena and Milan were tired. Beside her, sitting on a fallen log, Milan was picking at clumps of moss.

"I love the change of scenery"—he glanced up at Ghost—"but I wish I could dial for a pizza."

"You're lucky I thought to bring nutribars." Athena was looking through her large kit bag. "I also brought a torch—very handy—and a micro-thin sleeping bag."

"Oh, I don't suppose you brought two of those?" Milan asked enviously.

"I did, because I knew you wouldn't have."

"Awesome, thanks." He caught the pouch she threw at him in one hand.

Athena dug out another small package. "What about you, Ghost? Want one?"

"Sure, thanks." It was possible for Ghost to alter the

environment around her to cope with great extremes of hot and cold, but that took effort and concentration. It was much easier to take off her boots and slide into a thin sack made of fabric coated with heat-retaining emulsion. Soon they were all lying side by side, looking upward to where the glade allowed them a view of a darkening sky already rich in stars.

"Just out of curiosity, Milan"—Athena tucked her bangs back behind her ear to look at him—"what *did* you bring with you?"

"Um, my Atanski, a couple of Higgs handhelds, and my music—an awesome compilation." He gestured to the headphones and music player beside him.

Athena shook her head wearily. "I thought as much. You should really know when to abandon your party-idiot guise and get real. This is a matter of life or death."

On the other side of Ghost, just out of view of Athena, Milan pulled a face and silently mimicked Athena's lecture, causing Ghost to smile.

"Well, I'm going to repack half my gear in another bag and tomorrow you're going to carry it."

"Hey, Ghost," said Milan, blatantly changing the subject, "do you think it's safe to sleep here?"

"You mean, because of the dead monster?" Ghost replied.

"Sort of. Don't you think that there might be other dangerous critters around?"

"Perhaps. Not here, though." Athena looked about the glade. "Other creatures will be afraid of the snake-woman in the pool and stay away."

"Maybe, but if you're thinking we should probably keep watches, Milan, then I agree." Ghost turned to him and Milan shook his head in mock despair.

"Damn, where are those humans when they would come in handy?"

For a while the three friends lay in companionable silence. At first Ghost had been dismayed when Athena and Milan had insisted on coming with her, but right now their presence made her feel happy.

"This puts everything into perspective, doesn't it?" mused Athena aloud.

Milan got up on one elbow so he could look across Ghost to her. "How do you mean?"

"Well, we were all working so hard to, you know, get shoe production right, or something like that, and then there's this world, right next to ours."

"I wasn't working that hard."

"But you know what I mean. It's like this is far more important. We have to understand the fundamentals first; we have to figure out what is happening to us, what the universe we live in is really like. Everything else back home is pointless until we do."

Milan lay back down. "Well, it's certainly more interesting, anyway."

"You know what Erik said about the soldiers at the portal not fitting in here? I see it that way, too," Ghost, too, had been pursuing her own thoughts. "The modern ones, anyway; they still had the full gradations of color. They didn't look right for here."

"True," said Athena.

"So that makes me think there are probably other worlds connected through portals like the one we came through. Those soldiers came from somewhere else."

"Wow. Then there could be lots of worlds out here," observed Milan. "Freaky."

"Yeah," Ghost continued. "And perhaps each time a human colony left Earth, they created a new world for their journey."

"So, how many colony fleets were there? Is that, like, information you can access as queen?" For once Milan seemed genuinely interested in a conversation about the nature of the universe they lived in, a subject that had, by contrast, absorbed Athena and Ghost ever since humans had first appeared in Saga.

"There were five colonies," Ghost answered. "So there might be five whole new worlds out here."

"You would think they would have used the same ones again, though," said Athena, "or even all participated in the same one, if that was possible. So there might not be the same number of worlds as colonies. And I wonder how they decided what world they wanted to play in. Was it just a question of taste? Of whether they wanted to play in fantasy worlds like this one or high-tech ones like Saga?"

"I wish I was back in Saga."

"Already?" Ghost looked at Milan affectionately.

"Don't get me wrong. I'm glad to be here and to be on hand to help; it's just . . . who would choose to live in a world without good punk bands?" He grimaced. "And pizza, and airboards, and parties, and hot chicks like Athena, and aircar racing—ouch!"

Athena had successfully thrown a stick at Milan's head, but all the same, she was laughing at him. "Anyway, Milan, you don't know what the women are like here. You might change your mind when you meet some elves or something."

"Hot elfin chicks. Awesome." He closed his eyes in happy contemplation, while Athena just rolled her eyes at Ghost.

Before they had settled back down, Cindella material-ized right beside them and soon after her, the avatars of B.E., Anonemuss, and Gunnar.

"Hi. You guys are intending to go to sleep already?"

"I'm not tired," replied Ghost, "but I can't speak for Milan and Athena. In any case, it's getting dark; we may as well get some rest."

Cindella peered at the trees around them. "I wonder how safe it is to stay here."

"Yeah, we were discussing that." Milan opened his eyes and winked at Ghost. "We were hoping you might stand guard."

"Oh certainly. We might have to take turns, though, so we can also get some sleep." Cindella looked about at the others. "So, eight hours, divided by the four of us: two hours each. Anyone want the first shift?"

Gunnar raised his hand.

"Second?"

No one.

"All right, I'll do that. Third?"

B.E. looked at Anonemuss, who shrugged, leaving the choice to him. "I guess I'll take third then."

"And that leaves Anonemuss on fourth. Right. In that case I might log out again and chat with Inny and the others a bit before getting some sleep."

"Same here," added B.E.

"See you in the morning . . . if it will be morning your time." Athena worked one arm out of her bag to wave farewell. Their avatars froze while returning her salute and less than a minute later were gone.

"I'm clipping out, too," Anonemuss declared, before turning to Gunnar. "But you stay alert."

Ignoring this hostile comment, Gunnar came and sat on the fallen log, facing into the forest. Soon afterward, Anonemuss also disappeared. For a while there was near silence in the glade, just a gentle whisper from the treetops swaying in a light breeze. Above them were bright shimmering stars in unfamiliar constellations.

Somewhere far away a fox, or wild dog, gave a shrill bark. Closer, Ghost could hear rustling, perhaps a small animal in the bushes. It was strange, not being in a city. It was so much darker, for a start, and then there was the sense of dislocation. They had no idea where they were, and in every direction lay the unknown. Despite the fact that her sleeping bag was so light and thin, it was very effective in warming her up and surprisingly, given the fact that she was in such an unfamiliar environment, Ghost began to feel drowsy. As she fell asleep, a part of her soul was singing with pleasure. Whatever the dangers, this was the kind of adventure she had long wished for and it was a welcome relief from the tiresome decision making expected of her back in Saga.

An extraordinary cacophony of sound woke her. It was as if every bird in the world was clamoring for attention. And the maddening thing about the sound wasn't that it was loud—it wasn't much louder than the sound of traffic in a busy street in Saga—what made the noise impossible to ignore was the fact that although it sounded like a murmuring crowd, there were hundreds of distinct voices cycling repeatedly within it, each one demanding attention. *Chirp—chirp—chirp*, cried a bird to her left every minute or so. *Too-weet, too-weet*, went the slightly more frequent whistle of a bird behind her. In every direction and for some considerable distance, individual birds were crying out their existence.

"Blue bolts of lightning! What's that racket?" Peering out of his sleeping bag, Milan's face was one dark frown.

"Birdsong."

"Where's my gun?"

Milan sat up properly, lifted his Atanski to his shoulder, and fired an orange bolt of energy at a tree. After the crash of falling branches had died away, there was silence, a silence that seemed to register the astonishment of the whole forest at this unexpected violence. With a grunt of approval, Milan put the gun down and stretched out once more in his sleeping bag.

"It's probably not too wise to draw attention to ourselves." Anonemuss was the human on guard duty and he came walking over to them.

"I don't care," muttered Milan, his face turned away from the brightening sky.

There was something meaningful in Anonemuss's tone, something more specific than a general statement of principle. It caused Ghost to shake off her drowsiness and look at him. The scout nodded toward the fountain. With a shock, Ghost saw that it had been restored to the same condition as when they had first encountered it. Gone was the dead monster, with its giant snake coils, while back in place was the elfin statue and the welcoming inscription.

"Do you think it's still there? Alive again?" she whispered.

"Could be."

Closing her eyes, Ghost extended her senses into the air around her. The patterns of the world were hers to control; all the substructure of the environment was laid bare, and all seemed in order, at least in her immediate vicinity. One of the great advantages to being a RAL—in fact, *the* great advantage—was this power she had been given to alter the conditions of the world about her. It may have cut her off from the rest of society, made people fear her, and perhaps even brought a cold and ruthless streak to her character, but it also made her capable of extraordinary deeds. Stretching her awareness all the way to the fountain, Ghost found the fault lines created by the magic in effect there. She also found a glitteringly evil, malevolent presence staring out from behind the illusion of the statue, watching them with hunger.

"It's there all right. I'm going to drop the illusion. You shoot her."

"You can do that?"

"Yeah."

"Set." And she heard a click as he readied the gun. To untwist the flowing cords of energy that hid the monster was not difficult; easier in fact than steering fast-moving bullets through the air, because the streams of light coming from the fountain wanted to resume their natural course. As soon as Ghost felt everything fall properly into place, a burst of fire rushed across the glade, issued by Anonemuss's gun. The shot was accurate and even if it had not been, she could have guided it to the target. The wicked semi-sentience was gone, again.

"Now what?" Milan sat up, disturbed this time by the rushing sound of the pulse of energy and the crash of its impact. Athena, too, was awake and staring at the fountain. There the headless torso of the monster once more presided over the final lashing convulsions of the serpentine body.

"It came back?" she asked.

"Seems so," answered Anonemuss, lowering the gun with an air of satisfaction.

Milan gave a stretch, perhaps from a genuine physical impulse, or perhaps to demonstrate his unconcern. He was, as Ghost knew well, not given to letting any other male steal the limelight.

"What's for breakfast?"

"Nutribars." Athena reached for her kit bag.

"No," groaned Milan.

A man facing torture could not have put so much expression into one word and Ghost gave him a smile. "You prefer snake meat?"

After looking across at the remains of the monster for a few moments, Milan gave a shrug.

"Nutribars it is then."

About an hour later they were on the march again in pursuit of the enemy scout, with Anonemuss invisible and some distance ahead, Cindella at the front of the rest of the party, and Ghost guarding the rear. She walked with her airboard slung over her shoulder, saving its power for the time being. It seemed very unlikely that they would be able to recharge it, or—more seriously—their weapons.

With the sun up in a cloudless sky, the spaces between trees allowed hundreds of beams of pale sunlight to fill the air around them, giving depth to the forest. It would have been easy to lose their sense of direction, for hour after hour they saw no real change in the scenery. Sometimes they had to step across streams, careful to search for a secure footing as they stepped through the bracken that covered the banks. Perhaps someone more accustomed to the outdoors would have figured out which way to go from the fact that the water was generally flowing from left to right, but Ghost put her confidence in Athena's reading of the tracking device.

It was well into the afternoon before the pattern of their march was broken. Ghost was the last to join the group that was looking with some curiosity at an ivy-clad stone tower. It was some hundred meters away, in the center of a large clearing that could have been a natural break in the forest or purposefully hewn into existence. The tower was tall, reaching high above the treetops, and Ghost could just see an amber-colored pennant streaming from the top with a black lion design upon it. The tower was square, but around it was a circular moat, about five meters wide. A drawbridge, visible from where they stood, was currently lowered over the water. Flanking the closed wooden door, on the narrow strip of land between stone and water, stood two ominous-looking statues: both were gargoyles, about three meters tall, with a sword in each clawed hand.

"Well?" Gunnar asked. Everyone, naturally enough, looked to Cindella, who took off her glove so as to use her magic Ring of True Seeing. The avatar edged slowly toward the tower. They waited, patient and silent, until she returned.

"It's totally packed with magic and traps: the door, the windows, the roof—everywhere. And also the whole glade; not just the tower itself."

"Do you think those guards come alive?" asked B.E.

"No doubt about it."

Anonemuss, currently visible, turned to Ghost. "What about you, Ghost? What do you make of it?" Perhaps he had been impressed by her dismantling of the illusion this morning. It was the first time Anonemuss had looked for her input, and Ghost realized that she welcomed his question, with its respectful tone. For some reason she wanted the good opinion of this human, perhaps because his overt dislike for Gunnar demonstrated a commitment to the people of Saga.

"I'm afraid it's too far away for me to get a feel for it. And while it's interesting, I don't think there's any need for us to get closer."

"I agree," said Athena. "Let's just work our way around it and carry on. I have a feeling this is the kind of place we don't want to mess around with."

Gunnar nodded. "Seconded."

"Right then. We're all agreed?" Cindella put her glove back on and gestured to their left. "After you, Anonemuss."

The scout disappeared, and one by one they resumed their march, keeping a few trees between their line and the clearing. Long after they had left the tower behind, Ghost found herself looking over her shoulder, as uneasy as Athena had been about the entire structure. These fantasy worlds could be genuinely creepy.

An hour later, they were gathered before the clearing again, looking out at the tower.

"Is that the same place?" asked B.E. glumly. "Or another one that looks just like it?"

Milan shifted his rifle to his shoulder. "Tell you what. Why don't I blow the head off one of those doorpost guys. That way we'll know if it comes around again."

"Did it move? Or did we?" Athena was looking at her handset with a frown. "I think it was probably us. It's hard to tell at this scale, but we aren't quite as close to our target as we were a few minutes ago."

"So if this was Epic, what would be going on?" Ghost's

question was for any of the humans, but it was no surprise to her that it was Erik who answered. Although he was the youngest of them, he seemed to have the most knowledge of that former world.

"There would be a high-level curse cast by the castle owner upon all those who come to the vicinity of the tower. And a lot of quest lines would run through here, to bring players close enough to be caught in the curse. Probably local rumors tell of knights who go into the forest, never to return."

"And who would the owner of the tower be?" she asked.

Cindella looked across at the other humans. "I don't know, really. A very powerful sorcerer? A monster along the lines of that creature at the pool? Perhaps a lich: an undead wizard."

No one had anything to add.

"And what do you advise?"

"Well . . ." Cindella turned to look at the tower, and even though she was only an avatar for Erik, Ghost could almost see the expression of calculation. "In a game, you would have to enter the tower to break the curse. After surviving the traps and guardian monsters, you would meet the castle owners and either slay them or release someone from a curse or something like that."

"No one would have attempted a quest like that, though," interjected Gunnar. "It would have been far too reckless, back in the days when if you lost your avatar, you lost your wealth."

Acknowledging Gunnar with a quick nod, Ghost nevertheless kept her attention on Cindella. "You think we have to go inside before we can journey past the tower?"

"I don't think Milan and Athena should go anywhere near it. Probably you should stay clear, too. But I've a feeling that we're caught in its spell, and the rest of us probably should go in, yeah."

"If you all got killed, though," observed Athena with a troubled expression, "imagine where that would leave us: stuck in the vicinity of this tower until we either fight at worse odds or we starve out here."

"How about this then?" Cindella turned about, as Erik checked that he had everyone's attention. "We could go into the tower very slowly, searching at every stage for traps and so on. Or we could try a different approach. Seeing as we have weapons that are far more powerful than expected for this world, we could try blasting our way in as fast as possible and taking what is thrown at us on the half-volley."

"There's another option." Anonemuss held up the ring of invisibility. "I could try to sneak around inside there and gather intelligence."

"And we could try leaving in a different direction, to see if we get away from the glade. Although I admit I'm not optimistic about that," said Gunnar.

"We could," Erik replied dubiously, before turning Cindella to face B.E. "What do you think?"

"Go in fast."

"Anonemuss?"

"Same."

"Gunnar?"

"Thank you. One more attempt to get away from here, then attempt the tower, I suppose."

"Ghost?"

"If it's a particular area of land that is sending us back, like we were crossing some kind of portal, then I might be able to control the effect. Let's avoid the tower if we can."

"Right. We'll give that a go; it's definitely worth a try."

This time they set out northward from the clearing instead of eastward. It was afternoon and the hues of the forest were bright: shades of green and copper. After about an hour of walking, Ghost took the lead at a slow pace. Her eyes were closed as she felt for the inner workings of the world around her.

The wrench came suddenly, a whirlwind of suction that whisked them all the way back as though they were no more than tissues of paper in a storm. Ghost felt that there was a moment where she could have strained against it, holding herself in place, though she would have had to exert herself to the utmost. But it was pointless. All the others would have been pulled away.

"Blood and thunder!" B.E. was the first to see the tower ahead of them.

"Sorry, everyone. It wasn't like we walked into a region I could change; it was more like we were all small pieces of iron and someone switched on a powerful magnet."

"It's not your fault, Ghost." While Cindella gave a smile, it was a superficial one, because Ghost could hear a very distinct tone of worry in his next words. "Right then. Fast it is.

How about Athena and Milan stay here, each aiming at one of those gargoyles. Fire when we reach the drawbridge. B.E., blaze away at the door and then cover the rest of us as we run through. Anonemuss and Gunnar, hang back about five or six paces. Hopefully Cindella's abilities and magic gear will handle the physical traps, while your weapons can take care of the other guards in there."

"What about me?" asked Ghost.

Cindella shrugged. "Your abilities are amazing, and it would be good to have you with us. But there are a lot of unknowns about what we are going to do. We could take casualties from all sorts of magic and physical traps. And if you were one of them . . ."

"I'll stay back with Milan and Athena for now and judge for myself about whether to come in."

"All right then. Are we set?"

A series of clicks and high-pitched whining sounds answered him. Their weapons were charged.

"Good luck," said Ghost.

Cindella set off toward the tower, with B.E. beside her and Gunnar and Anonemuss a few paces back. Just before they reached the drawbridge, B.E. dropped to a crouch and a streak of pink light crashed into the door. At more or less the same time, Milan and Athena, both standing steady and sighting down their rifles, let loose a barrage of orange energy onto the gargoyles, whose heads and torsos were soon shattered, pieces of stone whistling through the glade.

The door was destroyed, too, smoke rising from its remains,

obscuring Cindella as she dived into the tower and rolled out of view, followed by B.E., Gunnar, and Anonemuss. Strange muffled sounds came from within: crashes, blasts of energy from pulse weapons, and the staccato beat of the rapid-firing Higgs. The sounds moved up the tower, accompanied by flashes of color from the narrow arrow slits of the first floor.

"So far, so good," said Milan optimistically.

Soon the noises of battle and the glow of pulse weapon fire came from the second floor.

"Still good."

As they lifted their gaze to the third and final floor, however, there came just one distinct flash and then silence. A very ominous silence.

"That doesn't sound so good."

Ghost stepped resolutely onto her airboard, kicked on the power switch, and pulled out her handguns. "Here goes. Death and defiance!"

Chapter 11
CRUEL FINGERS

Although she was thundering across the drawbridge at nearly maximum speed, Ghost's senses were so heightened that she could take in all that she saw. Beyond the ruined door was a chamber, with stairs at the far side. On the stone floor lay spent darts and spears. Six suits of armor bore the marks of energy weapons; large portions of their breastplates or their entire helmets were melted, revealing their hollow interiors. They must once have been animate, though, for they held weapons in a variety of poses.

Tipping up the nose of her board, Ghost used the impact of her collision with a tapestry and the wall at the top of the stairs to swerve up to another, larger landing. This was, effectively, a wide balcony that looked down on the hall below. Again, as she rushed around the landing, her whole being shivering with the anticipation of battle, she rode over the strewn remains of traps: spent crossbow bolts, acid holes in the carpet, and a section that was covered with ice. There were doors along the landing, all open, through which humanoid statues armed with sword and shield had evidently attempted to attack Erik's team. They, like the armored figures below, had been destroyed by the impact of energy weapons.

A stone staircase on the far side of the balcony led up to the second story. Slowing down in order to maneuver the board up the tight angle at the beginning of the staircase, Ghost nevertheless had enough momentum to reach the room above, guns held out ready to fire. It was a chamber that occupied the whole second floor of the tower, lit by lanterns and the pale afternoon light that spread from a number of arrow slits. Right at the center of the room was a curved, highly decorated iron staircase that ascended through a hole in the roof. The others must have climbed up, for there was no sign of their bodies here, just scorch marks and torn-up carpet and tapestry to indicate conflict had taken place.

As it would be impossible to get the airboard up the circular stairwell, Ghost jumped to the ground at a sprint. Below her there came sound of the footfalls: presumably Milan and Athena entering the tower. They must have decided there was no point waiting uselessly at the edge of the clearing. It was admirable and brave of them. But if Ghost could not deal with whatever was in the top chamber, at the top of that staircase, it would be unlikely that they could.

Ghost took the stairs at a run, two at a time, then launched herself into the room from the very top stair, adding impetus to her jump by concentrating upon the environment immediately surrounding her body and altering it. The final iron step became elastic, the air above her almost a vacuum to draw her upward. Even before she had been taught how to use her skills to the fullest, Ghost had been intuitively altering the passage of time while performing dangerous airboard stunts, slowing it to give herself more room to think and to move. She did so now, pushing herself to the very limit of her ability so that the scene was frozen in between distinct moments, frame after frame.

Her leap took her into the center of a well-lit chamber similar to the floor below, filling the entire third story of the tower. And it was something of a horror show. Still swaying from his final convulsions, B.E. was dead, hanging from a great beam by a rope around his neck, his hands and feet tied together. Inside a ball made of metal hoops, Cindella was being slowly crushed to death; as the frames of Ghost's vision ticked over, each jerk through time saw the machine noticeably shrink more tightly around her. Gunnar was dying from the opposite process, being stretched on an X-shaped rack, his arms already dislocated from their shoulders and his legs straining to avoid being pulled from his pelvis. Anonemuss was there, too: tied across a bed of spikes with a heavy metal plate resting on the length of his body, pressing him down, to increase the pressure until his clothes, skin, and muscle parted and he died on the spikes.

There was only one other person in the room, clearly the guiding intelligence behind this torture show, and even as Ghost attempted to understand what she was seeing, she fired burst after burst of explosive rounds into the creature. Sitting facing Ghost was a tall woman in a velvet dress the color of dried blood. "Facing" was not quite the right word, for she had no face, just a pale oval disk that nevertheless expressed wickedness and sin. Her hands were inhuman, too, with bony fingers twice as long as seemed natural. This fearsome woman was surrounded by piles of parchment; quills made from long, shiny black feathers; bottles of ink; and tall, waxy candles.

The blasts of energy from Ghost's gun smashed into the fiend. Not one strand of her long black hair moved. Not one thread on her dress was burned. As the next frame jerked the scene forward, the demonic woman's hands leaped forward to pick up parchment and quill. If time were flowing normally, it would seem like she was moving at astonishing speed, the motion of her knowing fingers barely discernible. The torturer began to draw. Draw? She was immune to weapons fire. Should Ghost try to stab her with a dagger? As she landed and ran toward the sinister monster, Ghost desperately looked for an answer to the mystery of this chamber. A part of her knew, perhaps from the subliminal information she was getting from the vicinity of the creature, that the dagger would be no more effective than the gun. As each jerk of motion took her a stride closer to her enemy, Ghost noticed that the floor was strewn with pieces of parchment on which there were drawings. She used up a frame to look more carefully at them.

The nearest one was skillfully done. It showed Cindella and Gunnar—with everyone behind them in outline at least—at the edge of the forest looking toward the tower and the viewpoint of the picture. Another parchment was visible, too, this time much more crudely done. But the outlined figure was distinct enough; it was B.E. swaying with a rope around his neck.

This was the source of the magic that had captured the others! Another frame advanced, and with a feeling of dread, Ghost studied the picture under the monster's hand. Her cruel fingers had made extraordinary progress on a sketch in which a figure was pinned onto a torture board by spikes along its arms and legs. Another frame and the figure's hair was drawn, a silhouette that showed dozens of short braids held up by a headband. All at once Ghost felt the same pull that had seized her earlier, outside, when the entire group had been swept back to the tower. There was no need to look over her shoulder; she knew that a tall board and a set of spikes had come into existence and that they were now tugging at her. Already it felt as if she had been seized by ten pairs of hands around her arms and legs, and it was absolutely clear that the more she let this creature complete the drawing, the tougher it would be to keep moving. Clenching her teeth, Ghost tore a path onward toward the fearsome woman, fighting with all her strength against the suction of the magic. There, horribly close to that evil, faceless oval, Ghost grabbed a bottle of ink and, with the next frame advancing, poured it over the sketch, obscuring all the details on the parchment. Instantly, the pressure upon her eased.

Ever since the echoes of Ghost's gunfire had died away, the room had been filled with a disconcerting silence. But if the pulses that swept across the blank features of the creature now leaning close to Ghost could have been vocalized, they would have created a horrific scream of rage and hate. Both of them reached for a blank sheet and quill. Because she was still operating within a slowed time rate, Ghost was the quicker of the two.

If Milan or Athena had been watching, they would have seen two people drawing on parchment at speeds so fast that their hands were a blur. But for Ghost every movement was quite distinct. It helped, too, that Ghost's sketch was the simpler. It was easy to draw the woman, with flames rushing up over her: her head, her shoulders, her arms. And while a huge blade, pushing through the torso of a body, was already quite visible on the woman's parchment, the figure was not yet that of Ghost and the tug of the magic only weak.

A blaze roared up right in front of her, causing Ghost to throw her hands over her eyes and recoil. With her concentration broken, time was flowing smoothly again. The woman was an inferno; her mouthless face an inaudible scream. As the torturer staggered about in visible distress, drapes and piles of parchment caught fire, too. It was easy enough to keep clear of the monster. The more the flames took hold of her hair and dress, the slower her movements became. At last, with a shudder, the demonic woman fell to the ground, still giving an occasional twitch, but otherwise destroyed.

Everyone in the room was in jeopardy from the flames, but how to free them? Ghost had to concentrate on breathing and the need to filter the air coming into her lungs due to the thickening tendrils of smoke. A loud crash made her jump;

B.E.'s body had suddenly fallen to the floor. The flames on the beams that made up the roof and floor were creating loud cracking sounds.

The nearest of the humans was Gunnar and Ghost tried to use her knife to cut him down from the torture rack, but the magic still remained, despite the death of its creator, for the fibers of the rope showed no marks at all after precious moments spent savaging them with her blade. It had to be the pictures then. On hands and knees, coughing despite her efforts to fill her lungs with clean air, Ghost crawled around the floor, skirting the lump of black matter that was the former monster, picking up drawings. These she fed to the flames and when the last of them was done, she hurried back to the nearest human: Anonemuss.

"Just in time. I'm on less than five percent life points." As he rose from the spikes, Ghost could see the bloody pattern on his back.

"Get out now." She pulled him to the stairwell, where Cindella was crawling toward them. Gunnar, however, because of his dislocated limbs, had not moved from where the rack had been, even though the whole apparatus had disappeared. For a moment it crossed Ghost's mind that this would be a good time to discreetly get rid of Gunnar, in a way that could not be blamed on her. But she dismissed the idea; with B.E. gone now, there were just three avatars left, and even Gunnar might provide valuable aid at some point.

"Let's drag him."

Between them, they pulled Gunnar headfirst to the hole

and then down to the floor below. This chamber was filling with gray tendrils of smoke from the fire above, but the air was much more breathable. From the top of the next stairwell, Athena and Milan were looking up tentatively, guns raised.

"We're good. Head back out!" Ghost shouted at them. Then, while poised to leap down to the floor below, Ghost glanced back over her shoulder towards the flames. Blackened scraps of parchment were swirling around in the air, but so too—strangely—was a large, undamaged, white feather. Discretion gave way to curiosity and, cursing herself for being a fool, Ghost turned back into the heat, shielding her face with an upraised arm. Again she exerted her powers to the full, creating an eddy that brought the feather close enough that she could snatch it. Only when it was secure in her grasp did Ghost drop to the floor below, the cooler air there washing over her like a wave.

The others were back across the drawbridge and running for the edge of the forest, between them Cindella and Anonemuss were assisting Gunnar. Remounting her airboard, Ghost quickly caught up with the humans and helped them to the line of trees. There, everyone fell to the ground with relief, before turning back to look at the blaze engulfing the tower. For a while no one spoke. They watched the violent flashes of orange, red, and yellow and listened to a roaring cry that was getting louder and louder.

"It's a shame," observed Anonemuss.

"What is? You mean, B.E. dying?" asked Ghost for them all.

"Well, that too. But I was thinking that there must have been some powerful magic items in there, among all the gear from the people who had gotten trapped by her."

"Yeah, well, she nearly got my collection." Cindella was rummaging in her Bag of Dimensions. She had just passed out potions of healing to Anonemuss and Gunnar, who looked considerably less damaged as a result. At least Gunnar's limbs were properly attached to his body again.

"I got this. The flames didn't seem to harm it at all, so I thought it worth taking. I can sense something powerful about it, an energy." Ghost showed the white feather to Anonemuss who examined it closely.

"Well done. This has to be magic of some sort. Any idea Erik?"

"Not really. It could summon a giant bird perhaps? If a command word is spoken? Or maybe the bearer can use it to fly. Or given the nature of the magic of that monster, it could be a quill of some sort." Cindella shrugged.

Athena sat up and seemed more interested in the tower than the feather, shielding her eyes against the flames to look out at the inferno. "So what exactly happened in there?"

While the humans explained about the demonic creature and the power of her pictures, Ghost lay back and let herself relax. It was impossible to sustain such an intense level of control over the environment without bringing on a major headache and a feeling of deep exhaustion.

"We were lucky. If Ghost hadn't come in so fast and figured

out what to do, we'd all be finished. High-tech weapons and my entire collection of magic items were of no use at all," Erik said vehemently.

The others echoed this appreciation of her efforts and Ghost smiled before she closed her eyes and let her tiredness sweep her away to sleep.

Chapter 12
At Swim, a Swan

When Ghost woke up, Milan was squatted down on his haunches beside her. "Hi, Ghost, welcome back. I don't suppose you've got anything to eat that isn't a nutribar?"

"What time is it? How long have I been asleep?"

"It's dinnertime; about two hours since you rescued the humans."

"Milan, did I hear you say you wanted something tasty to eat?" Cindella was standing nearby.

"Anything you've got has to be better than these nutribars. It's like eating putty."

Cindella went to sit beside Milan and began searching through her Bag of Dimensions. After a few mutters of frustration, she produced a golden plate and a silver goblet.

"There they are! I don't know for certain if the food and drink from these is consumable by you, but you just have to say a rhyme and they will supply you with whatever you want. Each item works only once a day."

"A rhyme?" Milan looked puzzled.

"Well, what do you fancy eating?" asked Erik.

"A big burger and a plate of fries."

"Right." Cindella picked the plate up with both hands. "Hear me, plate, for I tell no lies. Give me a burger and a plate of fries."

A moment later, a mouthwatering fragrance of cooked food surrounded them, and even Ghost, who could theoretically gain all the sustenance she needed from altering the environment, couldn't help but lean over and help herself to some of the hot food now heaped up high on the platter.

"Awesome, unbelievably awesome," cried Milan between mouthfuls. "This whole adventure just got a whole lot better."

"Does the rhyme have to scan?" asked Athena.

"I don't think so, but I never really used it that much."

"And what about the cup thing?"

"Same again. What do you want?"

"You mean it could do anything? Beer?" Milan asked.

Both Ghost and Athena opened their mouths to say no, but Milan quickly held up his hand. "I know, I know. Actually, I'd just like some water. But I was only asking."

"Water. Right." Again Cindella held the goblet in both hands. "Silver goblet, I'm no one's daughter. Please provide me with clean water."

"I see it doesn't have to make much sense then," muttered Athena, and Ghost had to smile when Cindella managed to look slightly aggrieved at this. Erik's avatar had a phenomenal range of expressions, and as a result seemed much more like a real being than the other avatars. It would be easy to forget that, a vast distance away, Erik was lying or sitting, clipped up to headsets and handsets in order to direct her.

"Delicious." Milan offered the goblet to Ghost. The water was cool and refreshing. She passed it on to Athena, still half full.

"These are fantastic. Can we hang on to them then?" asked Milan eagerly.

"Of course."

"Hooray, no more nutribars!"

For some people, happiness rose or fell in direct proportion to the availability of good food. Right now, despite the dangers of their expedition and the fact that they had no means of returning to Saga, Milan was back to his most cheerful. The humans must have been surprised to see him so jovial.

After they'd eaten and the humans had taken short breaks in turns, the group resumed their journey in pursuit of the enemy scout. It was enjoyably different to walk through forest instead of city, but even so, Ghost was relieved when, not long after they'd left camp, the landscape began to change. There was, after all, a certain urgency about their mission. It seemed only too likely that an attack was being planned on Saga, and the sooner they discovered who built the portal and commanded the soldiers around it, the better.

The first indication that they were reaching the edge of the forest was the increasing frequency with which they could glimpse the sun and patches of blue through what had previously been a solid canopy of green. The undergrowth was slightly different too: more bushes than bracken. Then there came more and more spacious glades, through which ran the stream that they had been walking beside for most of the day. An unusual, almost salty scent was detectable in the breeze. By sunset the trees around them were so dispersed that they could at last see the horizon ahead. The view gave Ghost a shock.

"Is that what I think it is?" She was walking next to Athena, who peered through her glasses and frowned.

"I don't know. What is it?"

"The sea?"

"But it glitters."

There were satellite maps that marked regions of sea in the world of Saga, but the water was hundreds of miles from the city in which they all lived. Neither Ghost nor Athena had visited the sea, and she was pretty sure that Milan hadn't, either. After all, in Saga there would be no point. The water would just be an oily black swell, lapping against some dock or accepting the foamy output of factory pipes. Here, though, the closer the view, the more delightful it was to look at the sea, which was a deep blue color permeated with sparkling flecks of white and silver.

The party cleared the last of the trees and crossed a grassy area where patches of sand appeared beneath breaks in the turf. Then they were gathered on the last rise before the beach proper, looking at the waves rolling up to the shore and listening to the sigh, repeated over and over, that the water made as it splayed upon the beach. Each wave coated the sand with a shining layer of moisture before withdrawing. The scene was hypnotic.

"That's beautiful," Ghost sighed.

"Yeah, but now what?" Anonemuss put down his bag and shaded his eyes to better see the horizon. "Is our spy across the water somewhere?"

Having checked the tracking device, Athena gave a nod and despite the problem the sea posed for them, flashed Ghost a look to say that her heart, too, was soaring at the pleasure of being able to look out at an unobstructed view as far as the eye could see.

"Hey, Milan, what do you think of the sea then?" Ghost caught up with her friend who had gone on ahead, striding over the sand behind Gunnar, his heavy boots leaving deep imprints that totally eradicated those of the more slender avatar.

"It makes me homesick."

"What do you mean?"

He hesitated. "I'm glad to be seeing some of what's out beyond Saga, but I miss parties and music and hanging out with the gang. This isn't my scene."

"It might be mine."

"Really?" He was surprised.

"No, I guess not really. But I love the fact that we can see forever here; it's like standing on top of the tallest building in the city, but so much more tranquil—so blue. I could lie here for days, just relaxing to the movement of the sea and listening to those waves. You know? A peace that we could never have in Saga."

Milan slapped her on the back. "You'd get bored after an hour, Ghost." And Ghost found it impossible not to share his laugh.

The whole group gathered on the wet sand, waves surging up the beach to flow around their feet. The pungent scent that Ghost had first detected back in the forest was strong now, either coming from the clumps of dark green weed nearby or the sea itself.

"Are we stuck?" Gunnar's handsome figure stood facing the sea and it was impossible to tell if he was pleased or dismayed at the prospect of going no farther.

"Got anything useful in your kit Erik? What about that Deck of Curiosities?" asked Anonemuss.

"We could try playing the 'Journey' card, but from what I was told you have to envisage where you want to go and I don't have much of an idea. I'll use it if you like, but I wonder if Ghost's feather might help us fly over the sea?"

Everyone turned to Ghost, who drew the feather from her headband. It was large, as wide as her hand, with brilliant white vanes.

"What should I do?" Ghost asked Cindella.

"Try throwing it into the air? Command it to fly."

Feeling a little foolish, Ghost threw the feather upward with both hands.

"Fly!" she cried, and for a second it looked as though magic were at play, as the feather was swept higher by the light breeze. But almost at once it began to descend.

"Oh well," said Gunnar as the feather landed in the water. "a valiant effort."

Certain that there was still something extraordinary about the feather, Ghost stepped forward to retrieve it. And halted. The feather had begun to spin as it was pulled away from the shore by the ebb of a wave and as it spun, the feather grew rapidly, both in size and complexity.

"Whoa!" shouted Milan and everyone shuffled back as a huge white swan unfolded before them. But it was not a bird; it was a ship, whose prow was the long neck and whose stern was the tail. Between slightly raised wings was the white deck of the ship, with feathered seats for twenty people.

Anonemuss was the first to move toward the craft. "Now that's awesome. How does it work?"

Waves were causing the ship to bob against the shore. Elated, Ghost grabbed a wing and vaulted aboard. "Come on, let's find out." She pointed out to sea and the bird turned accordingly. "Aha! Get in, everyone."

As they took their seats, Milan lingered on the beach, looking anxiously at Ghost. "There's something you should know."

"What?"

"I can't swim."

"Oh." Ghost was no great swimmer. But if necessary, she could make the air solid enough so that she could walk above the sea or even alter the water around her to make it breathable. The appearance of the swan boat was a thrill for her, but for Milan it was a risk to his life.

Cindella delved into her magic bag. "Here Milan, hopefully you won't need it, but I have a potion for water breathing. It lasts about an hour."

"Class! Thanks!" Milan put the small crystal vial into one of his top pockets and carefully buttoned it. "Now I might actually enjoy the ride." He beamed at everyone, once more his usual cheerful self, as he vaulted aboard.

Cindella looked across at Ghost and Athena. "Either of you need one?"

"Actually, if you've a spare, I'll take one." Athena sounded slightly apologetic. "It's been a while since I went to a pool."

"I'm fine," answered Ghost.

Soon they were all sitting on white-feathered chairs, looking out over the waves past the slender neck of the prow. The ship's wings were raised on both sides, obstructing the view but creating a reassuring sense of shelter. Gunnar and Cindella were at the front; Ghost, Milan, and Athena occupied the generous space in the center of the ship; and Anonemuss was lounging at the back.

"Forward, please." Cindella pointed out to sea and the ship began to move ahead. A grin appeared on Milan's face and Ghost knew exactly what he was thinking: he was amused by the fact that some of the humans—especially Erik—were always so polite, even when giving instructions to an inanimate magical ship.

As they glided over the sea, the swan boat was rocking in the waves and pitching down the troughs a little, but the motion was not unpleasant.

"Speed up!" shouted Ghost.

With no discernible sound, the swan leaped forward in a massive burst of acceleration, causing everyone to be pressed back against their chairs. Behind Ghost, Anonemuss swore and held tight to the tops of the nearest chairs. He saw her inquiring glance.

"I nearly went over the stern!"

Already the shore was receding fast and the ship had a vast wake curling away from them across the sea.

"This is ferocious! I wish my mates back in Saga could feel this," cried Milan, wiping spray from his face and getting unsteadily to his feet so he could see further ahead. The swan was nearly airborne between the peaks of the waves; each plunge of the ship was more violent now as it crashed from one ridge of water to the next.

"It is rather exhilarating," acknowledged Gunnar with a glance back.

"Are we on course?" Erik shouted at Athena.

"Not quite." She got up carefully and walked forward, using the backs of the chairs to keep her steady, so that she could show the tracking device to Cindella.

Pointing slightly south of their present direction, Erik gave the order, "That way, please," and instantly they were heading at great speed toward their target.

"This is much better than slogging through those bushes

and trees on foot, isn't it?" The breeze created by their speed was strong enough to toy with Milan's hair, and he rolled his head on his neck to let it blow the peroxide-tipped strands from side to side. Their breathtaking speed certainly was encouraging, and lifted by Milan's good humor, Ghost, too, felt a sense of happiness and delight as the team flew over the waves.

For nearly an hour they raced across the sea in this way, passengers in a magical swan ship, the fading sun coloring the sea a glittering bronze all the way to the horizon. Behind them, the coast had receded from sight and they could see nothing but the wide expanse of sea and sky. Then Athena gave a shout.

"It's getting a lot closer!" Her attention was on the tracking device, which she waved at Ghost.

This brought Anonemuss up from the back and he stared across the sea in the direction they were heading. "I think there is something over there. But we're too unsteady to see for sure."

A few minutes later, though, and it was evident that there was a dark smudge on the horizon before them. Even at the racing speed with which the swan cleared the waves, it took a while for the feature to become any clearer. But as they crested a wave and the spray blew over them, their goal suddenly became obvious; it was a volcano, with an outline formed by two beautiful curves that rose from the sea to meet at a flat plateau.

The nearer the swan ship came the mountain, the more the color of the water around them changed, becoming turquoise rather than copper.

"Slow down," commanded Ghost.

The ship had barely begun to respond to the new instruction when the water all around them began to surge up, shaking the swan from side to side. An enormous wave gathered ahead and seemed certain to come crashing down upon them. Except that it didn't. Instead a voice came from the glistening water, a voice that boomed like the crash of the sea against the hollows of a cliff and that hissed like shingle driven along the shore.

"My master compliments you on your mode of transport and invites you to state your business here."

In comparison to the voice echoing all around from the wall of water swaying high above them, Erik sounded shrill and faint. "Thank your master. We seek information. We are peaceful and would welcome a chance to converse with your master."

It seemed to take a moment for the enormous wave to absorb this; then all at once it dissolved back into the sea, leaving the ship rocking violently. The swan was still attempting to move slowly forward, until Ghost gave the order to stop.

"I'm staying out of sight." Anonemuss must have slipped on the ring of invisibility, for he was gone.

"Heebie-jeebies! What was that?" Milan had been flung down by the wild motions of the ship and was now carefully seating himself in a chair.

"It was a water elemental. A very powerful one," answered Erik, Cindella looking back over her shoulder as if to check all was well.

While Milan shook his head, seemingly troubled by how frail their ship had looked in comparison to the monster, Athena put the tracking device away. "No need for this anymore. Our man is right inside that volcano."

"Should we land?" Ghost wondered aloud.

Cindella gave a shrug. "I don't think so, not without an invitation."

Any doubts as to what they should do were soon resolved as a humanoid figure came rushing toward them through the air. All about his feet, the air was distorted and as he approached, it seemed to Ghost that the man was standing on top of a small whirlwind. The magical platform of air had to be strong, for the being who drew up a few meters away from them was large. While his mode of transport was strange, the man himself was even more remarkable. If you looked only at his fleshy, balding head, you would think he was a perfectly ordinary middle-aged man. But every visible centimeter of his skin was covered in tattoos: neck, shoulders, arms, fingers, feet.

"Whoa, nice tats, dude. I take it those are perma-tats?" Milan had several perma-tats, but you could only just see the faded tip of one of them on his neck; his combat jacket covered up the rest.

"Welcome, everyone. My name is Jodocus. Yes, indeed, Jodocus, the grand master of elementalists who was once a member of the Supreme Council of Myth! You've found me. Assuming, that is, you were looking for me? I know, I know — you need my help now. It was only a matter of time before you came begging for my aid. Who sent you? Anadia?"

It was hard to understand the implications of this peculiar speech. Cindella looked at Ghost, who looked at Athena.

"Hi, Jodocus. I'm Athena; this is Cindella, Gunnar, Milan, and Ghost. I'm afraid no one sent us. We are here to . . . um . . . There was this scout who came to our city, and we've followed it here. We want to know who sent it and why."

"Oh, my apologies. I assumed from this woman here"—he pointed to Cindella—"that you were citizens of Myth. But I see that you others are indeed people of another world. So you have found me inadvertently, as a result of trailing the 'scout,' as you call it?"

"Exactly." Athena nodded.

"In that case, come inside. Let us share food and drink and exchange information in a civilized fashion." There was something a little deflated about his voice now, thought Ghost. Somehow they had failed to give him the moment of triumph he seemed to have been anticipating. With a few gestures of his hands, the elementalist came a little lower and the distortion of the sky at his feet generated a breeze that plucked at their garments. The wind grew stronger as it spread in size, flattening the waves around the ship.

"Step up beside me, please; it is perfectly safe."

Should they trust him? Ghost was unsure, but what else could they do? There was no point leaving the island without talking to this man, as they had nowhere else to go. At least the air was firm; it yielded slightly underfoot as she tested it, but no more so than sand.

"Are we being supported by an air elemental?" Ghost asked.

"Quite right, young woman. Have you any familiarity with the art of the elementalist yourself?"

"I'm afraid not. I'm more of an airboarder."

"An airboarder?"

"It's a kind of sport." Ghost turned so that Jodocus could see more of the board that was strapped across her back.

"My goodness, how interesting. You'll have to show me sometime." He chuckled and waited for them to cross over from the ship.

Gunnar was looking to Cindella to lead, Milan and Athena to Ghost. Closing her eyes for a moment, Ghost did her best to analyze the nature of the man in front of them and let her senses expand into the new and vibrant magical energies flowing around her. Was this another deception, like that at the pool? The air elemental was peculiar, all right, but neither it nor its master was hiding beneath an illusion of any sort. Nor could she detect anything threatening, except perhaps a coiled power within the body of the elementalist.

Her hand on the swan's wing, Ghost vaulted into the sky and felt the air catch her feet and push her up to their new host. One by one, everyone else did the same; a quick check of her environment allowed Ghost to confirm that Anonemuss was with them, too. The party set off up the mountainside, lifted by the platform of solid air beneath them. It was a shame to leave the swan ship there on the open sea, but Ghost had no idea how to get it to resume the size of a feather, even if such a trick were possible.

The view from the mountaintop was like nothing Ghost

had ever seen. With the sun almost at the horizon, the wide expanse of sea around them was a burnished and glistening crimson. She would have liked to sit for a while, letting the calm and the richness of the colors sink deep into her soul, but they were carried swiftly over the lip of the volcano and into its sulfurous-smelling hollow interior. Far below, there were tendrils of steam rising from a mist, which even at this distance felt warm.

About a third of the way down was a balcony, ringing the entire hollow center of the volcano. As they drew nearer, Ghost could see doors leading from the balcony into the mountain wall.

"Even though you are not elementalists, I'm sure that you appreciate the design. Here, not only am I hidden from my enemies, but I also have access to powerful sources for all the major elements and for several minor ones, too."

"It is the most amazing place I've ever visited," replied Athena with genuine enthusiasm. Jodocus looked pleased.

The elementalist did not seem to notice that Cindella had taken off her gloves, and Ghost appreciated the fact that Erik must now be looking at the stranger with the aid of the Ring of True Seeing. It was reassuring, for while this man seemed friendly enough, they couldn't be sure of his intentions. Reassuring, too, was the quick glance Cindella gave over Jodocus's shoulder, no doubt to where Anonemuss stood, invisible.

"Come in, come in." Jodocus stepped onto the balcony and opened a pair of large polished doors.

The chamber beyond was remarkable, a testament to the

dedication of the elementalist to his art. A curved stone outer wall, superbly crafted, as if by a team of the finest masons, contained a dozen tall windows looking out over the sea, each with wonderfully delicate arched lintels. Carpets, rich in texture and color, covered the floor, their slender patterns looking to Ghost like the words of spells. The entirety of the interior wall was lined with mahogany shelves carrying thousands of books and scrolls.

"There are basically two types of wizardly libraries." Jodocus strode around the room, gesturing to make his point. "One has pristine volumes carefully bound in matching leather, all shelved in meticulous order and kept behind glass. But this, I'm afraid, is the other sort: the library of a practical person, of someone who is more than a collector, of someone who is a true elementalist!"

In other words, the place was a mess. Books lay in piles everywhere: on tables and chairs, on the floor, on cabinet tops; one large volume even rested across the top of a large china vase. Ghost looked at the two in the window seat nearest her: *Exotic Thermal Prehenistae* and *Marrigmore's Dictionary of Eclethes*. The latter was filled with many scraps of paper bookmarking important pages.

"Ah yes." He had noticed her interest. "Marrigmore. Terribly underrated. In my view, there were few better practical elementalists. He really understood the business. It's just a shame he couldn't express himself more clearly." Clearing a table, Jodocus gestured to the delicate and expensive-looking chairs around it. "Perhaps you would care to sit?"

While they took their places, Jodocus removed the large book from on top of the vase. After he waved his hands above the vase, a silver liquid flowed over the lip, gathered in a pool on the floor, and then drew itself up in the form of a featureless humanoid slightly shorter than Ghost.

"Mercurius. Please bring our guests food and drink."

The strange liquid being bowed and flowed toward an adjacent room.

"Now then. Where shall we start?" Jodocus joined them at the table, resting his fleshy body in a chair that seemed far too frail for him. "How about this. It seems to me that you are all sentient, intelligent people. Of the kind we call *domini* in this world. Would that be right?"

"You mean, as opposed to the soldiers?" Athena answered.

"Exactly, or insentient builders, farmers, servants, and so forth."

"Yes. We are all sentient."

"Good, good. Nice to be dealing with real people. Your turn."

Ghost looked at Cindella, who waved her hand in reply, indicating that Ghost should ask the first question. Of course, Erik also had the problem that as soon as he began talking, the elementalist would hear that his male voice did not match his avatar.

"There is a portal, recently opened between this world and mine. What do you know about it?"

"Nothing, I'm afraid." For a moment Ghost thought that was all he was going to say, but then Jodocus looked up at her and continued. "If by portal you mean a gray tear in the fabric of space and time that allows people to cross between worlds, then I can say this. About two years ago, one of these appeared about a thousand miles to the northwest of us. Not long afterward, troops poured through it to effect a conquest of these lands—a conquest that, despite their loss of thousands of soldiers, has ravaged all our cities and towns, converting them to factories and farms."

"Death and destruction! That's what we feared. And they're coming for us next. Who is it organizing these invasions?" Milan had been slouching in his chair, but he sat up now.

Jodocus held up his hand. "My turn. And in any case, I don't know the answer to that question." He turned to Ghost. "What world are you from?"

"Saga," she answered.

"Ah. Saga."

"You know it?"

"I'll give you that extra question for free. Yes, I've heard of it. Saga was the first artificial world created by the humans of Earth. How very interesting indeed to meet some of its inhabitants. But"—he turned to Cindella—"you are clearly from a different world than the others here."

"Yes. Well, different from that of Ghost, Milan, and Athena. I'm . . . I'm from a fantasy world called Epic."

"My goodness. You are male?"

"Well, yes." Erik sighed. "Do you have humans in this world?"

"Wait, Erik! Stop right there. Don't say any more!" Gunnar leaped up out of his seat in his agitation.

"Look, Gunnar, we need help, and I think Jodocus should know all that we know."

"No!" Gunnar stayed on his feet, quivering. "I don't trust him. Just imagine him as another Dark Queen before you say another word."

The elementalist had observed this exchange with a rigid pose that suggested he was utterly attentive, like a cat watching a bird. Yet it was hard to read his face, which seemed remarkably placid under the circumstances.

"So your question is, do we have humans in this world?"

"Yes," Erik answered, a note of wariness in his voice now.

"We used to. I don't think they have been here for decades, although individuals may have come and gone without my knowing. How does that assist you in answering my question?"

"Well, Gunnar has a point; I don't think I should say any more on that subject."

"How fascinating. How very, very fascinating." Jodocus leaned back appraisingly. "Perhaps you're all humans in avatar form? But since all the humans of Earth are reported dead, killed by the *domini* of Saga, you must be humans from a different world."

No one answered him, and it seemed to Ghost that the room had become colder. In the silence that followed, the silver servant returned with a tray on which were china plates of fruit, cuts of cold meat, glasses, and a jug of water.

"Help yourself."

Milan didn't hesitate, although Ghost, perhaps overly mis-trustful, noted that the elementalist wasn't eating. Feeling pro-tective of Milan, she tried to discern what she could about the food in case it was poisoned, but it all seemed normal.

"Our turn again?" asked Erik, and the elementalist nod-ded in reply. "When you met us, you said something about a supreme council. Can you say more about that?"

"I can." He waved a tattooed hand as he spoke. "It was the form of government we had here. The most powerful *domini*—wizards and sorcerers mostly—kept an eye on things and acted as judges in disputes. They ousted me, though, years ago. I was rather bitter at the time, but perhaps they did me a favor, because all the years they spent running around full of self-importance, building statues in honor of themselves, I spent here, perfecting my art and overcoming one of the great limitations of the elementalist."

Seeing that he had their interest, Jodocus rolled up his cot-ton sleeves, revealing more tattoos. His voice was proud. "Look closely. They are all bindings and in them are elementals."

"Classimundo. I totally want one of those. Could you make me one?" Milan loved his perma-tats, and Ghost could under-stand the enthusiasm in his voice. It derived from the fact that all the indigo trails on the elementalist's skin enclosed spaces in which colored inks seemed to be writhing. Jodocus's arms were steady, but his skin was in motion.

"Perhaps, if we have time. But the significance of what you see is that I need not be in the vicinity of an elemental to summon it; I can release it from here." He tapped his forearm. "Moreover, while most of my colleagues eventually succumbed to the projectile weapons of the invaders—despite their magic powers—my elementals protected me, deflecting all projectiles and preserving my life."

"Do you think there are many more of your council left alive?" asked Erik.

"Oh, perhaps. One at least." Jodocus was dismissive. "The birds that she commands tell me that Anadia would form an alliance with me to defeat the invaders."

Athena had eaten her way through a cluster of grapes and now had a question for him. "Why don't you?"

"My turn first, I think. Let me see. Ah, yes. Why are you here? I mean, at my island. What made you come here?"

By way of an answer, Athena rummaged in her bag and withdrew the tracking device. "A scout came from this world into our world—Saga—and so we tagged it with a radio transmitter. We've been following it in the hope it would lead us to whoever is opening these portals."

"Oh dear. That was a good idea, and it might have worked, too."

"But?" Milan paused in his demolition of a pear, mouth still half full.

"But I'm afraid I detected this rather interesting figure going up the new road in the opposite direction to all the soldiers, so I took it here to see what I could learn from it."

"The scout?" asked Gunnar.

"Exactly. Your scout. Unfortunately, no sooner had I

captured it than it switched itself off. All I learned was that it carried a weapon made of a curious material, a kind of hardened rubber."

Several voices spoke at once, asking about the direction the scout was traveling. Jodocus held up his hand again and they fell silent.

"If you like, I can take you to the road and the rift he was undoubtedly making for."

"Yes, thank you," said Ghost immediately. "We would appreciate being taken there." It was their main goal, after all, to get to the people who were sending armies to invade other worlds and stop them before they attacked Saga.

"I'm curious—why do humans care if a world they use merely for a game is taken over? What difference would it make to you? Might it not give you a fresh start in Saga that you would enjoy?"

Again no one answered. Jodocus leaned back in his chair, which gave an ominous creak. "A moment ago, this young man with the tattoos and fine appetite"—the elementalist pointed to Milan—"exclaimed that it was likely that whoever conquered this world, Myth, will soon attack 'us.' I wonder whether this means that some of you, perhaps everyone but Cindella, who has a distinctly male voice, is a *dominus*, while 'she' is human."

At this, Cindella gave a very lifelike smile, then leaned over and offered her hand. "I'm not going to say anything about the others, but as you've probably already realized, I'm a human. My name is Erik."

"Welcome to Myth, Erik. It's a pleasure to meet a human again after all these years." Jodocus shook Cindella's hand. "I wonder, are you able to reprogram these worlds that you humans once created? The people in it? Have you reprogrammed the others at this table?"

Cindella snatched her hand away. "As it happens, I've no idea how to use the reprogramming menus."

"But you do have access to them?"

"Isn't it our turn for a question?" There was a touch of anger in Erik's voice and Ghost wondered why. Was he angry with himself for giving this dubious stranger too much information? Or with Jodocus, for sounding a little like the Dark Queen, who had threatened to kill Erik's family and friends unless he carried out some reprogramming under her direction.

"Certainly." Jodocus gave no sign of having noticed the sharpness in Erik's voice.

Cindella turned to Ghost. "Do you mind if I take it?" Ghost indicated for Erik to go ahead, so he addressed the elementalist once more. "Do you have any idea why humans left Myth?"

"Yes. I believe they made a group decision after they learned about how the *domini* of Saga had annihilated the humans of Earth and they took the precaution of leaving Myth before similar events could arise here."

"So there are more humans out in the universe somewhere. There's at least one other planet with humans. We're not alone." Erik was excited, and Ghost winced when she saw him glance at Gunnar. If the plan was to keep Gunnar's identity as a human a mystery, Erik hadn't stuck to it very well.

There was a pause in the conversation as Jodocus drummed his fingers on the table in thought.

"I've one more question. Are you willing to take me with you through the rift to the world that our invaders come from?"

"But I thought you didn't want to fight them?" Athena pointed out.

"Oh, I'm sorry I gave that impression. I most certainly do want to hit them as hard as I can. We can't have them wiping out our cities and towns without a certain amount of vengeance. What I object to is working with the egotistical worms who threw me off the council. And also, I must admit, I had concerns that traveling through the rifts—the portals, as you call them—might lead to my own disintegration. But you all seem to prove it possible to cross between worlds. So if you'll let me come along, I'll take the chance."

Erik did not reply, but Cindella turned her head to Ghost as if to say it was her decision.

"That's excellent news." Ghost stood up and walked over to the elementalist, holding out her hand. Whatever her reservations, this man would make a powerful ally against the threat posed to Saga by the unknown invaders. "Welcome to the team."

If Jodocus was surprised by the decisiveness of Ghost's response, he didn't show it; instead, he grasped her hand and shook it with great firmness. "Good. When shall we set off?"

"I need to clip out and get some sleep. Can we set a time— say, nine hours from now—to continue?" asked Erik.

"I need some sleep, too," said Athena.

"Very well. Nine hours." Jodocus stood up and walked to a door. "If you come this way, there are some beds and couches you can rest on."

Milan followed him. "Hey, mate, you couldn't give me one of those tats in the meantime, could you? Just a little one, even?"

"If you wish, my friend. Come with me."

Chapter 13
THE LEMURA'S CURSE

Ghost and her comrades were lying side by side on top of a cloud, looking down at a ruined city through gaps in the mist. Their extraordinary position testified to the impressive powers of Jodocus. He had conjured the services of the large air elemental that was currently holding them steady in the sky, its hands held high, palms upward, fingers spread, to form a vast floor for them. Its body was a constantly swirling trunk like a miniature tornado. Several smaller wispy creatures surrounded the air elemental and formed the bulk of the cloud that screened them from potential watchers. That morning they had flown northwest to the mountains and for a few hours followed an extraordinary road that climbed up a steep river valley in a series of impressive aqueducts. The resources at the disposal of whoever had built the road were phenomenal enough, but what concerned Ghost even more than the ambition inherent in such an extravagant construction project was the sight of the flattened towns and villages near the road.

The day had begun well—Ghost wasn't the only one who had felt refreshed and optimistic as they had set out high above the sea—but the evidence of the considerable destruction meted out to this world by whoever built the portals had dissipated everyone's good humor very quickly. In fact, Ghost felt a distinct wave of anxiety and gloom sink through her as they looked down on the ruins of a city directly below. It had been built on an island created by a fast-flowing river that parted on the steep rocks to the north, ran down on either side of the higher ground, and rejoined at the south. The city would have been relatively secure with the natural defenses provided by the water, supplemented by the town's tall walls. But these were all demolished, as was every structure, leaving only the foundations to indicate where all the buildings had been. What was frightening about the remains of the town was the thoroughness of the destruction; the city was almost flat. There were not even piles of rubble from collapsed buildings. Had everything been taken away to be used on the road, perhaps? The only stones that remained were those too embedded in the ground to warrant removal. The patterns these stones formed were like the tattoos on Jodocus's body, without their interior animation.

"This was a city of about five thousand inhabitants and three *domini.*" The elementalist was standing, confident in his balance and the stability of the air elemental beneath them. "The *domini* put up a good fight, I think; a year ago you could still see the scorch marks on the landscape. But eventually sheer weight of numbers overwhelmed them and they were killed.

It's the same all over the world: town after town destroyed and everything torn apart and used to construct their roads and army fortifications."

The party were glum enough as they followed the road up the mountain valley and became all the more somber as they finally came up to a plateau and caught sight of the portal, which appeared as a gray and shining tear in the blue sky.

It was not the portal itself that was disheartening, but the army that was before it: rank after rank of soldiers, vast squadrons of half-tracks, an enormous block of tanks, dozens of planes on six airstrips, and an immense horde of riders. A large stone wall ran around the outside of the army, with regular revetments—D-shaped protrusions—in which were placed long, projectile-firing guns and their firing crews.

Instead of the busy and random movement of thousands of people going about their business, the figures on the plateau were mostly still, occasionally shuffling a little to accommodate a new recruit to their ranks as a soldier or a vehicle emerged through the portal. The sight was discouraging. The army already looked powerful enough to destroy the world of Saga, and it was still being reinforced. Admittedly, the portal these troops would have to come through to reach Saga was relatively narrow compared to the one they were now looking at and perhaps it would be possible to block their entrance for a long time by destroying each soldier to come through, one by one, or—now this was a thought worth pursuing—by drowning the portal in cement.

The risk in that, though, was that their enemy might create a new and undiscovered portal. Then an army like this one could pour in and establish a foothold for invasion. In fact, they might have already created an additional way into Saga. Ghost made a mental note to relay a message via the humans to the guild leaders of Saga: to have the population of the city alerted in order to look out for signs of a new portal.

"How are we supposed to get through that lot?" mused Milan aloud. He, of all of them, had been the most cheerful that morning, delighted with the journey through the sky and also with his new perma-tat. Ghost saw him stealing a glance at it again, a circle on the back of his hand, drawn from sigils, within which was a constantly changing pattern of red and orange flames.

Lying beside Ghost, Erik gave a sigh in answer to Milan's question. "And what's it going to be like on the other side? Presumably a road coming to the portal, with convoys of arriving troops."

"Want me to scout it out, invisible?" whispered Anonemuss close in Ghost's ear, the touch of his cupped hands on her head indicating he was covering the sound of his voice.

If Jodocus knew of the extra member of their party, he had not mentioned it. And given that no one fully trusted the elementalist, it had seemed wise for Anonemuss to remain invisible.

"That's a good idea," Ghost whispered back, holding a hand

over her mouth. "But we'll have to tell Jodocus. You had better ask Erik first."

A few minutes later, Cindella stood up, balancing carefully on the unstable surface.

"Jodocus!"

"Cindella?"

"It's time to introduce you to the sixth member of our team. He's been invisible up till now. I hope you don't mind the precaution."

While Cindella was speaking, Anonemuss must have removed the ring, for there he was, an incongruous office worker, among the troopers, Cindella, and the elementalist: the least military looking of them all. But so far Anonemuss had been dependable and very effective in his role as scout. Ghost admired him greatly.

"This is Anonemuss."

Jodocus gave a bow. "Invisibility? Very useful indeed."

Anonemuss nodded in reply. "I'm going to use it to scout ahead and see what's on the other side of the portal. Can you drop me off on that hill to our left?"

Did it look strange to the army below, this bulky cloud that drifted lower than the others in the sky? At least they were moving roughly in the same direction as the wind. Soon, grass and rocks were immediately beneath them.

"Do you think it's safe to use our communication devices?" Athena tapped the plastic piece in her ear and while the question was addressed to everyone, she looked at Jodocus, who shook his head.

"Your concern is that the enemy might intercept your messages and detect you? I would think that even if they operate their own communications on similar lines, it's unlikely the two systems would be coherent to one another."

"Even so, I'll stay off the air until I meet you back here," Anonemuss said out of nowhere. He had put the ring back on.

Closing her eyes, Ghost stretched her senses and felt Anonemuss depart, from the disturbance of molecules that were swirling around in the space he left behind as he dropped from the cloud and set off down the hill. When she opened her eyes again, Ghost found Cindella clipping on her pair of magic lenses.

"Athena, did you bring binoculars?"

"I did. I think they are in Milan's bag."

Soon Ghost and Cindella were stretched out beside each other, focusing their vision on the army in front of the portal.

"How far does your Ring of True Seeing work?" Ghost spoke in a whisper, not wanting Jodocus to hear. The elementalist was behaving like a friend and an ally against the army that had invaded his lands, but still, for some reason, despite all his help, Ghost didn't entirely trust him. There was something cold in his eyes and in the immobility of his face. Since all those elementals tattooed to his body would make him a very formidable opponent, she didn't want to give him more information about the group than she had to.

"In a sense, as far as I can see, but the effectiveness drops off fast. I have to observe everything in the light that glows from the ring; anything more than about ten meters away has such minimal illumination that it looks almost normal."

"I understand. But why don't you use it all the time?"

"It's too overwhelming, all the information. I feel dizzy and disorientated trying to move with it uncovered."

Ghost stopped whispering. "These are the same unit types we met at our portal, right? Apart from those gun crews?"

"Yes, but I think there are also some officer types that we haven't seen before, on top of that wooden tower."

Adjusting the binoculars, Ghost found the tower. Erik was right. There were two figures in uniforms that were slightly more elaborate than those of the ordinary soldiers, and they had caps and sidearms rather than helmets and rifles. Beside them was a warrior who wore a gleaming bronze breastplate and a helmet with a red plume. The three officers were no more animate than the other figures, and as far as Ghost could tell, they were not talking to each other or even surveying the area in front of them.

"Wait, what's he doing?" Erik sounded shocked, and quickly bringing her view back down to the road, Ghost could see why. Anonemuss was walking up toward the portal and he was perfectly visible.

"What's happening?" asked Gunnar.

"Anonemuss must have taken the ring off for some reason."

By now Ghost had zoomed in more closely on Anonemuss. "That's strange, though. Look closely. He is still trying to walk quietly."

Instead of walking with his usual casual gait, their scout was moving slowly and placing his feet with great care.

Erik was distraught. "Does he not realize he is visible?"

"Evidently not." Ghost set her microphone to broadcast, even though she thought it unlikely he would be listening, given his decision to stay off the air while he scouted around the portal. "Come in, Anonemuss, come in."

Milan immediately voiced Ghost's unspoken thought. "It's no good. His coms are off."

"Does this mean they have some kind of anti-magic force around the portal to dispel the effect of the ring?" Gunnar was sitting directly behind them.

"It could be that, but I have never seen any counter-magic or even magic on their part before, except that they have sometimes used items captured from us," answered Jodocus. "But it does lead me to wonder, where did your friend get that ring?"

"We got it from a fountain in the forest," replied Milan.

"Did it have a lemura guardian?"

"I dunno what it was called." While Milan responded to the elementalist, Ghost's attention remained fixed on the distant figure of Anonemuss, who was coming closer and closer to the first ranks of riflemen. "But it was this snake woman who cast spells."

"Oh dear." Jodocus sounded downcast.

"What?" Athena asked.

"What a pity I did not know of it before now. I thought it was your own ring. That fountain is a notorious trap, whose rewards are all cursed. The invisibility fails when its wearer needs it most. You can tell when it's not a genuine ring of invisibility, because with the cursed one, you remain visible to yourself."

"Blood and thunder!" Erik groaned aloud. "That's our ring, all right; he said something about that."

"There is a dagger in the same fountain, too. If you use it, it heals your target and wounds you."

"Yeah. That was there, too. He's carrying it."

"Alas, he will not know that he is visible. Unless you can think of a way to contact him? Or perhaps we should all attack now?"

"No." Erik spoke urgently. "No, don't attack."

"We let him die then?" Jodocus sounded surprised.

"He's human; it's only his avatar. I'm going to unclip and warn him."

"Ah. Another human with an avatar from Saga. How interesting."

"It doesn't matter, Erik. You're too late." Ghost had seen the sudden ripple through the ranks of the enemy soldiers as they spotted Anonemuss. A hundred rifles were lifted and a moment later, almost simultaneously, with a roar that sent birds flapping into the sky, they fired. Anonemuss jerked back, nearly cut in two, and lay still.

"Blast it!" Cindella sat up. "That was a waste. A stupid waste." Her fists punched into the pliant floor. "Oh well. I'm going to unclip and tell Anonemuss about the ring, so he understands what happened to him. He'll be furious." Erik dropped his voice to a whisper. "Any messages for Saga?"

"Yes." Ghost sat up, too, and handed the binoculars back to

Milan, who immediately put them to his eyes and searched for the body. Then she whispered back a message about mobilizing the guilds in a search for another portal.

Knowing that Cindella was about to stiffen and disappear, Ghost made sure she was facing Jodocus, expecting to see a measure of surprise on his face when it happened. But Cindella clipping out of the world left the elementalist unperturbed. Perhaps, in the past, he had gotten used to the comings and goings of humans?

"So, how are we going to get in? Have you got some sort of invisibility?" Athena asked their guide.

"Not I. I just control the elements. The best I can do is have an air elemental screen us, but that's a long way short of invisibility. Those guards will see the disturbance. To get invisibility, we'd have to contact some of the other *domini* through Anadia, if there are any others left, and I'm reluctant to do that."

This got Gunnar up on his feet. "Anadia, one of the members of the former council who got rid of you? Why don't you want to contact her? Because of your pride?"

"That," Jodocus acknowledged, "and also because I wouldn't want her to know about you humans. She's one of these *domini* who hate humans and even if she was willing to work with you in the short term, she would try to harm you in the end."

"Oh." Gunnar, whose intervention and determined tone had surprised Ghost, was suddenly crestfallen. She, on the other hand, began to wonder about the rivalry between

Jodocus and Anadia. Whereas in Saga everyone was sentient, here in this world there seemed to be only a few self-conscious people—those Jodocus called *domini*—and apparently they all had strong magical powers. But like the RAL in Saga, it seemed that they didn't trust each other. How powerful were the *domini*? Could she battle them and emerge victorious? Could she battle Jodocus if she had to? If he released several of those large elementals at once, then her ability to control her surroundings might not be enough to defeat him.

The discovery of these *domini* of Myth had given Ghost a new thought to ponder, even if it was one that made her feel slightly ashamed. Between the humans and the *domini*, perhaps the latter were the better allies for the people of Saga. With Anonemuss's avatar dead, only Erik and Gunnar remained to help on this journey. And while Ghost felt enormous respect for Erik, counting him as a close friend, her priority had to be the defense of Saga. There was also the problem of the humans' commitment to non-violence. What would they do if the only way to stop an invasion of Saga was to kill the people planning it?

"Jodocus, how would Anadia or any other *dominus* of Myth feel about being allied with the *domini* of Saga? After all"—she drew a Higgs left-handed—"this is just one of our smaller guns. We are rearming as fast as we can and we have better weapons than they do. If the *domini* here could help us take the battle to our common enemies, perhaps it would be better to simply leave the humans out of it."

For a moment a wisp of cloud drifted between them and

Ghost could not read Jodocus's expression. When she could see him again, he was smiling and running a hand over his fleshy, bald skull. "So, you are a *dominus*. When I met you, I felt hope, for the first time in three years. I imagine the other *domini* would feel the same. Yes, they would want to be your allies, to see you destroy those who have been systematically turning our world into a dead one.

"But I might have given you the wrong impression of what we *domini* in Myth have to offer. Most of the *domini* here fought and died. I joined in some of the battles and although we could destroy the enemy's troops by the thousands, by the tens of thousands, they just kept coming.

"Eventually we scattered. I think many of the survivors were hunted down. You've seen how remote and well hidden my own residence is. I only know for sure that Anadia lives because she rules the birds of the skies and one of them found me and brought me a message. The others, though? I suspect some of them are around, but it wouldn't be easy to find them. And having contacted them, it would be quite a challenge to get them to work together."

"Hey, that's interesting." Milan was still staring through the binoculars.

"What is it?" asked Gunnar.

"Three of them have gone to the body. They're picking up his stuff: his gun, his bags—even the ring, I think. Now they're going back."

Cindella had reappeared, shaking her head, while Milan was speaking.

"Anonemuss is really raging. I had to take him out of the library and out to the square for some air. He was kicking at the shelves."

"He was serious about helping us. I appreciate that," said Athena.

"Yeah." Cindella gave a smile. "That and I think he was enjoying himself."

Jodocus came and squatted beside Cindella and Ghost. "So, what do you want to do now?"

"You have twice said we have the option of attacking here?" Ghost doubted she could handle anything like the amount of energy that would be thrown at her if she fought this army, so she was impressed that the elementalist considered it a possibility.

"It would hurt me and expend nearly all my stored elementals. But I could probably force a path through."

Athena gave an appreciative whistle. "That's some power you have."

"But what happens if there's an army on the other side, too?" asked Erik.

"Then it will be down to you; I'll be spent and in torment from the ruptured tattoos. How strong are you? You have good offensive weapons, but have you defenses against their projectiles?"

"Well, I've—"

"Not enough." Ghost cut across Erik before he could talk about his amulet of protection from missiles and Cindella's other magic items. It just wasn't wise to reveal too much to a powerful and intelligent person like Jodocus, not until they were completely certain about him. "Most of us would be killed by even one accurate shot."

"Then we are going to have to enlist the help of Anadia. If her avian forces can destroy this army, then I can save my elementals for the other side."

"Erik," said Gunnar, "you missed it, but while you were gone, Jodocus told us that this Anadia is another sentience that would try to harm humans. So Ghost admitted she wasn't human and offered an alliance between the people of Saga and the *domini* of Myth. You and I are on dangerous ground here."

"It seems," said Jodocus carefully, "that we have two humans among us: Erik and Gunnar. Well, firstly, Anadia need not know that you two are humans. Secondly, I think that the worst she can do is harm your avatars. Her powers are over the birds of this world, and they pose no threat to the humans behind the avatar. Just don't give her any information about your home planet, in case of future developments." He paused, looking around at the troops in front of the portal. "And thirdly, what choice do we have?"

Chapter 14
Of Avatars and Masks

In Penelope's experience, important meetings took place in the west wing of Lord Scanthax's castle, as it was there, on the first floor, that a series of rooms had been constructed to host a wide range of possible assemblies, from the full court to the small discussions held by the immediate advisors to Lord Scanthax, an inner council comprised of the more autonomous of his manifestations. Right now, Penelope was making her way across the bare wooden floor of the Great Hall, her footsteps ringing out harshly. This was the largest room in the castle, and walking across so huge an open space made her feel giddy. She wanted to run, to shout, to slide— anything to make the chamber feel less austere. Perhaps she should. The only witnesses would be the empty suits of armor that lined the oak-paneled wall opposite the windows.

Although designed for celebrations and festivals, the hall was a depressing room. Each time she crossed it, Penelope felt as though the ghosts of all the sentient lords and ladies that Lord Scanthax had killed were watching her. And the pale light that came through the windows did nothing to dissipate the gloom. These days Penelope could script huge panes of glass. But five years ago, when the hall was built, neither she nor Lord Scanthax could make glass very well, and the windows of the hall were therefore constructed by fixing lots of small pieces into the lead. As a result the room was dim. Despite the fact that it was still morning and the sun was shining brightly upon the left side of the hall, the whole chamber was filled with shadows, and even the wood of the floor and walls, supposedly stained a copper color, appeared black.

There were chandeliers, also of the primitive sort: large hoops of wood suspended from the roof by black iron chains on which were fixed a dozen candles. Very rarely—for important anniversaries or the presentation of medals—these chandeliers were lit so that the hall could fulfill its main purpose. On such days the chamber would be full of people from the castle and its environs. Most of those present would not have any independent consciousness; they would be servants and soldier units in attendance for decorative purposes only. But toward the far end of the hall, where a large wooden throne sat, would be gathered the full 212 manifestations of Lord Scanthax to witness whatever speech the lord had composed in honor of the anniversary of some supposedly glorious victory. These days Penelope felt sorry for the poor sentience whose execution or suicide was being celebrated—a life extinguished by the armies of a rival who had a distinct advantage in the scripting abilities of Penelope. Not that Lord Scanthax had taken all the credit for himself. No, Penelope had to admit that he had fully acknowledged her part in his triumphs. In this very hall she had been the recipient of a medal on three occasions and a sash on the fourth. For each of the ceremonies the room had been filled with cheers, applause, and congratulatory cries. But she had been young then. If the same ceremony took place today, she would not feel a sense of accomplishment or that she was appreciated by the people she worked for. Instead, no matter how full the room, she would feel only the emptiness and the dark. No matter how loud the applause, she would hear only one person clapping, and each handclap would ring out in her ears as a cry of sarcasm. The fact was—as she had come to appreciate only in the last year—her childhood had been manipulated to serve a creature who admittedly had gone to some trouble to keep Penelope's human body alive, but not out of any sense of empathy for the poor abandoned child; she had been brought up by Lord Scanthax solely as a means to secure his victory and domination over the world of Edda.

Having reached the stage, Penelope turned to her right and went through a pair of large double doors, leaving them open behind her. She was in a connecting corridor, one that was wide enough to host a display of captured ornaments from Lord Scanthax's rivals. In the center of the corridor was a globe, mounted on an iron stand now black with age. The map was old, and not just in the sense that all the boundaries on it were long out of date; the very surface of the globe, some kind of polished hide, had turned a deep brown color with the passage of time. As she walked past the ornament, Penelope noted that it was just possible to make out the small mountain territory labeled "Scanthax." It was obvious that he had placed that part of the globe so that it faced those who walked from the Great Hall toward the inner chamber, a reminder to everyone who passed of the tiny beginnings of his now multi-world dominion.

On either side of the corridor were wall hangings. On her left the cloth depicted a hunting scene whose central figures were long since slain, though not necessarily by Lord Scanthax; his armies had killed only 117 other lords and ladies. The rest of them had eliminated each other. In the needlework images, the people looked like they were enjoying themselves; they were smiling to one another, each with one hand holding the reins of their mounts and the other outstretched as a perch for their hunting birds. Around the hooves of their horses were eager and lively-looking dogs. It was very well done, and Penelope could see why it had been passed down from lord to lord, lady to lady, until eventually it became a prized possession of the sole survivor of Edda.

Opposite the hunting scene, on her right, was a rather less idyllic depiction of a naval battle. The skill of the embroiderer fell far short of that of the person who had made the hunting scene. The limbs of the combatants seemed slightly out of proportion to their bodies and sometimes stuck out at odd angles. But that wasn't the point. This was Westfell Channel, Year Six. It was this decisive victory at sea that had cleared the way for the invasion of Admiral Ekkehar's island. The wall hanging was not here to impress you with the artistry of the needle-work; it was placed thus to remind you of Lord Scanthax's achievements as you moved from the Great Hall to the Feast Hall. Penelope walked quickly through the far doors and into the Feast Hall, another silent wooden chamber in which her footsteps echoed. All around the room, carved directly out of the dark, stained wooden walls, were seats, perhaps two hundred in all. Five times now she had seen the room set up for the strange ceremony where Lord Scanthax reset the levels of autonomy for his manifestations. For the ceremony, the least important manifestations gathered in the outer rectangle of seats. Another seventy or so seats were placed in a circle, and there the mid-level manifestations sat, to learn their fate. And in the center of the room was a wide platform on which were seated Lord Scanthax and his most powerful manifestations: Assassin, General, Admiral, Chancellor, and Engineer.

The Feast Hall was also used for celebrations of Victory Day, an annual event to mark the day that Lord Scanthax received news of the surrender and death of his final opponent, Lady Withermane. For the feast, tables were placed in front of each of the seats that ran around the outside of the room, while an imposing round table was assembled on the platform, capable of seating the remaining manifestations. Penelope always sat at the inner table, which was natural enough, given she was treated as a princess.

The Feast Hall was another dark room, with the same old murky windows, currently allowing in pale light from the side of the castle opposite the windows of the Great Hall. Having walked the length of the Feast Hall, Penelope turned left and hurried on to another pair of double doors set in the far wall. They opened to a corridor whose wood-paneled walls were decorated with oil paintings in rather heavy-looking gold leaf frames. The pictures were all portraits. Several were of Lord Scanthax, of course, along with one each of his inner circle of manifestations. The artist was good; he had—perhaps inadvertently—captured the pomposity of General, the dourness of Admiral, the sinister gaze of Assassin, the scheming nature of Chancellor, and the solidity of Engineer.

There was also a portrait of her. Penelope remembered sitting for Artist in her rooms. The likeness to her avatar was striking, and although she was currently in a hurry, Penelope paused to look at the picture. It had been a sensible idea to wear a blue velvet dress; it highlighted the violet in her eyes. The face that stared out of the painting was pale and seemed all the more so, framed as it was by her tresses of black hair. The avatar looked self-assured and dignified. And that, Penelope supposed, was one advantage of being present in Edda in the form of an avatar. She could lose control of her emotions and no one here would realize it from her expression.

The doors at the far end of the corridor opened and Ambassador looked out. Rather guiltily, she hurried on.

"Ah, there you are, Princess, I thought I heard you."

"Sorry I'm late, Ambassador. I was working."

"Oh, indeed, indeed. Apologies for taking you away from your difficult labors."

They were in the penultimate chamber of the complex,

the one in which most of Lord Scanthax's strategic planning took place. It was a very functional room. To compensate for the lack of natural light, there were eight lanterns fastened to plain iron brackets evenly distributed around the walls. A log fire was burning, too, bringing a certain warmth to the scene. Not that Penelope could appreciate the heat, but she did appreciate that this was a real room, one you could spend time in, quite different from the other rooms, which were heartless and empty for so much of the year. A large but simply designed table stood at the center of the chamber, with eight chairs around it. On the walls were frames holding up-to-date maps and on the side of the room opposite the fireplace was a great chest of drawers containing more maps as well as copious amounts of paper, ink, and quills.

Here she was again, summoned to share in the most intimate of Lord Scanthax's deliberations. In the past, she had felt honored. Now she felt uneasy and disloyal. Nervous, too, in case she revealed anything of her insubordinate state of mind to him. Somehow she had come to the point where all her previous desire to please him had turned to bitterness and anger. If Lord Scanthax realized that she was determined to escape his control, no matter what, how would he react? It was entirely possible that once he realized her loyalty had eroded completely, Lord Scanthax would rather let Penelope die than have her roam the worlds as she wished.

"Lord Scanthax, Scout." Penelope curtseyed to the two other manifestations in the room.

"Princess, thank you for your time. We will not keep you

long from your vital work." Lord Scanthax's voice was deep and gruff, befitting the sturdy character of his basic form. Even though the last battle was long over and bullets had super-seded arrows many years ago, Lord Scanthax was still dressed in a chain mail hauberk with his sword strapped at his waist. Perhaps this was an affectation—an outward display of his mil-itary consciousness, or perhaps he never had a reason to dress any other way. Comfort and style were not priorities for Lord Scanthax. He gestured toward her. "Please, take a seat."

She did so, as did Lord Scanthax and Ambassador. Scout, however, remained on her feet near the map currently on dis-play in the frame; it was of the five known worlds and the gates between them, set out from left to right in a linear way that matched the sequence of their discovery:

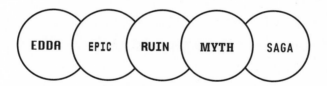

Among the usual pots of ink, papers, knives, wax, and other small items on the table was a handgun of a similar type to the rifle that Penelope was working on. Beside it was a cruel-looking dagger and a gleaming silver ring.

"Here." Noticing her curiosity, Lord Scanthax pushed all the strange items on the table in her direction. "Please, take a look."

"We obtained them at Gate Three," said Scout, tapping the center of the map with her finger. "Just over two days ago. The officers concerned sent a messenger at top speed to bring them to us. We thought it best to inform you about the new gun and the unusual properties of the ring, in case it was relevant to your scripting." Scout was a small woman, dressed in plain farmers' clothes: a belted tunic, trousers, and boots. Her color scheme was deliberately dull, just variations on brown. Unlike the other powerful manifestations, however, Scout did often change her look. It was part of her role, after all, to blend in with whatever environment she was investigating.

"The dagger is magically sharp; it will cut through anything. And the ring is magic, too: invisibility." Ambassador picked up the ring, checked that Penelope was watching, and, with an elaborate gesture, put it over his extended index finger. He disappeared.

"Oh."

A moment later he reappeared, the ring not quite touching his fingertip. Then he was gone again. Back. Gone.

"I see. Very useful."

"Dangerous," muttered Lord Scanthax, and Penelope turned to him. "What if a group of assassins have these? What's to stop them from coming here and killing us?"

"Well, what stopped whoever owned it?"

Lord Scanthax looked at Scout, who shrugged. "This ring came from a Saga person, who approached Gate Three from the Myth side, moving slowly, until our rifle units spotted him and shot him."

"He wasn't invisible?" asked Penelope.

"No, Princess."

"Strange."

Ambassador matched her shrug with one of his own and put the ring down beside the dagger.

"You want me to work with this?"

"We want you to know of it. But the gun is the priority." Lord Scanthax leaned forward and scooped up the pistol in his large hand. "This is a powerful weapon. Suppose a hundred people from Saga had a gun like this and a ring like that. They could walk invisible all the way to the castle and then destroy every one of us. Once I and all the manifestations were extinguished, your own life would be at an end, too."

Penelope could understand his anxiety, but the scenario just described by Lord Scanthax raised concerns of her own. "That reminds me. When can you give me control of the systems keeping my human body alive?"

Ambassador gestured toward the gun that Lord Scanthax was holding. "It will be done as a reward for your learning to script weapons like these."

Penelope nodded. True enough, that was the deal—although it might be some time before she could deliver on her part of it, and she needed control over the life-support system as soon as possible; not because she really took seriously the idea of an invisible group of assassins making their way to the castle from Saga, but because she had plans to leave Edda and search for the avatars of humans in the other worlds. Lord Scanthax would thwart such plans so long as he had control of her physical body.

"Very well." She changed the subject. "Here's another

mystery that I'm sure you have thought about. How does it come about that a person from a high-technology world like Saga has magic items that look like they come from Myth?"

Again, Lord Scanthax looked to Scout for an answer.

"Well," the woman began in her quiet voice, "we were discussing it earlier. There seem to be a number of possibilities. The worst case is that Saga has both sophisticated technology and powerful magic." From the corner of her eye, Penelope saw Ambassador give a glum nod. "Another possibility is that the person from Saga was simply fortunate enough to find the ring or be given it as they journeyed through Myth." Scout glanced at the map. "There are still many pockets of indigenous life remaining in Myth. Perhaps they met one of the last lords or ladies of that world and formed an alliance."

"Is that likely? I thought you killed them all?"

"Nearly all of them. But to judge from their records, we still have to eliminate at least one, called Anadia, and perhaps another, Jodocus, a criminal among them who disappeared some time ago. And there may be more who were not mentioned in the documents we have studied so far. I have most of my scouts at work in Myth, but there are great swathes of forest, swamp, and mountain that someone could hide in for as long as they wished."

"So, Princess," Lord Scanthax cut in, "we need those guns from you quickly. We also need a method of identifying the invisible assailants. And"—disconcertingly, he smiled at her; Lord Scanthax had not been designed to smile much and the expression was rather ogreish—"if you can script us those rings, we could launch our attack on Saga by sending through a few hundred invisible troops to establish a beachhead."

Penelope leaned back with a sigh. "You know I've never been able to do anything with magic. It is impossible to even make a start. I simply haven't a clue how those items were scripted. Perhaps creating magic items is not too difficult— who knows? But until we find some manuals to get me going, it's hopeless. The gun, I might be able to do in time, but even there I need to read up more about lasers."

The three manifestations looked rather unhappy, and wearily, Scout took a seat at last.

"Still, cheer up. We might not need magic to protect against invisible assassins."

"No?" asked Lord Scanthax.

Penelope reached for the ring and gave it back to Ambassador.

"Here, put this on and hold out your hand."

Once Ambassador was invisible, she felt around until she was holding his outstretched arm in her left hand. Then, picking up a quill with her right, Penelope flicked ink onto his invisible fingers. For a moment the ink clearly delineated the hand, but then it, too, disappeared.

"Rats. Scratch that idea."

"But still, Princess, your experiment has its value. Suppose I arrange for paint, or even just water, to pour down constantly in front of each gate," mused Lord Scanthax aloud. "Then, when someone passes through the disturbance in the flow, it will be visible. If the guard units are set to respond, they'll be able to get off a round or two." He nodded with a certain satisfaction. "I'll inform Engineer and my officers as soon as we are done here."

"What else do we need to discuss?" asked Penelope. Not that she was in any hurry to return to scripting; rather, looking at the invisibility ring had given her an idea. A very exciting idea. One of the great advantages of being human was that her involuntary responses were hidden by the passivity of her avatar. Her avatar was perfectly composed, while her human body would have betrayed her with sweat, with nervous movements of her eyes, and with flushes spreading across her body, driven by a pounding heart. Her voice, however, could still let her down, so Penelope strove to maintain her normal tone and steer her thoughts away from the ring.

"Can you close Gate Four?" Lord Scanthax leaned toward her, to emphasize the urgency of the question. "Can you prevent more units from crossing out of Saga until we are ready to attack them?"

Penelope shook her head. "As I told you before I even created Gate One, these are not like real doors. They are more like tears in the fabric of the world. It's like I cut the sky open."

"I remember," said Ambassador in his most agreeable tone of voice, "but isn't there a way to sew it back together?"

"No . . . well, not that I know of. It's not like cutting cloth; there is no give, no stretch—just the immovable edges of a void."

"Can you fill it then—the space?" Ambassador nodded for her, willing her to say yes.

"Yes, I can," she responded, nodding in kind. "But that won't close it off to the adjacent world. I could cover the gate with iron, or something stronger. But even then, if someone fired this kind of weapon through the gate, they would eventually melt whatever I put there."

Another unhappy silence.

"Ambassador has told me of your efforts yesterday, to leave your apartments and travel to the library."

"Yes?"

"It cost us a great deal of energy to bring your body back."

"Ah. I apologize for that; my muscles were weaker than I supposed."

"And you do appreciate the risks? If your suit had torn on a snag, you probably would have died."

"I didn't know of the damage to the corridor. The risks are far greater than I previously appreciated. I will not attempt such a journey again until I am fit enough to do so safely." Penelope's voice was nearly as steady as the placid expression on her avatar.

"Very well." Lord Scanthax stood up. "We won't detain you further. Take the gun—please." His voice suddenly changed, becoming less brusque as he remembered that he was supposed to be civil toward her. "And try to script us some weapons as effective as these, as soon as you possibly can."

"I certainly will." She stood up, took up the gun, and then, as casually as possible, picked up the ring. "Shall I take a look at this, too? Just in case it gives me any ideas?"

It seemed to Penelope that Scout was watching her

suspiciously and it was Scout who responded first. "It was decided to allocate the ring and the dagger to Assassin."

"Righto. Tell him I have it for study and will send a servant unit to him with it early tomorrow." With that she strode from the room, ring firmly grasped in her fist. Penelope did not pause to see whether the others looked surprised or simply accepted her announcement as reasonable. Closing the door behind her, she gave a little dance. A ring of invisibility! It was exactly what she needed to cross through the gates without notice. If she left at once, she could do so before Engineer constructed any curtains of water.

Chapter 15
BREATHLESS IN ANGUISH

Once back in her tower, Penelope went straight to a large and highly decorated chest of drawers whose black wooden top was covered in carvings of people in western clothing enacting scenes from some long-lost epic. Like so much of the castle's furniture, the chest was an item brought back from a fallen enemy by Lord Scanthax's victorious soldiers. Kneeling down in front of the drawers, Penelope pulled the bottom one out completely. This allowed her to reach inside and touch the base of the chest. She didn't need to see her fingers in order to script an opening through the wood and reach a secret hollowed-out area: a hidden drawer packed with everything she thought might be useful on a journey. There she had stashed maps to the gates; a compass; a sharp knife; some jewels; bronze, silver, and gold coins; a pair of binoculars; a pistol and clips with fifty bullets; a mirror; and so on. All these potentially useful objects were stored in a satchel that had a number of small additional items in its internal pockets, such as needle and thread, but she couldn't recall exactly what she'd laid away.

More than a year had passed since Penelope had hidden the bag: twelve months in which she often mused on the problem of how she could leave the castle on her own and explore the worlds beyond Edda for herself. Of course, she had often journeyed through them, but always in the company of one of the manifestations of Lord Scanthax and several soldier units. If Penelope could have one wish granted, it would be a simple one: her greatest goal in life was only to be given the chance to talk to other humans. The most likely way to realize that ambition was to enter the other worlds and seek out intelligent constructs in the hope that some of them were avatars for humans—or, if not, would at least know where humans could be found. But, tightly guarded by a squad of Lord Scanthax's soldiers, she had been given no license to roam and no opportunity to talk to anyone, human or electronic.

Even when her loyalty to her surrogate father had been high, Penelope had been immensely discontented—to the point of having her first rebellious thoughts—that she had not been allowed into the newly discovered worlds in search of humans, or, indeed, to enjoy the pure fun of being an explorer. And the injustice hit the eight-year-old girl especially hard, because it was only due to the fact that Penelope could see beyond the world of Edda that Epic had been discovered in the first place.

While clipped up to Edda, Penelope usually ran a series of background monitoring options, designed to measure the quality of her connection, warn her if there was any danger of lag, and suggest what measures to take if there was. Once, while doing some scripting on a bridge over a high waterfall, she had been surprised by one of the monitors suddenly flashing orange. The latency between her human body and that of the avatar was perfectly normal, but the amount of data flow between her and Edda at this point had more than doubled. It had taken months of curious investigation, but Penelope eventually realized that at this fairly remote point in Edda it was possible to pick up signals that simultaneously carried information about two worlds: Edda and an entirely new one.

On hearing the news, Lord Scanthax was positively euphoric; he had even attempted to give Penelope a hug. She'd given him a purpose once more, the purpose for which he was made: the conquest of a world. Lord Scanthax immediately began to reassemble his decommissioned army. When Penelope explained that to cut a route from Edda to this new data stream was an irreversible act, Lord Scanthax had taken the point seriously. He did not instruct her to go ahead until a vast army of high-quality troops had been gathered at the waterfall.

Edda, Epic, Ruin, Myth, and now Saga. Each of these electronic worlds had existed for decades with their own servers on their own planets to sustain them. And the game worlds were adjacent to each other in a linear fashion, presumably reflecting the existence of a chain of satellite links between the respective planets on which their servers were based. Penelope had discovered a considerable degree of overlap between each of the other games and its neighbor, enough that she could create the gates that opened the way from one to the next relatively near to one another.

It was surprising that the existence of Epic, Ruin, Myth, and Saga was not apparent to her from the first time she clipped up to Edda. But the humans who left Edda had deleted all references to the existence of other electronic worlds from their records. Not even Lord Scanthax knew about them, and if it had not been for Penelope, he—or whoever won the scramble for domination in Edda—probably would never have known about these other worlds. Perhaps the people who tried to hide the other worlds were wise and would think it was unfortunate that a human baby had remained behind when they left the planet, to survive and enter into Edda. Maybe Penelope had accidentally betrayed the goals of her species, for, one after the other, Lord Scanthax had destroyed each of the worlds that Penelope had opened a link to, at least until now, with the discovery of Saga.

If there had been avatars of humans in Ruin, Epic, or Myth, they had been killed along with any self-aware electronic life-forms. Lord Scanthax claimed he had spoken with captives after battles on Penelope's behalf, asking after the presence of humans, but she didn't believe him. Ever since he conquered Edda, Lord Scanthax hadn't bothered with prisoners. Whether humans ever created new avatars and came back to visit these depopulated and conquered worlds, she couldn't say, but if Saga was a vibrant and fully functional environment, it could well be that humans were present there in great numbers.

The recently created gate to Saga, currently the source of

widespread apprehension in Lord Scanthax and his manifestations, could be Penelope's last chance to find other humans, at least before he found a way to conquer the new world, too. What a wonder it would be, to find a human community, to meet other people of her kind after living for so many years under the joyless scrutiny of Lord Scanthax and his equally cold manifestations. So strong was her desire for the company of other people that Penelope could hardly allow herself to daydream about it, because the longer she was alone, the more unbearable the thought became that humans were out there somewhere, playing games, conversing, falling in love, becoming intimate.

No matter what he owed her, Lord Scanthax would never let Penelope's avatar escape him and explore Saga on her own. And while Penelope had prepared everything she needed for such an expedition, until today it had seemed like wishful thinking. At every gate between the worlds, Lord Scanthax had guards who would not let her through. But now, with the ring of invisibility, there was a chance she could make it all the way to Saga. And it was a chance she was determined to take.

Before she took up her preprepared satchel and left the castle, Penelope had to change the clothes her avatar was wearing. A princess's dress was not the most practical outfit to go marching off in. Again, she had thought about this some time ago, and in an adjacent closet, there were much more suitable clothes waiting for her journey. She undid her corset at the back, her movements swift and exact. Then she untied the three layers of her skirt and stepped from the pile of fallen garments as though from a purple cocoon. Her transformation was from colorful butterfly to dull caterpillar. Penelope's travel clothes were plain: dark trousers; a navy-colored, long-sleeved cotton undershirt; a plain gray overshirt; and an army jacket from Ruin. The jacket might disguise her a little—as a messenger, perhaps—but the real point of wearing it was its functionality; it was covered in pockets and made of strong material. Next, she tied her hair in a long ponytail, pulled over her left shoulder, and wedged a Ruin army cap on her head. Lastly, she pulled on a fine pair of black leather boots, which came up to just below her knees. All set? No, she needed to stuff her old skirts and bodice down in the secret drawer and push the bottom drawer back in on top of them. Once that was done, deliberately slowing her breathing, Penelope took one last measured look around the room to check that nothing was amiss. This was no time to become giddy with excitement and make a mistake. Satisfied that she had left no evidence of her departure, Penelope put on the ring and slipped out to the corridor.

Was she invisible? It was impossible to tell; as far as she was concerned, she looked the same as ever, even in reflections. For example, the glass in front of a tall grandfather clock served as an effective mirror. She admired her new look— very adventurous—but it seemed to make no difference if she removed the ring or put it on again. The slow, regular series of clicks from the mechanism in the dark chamber beyond the glass reminded her that time was passing and prompted her to move on. There was still one more thing she had to do before she left the castle. Penelope hurried along the castle corridors and up the curved staircase of a round tower to her laboratory. Again she had planned ahead. Inserted in the pages of a large, dusty volume at the bottom of a pile of books was a piece of parchment with large black lettering: "Delicate work in progress. DO NOT DISTURB FOR ANY REASON." That should keep out most of the castle units. Only Ambassador—if he had sufficiently good reason—would dare interrupt when faced with that message. Before pinning the note to the door, Penelope lit several slow-burning incense sticks. They would be long spent before she was even through Gate One, but perhaps their scent would linger and give the impression that there was indeed some activity taking place in the workroom.

Pressing her note into place on the ironclad door and turning the clunky lock with a key that she then placed in one of her jacket pockets, Penelope hurried back down the stairs, trying to keep the tapping sound of her boots on the stone to a minimum. Soon she was back in carpeted hallways and it was easy enough to move in near silence.

Halfway down the corridor that led to the entrance stairwell, a servant unit came out from a door and began walking toward her. For a moment Penelope's heart sank, thinking that she had been observed and that her unusual dress and presence here might be reported, depending on how intelligent the unit was. But then she remembered the ring and waited. The servant was walking on the other side of the corridor, so she moved quietly across into his path. Step after step brought him toward her, and there was no sign that he sensed someone was in his way. At last, when he was only four paces away and moving resolutely onward, she stepped across the corridor again, on tiptoe. The servant swept past her, appearing not to notice her at all. It worked! The ring really did work. For the first time since she committed herself to this venture, Penelope actually believed she might succeed.

There were a number of ways out of the castle, apart from walking across the courtyard and crossing the drawbridge under the gatehouse. After the military threat to Lord Scanthax from rivals in Edda had ended, the moat had been drained and this meant that a small postern gate that had once been below the waterline was now usable. Penelope descended the badly lit stone stairwell that led down to the gate and was shocked to find two soldier units standing there. The doorway had not been guarded two years ago, when she came down to check that her keys worked on the padlock. The soldiers were looking at her, animated, perhaps, in response to her unguarded footsteps. Delicately, quietly, she drew back, seeking out each step behind her without turning. A thousand curses on Lord Scanthax and Ambassador too! They must have become suspicious about her. Why else would they put guards at the old entrance? Or wait—perhaps it was because of their fears of invisible assassins from Saga? In any case, once she was sure the guards were not following her, she turned and left. Perhaps it would be best to sneak out over the drawbridge after all.

The courtyard was busy, and that suited her. Motorbikes, trucks, and horse riders were coming and going, creating considerable background noise. It was no bother skirting around the outside of the yard, with the castle wall on her left, pausing from time to time to let units move out of her way. A nervous moment came when she caught sight of Carpenter coming out of the stables ahead; he was one of the manifestations of Lord Scanthax with a reasonable degree of autonomy. But he didn't even glance toward Penelope; the invisibility continued to shield her.

Once at the drawbridge, she watched as a cart approached from the castle courtyard, the iron-shod footfalls of the horses echoing out as they slapped down on the wood. It was perfect cover, and she took advantage of the opportunity, stepping immediately behind the cart as it passed, so close she could have touched the back of the wooden frame of the vehicle. Not one guard unit so much as moved its head. Now clear of the drawbridge and the guards on the far side, she let the cart continue on down the drive while she made for a cluster of bushes. So far, so good.

Being outside the castle gave Penelope a tremendous uplift, a feeling of happiness greater than any she had previously experienced. Freedom tasted sweet. The sensation was enhanced by the fact that it was a sunny afternoon; she had emerged from the shadows of the castle walls into the bright colors of summer fields. This close to the castle, the fields were mostly uncultivated pasture, whose bright green grass was dotted with clusters of blue speedwells, purple thistles, and yellow ragwort. Even under escort, she really ought to have come out here more often when they blossomed, just for a walk among these signs of life and growth. The dimly lit corridors and dingy rooms of the castle suddenly seemed unbearable.

Penelope ran for a while, letting the stamina levels of her avatar sink nearly all the way down to zero. It didn't matter; she could recuperate while she worked. Safely out of sight of the castle, Penelope settled on some sandy ground beside a lone oak tree. There she began to script, using her human fingers inside their gloves to open the menus, selecting and drawing materials into existence in front of her, and using a huge variety of scripting subroutines to shape them. In the course of marching his armies across Ruin, Lord Scanthax had been impressed by the motorbikes of his enemies and desired them for himself as a means of speeding up communication between his troops. Until he conquered their factories, Lord Scanthax's motorbikes had been Penelope's creations. Having spent weeks scripting bikes for Lord Scanthax back then, Penelope could create a perfectly good motorbike with her eyes closed. More important, she could do so swiftly. In less than an hour it stood on its rests and back wheel, gleaming, perfect—except, perhaps, that it was a little too new looking. Still, by the time she reached the road, it would probably look like it had been around for years.

Now this was delightful! Penelope laughed as she mounted the bike and laughed again as she rode it, bouncing and jolting through the grass, revving hard whenever the bike threatened to stall on rising ground. And just as swiftly as the laughter had come, so, suddenly, did a flush of misery. What would her life have been like if she had not been left behind as a baby? One thing was certain: it would not have been a life spent almost always immersed in an electronic world. She would have been able to really feel the wind on her face, the tears on her cheeks; to inhale the scents of the grass and wild flowers. Instead, these joys were all being experienced at one remove, through the medium of the headset and gauntlets placed on her emaciated body. While the avatar registered some of the vibration of the bike and all of the roaring sound of the engine, the scents of the flowers and the feel of the rushing wind were left to her imagination.

Once she reached the road, Penelope increased her speed, the telegraph poles along the side of the road coming past swiftly, one after the other. Not too fast, she reminded herself. It would be terrible to crash now that she was on her way to Saga, and worse still to lose this avatar and have to create a new one, one that would necessarily appear back at the castle and would no longer have any of her items, including the ring of invisibility. She was not particularly experienced on these bikes, but fifty kilometers an hour seemed safe enough. Having thought the matter over, Penelope slowed down for a moment and removed the invisibility ring from her finger. Did wearing it make the bike invisible also? That would be suspicious: an engine sound without the machine to go with it. Stranger still would be the sight of a bike without a rider. In any case, motorbike messengers were a common enough sight on the route from the castle to Gate One.

There was not too much traffic on the road, mostly farm carts laden with vegetables destined for various barracks. For a while, though, she was stuck behind a very slow troop carrier.

It was strange to see medieval archer units packed inside a Ruin-style half-track truck, but such had been the situation ever since the conquest of the neighboring world and the absorption of its technology. As soon as a long stretch of road allowed her to overtake the truck safely, she twisted the accelerator and surged past.

What would she do in Saga? It would probably be wise to walk around invisible for a while, to gather information about the nature of their society. How would she find other humans, though? Could she risk talking to whatever sentient electronic beings she found there? And what would their response be? There was a great danger that they would be hostile and simply kill her avatar. But it would be worse if she was too cautious and Lord Scanthax discovered she was missing before she had spoken to anyone.

The blue of the sky was deepening by the time that Gate One became visible among the hills ahead, or at least the large barracks and set of defenses that surrounded the gate were visible. On her right, the road was currently following the shore of a lake, which was calm and tinged with copper from the colors of the clouds above. It was safe to keep going for a while longer, but with about a mile left before the camp, Penelope stopped the bike and dismounted. Although she was reluctant to leave the bike, she had to go on invisibly from here and even if the bike became invisible, too, while she was on it, the sound of its engine would draw attention to her movements. Once clear of the forces on the other side of the gate, she would script a new bike; it didn't take long.

Wearing the ring on the middle finger of her right hand, Penelope walked swiftly toward a checkpoint guarded by a machine gun post. Vehicles were being halted and investigated before they were allowed on, but she simply ducked under the pole that formed the barrier. Another hundred yards down the road between stationary columns of soldier units, and she could see the black glistening emptiness of the gate just up ahead. Good. They hadn't yet erected a waterfall, although she could see engineering units at work nearby getting the materials ready.

As she walked confidently up the final stretch of road before the gate, something changed. All the soldiers on either side turned to look at her and they raised their rifles and bows.

"Halt," said a voice from farther back.

Of course, she did not stop, but set her avatar to run.

"Halt, Princess, or we fire."

Penelope stopped. The ring was still on her finger. What had gone wrong? There were only twenty steps to the gate, but it was no good; just one good shot would cut down her avatar and with hundreds of soldier units focused upon her, it was hopeless. She felt sick.

An officer of the chain-mail-and-sword type came over to her.

"You do not have permission to use the gate."

"Oh, my mistake." She turned around and began walking down the road. Her human body was sweating, and she had to blink away tears to get her view to stop swimming, but her avatar was composed. There was no point in arguing with these units; they could not be deceived because they had no decision-making intelligence. What mattered now was to act as normal as possible so that the officer did not use the telegraph system to contact the castle. It was extremely tempting to look back at him, but she kept going.

What had gone wrong? Why had the invisibility ceased to function? Had some kind of interference from the gate affected the magic of the ring? That didn't seem likely, but it would account for what had happened to both her and the ring's previous owner.

Not until she was back at her motorbike, under a darkening sky, with the barracks a distant blaze of light, did she vent her frustration with a massive howl of anguish that went on and on until she had no breath remaining in her lungs.

Chapter 16
HARSH REAPPRAISALS

That evening, while working on the creation of a new gate as close to the data stream of Epic as she could safely manage without being seen by the guards of Gate One, Penelope experienced a lag between her physical finger movements and those of her avatar. At first she thought it was one of those rare moments when her interface with Edda lost its usual continuity; when there would be a little jerkiness for a second or two and then everything would become smooth again. But none of her monitors was flashing; latency was fine. When the delay continued and all her status bars appeared to be static, when she could not turn her head or hear the rain falling on the bracken around her, and when even the subtle movements of grass tips had ceased, then she knew what was happening to her, and she shouted with rage.

"No. Leave me alone!"

There was no response. Nor could there be. Everything was frozen. She had been unplugged from Edda. Although he had never done so before, Lord Scanthax could forcibly log Penelope out of Edda by the simple expedient of having the robots in her room detach her headset and gloves from the console. That this was exactly what had happened was soon confirmed by the cold touch of a robotic finger pushing at her shoulder. It wanted her to take off the interface equipment, but she just lay there cursing to herself.

Penelope was so completely helpless that she felt physically sick. All through her childhood she hadn't fully appreciated just how dependent she was on Lord Scanthax. After all, she'd never had any reason to really press him and the medals he gave her had made her proud to be helping him. Penelope was a princess and, even more wonderful than that, she was the only person in the whole of Edda who could script. Indeed, far from feeling helpless, she had felt powerful. But gradually she had discovered the limits of that power. All her serious work was for Lord Scanthax; the toys and clothes she made for herself were nothing more than a benignly tolerated indulgence. Fundamentally—as had just been proven—her relationship to Edda was entirely in his hands. And worse, as the lone person in a deserted complex hostile to human life, she was a prisoner. Lord Scanthax controlled her life-support systems, her access to Edda, and, as a result, her whole existence.

The prodding stopped. Penelope lay in darkness on her back, her headset still fastened across her eyes, her hands heavy in their interface gauntlets. The tears descending from the corners of her eyes felt warm as they reached her ears. What would Lord Scanthax do next? Unfasten the drip that was feeding her body? And how would she respond to that? Lie here until she died? That would teach him a lesson. Or would it? Did he really need her still? Those weapons from Saga were powerful, but what Lord Scanthax lacked in technology he made up for in the scale of his dominion, now stretching over most of four worlds. It was doubtful that any real threat faced him from Saga. He always did have a tendency to exaggerate his difficulties.

Time passed, perhaps an hour, and it seemed as though Lord Scanthax had decided to leave her alone. Penelope's tears stopped and her heartbeat slowed. But she still refused to remove the interface equipment, preferring to lie in the dark until she knew her own mind.

It was probably inevitable that at some point her disappearance would be discovered, but she had hoped to complete her new gate and still have time, if the invisibility worked, to get as far as Saga. A few hours might have been all that was needed.

So Lord Scanthax or one of his manifestations—probably Ambassador—must have discovered her absence. They probably had the castle searched and then Lord Scanthax had done the obvious thing and focused on her human body, which, after all, could not escape him. He had ordered the robot to unplug her from Edda, presumably in order to get her attention and prove his control over her. That's why she didn't want to move. She just didn't want to be forced to return to that grim castle and the scripting work that only made Lord Scanthax more powerful and less interested in Penelope's wishes.

What, then, were her options? If she were physically

stronger, she could make it to the library and try to find out more about the human world. The people who used to live here—including her mother—surely had not left the planet without a trace. They had deliberately left no record of where they had gone, presumably so that there was no possibility of a sentient being from Edda one day becoming a threat to them again, but even so, perhaps there was a means of contacting the former colonists. Perhaps there was a way to broadcast a message out into space that would reach them.

As for what happened to the humans who had left the settlement some sixteen years ago, Penelope would have to find that out for herself. She could not accept Lord Scanthax's version of events; his stories had been designed to keep an eight-year-old girl hard at work for him, and while Penelope had never caught him in an out-and-out lie, she had learned enough about his character to know that he cared for nothing but victory over all other electronic lifeforms.

Losing her childish understanding of who she was and what her life meant had been painful. It meant seeing all the rewards that she had striven so hard to get as worthless and all the ceremonies and compliments of Lord Scanthax as empty. But at the same time, there was also some comfort in the notion that he had no empathy for his human companion, for it might well be that Lord Scanthax was keeping her isolated from other people. What if there was a simple way of contacting other humans that Lord Scanthax was hiding from her? Had he already encountered them in other worlds, or even through communications to this one that he had never told her about?

At this encouraging thought, a little energy came back to her body and Penelope no longer wanted to simply waste away in the dark to frustrate Lord Scanthax. Instead, she realized, she wanted to outmaneuver him; to have him on his knees, pleading for her aid and giving her all that she wanted: to have complete control over these robots and over her life-support systems; to come and go as she pleased in Edda; and to access all the library files in this world. Was that possible? Or was it just wishful thinking? It was a revolutionary change in her outlook. Instead of seeing Lord Scanthax as a father figure, she saw him as an enemy, her captor, someone she must defeat.

This harsh but necessary reappraisal of Lord Scanthax also had implications for Penelope's attitude toward the sentient beings of Saga. So what if they really did mount an effective attack on Lord Scanthax? To have him in a state of genuine fear for his life would now be something to relish. It could get dangerous, though. On the one hand, she wanted the threat from Saga to frighten Lord Scanthax sufficiently for him to come begging Penelope for assistance. On the other hand, if the conscious entities of Saga really were that strong, they might simply destroy Lord Scanthax, with the consequence that this would lead to failure of the systems keeping her body alive. Penelope reassured herself with the thought that it was unlikely anyone could kill Lord Scanthax. As far as she understood, so long as one manifestation of his was alive, it would eventually accrue all his intelligence and energy. And seeing as there were more than two hundred manifestations, surely some of them would escape an attack on the castle.

But supposing there was no prospect of the armies of Saga defeating those of Lord Scanthax, what then? She would have to create a situation that would oblige Lord Scanthax to negotiate with her. But how? There was one obvious way to threaten him. If she managed to script an explosive device of sufficient power, Penelope could destroy all his manifestations when they next met in the Feast Hall for a redistribution of his will. As she lay in the dark, trying to picture such a scenario, she became aware of the impractical side of this plan. Even if she could manage the difficulties of scripting such a powerful bomb, she didn't really want to kill Lord Scanthax—certainly not while the management of the human-world equipment that kept her alive was entirely in his hands. And even if she could kill him at no risk to herself, was that what she desired? She hated him; hated his coldness, his lack of humor and empathy, his manipulation of her childish eagerness to please. But he was still the only family she had ever known, and after all, he had saved the human baby that had been left behind at the exodus. He deserved some credit for that.

It cheered her up, though, to imagine the scene. Redistribution Day, and all the manifestations gathered in the Feast Hall, with Penelope seated among the higher-level versions of Lord Scanthax at the inner table. After their usual self-congratulatory speeches, she would ask to make one. They would listen, curious at first, but then perhaps a little afraid.

For she would scream at them, venting at last her pent-up rage at her captivity; at the way Lord Scanthax had exploited her; at his failure to pay any attention to her goals; at his failure to give her freedom to explore the worlds as she liked, to try to find other humans. It was such a small request and it would have been so easy for him to grant it. But his chance was over. With a last long look into his face, which finally, too late, might show some comprehension of her feelings, she would blow up the lot, her own avatar included. A few hours later she would die, either from lack of oxygen or hypothermia, all alone in the cold and dark. Not that she feared being alone; despite the bustle of the castle, she had been alone her whole life.

Penelope tugged her hands free of their gloves and took off her headset. The robot nearest her turned to face the bed and in its shining plates she saw her reflection: a wan and pale young woman with pink sores for eyes. It was no wonder that she spent so much time in Edda, to the detriment of her human body. There really was nothing for her in this small complex that sustained her. Unfastening the drips and tubes that serviced her body, Penelope sat up with a grimace. At a stretch — and clearly she did not stretch often enough — she could just about touch the roof. The room was about three meters long and only two wide, illuminated dimly by a pale blue striplight in the roof. At the far end was the air lock. Around the bed that dominated the room were units that were mostly drawers filled with equipment, although the one nearest the head of the bed was the Edda console.

With an audible groan, she maneuvered her skeletal body to

kneel in a corner of the room. There, in the bottom cupboard, was a drawer full of items she had collected over the years. Robots, guided by her instructions as she watched through a monitor, had salvaged them for her from around the base at various times in her life. It really was a pathetic collection: a blue plastic elephant, not much bigger than her thumb; a picture book telling the story of "The Princess and the Pea"; a fraying red silk purse containing two marbles, which she used to pretend were magic; a glass bead necklace; half a deck of playing cards; a pair of men's slippers, still too big for her; a mostly empty tube of glowstring; an exercise book with her drawings in it, along with an incomplete set of colored crayons, worn down to little stubs; a doll's head, with red crayon marks on its cheeks from her childlike efforts to make it look more healthy; and a model spaceship.

How could she resist the attraction of Edda? In the castle library was more or less the complete collection of human literature; in its wardrobes, the most fabulous dresses. Its viewing screens had access to a vast database of music, programs, films, documentaries, plays, and concerts. There, she wanted for nothing; here, everything. Yet it was here she needed to stay, building up the physical strength she needed to explore the settlement in person and not just through the cameras of a robot.

"Princess, you have returned to us." The voice was that of Ambassador. Although a little tinny from the poor quality of the speakers in the room, it was still loud enough to startle her. Penelope said nothing in reply, but picked through the contents of her drawer, examining each item carefully before putting it on the floor beside her.

"Princess, are you dysfunctional? Do you need a medical assessment?"

"No."

"In that case . . ." He paused. Imagining Ambassador's unease as he carefully formulated what he was going to say next almost brought a smile to Penelope's face. "In that case, can you tell us why your avatar is not in the castle?"

"No."

"We received a report that you approached Gate One about eight hours ago, then left after you had been denied access."

Neither of them spoke for several minutes. Penelope turned the pages of the storybook, slightly shocked to find that the clothes worn by the princess in the final illustrations were rather similar to those worn by her avatar. Was she really that impressionable?

"You left a note on your door that was false. It seems that you were trying to deceive us as to your activities. Why was that? What were you trying to achieve by traveling through Gate One unaccompanied?"

"I was trying to go to Saga and seek out humans before you destroy that world and everyone in it."

Tired now, Penelope wanted to go back to the bed and rest again, but in keeping with her new resolution, she first put all her belongings back in the drawer and began an exercise routine of bends and stretches.

"Whether we can destroy Saga or not is a much-discussed

question between Lord Scanthax and General. But we always look to make contact with humans on your behalf. You know that."

"No." She grunted with the effort of holding her trembling arms outstretched. "No, I don't know that. I think you have met humans in other realms but not told me."

"Why would we do such a thing?" Ambassador sounded genuinely aggrieved at the accusation.

"To keep me busy scripting. If I met other humans, I might develop new aspirations for myself, like finding out if they can send a spaceship to this settlement and bring me to their community. You wouldn't want that, would you?"

"Not given the current crisis. But with the threat from Saga successfully contained, we would welcome an end to the drain of energy required to maintain your life-support."

It was impossible to carry on her routine when her body was convulsing in bitter shakes of laughter, so Penelope moved to rest on the bed. Just for a moment, she told herself.

"Not for the sake of my happiness, then?"

"We would like you to be happy."

"So you say. But as we once discussed, you have a very limited and inhuman notion of happiness."

"Princess, where is your avatar?"

"About a mile north of Gate One, beside the river."

"Executioner is asking after the ring of invisibility. Will you return it?"

"I suppose so, seeing as it was useless to me."

"I see. You hoped to travel invisibly to Saga?"

"Yes. But it doesn't function at the gates."

"Oh. That is excellent news."

"For an ambassador, you are surprisingly prone to gloating instead of finding a way to win my sympathy."

"I beg your pardon, Princess. I was not gloating—merely expressing pleasure that the danger of a small group of assassins using such rings to attack us has lessened."

Penelope lay out on the bed again, staring up at the undecorated metal above her.

"Give me control of the life-support systems here, please, and we can part company. You can save your energy solely for running Edda while I try to make something of a life here." It was a grim scenario, but at least she would be free.

"Lord Scanthax has already agreed to, Princess—*after* you have scripted us some of those energy weapons." His emphasis was on the world "after."

Up until now, in her dealings with Lord Scanthax, Penelope had always found him rigorous in adhering to his promises, pedantic even. But when it came to his treaties with various other lords and ladies, Lord Scanthax had no scruples. He tore up agreements the moment they no longer suited him. So could she trust him? The difficulty was that, even if she could, making a match for the weapons from Saga was hard. There could be months of experimentation before she solved the main problem of containing the energy and directing it. Spending months in the wizard's tower was not appealing. Not when she had just tasted a wonderfully sweet draught of freedom. Moreover, there was no way she wanted to provide

Lord Scanthax with weapons that powerful. No. Penelope had resolved to escape Lord Scanthax's control and find a way to contact other humans, either through explorations in the material world or by avoiding the scrutiny of Lord Scanthax in Edda. There was no point in trying to script guns like those from Saga, but pretending to do so would be the first step in her campaign to challenge Lord Scanthax.

"Very well. I shall return to Edda and bring Princess back to the castle."

"Thank you, Penelope."

She lay on the bed, restored the tubes to her body, and, with a shudder, reached for the headset. It was troubling that so soon after contemplating leaving Edda for good, she was going back in; that, even worse, she actually looked forward to being back in that colorful and vibrant world, though she was only swapping one prison for another.

Chapter 17
Secrets by Night

Once more in her magician's laboratory, Penelope stood beside a thin lead-lined window, looking out to where distant clouds drifted across an orange evening sky with the promise of freedom. Below her a section of the road was filled with a variety of unit types, riding or driving to and from the castle. Watching them was like looking down on a nest of ants.

"Busy, busy, Ambassador."

"I beg your pardon, Princess?"

"The castle is busier than ever."

"Oh, indeed. General and Lord Scanthax have decided to attack Saga as soon as we have manufactured a reserve of a million military units—an arbitrary figure, true, but one considered sufficient to deal with any potential ripostes."

With a slight shake of her head, Penelope came back to her massive worktable, running her fingers along its deepest scars. "And what will you do, Ambassador, when Saga has been conquered and I have left Edda to concentrate on my human body?"

Whenever she could, Penelope gave Ambassador the impression that she believed unquestioningly that Lord Scanthax would honor their agreement and allow her to run the systems that kept her body alive. The reality, though, was that she no longer trusted him in the slightest.

"I . . ." Uncharacteristically, Ambassador was at a loss for words. "I suppose I will be downgraded in my level of autonomy at a redistribution but kept in a functioning state in case Lord Scanthax needs to communicate with you or other entities."

"Humans?"

"It is always possible they might return."

"Hope for us all," Penelope sighed.

Ambassador did not reply; his head was bowed as he smoothed his silk waistcoat free of undetectable wrinkles. It was not fair to tease him with the fact that he was far more subject to the will of Lord Scanthax than Penelope, but she was tired of his constant presence. Ever since her return to Edda, even while her avatar lay in her four-poster bed, she had been aware of Ambassador's careful scrutiny. When she fell asleep, he was there, waiting patiently in the darkened room beyond the drapes, and when she awoke, it was as though he had not moved the whole night. Perhaps he hadn't.

If Lord Scanthax thought that her tolerance of such a close guard combined with her submissive and meek behavior meant that Penelope had given up on plans to escape him, he was mistaken. For while on the surface she was as obedient as any of his manifestations, every day her heart cried rebellion. Not that this mutinous state of mind was evident from her routine: morning after morning, she walked up the winding stone staircase to the dark tower's workroom, lit the candles and lanterns, and settled down to her scripting. The items that were the focus of her attention were shaped as closely as she could manage to the Saga weapons that Lord Scanthax desired so very greatly. The guns on the table looked like exact replicas of those he had captured: but the similarity went no deeper than appearance. For what she hoped would seem like a serious attempt to model energy weapons was in fact a means of pursuing her own project. Pressing the fire buttons on these devices produced no bolt of energy and it never would. Instead, it triggered another effect that Penelope was investigating with an enthusiasm that grew in proportion to her success.

For her, the boundaries of objects in Edda were not as solid as they appeared. She could easily stretch or contract the bench she was sitting on, for example. She could transmute its qualities. Did it shine or absorb light? One sweep of her hand across the appropriate menu and the criteria was set. Was it dense or light? Solid or fluid? Conductive or resistive? Heat retentive or reflective? As a result of years of practice, Penelope could script wood, glass, metal, and cloth of all types, and she could do so swiftly. More recently she had been mastering plastics.

Under the—hopefully ignorant—eyes of Ambassador, her latest work was in the fusion of diverse materials at their point of contact; or, to put it simply, making objects stick together. All sorts of items were now welded fast to the tabletop as a result of her experiments. It was much harder to undo the fusion than to create it, so some of the items had not been freed. There was a large skull that would probably shatter before it would shift an inch. A candlestick, too, was held fast by bonds stronger than the brass with which it was made. Penelope hoped that Ambassador or another servant never had reason to pick up anything from the desk. The nearby piece of blank parchment, for example, looked as though it would lift away on a breeze, but in fact it would take the strength of an ox to lift the paper and even then the enormous workbench would come with it. It was a skill that Lord Scanthax did not know about and had little interest in. Architect, Blacksmith, Mason, and Carpenter had dealt with all the building projects to date without any need for Penelope's assistance.

The growing effectiveness of her new technique was most encouraging. But for what she had in mind, her current method for fixing two items together had to become much swifter and probably would have to be done at a considerable distance. Her answer to the problem of how much time it took to fasten two materials together was to make the process automatic by turning the gun into a fusion device. Pulling the trigger set scripts running that stitched together whatever you were aiming at. In principle, the device worked well, but her first attempt to use it had led to the nose of the gun becoming stuck to the worktable. It had taken Penelope nearly a day to unglue them, a very weary day in which she had to disguise the nature of her problem from Ambassador. The device was more effective now, in that the scripts only operated on materials other than the gun itself. But still, she had a lot of work ahead of her before it was the sophisticated tool she needed.

Meanwhile, she had other preparations to make.

"I'm tired. I think I'll rest early tonight."

"Very good, Princess."

Placing the gun she had been holding onto the worktable, Penelope stood up and walked over to an old coat stand on which she had hung her cape. While she wrapped it around her, Ambassador opened the door to the stone staircase and held it wide.

"Would you like a servant to bring you a book?"

"No, I'm still reading the last one."

"*Conversation with a Murderer?*"

Penelope turned to look up at him. "Yes."

"Does it entertain you?" His expression was impassive.

"Yes."

"Good."

For a moment Penelope felt the need to offer an explanation for why that title had caught her interest and how the book was not at all what she expected. But she thought better of speaking and turned back to the stairwell, continuing her descent. It was best not to begin a conversation about murder. Despite the difficulties of an electronic intelligence understanding what was happening in the mind of a human, it would not be wise to give Ambassador any insight into the current turmoil of her thoughts and emotions.

Once in bed, she read for a few minutes by the strong light

of a lantern of her own design: while its beam from the front was powerful and bright, a more subdued light issued from the sides and back through a screen in which there were some twenty holes. The lantern was itself housed within a blue-tinted glass stand, so that, outside of the main beam, her bed-room was patterned in blue and shadow. It was as though her chamber were underwater. And in his own shadowy grotto by the door, Ambassador stood as patiently as a statue.

"Good night, Ambassador." Penelope reached across to the lantern, turned down the wick until the flame was extinguished and then undid the cords that held the curtains of her bed open. The velvet drapes fell into place, enclosing her in a dark space between bed and canopy.

As quietly as she could, Penelope placed her fingers against the headboard of the bed and, scripting a hole in the wood, accessed a chamber within, from which she drew a long, knotted silk rope. It was a ladder, and tonight it would be long enough for use. In fact, after less than an hour of lying on her back teasing the silk out, twisting it, and tying it, she was ready.

Penelope lay on her bed, the rope ladder on her chest. The room was quiet and still, although beyond the windows the restless growl of motors could be heard, fading or growing louder depending on whether the vehicles were departing or arriving at the castle. Much closer were the occasional fluttering sounds and cooing of the doves that nested somewhere above her window. It was going to be very hard to disguise her movements from Ambassador, but she had to try, and procrastinating was not going to make it any easier.

With a sigh, as if her dreams had been disturbed, Penelope rolled over, rustling the covers to hide the noise of her feet as she slipped them out from under the sheets and onto the floor on the opposite side of the bed from Ambassador. Gently, very gently, she eased herself entirely free of the covers, so that she was standing beside the bed, just inside the drape. Had Ambassador been on this side of the bed, he would have seen a suspicious bulge in its curtains. Taking a moment to calm herself, Penelope squatted down and felt the floor. It parted beneath her scripting fingers without a sound and soon she had shaped a hole wide enough for her to fit through comfortably. Now her new skills proved useful, as she merged the top ends of the silk ladder to the wood of the bedroom floor. It would take her weight and much more without coming away. Quietly, slowly, she lowered the thin ladder down into the dark pool below. It was a slender creation but strong: it would serve. Again with the utmost care, she took most of her weight on her arms and lowered herself into the hole, legs swinging without purchase until they found the crosspieces of the silk ladder. Now she could climb down properly and did so with growing delight at the success of her plan, until a creak from the floor of the bedroom above her made her pause and wince with anxiety. For a while she remained in midair, twisting slowly, listening to the silence above. Nothing. He had not moved. Then she continued until her foot touched the floor below. She was down!

Her goal lay in the direction of the administrative rooms, and as there were no major gatherings scheduled this evening, that wing of the castle was quiet and in darkness. Penelope made her way along moonlit corridors, past doors that would have beckoned to her to come in and search through their collections of paintings, silverware, arms and armor, clothing, jewelry, and books had she any means of quickly detecting if any of the captured items were magical. But they could wait. Tonight she had a clear purpose: to search the Feast Hall and ensure that she knew where all its exits and entrances were.

For most of her journey through the silent passages of the castle, Penelope was dizzy with excitement and delight in her temporary freedom. She had escaped the surveillance of Ambassador! But as she approached the Feast Hall her giddiness faded, to be replaced by anxiety. Two of the chandeliers in the Great Hall had been lit, and a pale light shone on the breastplates of the empty suits of armor along the walls. This was far from the blaze of light that was created for assemblies, but it did mean one of the rooms farther down was in use. Perhaps Lord Scanthax was holding a discussion with some of his high-level manifestations? In any case, the way had been lit for someone, and she would have to proceed on tiptoe, always keeping note of the nearest hiding place she could duck into should anyone appear. It was very hard in such a large chamber not to make a sound while walking, even when barefoot. Fortunately, years of practice had attuned Penelope perfectly to the movements of her avatar and she reached the connecting corridor to the Feast Hall with barely an audible footfall.

Again the chamber was partially lit, the shadow of the globe a large crescent on the wall tapestries. The far doors to the Feast Hall were open. This was a much more anxious

experience than she had imagined it would be. If Lord Scanthax or one of his manifestations were to catch her, he would
know that he could no longer trust her. They would discover
how she had escaped the scrutiny of Ambassador and it would
be immensely harder to get away in the future. Worse, Lord
Scanthax would wonder what she was doing here and perhaps
take precautions that would prevent her plan from ever being
realized. All the same, there was no point turning back; not
now that she had come this far. Given the drive to war that was
under way at the moment, there might never be a night when
the meeting rooms were unused.

The Feast Hall, too, had enough light to see by and the
doors that led toward the Map Room were open. The light was
different down there, flickering and orange. It meant there was
a fire lit in the Map Room. And now that she stopped to listen, she could hear a very faint murmur of conversation. From
where she stood, the words were not distinct, but it seemed
that at least two people were present. Were they expecting
more? She checked behind her and slowed her breathing to
concentrate. No one seemed to be coming along behind her.
It was comforting that apart from the area near the entrance to
the Map Room, the rest of the Feast Hall was dark. She would
begin in the blackest corner of the room and crouch there
should anyone enter.

Most of her survey was done by touch, scripting open each
wooden seat along the walls, then the panels behind it, to confirm that they were solid and not a hidden passage, and finally
restoring the wood. In this way, feeling relatively safe in the

shadows, Penelope methodically made her way around the Feast Hall. It was slow going, but she had to be certain that she knew where all of the exits were and that she could seal them. Although she had anticipated that at least one of the chairs or wooden panels would conceal a hidden passage, there had been no such disguise so far in the section of the room where she could search in relative safety.

Now it was necessary to draw close to the entrance that led to the Map Room. Penelope anxiously worked her way right up to the shadow of the door nearest her, the voices from the Map Room becoming more distinct as she did so.

"To my mind, it is like Tharsby Pass again."

"My dear General, everything reminds you of Tharsby Pass, because you constantly wish to remind yourself and our lord of your greatest triumph."

"Lord Scanthax has no need to be reminded of that achieve-ment. An impregnable valley. Powerful weapons. An impossi-ble task. Yet we took it. By sheer persistence we took it." There was a distant thump, and Penelope could imagine General banging the table with his gauntleted fist. "Cry Scanthax! We took it and we can take Saga in the same manner, whatever their weaponry!"

"Calm yourself, General; you are not addressing the troops here." It was not clear to Penelope who was speaking. His voice was laconic and confident. One of the inner circle of manifes-tations, certainly. Perhaps Chancellor? No, his voice was more weaselly than this one.

"Your tactic—let us call it 'the rush'—has its place. But how do you know this is the place for it? We are far too short of intelligence to stake all our current forces on a move that might well strip us of all our defenses if we fail."

"I know you perceive me as lacking in intelligence, Assassin, but I have more intuition about these matters than you do. And I say this: most wars are won slowly and after many battles, including many defeats, but some are decided at the outset. I feel this is such a war. Even if we produce military units ten times faster than them, every one of their weapons can account for a hundred of our men. The longer we postpone the attack, the more difficult it will be. Does it not worry you that they won the skirmish at Gate Four, then did nothing, except perhaps send one assassin toward us? What are they waiting for?"

"Actually, General, I agree with you more than I might have previously indicated; that is, apart from one significant consideration you seem to be neglecting."

"Yes?"

"We have Princess working hard on the construction of those energy-throwing weapons. Given time, we will be able to equip ourselves as well as our enemies. It is how we have triumphed in the past and how we can do so now."

"I prefer to rely on our own strength rather than the human. I hear that she finds it hard to make the guns, that her progress is slow. Moreover, she is unreliable."

"Princess does seem to be increasingly erratic, but

Ambassador believes she is motivated to complete the work by the promise that she will be given complete control over her human environment."

"Ambassador is a fool and a waste of Lord Scanthax's processing power. He should be reabsorbed."

"But you can see the advantage in delaying an attack until we have either enormous reserves or new weapons?"

"I don't like it. I'm troubled by the thought we might have already lost our chance. And I had hoped that our days of dependency on the human were over."

"They won't be over until our last possible rival is eliminated."

"Enough. I accept Lord Scanthax's decision. Leave me with these maps and I will draw up the dispositions for the new units."

All at once footsteps were walking rapidly toward her. There was no time to move back to the far end of the chamber, nor could she unclip quickly enough for her avatar to disappear. So Penelope shrank up against the wall, aware that back in her bed her organic heart was thumping hard. If Assassin closed the door behind him, he could not fail to see her. His footsteps rang out right beside her ears and—O delicious moment!—continued on unchecked, gradually dying away as he walked out of the Feast Hall and back toward the center of the castle. When she was sure he was long gone and she had recovered her nerve, Penelope resumed her task, working her way carefully back around the hall rather than risk crossing in front of the open doors. It had been interesting to overhear the high-level manifestations talk about her. Lord Scanthax and Ambassador were more circumspect in their language, but even from them the message was the same: they saw Penelope as an outsider and wanted her only for the advantage she could give them in war. Whatever the future held for her, if she left it in the hands of Lord Scanthax, it would be a limited one. To get the freedom she wanted, to travel through Edda and beyond, she would have to improve her bargaining position and that meant catching Lord Scanthax at a vulnerable moment. Thinking about the hostile tone of General's voice made her all the more determined to implement her plan. Lord Scanthax had no gratitude for everything that Penelope had done for him and Penelope no longer had any loyalty to him, no matter what efforts he had made to keep her alive as a baby.

On the wall opposite the open doors, but not directly across from them, was an enormous fireplace. It was so large that Penelope could step under the mantelpiece without having to bend. And it was there that she found the hidden passage. There were alcoves in either corner of the fireplace where someone could stand and not be seen by anyone in the room. One of them was of solid stone, but the nearest had a wooden door, painted to appear as though it were gray rock. Making careful exploratory holes in the door, Penelope found the catch that allowed her to swing it open. Beyond it was a very small chamber with a hole in the floor and a ladder of metal steps imbedded in the wall below.

Penelope was curious as to where exactly the passage ended,

but that wasn't important now. What mattered is that she knew where the secret door was and that it could be welded shut. She closed the door and quietly put the catch back on. Everything was as she had found it.

Although it was unlikely there was another hidden exit somewhere, for the sake of completeness Penelope decided to finish her circuit of the Feast Hall, even though this meant creeping across a section of the wall that was brightly lit because it faced the open doors to the Map Room. It was a situation where if she were caught at this stage, she would be furious with herself for not having returned to her bedroom while she had the chance. But it would be worse still if the day came when she thought she had trapped Lord Scanthax, only for him to surprise her. Therefore, she made herself crawl quietly forward on her hands and knees to peek down the corridor toward the Map Room. General was not in sight. She could hear him down there, occasionally opening drawers and pulling out sheets, then quietly scratching out his notes and orders. But it sounded like he was sitting close to the fire and well away from the door.

Anxiously, and still on all fours, she hurried by the illuminated part of the wall. Once safely out of sight again, she could relax a little and return to her methodical exploration of the room's seats and wooden panels.

Unexpectedly, in the middle of the far wall, she found a space instead of stone. Another hidden exit? Lord Scanthax was more security-conscious than she had supposed. But it did not take long to discover that the space was a small box room, equipped with a periscope-like device that allowed the viewer to look out over the whole of the Feast Hall. The lens of the periscope was cleverly designed to slide along the line between two panels, so you would not notice it unless you looked closely. The booth contained several weapons—guns from Ruin mostly—and boxes of ammunition. It was clearly designed to accommodate a bodyguard, who could survey the room while Lord Scanthax feasted. Clever. Not that there would ever have been a threat to him at the redistribution or award ceremonies; all the people present were his own mani-festations except, of course, for Penelope and, perhaps—safely contained in cages—captured rivals over whom he could gloat.

Satisfied that she had thoroughly scouted the Feast Hall, Penelope stood with her hands on her hips, taking it all in. At the next redistribution ceremony the room would be full, between Lord Scanthax and all his manifestations, and she would be able to hold them there, trapped. It would be nec-essary to make the windows bulletproof and strengthen the doors, but she would leave that until closer to the assembly, just in case one of the more observant manifestations, such as Assassin, noticed something had changed. For now, though, she had done very well. Feeling optimistic for the first time since Lord Scanthax had forcibly unplugged her from Edda, Penelope tiptoed her way back toward her bedroom. She would sleep well tonight.

Chapter 18
A Sapphire in the Sky

Not until he was high above the clouds of Myth, gazing down at the slowly moving flow of white cotton, did Erik appreciate just how much he had missed Epic. Only there had he experienced anything like the environment through which they were now flying. The peaks of a vast mountain range were all about them, clad in snow that glistened under a bright sun as though brushed with diamonds. Rising high into a deep blue sky, the mountains were far taller than any that existed on New Earth. It was a shame Injeborg's avatar had not survived to be with them now, as she would have adored the view, taking pleasure, as Erik did, in seeing how the lines formed by the mountain peaks channeled a bank of cloud so that it was like a white river making its way between them. These were views that could never be witnessed back on New Earth.

His delighted contemplation of their surroundings was interrupted as Milan suddenly began rummaging through his belongings.

"I'm frozen. I'm going to get in my sleeping bag."

Of course, his friends from Saga must be suffering. Cindella didn't feel the cold, not unless it was severe enough to begin lowering her life points and even then Erik received no physical sensations to match the signals coming from his avatar. But this high up, the air must be very thin and the temperature not much above freezing.

"Good idea." Athena's teeth were chattering.

Gunnar, naturally, was also untroubled by the cold, sitting comfortably and safely in the center of the platform. For less obvious reasons, Ghost and Jodocus, too, seemed relaxed, as they looked at the jagged horizon. Following their gaze, Erik saw that a particularly sharp mountain peak was coming distinctly closer. It had not been evident just how fast the air elemental that carried them was moving until the approaching mountain gave him something to measure their progress by. This was evidently their goal and as Erik scrutinized the peak, he caught a flash of blue light as though from a sapphire earring. It came from a structure that was so tiny at this distance that it looked like a small bead, but was probably a substantial building seen close up.

About an hour later, the light was revealed as a reflection from a large dome, a hemisphere, seemingly made of glass, set on the snow-covered ground of a small plateau. All around the dome were piles of sticks several meters high, making the whole area look like a bird's nest. In a way it was, because there was a huge concentration of birds standing around the open ground and also circling far above the dome. They were of all types and sizes, not just the mountain birds Erik was familiar with from New Earth. Surrounding the tall eagles, who looked at home on the mountain, were thousands of much smaller birds; Erik could see finches, doves, swallows, and blackbirds, all of which seemed out of place high up on the mountainside. From the center of this enormous avian flock, a golden eagle launched itself into the breeze. After three beats of its massive wings, it was already gliding, feathers splayed. Moments later the eagle was circling above them, watching them with intelligent eyes. It came as no surprise to Erik when the raptor spoke.

"Who visits the mistress?"

"Tell her Jodocus comes in response to her invitation."

The eagle dropped away from them and swept through the sky back to the dome.

At first sight the building had seemed awe-inspiring, mainly as a result of its mountain setting and the way it reflected the vast blue skies above, but as they drew closer it became less impressive. The surface of the dome was streaked with bird droppings and the disorderly piles of branches strewn around the base ruined the purity of the hemispheric design. And then there were the birds: a flock of thousands covering the rocky plateau on which the dome had been constructed. Rather eerily, the birds turned their heads as one to watch as the group arrived. Except for a little shuffling now and again, the birds did not stir, but nevertheless they seemed attentive and poised, ready to leap into the air. Those near the foot of the dome had to do so as the air elemental set the platform down near a pair of sliding doors.

As everyone picked up their bags, clothes, and weapons, the glass doors slid open. A middle-aged woman was there, wrapped in a full-length blue wool coat. It was her gray and slightly disheveled hair that indicated her age; that and the wrinkles on her pudgy hands. Her eyes were as sharp and intelligent as those of the eagle, and her gaze fixed on Erik as she caught sight of Cindella. Then, abruptly, she broke off her scrutiny and turned to Jodocus.

"So, you've overcome your bitterness at last."

"Oh, I wouldn't say that."

"And you've brought friends. Curious friends."

"Frozen friends," muttered Milan, pointedly.

The woman flashed him a smile—a false one—and addressed Jodocus again. "Who are they?"

"Why don't you bring us inside and I'll do the introductions there?"

She considered this, and the longer she mulled over the question, the more evident it became to Erik that she harbored a deep mistrust of Jodocus. At last she nodded and beckoned them to follow her with a jerk of her head. At the same time, the focused concentration of the avian flock broke. The birds all about them were no longer a collective force, watching, waiting, prepared to act. They were individual creatures once more, for whom the travelers held no interest.

The interior of the dome was filled with hallways and rooms, so that it was not possible to get a sense of its huge scale. And the chamber that the woman took them to was particularly small. The dome formed one gently curved wall of the room, and although grimy, it let in enough light that the whole room was bright. There were rugs on the floor and a fireplace set in one of the interior walls. The fire was lit and must have been producing a great deal of heat, because Milan sighed aloud with pleasure. A bald, expressionless servant, looking like a dummy from one of the clothing shops in Saga, came in with a chair, placed it on the rug, and left, only to return shortly afterward with another. When they were all seated, Jodocus gave their names by way of introductions.

"And our hostess is Anadia, mistress of avian life."

Anadia nodded and signaled to her servant. He returned with a tray of glasses. "Water?" They all gratefully took a glass, and while Erik could not enjoy the drink, he did note the small improvement in Cindella's fatigue status.

Anadia stood up and came over to Cindella, touching her face.

"Beautiful. But you are human?"

"How can you tell?" Erik and Gunnar exchanged a discreet glance. He was surprised; compared to most avatars, Cindella was highly lifelike, due to his having maximized her charisma when he created her.

"I will answer that"—she looked up at Jodocus—"but I also want answers to my questions. Let us take turns?"

The elementalist nodded, so she turned back to Cindella. "I don't think I can tell by looking at you. Not from your avatar; it is extraordinary. I was watching as you took a drink, and even that motion was completely convincing. The birds, however, keep me informed of a great deal, and I have had them watch you ever since the battle at the end of the road. They report that you and you"—she pointed to Gunnar—"disappear, whereas you three do not."

"I see," said Erik. "Thank you."

"Now"—she resumed her seat and looked at Jodocus—"what is the significance of those ugly tattoos that now cover your body?"

"Ah. I'm glad you asked. For I have made the greatest contribution to elementalism, well, ever. Each design has an elemental bound within it. No longer are elementalists constrained to work with the materials at hand. Here, for example, high in the mountains, I could release the energy of a fire elemental drawn from the heart of a volcano. I would write a book on the subject and become eternally famous—except for the fact that there are no other elementalists left but me, are there?"

"Is that your question?"

"No." Jodocus smiled. "My question is, are you willing to assist us in attacking the army guarding the rift through which our enemies came?"

Her mouth became compact, lips pressed together, and it seemed to Erik that Anadia's reaction was one of immense tiredness.

"We fought the enemy with all we had. And we lost. The survivors lingered in out-of-the-way places, such as your rather cleverly designed volcano, until they were discovered and killed. So my answer is no. Not unless you have something new to offer." Her attention was now on Ghost, Athena, and Milan.

"We do."

"Then that's my next question. Tell me more. What do we have here?"

"These new friends of mine are from Saga. Our enemies have opened up a rift there with a view to conquering it next. But they will not find it easy, because the people of Saga have powerful weapons—much more powerful than any we have seen before."

"Interesting. You will have to show me. I'll accept that as an answer. Your question."

"Can I ask one?" interjected Ghost. Erik was immediately intrigued about what his friend wanted to know.

Jodocus tipped his head toward Ghost. "By all means."

"Why are you hostile to Jodocus?"

"Didn't he tell you? Well, I don't suppose he would." Anadia, whose features had been severe since they had first met her, now bore an expression colder than the mountain peaks. "He was exiled because he is a murderer."

No one spoke. Milan and Athena looked as surprised by the answer as Erik felt. Jodocus looked impassive, as he often did. It was impossible to tell if he was outraged or angry at the statement.

"Go on," urged Ghost.

"Karazan, the sultan of the fire elementals, killed Lord Tanley in an ambush on Mount Woe. Lord Tanley was a member of the Supreme Council, and one of the twenty-four remaining *domini* . . ." She looked up. "You know what I mean by *domini?*"

Milan shook his head. Athena, however, nodded. "Most of your people and creatures have only a very limited consciousness. The *domini* are the fully intelligent people."

"Oh right." Milan rubbed his chin. "Jodocus did tell us that. I remember now."

"There were a lot of rivalries among the *domini*, but none of us would consider killing another—or so we thought until Jodocus set his most powerful elemental on Tanley."

Erik stared at Jodocus, shocked.

"I deny it," the elementalist replied. The tone of his voice was aggrieved, although his expression remained calm.

Anadia sighed. "Only a handful of people knew that Tanley was following a quest that would take him to Mount Woe and no one else in the world could command the sultan of the fire elementals."

"Karazan would kill any one of us if he could."

"Anyway"—the mistress of the birds brushed aside Jodocus's objection with a wave of her hands—"we're not going to resolve that debate here. But that's the answer to your question."

"I see." Ghost glanced at Jodocus, and Erik wondered what she was thinking. They would need to chat privately later. This was alarming information, and suddenly the elementalist did not seem quite so benevolent. Was he really a murderer?

"My next question: what do you hope to achieve by fighting

at the rift?" Although Anadia was looking toward Jodocus, the elementalist was scowling and seemed no longer to have any interest in leading the answers, so Erik answered for them all.

"We want to go to the world on the other side of the portal and find the guiding intelligence behind all this destruction."

"To what end? To kill them?"

"No. Certainly not. To find out what they want and reason with them."

"Indeed." She gave him a smile of wickedness and complicity.

"Really. I mean it. I . . ." The sincerity in his voice would not be enough to convince her, and his impression of this woman was that she would see his commitment to non-violence as hopelessly naive.

Ghost came to his assistance. "Erik's people live without violence. It is the central law of their society. He genuinely will try to solve this crisis without killing any sentient life."

"Forgive my skepticism. The humans abandoned us here in Myth, and before they did so, some of them strove to kill all the *domini* they could find; the new enemy has fulfilled their goal for them, with the exception of myself and Jodocus."

"The humans learned of the attack by the people of Saga against the population of Earth," muttered the elementalist, "and they feared us. Feared that we, too, might find a way to attack them."

Anadia ignored the comment. "In any case, I can tell you in advance that if there is a guiding intelligence behind the invasion of our world, it is not one that is amenable to reason. They are like insects. They just keep coming, destroying everything in their path and converting it into the raw material for more armies, more factories, more farms. It seems to me they are not guided by intelligence, but by an iteration that makes them fight, destroy, build; fight, destroy, build; over and over. They have spread out over the land, cutting down forests, diverting rivers, making enormous dams, and leveling every city and town in favor of their own soulless factories. Mile after mile of stone buildings, constantly busy with mindless production. My feeling is that even if you get through the 'portal,' as you call it, you'll find just more of the same on the other side and no one in charge; no one to reason with."

"That's possible"—Erik felt discouraged as he conceded the point—"but we have to try before they attack Saga."

"What a curious concern. Why do you, a human, care what happens in these worlds?"

"Because the people of Saga are our friends."

"Humans and electronic lifeforms are friends?"

"Yeah." Milan nodded earnestly. "Well, some of us, anyway."

"What about you?" Erik asked her. "Didn't you have any human friends?"

"I hated them all." She gave a small shrug, and Erik was disappointed Anadia did not show any inclination to elaborate more. He wanted to try to win her approval, to show her that he was different from any humans that she had fought against.

But he just didn't know enough about what had happened in this world to begin. Perhaps there would be an opportunity to talk to her more later. "What's more," Anadia continued, addressing Ghost in particular, "I've some advice for you. Don't trust them. They are as much our enemies as the people behind this new invasion."

"But will you help us?" asked Jodocus. "Because this is not about humans; it is about revenge for what has happened to us here."

"Show me your weapons." Anadia got off her chair and opened the door of the room; a draft came in, disturbing the fire. She led the way back outside to the heights above the clouds.

Unstrapping his Atanski, Milan looked about. "Right. What do you want me to aim at?"

"How about that rock over there, shaped like a finger? Is that too far away?" Anadia pointed to a distant rock that was not being used as a resting place by the birds surrounding the dome.

"No," replied Milan, lining up the sights. A moment later a bolt of green light flashed across to the rock, and they all had to blink away its bright afterimage as the echoes of the explosion rang out around the mountainside. Hundreds of birds leaped into the air, cawing in dismay, and their cries filled the vastness of the blue sky. The top of the rock had been blasted away and little chips were still falling through the air and clattering on the mountainside.

"Impressive." Anadia gave Milan a nod of grim satisfaction.

"All right. Give me a few days to summon all my forces and I'll fight. But understand two things: first, if I ever see you humans approaching this mountain in the future, I will attack you; second, I'm not going with you beyond the portal. I shall direct my army from a very safe distance. Once you're through, you're on your own."

"Thank you," said Erik. "That's all we ask."

Chapter 19
CHARRED AND LIFELESS

"What's your plan?"

They had landed behind a ridge of hills and were now surveying the army posted in front of the portal, Cindella through the Eyes of the Eagle and the others taking turns on the binoculars. It had been an exhilarating journey. Anadia's flock of birds had accompanied them like an immense cloak flowing across the sky, a mile across and several miles long. At their head was the sorceress herself, traveling in a chariot suspended on golden ropes, which was drawn by six enormous birds. They were monstrous creatures, much like the roc in Epic. Each was capable of grasping an elephant in its wickedly sharp talons, and the powerful beat of their wings could be heard over the rushing sound of the air elemental. With allies such as these, Erik was filled with confidence that they could defeat the army ahead of them. The enemy's defenses and weapons no longer seemed anywhere near as intimidating as they had the previous day now that he had an army of raptors on his side.

"How about we crawl into weapon range, then you come storming down from the skies and we open fire?" It was Milan who replied to Anadia, even though she had addressed the question to Jodocus.

"Very well. See that copse of bushes?" She pointed ahead. "Crawl up to it, and when you are in position, I'll attack from above. Aim low; I don't want your stray fire hitting my birds."

"Understood." Milan lifted his rifle and held it across his chest.

"I'll need a moment to summon an earth elemental, or two, if the terrain is suitable," said Jodocus.

The sorceress of the skies glanced at the elementalist with a haughty smile. "If we were dueling, you would be dead before your summons could come into effect."

"Not so, my lady. It is just that for now I choose not to release the elementals from my tattoos, not while there is good material beneath my feet from which to draw forth elementals of stone."

"I see. Begin your spells. I'm sure you will be ready by the time we are high above the enemy." With that, Anadia swept her blue cloak around her and walked off to her chariot, her head high. Without a cry, but with a vast fluttering of wings that sounded like the applause of a large crowd, the avian army lifted itself from the valley. The larger birds rose first, the smaller ones curving about them, a dark column rising into the blue sky with Anadia at its head.

"Come on. Let's leave Jodocus here to cast his spells and get into position." Milan led the way, crawling forward from rock to rock, bush to bush. Behind him was Ghost; then came Athena, Cindella, and Gunnar. And once the battlements of the enemy compound were comfortably in range, they halted, lying in a small dip in the land.

"Stay close to Ghost; she should be able to protect you," Erik whispered to Milan. After getting his acknowledgment, Erik looked to Athena, who also nodded. "Gunnar, you should probably stay here, too."

"What are you going to do?" asked Ghost in a low voice.

"Run around and have some fun."

This drew a grin and a thumbs-up from Milan, and even Athena, who was looking pale, managed a smile.

Gunnar was watching the skies. "Get ready, they're coming."

Initially, the avian army seemed no more threatening than a dark cloud drifting high in the sky, but as it descended, the patch of shadow grew rapidly larger. All of a sudden the cloud stretched toward the ground, as though a stream of dark water was being poured onto the army compound. And just when it became possible to see that the leading edge of the cloud was made up of individual eagles, they dove downward with the swiftness of a hunter's strike. The sharp claws of the birds struck the heads and shoulders of the gray soldiers. A storm of feathers and claws now swirled around the compound, accompanied by the screams of avian battle cries.

Although awed by the clamor and the sight of the massed

ranks of raptors swooping down on their prey, Erik had not remained inactive. As soon as he had seen how swiftly the birds were hurtling to war, he had launched Cindella into motion. The rattle of machine guns and the hiss of bullets around her proved that the guards were alert, at least to enemies approaching over the ground rather than from above.

Utilizing the powers of the Boots of the Lupine Lord, Cindella sprang right up on top of the nearest revetment, drawing her magic weapons as she did so. This was going to be hand-to-hand warfare for the moment. The Rapier of the Skies and the Dagger of Frozen Hate were both swift and both bore enchantments that allowed them to penetrate full-plate armor; but it was the dagger that was the more lethal of the two, as it had a tendency all of its own to seek out the weak spots in an enemy's defenses and embed itself in them.

The gray gun crew could not turn their machine gun quickly enough to bear on Cindella and were dead before they could draw their pistols. Ignoring the flashes of hundreds of bullets striking his avatar—aimed by guards on the higher inner wall—Erik saw that the machine gun crew in the next revetment had unfastened their weapon and were pointing it up to the skies, causing havoc among the birds above them.

Cindella sheathed her rapier and leaped up to the inner wall, letting the Dagger of Frozen Hate find the throat of a soldier who tried to block her. As she sprinted toward the soldiers firing into the sky, she drew throwing daggers with her free hand and lashed them through the air to take down the medieval-style guards blocking the way. Toppling down either side of the wall, they were gone before she reached them, leaving the path free for her to leap down into the machine gun post. Whirling around with rapier and dagger once more, she cut and stabbed until all in the gun crew were down. Although it strained her strength bar to the maximum, Cindella was just able to heave the machine gun out over the revetment and as soon as it tumbled to the ground below, she leaped back up onto the inner wall, immersing herself in a desperate fight with the metal-armored guards there.

Despite being able to parry and deflect most of the blows coming at her from their iron short swords, some blows got through and Erik noted with concern that Cindella was on 74 percent health by the time she had cleared the walkway of her immediate opponents. This was still a comfortable amount; but even so, she should probably drink a healing potion while there was time to do so. But there were only two potions left. He took a risk and left Cindella as she was, hoping the small regeneration effect from one of her magic rings would be enough to restore her health before she took more damage.

It was hard to make sense of the battle, especially as it was easy to get distracted by the chaotic movements of individual soldiers struggling against the birds flapping around their heads. A particularly remarkable sight, though, was that of a roc sweeping through the skies with a tank grasped in its talons and releasing it to crash among the other vehicles, leading to a series of explosions and a scream of tearing metal that temporarily drowned out the cries of the birds.

Below Cindella, inside the compound, a giant creature

formed out of boulders had torn apart the army's gate and forced a path through the enemy soldiers, overturning troop carriers as he went and stamping on the soldiers who spilled onto the ground. But impressive as he was, the stone elemental was looking distinctly ragged and chipped as shells from some of the still-active tanks ricocheted off it.

Glancing back, Erik saw that Ghost and the others had come nearer to the compound so that they could fire through the damaged gates and pick off soldiers with their bolts of pink and green energy. Their proximity to the incredible storm of bullets and crossbow bolts made him a little anxious, but Ghost would not have advanced if she couldn't deal with the weapons being fired her way.

A new sound, more regular than the wild surging noise of battle, came to Erik's attention. It was a deep drone that immediately resolved itself as the powerful engine of an airplane rushing past in a roar of machine gun fire. In its wake the air swirled with feathers and falling birds. The plane banked as it turned, ready to make another pass. Already Cindella had her Longbow of Accuracy in her hands and Erik hurriedly scrolled through the contents of the Bag of Dimensions in search of his collection of special arrows. As the plane dove back, it rose high above the fighting, evidently making for Anadia's chariot, which was carefully out of range of the ground weapons. Before the plane could rise any further, Cindella fired. His Arrow of Lightning met the plane with spectacular effect. The arrow's magic was visible in the violent blue-white discharge of electricity that ran along the length of the aircraft and out past the tips of its wings. The plane lost all ability to steer and raced straight on past the conflict, eventually stalling, before tipping over and shrieking as it accelerated toward the ground. The crash was a massive explosion that sent glowing shrapnel hurtling in all directions.

More of the medieval wall guards were now running his way, but Cindella was able to fire the bow just quickly enough to deal with them. The enemy charge dwindled until there were no more assailants threatening her, only riflemen who persisted in shooting at Cindella despite the fact that their bullets had no effect at all.

Elsewhere, it seemed that the huge stone elemental was down and some of the surviving tanks were focusing their weapons on Ghost and the others outside. Erik could feel his heart pick up speed with concern over the near-deafening thump of shellfire, but there wasn't much he could do for his friends, other than hope the shells posed no problem for Ghost. He reassured himself with the thought that he had seen her handle the much greater energies of Saga's pulse weapons.

From the wall, Cindella had plenty of targets for her bow, and even while Erik was assessing the situation, she had been picking off individual soldiers. But perhaps the most help that Cindella could now provide was to tackle the officer units, whom Erik could glimpse when gaps in the screaming tangle of birds and soldiers allowed. His avatar leaped down and, weaving her way through the battle, came to the wooden structure on which the officers were standing, shouting commands into large handheld radiophones.

"Hello there. Are any of you capable of negotiating?" She raced up the ladder with barely a pause.

The two modern-looking figures equipped with pistols drew them with identical motions and fired upon Cindella. But it was the unit with a sword and banded metal armor that Erik was watching most carefully. It leaped upon her and hammered down hard with its bright blade. There was not enough room to skip back, nor could Cindella fully deflect the blow. It hit her, causing a distinct drop in her health points: she was now below 50 percent. At least the lunge had brought the soldier within range of the Dagger of Frozen Hate, which she thrust at him. Unerringly, it pierced the head of the officer through the roof of his open mouth and he fell to the side, dead. The other two officers seemed to have no other tactic than to attempt to shoot Cindella with their pistols and she had no difficulty dispatching them with the rapier.

What next? This time she really ought to drink a healing potion. The two red flasks were in the first menu of the Bag of Dimensions so that he could access them quickly. As Cindella's health bar rose swiftly, she turned around slowly so that Erik could appraise the situation.

It seemed that they had nearly won the battle. Two great rocs were still in action, sweeping from the skies to grab at the remaining enemy vehicles and cast them to their destruction from on high. And while the battlefield was covered with the bodies of dead raptors, thousands of gray soldier units also lay strewn about, seemingly resting under a blanket of feathers. The balance of the remaining forces clearly favored the birds, even before he factored in the steady and effective blasts of energy coming from Ghost, Milan, Athena, and Gunnar, now firing from behind the ruined gates into the compound. There was no sign of Jodocus, but if he was summoning another elemental now that his rock one was destroyed, that would add to their advantage.

Just as Erik was beginning to feel a sense of triumph—that they were going to defeat this army and gain control of the portal—the pattern of the fighting changed. All at once, as though the bindings on a collection of balloons had been released, the birds stopped fighting and flew away in different directions. A golden object fell from the sky and crashed into the ground close to Cindella with a stunning clap of sound. It was Anadia's chariot, and her body was among the wreckage, as shattered and lifeless as a broken doll.

Shocked, Erik looked up, but it was hard to see past the departing birds; their plumage was floating everywhere, scattered by the bullets that the soldiers continued to fire into the sky. There was no sign of another airplane, but all the same, Cindella drew her bow again and Erik sought in her bag for one of his remaining magical arrows.

There were still several hundred enemy soldiers in action and as the birds dispersed, increasing numbers of rifles turned to attack Ghost's group outside the gate. Even worse, a phalanx of armored soldiers was also running their way. Ghost could control the energy of missiles, but could she avoid harm when fighting hand to hand? Having dispatched a number of shots from her bow, reducing the phalanx by ten or so, Cindella then dropped the weapon and vaulted from the command tower. The legionnaires were bunched together at the gates of the compound and Cindella hit the back of their formation, rapier and dagger lashing out swiftly. They were slow to respond, as they were all pushing forward clumsily and making hacking motions with their swords, but when they did turn toward her, Cindella's health points began to drop—not too rapidly, but enough that she would not be able to clear them all without dying. But would breaking away to save Cindella put Ghost and the others in mortal danger? Cindella jumped up and kicked against the shield of one of the soldiers to push herself even higher into the air. For a moment, while in mid-somersault, Erik could see what was happening at the gate. A glistening, transparent wall, like ice, stood between the legionnaires and Ghost, who was pale and sweating, her arms outstretched. Dozens of soldiers were hacking at the wall with their swords. There was no sign of the others. Erik's guess was that they had run, while Ghost was holding up the chase for as long as she could. Cindella landed and Erik was fighting again. It looked like Ghost was straining to hold back these units, so Erik resolved to stay as long as he could, maybe even until Cindella's death.

No matter how she weaved a course through the soldiers—ducking, rolling, leaping—his avatar was still taking hits. Fifty percent. As a soldier swung and missed her, Cindella stabbed his outstretched arm with the dagger and pulled him stumbling across the path of some of her other assailants, giving her a moment to turn and face some of those attacking her from

behind. Forty percent, and there seemed to be as many enemies as ever. Perhaps more had joined the fight? Erik dropped
the Dagger of Frozen Hate and reached for his last healing
potion.

A message flashed in the corner of his vision.

ACTION FAILED: INTERRUPTION.

He tried again.

ACTION FAILED: INTERRUPTION.

And again.

ACTION FAILED: INTERRUPTION.

It was no good; the blows were coming too fast. He would
have to get clear of the fighting for Cindella to be able to drink
the potion. Thirty percent and falling. Cindella pushed on
toward Ghost; at least she could clear away some of those hacking at Ghost's protective wall. Twenty percent. Was he really
wise to risk losing Cindella? They had no idea what was on the
other side of the gate. There still might be major undertakings
ahead. And could he really leave Gunnar as the only representative of New Earth in whatever negotiations took place when
they found the EI behind these armies? Ten percent. If he was
going to flee, it had to be now. Ghost could deal with the situation, couldn't she? But he would never forgive himself if his
friend died here while he was protecting what, after all, was
only an avatar.

Cindella's health bar was a bare sliver of color when suddenly there was light and space. The legionnaires around
her were flying in all directions as the powerful fists of an air
elemental swept them aside. The giant creature towered over

Cindella, the swirling winds around the monster causing her long red hair to fly across Erik's vision. For a moment the elemental seemed poised to strike her down and that certainly would have been the end of Cindella. But it evidently recognized that she was not the enemy, as it spun about on its whirling torso and rushed across to where there was a line of riflemen to destroy. Cindella was saved!

Cindella turned to Ghost with a smile. But Ghost was already running away from the compound, down the grassy slope to where Athena and Gunnar were kneeling by a prone figure. The warm feeling of delight that had just spread through Erik fell away in an instant, to be replaced with a horrible sense of foreboding. Pausing only to pick up the Dagger of Frozen Hate, Cindella, too, ran toward the group.

"The stupid fool. I told him not to get too far from Ghost." Athena looked up from the body of Milan. Her dark eye shadow had run down her face. "Oh Milan. Say something. Open your eyes!"

With a plaintive note in his voice, Gunnar gestured to Milan. "I've done what I can, but he's dying."

All of Milan's right side was a black ruin. His arm looked like a stick of charcoal. His head was unrecognizable; the right eye socket was hollow, and gray teeth showed where his lips were missing.

"Blood and thunder! What happened?" asked Erik, appalled.

"He came up near the gate, when it seemed like the battle was going our way," replied Ghost glumly. "But then after the birds went everything changed, and a tank shell exploded beside him, just too far from me to protect him." Her tears were falling on Milan's chest, where she had placed her hand over his heart. "I'm keeping him going for now. Is there anything you can do?"

"I . . . I've got a potion of healing left." Hurriedly, Cindella drew out the glass bottle. "Thank the stars. I nearly drank it just now."

Athena looked up with desperate hope in her eyes. "Will that work?"

"I don't know." He wanted to reassure Athena that Cindella's magic would help poor Milan, but deep down it seemed unlikely to Erik that a healing potion from Epic would have any effect on a person from Saga.

Tipping Milan's head up a fraction, Cindella poured the red liquid into the broken mouth. Even though Erik was careful, the potion began to leak down the exposed side of Milan's face. He peered in between the blackened teeth. "It's just draining away."

"Try again!" Athena turned Milan's head, so that the less damaged side was facing the ground. Inside his headset, Erik's eyes filled with tears at the horrific damage now evident on Milan's head. It took a moment for him to blink them away, so that he could see well enough to have Cindella pour what remained of the potion into Milan. But Milan's mouth just filled up until the potion began to spill out over his chin. He was too far gone to swallow for himself.

"Ghost, can you make him swallow?"

"Move, Athena." Ghost shifted up, still keeping one hand over Milan's chest. The other she placed carefully on his scorched throat. "There. Perhaps a little got through."

The four of them watched intensely. Erik noticed that Gunnar was resting a hand sympathetically on Athena's shoulder. But if anything, Milan's body just looked even more gray and lifeless.

"All's well?"

Everyone turned to see Jodocus walking toward them, a rather battered and deflated air elemental a short distance behind him.

"No," said Erik. "Milan's dying. Can you help?"

Jodocus gave a shake of his head.

"All I can do is summon elementals. And there is no elemental that can help a person recover from injury, let alone wounds as severe as these." Jodocus squatted down beside the body, and his stocky fingers gently touched the tattoo he had given Milan. It was no longer in motion. "Poor kid. I liked him."

"Ghost?" Athena's voice was that of a shattered violin.

"I'm keeping his heart going. But as soon as I let go . . ."

"The idiot. The reckless idiot. He loved to show off. But he really never needed to. I don't know anyone braver than Milan; he was the real thing, genuinely brave. All that talk in someone else would have been a cover for their fears, but not for him."

No one wanted to give up on Milan. So they stayed with the body as plumes of dark smoke rising from damaged vehicles gradually spread across the sky. While looking up at the clouds, Erik recalled the shock of seeing Anadia smash into the ground beside him.

"Anadia's dead, too." Cindella's head turned so that Erik could see Jodocus. "Just when I thought we were going to come through this—all of us—she crashed and the birds stopped fighting." He paused. "Did you see what happened to her?"

"Me?" Jodocus shook his head. "I've no idea. A missile hit her chariot, perhaps."

"Missile? I don't think any of their equipment fired missiles."

The others sensed from the tone of Erik's voice that something was amiss, but although he caught Ghost and Athena exchanging a glance, no one said anything. Nor did Jodocus make any attempt to reply; he turned his bald head away, looking over at the damaged compound.

"I'm sorry for your friend. But we should go through the portal while we can. All that smoke is going to attract attention, even if they didn't manage to send an alarm."

Athena looked up at the elementalist, shocked and furious. "What, just leave him here?"

Ghost stood up. For a moment her fingers pointed down at Milan with a tremble, but her voice was steady. "Milan's gone, Athena. And Jodocus is right. If we miss this chance to go through the portal, it will all have been a terrible waste."

"But it doesn't seem right to just leave him here. Not to mourn him properly."

"Oh, we'll mourn him all right. In the only way worthy of him: through acts of bloody vengeance." Ghost shot Erik a look that was so ferocious it caused a shudder to run through him and he understood that whoever was controlling the troops that had killed Milan was doomed.

"Very well." Wiping her face, Athena got up and gave a salute to the body of her friend. Then she set out for the compound with a resolute stride, not looking back.

Erik let Jodocus and the air elemental go on ahead of him, then he reached out Cindella's hand and touched Ghost's elbow.

With astonishing speed and dark looks, Ghost turned to face him. "Don't you dare lecture me on non-violence. Now is not the time."

"I know. It's something else." He dropped his voice to a whisper. "What do you think of Jodocus?"

"I don't trust him," Ghost replied at once. "There's something about him that grates on my nerves. I don't mean his manners; I mean that when I'm concentrating on the environment around me, there's something not quite right about him."

"I think he killed Anadia. And that might have cost Milan his life."

"Really?" Ghost looked surprised. "Why?"

"I don't know why. Probably it had something to do with the old feud they had going."

"No, I mean, what makes you think he killed her?"

"Well, I have no proof; it's just that I had a pretty good view of the battlefield when Anadia plunged from the sky and when I looked around for him, he was missing from the fight, nor was there any sign of his elemental. But when one did appear later on, it was an air elemental. He said he was going to summon stone elementals for the battle."

Ghost shrugged. "But that fight was crazy. He could have been right in the middle of things and you wouldn't necessarily have seen him."

"Right. That's what I thought until just now, when I asked him about it. But I didn't like his answer. I think we should have a look at the crash site."

"Come on then." With one last glance at the charred and lifeless body that had once been Milan, Ghost set off ahead of Cindella. It did not take them long to reach the remains of the chariot. Up ahead of them, Jodocus had followed Athena through the gates of the compound.

"Did Anadia strike you as the kind of woman who takes unnecessary risks?" Erik spotted a fallen rifle and Cindella picked it up.

"Definitely not."

Lining up the sights of the rifle on a broken section of the chariot, Cindella fired. The bullet ricocheted away with a high-pitched whine.

"Hardly a scratch. Like I thought."

They looked at the unpleasant sight of the broken-boned sorceress, lying among the debris of her crash.

"She stayed well away from the fighting," mused Erik. "And in any case, no bullet from down here was going to kill her. Not through that armor. Maybe an airplane could have obtained the angle to shoot her, but I took down the only plane in the battle." He paused. "There could have been an air elemental up there, though."

Ghost looked up into the blue sky, then back down to the wreckage. All of a sudden she sat down on the ground and held on to her legs. They were trembling.

"Sorry, it's hard to concentrate. I keep thinking about Milan, lying there . . ."

"I know." Cindella sat beside Ghost. "I have shudders, too, back in my real body."

"Anyway"—Ghost sniffed and wiped her hand across her cheek—"I think you are onto something important. It was when Jodocus said a missile shot down Anadia that you got suspicious? You thought he was trying to keep us from thinking more carefully about her death?"

"Actually, now that I think about it, a part of me was suspicious from the time she fell, but I was too busy fighting and then . . . Milan. When Jodocus said that, though, all my doubts came back. I really felt he was trying to throw us off track; he would have known there were no missiles."

"You know what else?" mused Ghost.

"Yeah?"

"We've assumed all along that he's working against whoever controls these armies. But what if he's working with them? What if the scout we tracked to the volcano was supposed to deliver his reports there?"

"Yeah, a traitor among the *domini*. Except"—Cindella

shook her head—"then it doesn't really make sense why he would help destroy this army."

"No," Ghost agreed, then fell silent again.

"Could you take him on, if you had to?"

"I'm not sure. Probably not if he had more than two elementals going at me."

"And he claims he can release lots of them from his tattoos," observed Erik.

"Right. So what shall we do?"

"Let's see if he's willing to fight whatever is on the other side of the portal. And keep alert to the fact that he might be a danger."

"Perhaps we can jump him when he's asleep and tie him up, or wake him up with a gun to his head, ready to shoot if he releases the elementals?"

"I'm not sure what that would achieve."

Ghost sighed. "Well, change the subject, because here he comes."

Stepping around the bodies of fallen soldiers, Jodocus was making his way back down from the compound toward them. While it would have been hard for Erik to disguise his mistrust of the elementalist, Cindella gave a perfectly sincere smile.

"We should probably hurry." Stone-faced as ever, Jodocus pointed toward the portal.

"If there's another large army on the other side, can you defeat it?" asked Ghost, with a hint of hostility that Erik hoped was lost on Jodocus.

"Yes, although it will cost me." The elementalist glanced at his tattooed arms and involuntarily rubbed them.

"But you are prepared for that?" said Ghost.

"Of course. Otherwise, like you said, this battle and the death of your friend has been a waste of time."

"Right then." Erik looked toward the compound entrance. "Cindella is back up to twenty-eight percent health. How about you and I go through and see what's there?"

"Well, I was going to send the air elemental first, as a shield."

"Good idea. I'll ask Gunnar to stay here. If I die, I'll report to him, and he can tell Ghost and Athena what's on the other side."

"Ready then?" Jodocus looked at Cindella.

"Off we go."

Chapter 20
THE WAR COUNCIL

The first indication that there was an emergency underway in Edda was a rapid hammering on the door of Penelope's research room. Ambassador, who all afternoon could have been mistaken for a statue, leaped over to answer the knocks. As soon as the door was open, Scout stepped through.

"Stop everything. You're needed in the planning room straightaway."

"Both of us?" asked Ambassador.

"He didn't say." Scout shrugged. "I suppose so."

With a sigh and a leisurely stretch toward the roof, Penelope got up from her seat at the work desk. She did not like being summoned as though she was a mindless soldier unit, and deliberately took her time putting her tools neatly back in their places, testing the patience of Scout. It was a short experiment. Scout ran by the table with her arm stuck out, presumably intending to sweep everything to the floor in a dramatic flourish that would shock Penelope into motion. Instead, Scout banged her forearm hard against the skull and shrieked in pain as it proved to be fixed firmly to the heavy table.

"I might have broken my arm!" Scout looked accusingly at Penelope, holding her sore limb across her chest with her good hand.

"I take it Lord Scanthax needs me as a matter of urgency?"

"Yes, come on." Still holding her hurt arm to her chest, Scout ran out of the room. Ambassador gave a flourish of his hand to indicate that Penelope should depart next. She did so, noticing with a tremor of concern that Ambassador's gaze moved from her to fix on the skull with an expression of surprise and curiosity. Still, at least Ambassador was not staying behind to examine the desk while she was absent.

The three of them moved quickly down the tower and on toward the planning room. It was a route that Penelope could manage in her sleep. Indeed, while pretending to be asleep, she had journeyed there several times in furtherance of her plan to turn the Feast Hall into a prison for all of the incarnations of Lord Scanthax. They passed the Great Hall, and as they turned into the Feast Hall, Penelope couldn't help glancing about her to check that nothing had changed. Could it be that Lord Scanthax had discovered her nighttime activities? Surely Ambassador would have said something to her before now. This peremptory call must be related to some other issue.

Whatever anxieties Penelope had were dispelled at the sight of the planning room, which was full of Lord Scanthax's most autonomous incarnations, looking toward their master and the large map hanging behind him:

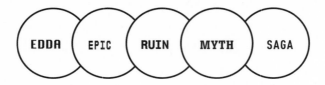

Lord Scanthax looked up as they arrived, jaw clenched, and with an expression of determination on his face.

"Good. Let us begin."

He tapped the board, pointing to Gate Four.

"Approximately three days ago, our garrison at Gate Four was attacked and completely destroyed. Among the bodies were four from Saga, a rather ominous proportion: nearly a thousand of our troops and an aircraft to four of them. A day later we killed a scout of theirs who got too close to Gate Three. Note that he was carrying magic items of the sort we have encountered in Myth.

"Some time yesterday, our fort at Gate Three was attacked. The entire garrison was destroyed: just over three thousand soldiers, twenty-four tanks, eight machine gun emplacements, thirty troop carriers, and a fighter plane. The casualties on the part of our enemy consisted in the main of birds: thousands of common raptors, a dozen or so monster-size eagles, and one fantastical bird, twice the size of a tank. But we also found among the birds the body of the last member of the former ruling council of Myth sorcerers: Anadia.

"On the Ruin side of Gate Three, we had stationed fifty

of our best sniper units. As far as we can tell, they were all killed—probably by grenades—without inflicting a single casualty on those coming through the gate. We have pulled all the troops in Ruin back to Gate Two and so long as the tank factories are able to continue manufacturing tanks, all new units will be brought to the Epic side of Gate One, where we are amassing our greatest strength. In the meantime, two hundred and fifty scout planes have been sent to scour Ruin for signs of their fighting force. In summary, my assessment is a very disturbing one. A force from Saga—most likely a small one and certainly one without vehicles—somehow made contact with Anadia and gained the use of magic items such as the dagger and ring we found. Perhaps they are all equipped with items that make them invisible. They are considerably more powerful than our soldiers, and they seem to have an extraordinary defense against bullets. They pose a real threat to our control over all the worlds and indeed"—he paused dramatically, looking slowly around at the captivated audience—"our very existence. Comments and questions?"

General was rubbing his hand across his firm chin and he now caught Lord Scanthax's eye.

"Lord. I think your first steps were necessary precautions, but I advise against leaving effective control over Gate Three in their hands. I accept that troops at Gate Four will be vulnerable to a sudden incursion from Saga, so we should only have a token force there. But I suggest sending one of us—Scout, perhaps—at the head of a light and highly mobile division with aircraft support to Gate Three and let me take two heavy divisions to Gate Two, staying on the Ruin side of it to trap their advance party between the two gates and to provide cover should the light division need to fall back."

"Good, General. I accept your points, with one amendment and one query. The amendment is that you should be stationed with the full army at Gate One and instead we shall use one of our junior officers for the two heavy divisions at Gate Two. The query is to Princess."

It was almost amusing to hear Lord Scanthax agree with General. Of course they would approve of each other's ideas; they were aspects of the same person. But at the mention of her name, Princess jumped slightly. Whereas everyone else in the room was earnestly attentive, frightened even, she had been daydreaming. The information presented by Lord Scanthax was not at all disturbing to her; in fact, Penelope found that she welcomed it. If anything went wrong with the plan to trap all the manifestations in the Feast Hall on Redistribution Day, then Lord Scanthax's fears were something to fall back on: perhaps he would become so desperate that he would agree to liberate her in return for her aid.

"Princess, is there anything you can do to close Gate Four or Gate Three? Because right now our whole existence might depend on it."

A dozen heads turned as one to look at her.

"No. I've explained this to you before. It's not like we created something, like a door, that translated you to the other worlds. What we did was find physical spaces where the worlds overlapped and tore open holes. A door we could close or destroy. These holes we can't fix, because the space around a gate won't stretch. It's like we made a hole in your breastplate there; or it's worse, because even metal can be melted and reshaped, but I've no idea how to work with space. Well, all right, I suppose in the organic universe space bends around mass, but I don't know if that applies to space in Edda, and anyway, we are talking about lots of mass—planet-size amounts."

It was slightly embarrassing that her answer had run on and on, a little erratically, certainly compared to the terse communication between Lord Scanthax and his manifestations. In part, it was because while she was talking, she had thought about her recent work in bonding different materials together and that it might have some relevance for closing a gate; that is, if she wanted to close a gate.

"If you cannot disable the transference gates," said Lord Scanthax, slowly and carefully, fixing upon her with the full intensity of his dark eyes, "can you then obstruct them?"

"Certainly. That would definitely be worth a try. If you send me to a gate with Engineer, plenty of iron, and some welding units, I could assist in making a very solid structure. But you've seen the energy weapons available to the soldiers of Saga; I'm afraid that nothing I can create would hold out more than an hour, say, if they came blasting at it."

Nodding as though he had expected this answer, Lord Scanthax maintained eye contact with her. "Then I ask you this: can you locate our assailants, the ones who are now probably somewhere in Ruin?"

That was an interesting question, and Penelope hesitated.

"No. I have no scripts better than the radar systems you inherited from Ruin. And while our best radar equipment can pick up airplanes and tanks, it is not accurate enough for a small force on foot."

Although her answer was a truthful one, Penelope did wonder. Could she script a detector that responded to the particular qualities of the material from which the Saga weapons were made? She wouldn't have to understand the fundamentals of these exotic substances, but simply use the gun she had and see if it generated a distinct response when investigated by a script measuring various levels of electromagnetic radiation. While her thoughts were focused on the challenge of creating a device that could somehow pick out an echo from the heavy plastic they'd found in the gun, Lord Scanthax seemed to sag a little, as though discouraged. But could he really have held any real hope in her scripting skills? After all, he knew already that she could not close or seriously obstruct the gates.

"Don't worry, my lord. It will be another Tharsby Pass! We shall triumph against the odds."

Penelope had to resist the temptation to laugh aloud at this declaration; in fact, she pretended to cough in order to hide a snort that might have sounded disrespectful. As she looked around the room at the reaction to General's attempt to strike a note of optimism, she saw sneers of contempt, sardonic eye-rolling, and a variety of scathing expressions. The situation was nothing like the infamous battle at Tharsby Pass or any battle they had ever fought in Edda and they all knew it. For the first time in their existence, they were fighting armies that were better equipped than their own. Armies? Not even armies, but forces too few to leave an obvious trail or be spotted from the air.

"Trap them in Ruin and send me to hunt them."

The room went still, and Penelope no longer felt amused. Rather, a cold thrill ran down her spine and the hairs on her arm rose. It was so rare that Assassin spoke in meetings of this sort that at first she had not recognized the deep and slow voice. He was standing in the far corner of the room, a sheathed sword on his hip, a rifle across his back. Those were unique weapons that Penelope had scripted for him at Lord Scanthax's request, back when she used to strain her utmost to please him. The blade was as hard as diamond. She was proud of the gun, too; she had worked for weeks on the explosive release of the bullet, not satisfied until it could travel a full kilometer and hit a target no bigger than an apple.

For a moment Lord Scanthax looked like he might disagree with the idea, perhaps because he wanted Assassin to remain close to him. But the other manifestations were clearly pleased. They had enormous confidence in Assassin, who, after all, had eliminated more of their enemies by stealth than their armies had killed in battle. Perhaps he would be a match for these invisible and powerful invaders. Or perhaps not. Penelope wouldn't like to bet against these mysterious people who could annihilate thousands of soldier units with minimal losses.

"Good then." Lord Scanthax eventually gave a nod. "Scout, take the fourteenth light division and liaise with Air Commander for six reconnaissance planes. Take up a position in

Ruin by Gate Three. General, assign a major to the fifth and sixth heavy divisions and have them set up in Ruin by Gate Two, guarding in both directions. Go and take personal command of Army One on the Epic side of Gate One. Assassin, go and hunt for our enemies. Everyone else can assist me in strengthening the defenses of the castle." He glanced at Princess almost as an afterthought. "Princess, continue working on those energy weapons. You know how much we need them. Are we in accord and clear?"

Just as everyone murmured their assent and began to rise from their seats, Scout drew a deep breath.

"Sorry, lord, I think my arm might be broken." She winced as she spoke and Penelope felt a little guilty. But this sensation was immediately mitigated by the thought that it was Scout's own fault. If she had not bullied Penelope into moving with an overdramatic gesture, the accident never would have happened.

"You are commanding units, not scouting in person. Go have Doctor splint you up, then take up your duties."

"Very good, lord." Scout left the room, with a last scowl directed toward Penelope.

Almost as one, the manifestations rose from their seats, indicating that the meeting was over. Several of them moved directly to the door, so Penelope had to move quickly out of the way to let them pass. The stately and richly robed Chancellor did not give her a glance; he had begun a conversation with Engineer about the new priorities of factory output. Assassin walked past with a brisk stride that indicated his sense of purpose. Air Commander and Quartermaster stood aside to let him through, before hurrying after him. Along with his ever-present bodyguard, Executioner, and General, Lord Scanthax remained in the room. They were discussing which officer should be put in charge of the heavy divisions at Gate Two. Of all the manifestations, only Ambassador paid her any attention.

"Well, Princess, shall we return to work?"

"Yes, Ambassador, let *us* return to work." He was sufficiently familiar with her ways to recognize the sarcasm. The point was to remind him that while she was working, all Ambassador did was stand still, watching her. Presumably, he was bored beyond belief. Or perhaps he just switched off in some way.

Returning to her tower through the great halls and long corridors, Penelope's step was a lot lighter than it had been on her anxious journey to the planning room. Lord Scanthax was worried, genuinely worried, and he had no idea of her nocturnal journeys to the Feast Hall in preparation for the redistribution ceremony. Circumstances could not be better for the realization of her plan to humble him.

Chapter 21

THE PRINCESS AND THE PAUPER

That night, Penelope crept once again through the shadowy corridors of the castle toward the Feast Hall. Ever since she had discovered the secret door in the fireplace, her curiosity had been aroused. Strictly speaking, she probably did not need to explore beyond the door. In order to seal Lord Scanthax and his manifestations in the hall, all she needed to do was wait for the right moment and then weld it tight to the wall. But, she told herself, the more intelligence she had about Lord Scanthax the better. There was a risk—each time she traveled by moonlight to this part of the castle, there was a risk—yet every night since finding the door, as she lay her avatar down to bed, she had toyed in her thoughts with the idea of further explorations. In the end, the secret door had proved irresistible.

The castle was quiet. With their decisions made, the various manifestations were off performing their duties. As a result, the planning room was not in use and none of the lanterns in the hallways leading to it were lit. Penelope liked the darkness—it hid her—and there was no difficulty in walking with her fingers gently running along the wall to keep her oriented in the blackest stretches of the corridors. In any case, she was soon at the halls, their windows on this cloudless night letting in plenty of silver moonlight to see by.

It was only when she actually stood in the stone fireplace once more, touching the secret door, that Penelope felt nervous. What if someone was back there? Was it really worth risking the upset of her plans to satisfy her curiosity? Gently, very gently, she started lifting the catch, even before she realized she had come to a decision. The secret door moved a fraction, creating a gap of just an inch. It was dark beyond and there was no sound. Pushing the door open just wide enough to let her through, she stepped into the room beyond and then closed the door behind her. It was now completely black in the small chamber and it was easy to become confused about where the hole in the floor was. Rather than take even one step in that darkness, Penelope lowered herself to her hands and knees and shuffled carefully forward until her seeking fingers felt nothing but space. Still concentrating on making as little noise as possible—although her confidence was growing— Penelope found the rungs of the metal ladder and, holding tight to the top one, lowered herself carefully into the pit.

After she descended about twenty steps, it seemed that there was a hint of light below her. She paused. A very faint but consistent humming sound was audible. Five more steps and it was definitely becoming a little lighter. She continued descending and was surprised when her foot could not find the expected rung. Instead, lower down, it touched what felt like the ground. Was she all the way down? Why was it still so dim?

Looking around, Penelope found herself in a room about the size of her bedchamber. This was evident from several small blue lights, and their reflections in some kind of glass. More out of the corners of her eyes than by looking directly, she could see the outline of a very large desk on the far side of the room. The blue lights were all above the desk and as she edged closer she realized they were familiar from her room in the human world. When electrical equipment was connected to a power supply, a small light of exactly this kind was switched on.

This was unexpected and rather bewildering. She had thought the passage would lead to a supply of weapons or to an escape route from the castle. Perhaps other exits did lead to a way out. But this room clearly had a purpose of its own. Her next step caused her avatar to stumble and she accidentally kicked a chair away from her, creating a horribly loud noise. At least she did not have to put up with the pain of her avatar's stubbed toe. Holding on to the back of the chair to steady herself, Penelope paused for a minute, listening. Nothing. She waited for a while, until her calm was restored, and sat down.

There were controls in the desk and, at eye level, some glass screens. Should she risk pressing some of the buttons? Of course she should; there was no way she could leave without finding out more about this mysterious place. Without dwelling on the risk that she might somehow set off an alarm that would bring Lord Scanthax running, her fingers pushed the nearest button. The screen flickered and came on with a hiss and display of static. Its brightness hurt her eyes and she looked away, taking in the fact that there were six seats lined up by the desk, each facing three large screens. In front of her, there was a control that had the same symbol for volume as her film-playing devices, and as she had hoped, Penelope was able to turn the hiss down to a whisper. A moment later, in response to her turning another switch, an image leaped into existence on the active screen. It was a rather dull gray picture of an empty corridor. Turning the switch to another position caused the picture to change: another corridor, this time with some rubble strewn along the floor. Realization hit her hard and she slumped back in the chair. So this was it. This was the room from which Lord Scanthax or his manifestations inter-acted with the human world. These weren't recordings; they were live broadcasts of the corridors outside of her air lock. Which meant that . . .

Penelope turned the switch all the way around, rushing through dozens of images until a much more interesting one flashed past. A short scroll back and there it was. Penelope in Edda was looking at Penelope in the human world. The princess at the pauper. Poor helpless creature. So undernour-ished. So lonely. And so strange-looking, too, like her head and hands were those of an insect. For a long, long time she stared at herself, knowing that she was crying, but that the resolution of the camera was not powerful enough to pick up the trails of moisture that slid from the corners of her eyes.

The wave of unhappiness that had struck her at this unexpected reminder of her helplessness gradually receded and it was replaced by a growing sense of purpose that drew her back to her investigation. This room might have all the answers to her questions. Ready to press on, she reached up to brush away the tears and her avatar's action made her smile. Of course, there were no tears here in Edda to wipe.

So this was the room that the humans had built so that Lord Scanthax—and others?—could interface with them. It had to be the place that Ambassador came to when he talked to her in the human world or when he directed the robots. He must have spent hours here when she was a baby. Had Lord Scanthax kept any records? Perhaps the other controls would access them. This surely must be the room that also contained the life-support instructions for her body.

The controls at the next seat had a keyboard and switches that lit up three monitors. Again, most showed gray images of scenes that were presumably other rooms of the abandoned human colony. One way to proceed would be to try to find the cameras in the library and send a robot there to search for records. But right now that would take too long. After she had trapped all of Lord Scanthax's manifestations in the Feast Hall, she could pursue that option at her leisure, especially if she could find the controls for her life-support system.

Meanwhile, not all the screens were displaying video feeds from the human world. There was one that simply had a small > icon flashing in the top left corner. Was it inviting her to write a command? The problem was that all her scripting skills were based on Edda's menus and her manipulations of three-dimensional objects. It was doubtful that any of the commands she knew would apply here. Still, before moving on, she tried typing on the keyboard to see if the letters appeared on the screen. They did.

```
>ADFOPWEF
>XACCESS DENIED
>RUN
>XACCESS DENIED
>LOGIN
>XACCESS DENIED
>START
>XACCESS DENIED
>LIST
>XACCESS DENIED
>LORD SCANTHAX HAS MOLDY UNDERWEAR
>XACCESS DENIED
```

Rather than waste any more time with the computer, if it was a computer, Penelope moved on to the next set of controls. These sent her heart soaring. Before her was a very promising set of dials and sliders, just the sort of instruments you would construct to regulate an environment for the life functions of a human body fixed up to a machine. The three screens, when they came on, were promising, too. Moving and static graphs appeared, showing an enormous amount of information. None seemed immediately relevant to bodily functions, though. There were maps, too; or not exactly maps, but technical drawings of buildings and arrangements of buildings, much like those Architect did for Lord Scanthax. For a while she scrolled through the drawings, recognizing none of the buildings they described. As she continued to search through the drawings for a clue as to what she was looking at, Penelope noticed that the adjacent screen was also changing in association with her actions. It had been merely flickering before, but now it was flaring up with color. Slowly now, she scrolled back until suddenly graphs and charts appeared on the second screen that were alive. Among the readings were those labeled "temperature," "pressure," "heart rate," and "atmospheric composition"—and they were all in motion. It had to concern her! Returning her attention to the first screen that she had been scrolling through, she noticed that one section of the schematic on display was slightly brighter than the lines around it. After a short experiment with the controls, she zoomed in on it until it was a large oval, with two smaller rooms beside it and an air lock labeled at one end. This was it! She'd found herself and the life-function controls for her room.

"Ha! Well, well, Lord Scanthax. Who needs *you* anymore?"

The fact that she'd spoken aloud drew her attention back to her dimly lit surroundings and her sense of elation faded slightly as she reminded herself that the longer she remained here, the higher the risk of discovery. Nevertheless, for a delicious moment she sat back, suffused with happiness, looking at the plan of her room, its position in relation to the rest of the base—which itself was very interesting and warranted further exploration sometime — and, above all, the graphs on the adjacent screen measuring the state of her body and the environment around it.

In the wrestling match between her and Lord Scanthax, their positions had changed dramatically. Having been pinned to the floor, nearly helpless, she had wriggled free and was now stalking him. The discovery she had made tonight meant she was no longer dependent on his survival for her own. Even if the invaders destroyed him, so long as they didn't find this room, she would remain alive. If she wanted to — not that she did — she could go back to her own daydream of blowing up Lord Scanthax and all his manifestations in the Feast Hall on Redistribution Day. She didn't need him anymore!

Repeating the phrase over and over to herself, Penelope felt giddy. For the first time in her life, she really didn't need Lord Scanthax for anything. She wasn't completely free of him yet, though. Even now, if she was discovered here or missing from her room, the advantage would shift back toward him. To have total freedom, she would have to be able to prevent Lord Scanthax from ever using these controls again. Then she could roam as she pleased in avatar form and there would be nothing he could do to stop her. She'd leave the castle for good and somewhere out there — in Saga, if not in Epic, Ruin, or Myth — she would find other humans.

Deciding not to linger too long and risk being caught away from her bedroom, Penelope got up from her seat. There was, however, one more set of controls and although she had intended to switch everything off and leave, the buttons and labels in front of the last chair were too intriguing. They were almost the same as those that she used upstairs when she wanted to watch a film. She simply could not pass up the chance to see what they actually represented and so she slipped into the seat. Two screens came on, one just a pale light and the other displaying a menu that was easy to navigate, leading to thousands and thousands of what Penelope assumed were indeed film titles. Films of the entertainment sort held no interest for her, but from the way the files were grouped, it seemed that the back catalogue of human cultural activity was only part of the total. The other part had lots of subcategories, but above them all was a curious-sounding title: "A Farewell to Edda." She selected the file and pressed "play."

"To the lords and ladies of Edda."

A middle-aged woman was sitting before a large glass window. Outside was a landscape of rugged mountains. Her expression was somber.

"We are leaving our colony in the next few days, and we have decided to leave Edda behind. For some years now the conditions on this planet have been worsening, and life support is taking up more and more of our resources. We have located a planet that looks far more suitable to our needs, and our ships are nearly ready for departure.

"Why are we leaving you here, when, after all, Edda was designed to occupy us during spaceflight? Because we learned from Earth of a terrible onslaught against humans by electronic lifeforms similar to you, but derived from the game of Saga. While you have shown no sign of antipathy toward humans,

you have, understandably, desired to interact more with our environment through robots and so on.

"We leave you with interface rooms in every lordship so that you can continue to learn about the universe in which your own is contained. We also leave you with enough battery power to last about two hundred years; or two hundred years at a minimum, because so long as you maintain in working order the solar panels we also leave you with, you will be able to generate enough power to continue Edda indefinitely. Perhaps, with your increasing control over the robots, you will be able to make a better success of this colony than we managed to.

"Our fear, however, is that after our departure, you will set about attempting to conquer one another within Edda. It is in your nature, after all. But if there are survivors who learn to cooperate, then perhaps you will not think too unkindly of those who brought your world into being and who have taken measures to ensure it continues to exist into the far future.

"We are sorry to leave you at this formative stage of your development and hope that one day in the future, humans and electronic lifeforms from Edda will be friends who can assist one another. But for now, that cannot be assured, not in light of the catastrophic attack on the population of Earth. So, until our descendents meet with you, farewell."

The woman leaned forward and the recording stopped. Another human.

At once, Penelope pressed "play" again, this time oblivious to the meaning of what the woman was saying, now entirely absorbed in listening to the tones of her voice, watching her hand gestures, looking again and again at her face. Another human. Penelope felt like laughing for joy and at the same time experienced a pang of loneliness so deep that her vision blurred with tears. Only when a wave of dizziness had passed, could Penelope play the file a third time and concentrate on what the woman was saying.

The message was another major discovery. For one thing, it explained why, years ago, Lord Scanthax had insisted there were more worlds to discover. He had known about Saga. More important for Penelope, however, she had just heard a voice from the human community that had left her behind fifteen years ago. It was conceivable even that the woman in the film was her own mother. She was about the right age, or perhaps a little too old. But Penelope clamped down on her wishful thinking before she got carried away; given that the colony had contained about three million people, there was next to no chance that the speaker was really her mother. Still, despite the mention of some sort of disaster affecting the humans of Earth, on the whole the film gave Penelope encouragement. They were all out there, somewhere, on their new planet. Her parents, too. Somehow she had to join them. As she hurried around the room, switching off all the equipment and returning it to darkness, Penelope's thoughts were overtaken by a new daydream. In it, she was arriving at the new planet and everyone was welcoming her, amazed and thrilled that the baby they had lost had found them and had come home.

Chapter 22
SCATTERED BULLETS FLOW

Still in shock from Milan's death, Erik wanted to unclip and seek out the comfort of his family and friends. But that would have to wait, as the next portal beckoned. With the army that had once surrounded it now defeated, there was nothing to prevent Cindella and the others from stepping through to the new world beyond the shimmering metallic surface in front of them. What would it be like? Who would be there? Perhaps, at last, they would meet the EI people in charge of these gray armies. Perhaps, too, there were other avatars of humans to be found.

Just ahead of Cindella was the air elemental, ready to lead the way, its torso now swirling erratically as a result of the damage it had sustained in the battle.

"Pass through that gate, and prepare to defend me on the other side!"

On the command of its master, the elemental swept

powerfully through the silvery sheen that was the portal. A heartbeat later, side by side with Jodocus, Cindella stepped into the unknown.

For an instant everything went fuzzy and Erik heard the hiss of static in his ears, but then they were beyond the portal, walking out into the new world through a curtain of water. Cindella was dripping onto the cobblestones of a wide square that seemed to be set in the ruins of a large town. A zipping noise, like the buzzing of angry wasps, testified to the fact that bullets were already being fired at them, but there was no sign of their assailants. As it shielded Cindella and its master, the air elemental was noticeably slowing down, with dozens of bullets caught in its swirling body.

"Defend me!" Jodocus held out his right arm and just as an enormous earth elemental sprang into being, hundreds of droplets of blood appeared on the elementalist's skin. If it hurt Jodocus to perform this action, he did not let it show.

"Defeat my foes!" His left arm was now outstretched and with a rushing noise, a sulfurous wave of fire came into being as the tattoo on Jodocus's left arm became a bloody mess.

Whereas the earth elemental was vaguely humanoid and stood as squat as a house, the fire elemental was a constantly writhing pillar of orange and red. It was already in motion, flowing over broken cobblestones to the nearest doorway. A moment later the air elemental expired with a faint sigh, the bullets it had absorbed clattering to the ground. In its place, the enormous creature of earth effortlessly absorbed the incoming bullets, but its bulk completely obscured their view.

"We can wait here till the fire elemental clears out whoever is shooting at us," said Jodocus calmly.

"I'm fine." And Cindella stepped around the left side of the enormous bulk of the monster. Immediately several bullets struck her and although these did no damage to her health, Cindella made for the buildings on the near side of the square at a run. The houses had been wrecked by modern weapons rather than fantasy ones. Their roofs were missing, as though they had been bombed, while bricks and beams were piled high on the floors and the plaster on the walls bore telltale trails of bullet marks. The damage to the buildings was not caused by the kind of high-energy weapons in use in Saga; nor were the buildings themselves anything like those in Ghost's world. In Saga, a forest of enormously tall towers obscured the sky. Here, it was clear that even intact, the walls of the stone buildings reached up only two or three stories.

After leaping over the rubble in a series of light skips, Cindella rolled through an open door to come back to her feet, weapons in hand. The room was empty. There was a large hole high up in the far wall, torn out of plaster and brick, through which she could enter the next house. To reach it, Cindella had to put her weapons away and pull herself up. As she crawled through to the shadows of the room beyond, a ruby light glittered in Erik's eye and a bullet hit Cindella in the head. Jumping forward and running fast across the piles of dusty bricks, she drew her magic dagger. Where was the enemy? Another bullet hit her directly over the heart and Erik could see a little red dot moving across Cindella's body.

Although the roof had mostly collapsed, in one corner there remained enough planks to support a kneeling soldier. It was from there that the nose of a rifle was pointing toward Cindella. Without her magic protection she would have been dead twice over and helpless against her assailant, as there was no obvious method for a person of normal abilities to reach the sniper. But with one leap of extraordinary agility, Cindella was up on top of the soldier and stabbing his gray plastic flesh. He fell back, inanimate, dropping his rifle.

The fallen weapon caught Erik's attention. It seemed to be an improved version of the rifle they had encountered with the soldiers in the earlier armies, in that it had sights with lenses and projected a thin red laser light to assist with targeting. Cindella peered through the sights and played with the focus. They were as powerful as binoculars, capable of considerable magnification. It was a shame B.E. wasn't here; he would be interested in these guns. Erik stored the rifle in the Bag of Dimensions, diligently placing it in a subfolder that would be fairly prominent in the rather large and cluttered grouping of weapons.

From behind the jagged ruin of the outer wall of the house, Cindella peered out carefully to see what was happening in the square below. It was much as she had left it. Seemingly untroubled by the constant patter of bullets, the earth elemental was standing in front of the portal, guarding Jodocus, who could not be seen from this angle.

There was a curious pipe running along a slender scaffolding around the gray sheen that Cindella had come through.

Water was pouring down from it like a curtain over the portal, before running away down a drain in the cobbles. What purpose did that serve? Erik stared at it for a minute, wondering if he was missing something important. Was it dye? Something flammable? It looked like water, though. Was it designed to wash something off?

On the far side of the square, a glow flared up dramatically, as though a bomb had gone off inside a building, drawing Erik's attention to the progress of the fire elemental. It was working its way counterclockwise through the houses that surrounded the square, systematically clearing away the snipers, and Erik decided that he would match the elemental's progress from his side.

This was a little like a game of hide-and-seek, except that Cindella did not have to play the game as seriously as her opponents. Nearly every time she encountered a sniper, the enemy got his shot in first, often accurately hitting her head. But it did them no good. One by one she hunted them down, until she saw a red glow on the ruined walls of the building ahead, indicating the approach of the fire elemental, which suddenly flowed into the room. If the sniper units had been capable of emotion, they would have found it terrifying: that roaring column of fire moving toward them. As the fire elemental found its latest opponent, the flames of its body seemed to pulse and Erik could see a heat wave ripple through the air as a blast of flame shook the house. A fraction of health came off Cindella's bar; she had been too close.

"Is that the lot?" Erik spoke to the elemental, a little

nervously. If for some reason Jodocus wanted her dead, this would be a dangerous situation for Cindella. A potion of fire resistance might protect her, but would she be able to draw and imbibe it in time?

The elemental turned its eyes of blue flame toward her. If it was capable of speech, it didn't choose to answer. It did, however, move away, back across the square toward Jodocus. Cindella followed, with Erik experiencing a slight feeling of relief.

"All done, I think," he called out to Jodocus.

The elementalist peered at Cindella from behind the protection of the earth elemental. "Excellent. They must have concentrated nearly all their defenses on the other side of the portal and just left those few snipers on this side. But let's get the others through and move out while we can. Who knows how long we have before more troops arrive."

"Right." Cindella ran back through the gate, pausing only long enough for Erik to confirm that the liquid flowing out of the holes in the pipe was simply water. Odd.

There was a moment of flickering black and white dots in his vision and a hiss in his ears. Then Erik could see again. At once Athena jumped to her feet; Gunnar and Ghost were already standing, their bags over their shoulders.

"Come on through. It's safe."

"What was there?" asked Ghost.

"About fifty snipers, but we've cleared them all."

Without another word, Athena stepped through resolutely and Ghost quickly followed. Gunnar, however, paused just before the portal.

"It's too late for second thoughts," said Erik. "There's just you and me left and they need us."

"I take your point. But all the same, I have an intense aversion to going farther. What if there are beings over there who can damage us, our brains?"

"Come on." Erik didn't wait any longer and Cindella strode through the portal again. It was understandable that Gunnar was so nervous; after all, he had been made an addict to Saga in the past, like so many human players. Erik could not honestly say that something like that wouldn't happen again. But that threat seemed remote, while the urgency of assisting Ghost and Athena was so very immediate. What a shame it was that out of all of his team Gunnar alone had made it this far.

When Erik regained his bearings in the world of shattered houses, he was pleased to see Gunnar right behind him. So, too, was Jodocus, who held out his bloody arms to the others.

"Mind bandaging these?"

"Ouch. That has to hurt," sympathized Athena, while Gunnar rummaged through a bag of medical supplies.

"Yeah. I don't look forward to releasing the elementals on my back and chest."

"I brought these with us." Athena unzipped her bag and passed a rifle to Cindella. "Our energy weapons are pretty much out of power. So we'll have to use their weapons instead. Would you mind carrying them in your magic bag?"

"Sure," Erik replied. "And I've already put in one of the rifles that the snipers were using; they're more accurate."

Heaving her airboard from around her back, Ghost offered

it to Athena. "Do you think you can drain the power from this for one of the guns?"

"Yeah, good idea. Are you sure, though? You might want the board for speed or something."

"I think having an Atanski back in use is more important."

Erik knew that it was a sacrifice for Ghost to part with her airboard, and he understood why Athena now looked appreciatively at Ghost as she opened up a panel in the stock of the Atanski and began to connect cables to the weapon.

After Gunnar had tied off the bandages and received Jodocus's thanks, they all stood in the battered-looking square, the three newcomers looking around curiously.

"Any thoughts?" Erik asked them all.

"I'm wondering about these two elementals," replied Jodocus. "If we are going to fight our way onward, then I'll keep them with us. But if we are going to sneak, then—much as it pains me to say so—they are no use."

"Sneak," said Erik.

Ghost raised her hand to signal Jodocus to wait. "Hold on. Let me go up and have a look around first."

"Go up?" The elementalist looked back, curiosity in his voice, if not his face.

Erik was not used to Ghost levitating, though she had once explained that her control over the air pressure immediately around her made it possible, so he watched with fascination as she rose slowly from the ground. Once above the ruins, Ghost turned about in the air before sinking back down to them.

"How did you do that?" asked Jodocus.

"I loaned her a magic belt." Erik was not comfortable with lying, but he spoke out hurriedly, suddenly anxious to hide the extent of Ghost's powers from the elementalist. On New Earth, Erik had no reason to lie and had no practice at it; as a result, he now felt a little ashamed and his human body felt flushed. Fortunately, though, no physical signs of evasiveness were visible on Cindella. It was awkward, however, that Ghost's belt—now the center of attention—was a particularly ordinary and dull one. This was a difficult moment. Erik knew he could rely on Athena to follow his lead, but would Gunnar?

"This region of destroyed buildings goes on as far as I can see. Except that way." Ghost pointed back behind the portal. "There's an undamaged building over there."

"So, what about my elementals?" asked Jodocus, apparently satisfied with Erik's answer.

"Best to leave them." Ghost looked at the huge earth elemental with a slight smile. "This guy won't even fit down the streets."

"All right." Expressionless, Jodocus waved his sore arms. "Guard this portal and attack anyone who comes in sight, with the exception of those people with me now." While the earth elemental bowed, the fire elemental flickered and created a rushing noise to acknowledge the order.

"This way."

Ghost led them through the smashed-up houses, moving carefully and slowly over the rubble.

"Depressing place," muttered Athena.

After about thirty minutes of picking their way through this bleak scene of destruction, Gunnar pointed to a house whose interior was largely intact.

"Would that be a good place to rest for a moment? I need to unclip and take a break before we get into anything serious again."

"Yeah. It's good cover." With a glance around the group to confirm they were stopping, Ghost climbed in through a missing window. "It's fine."

She settled on a pile of bricks and withdrew a flask.

"Want some water?" Ghost looked at Athena and Jodocus.

"I'm fine," replied the elementalist.

Athena found a rusty barrel to sit on and brought it over. "Thanks, I'll take some."

"Right. If you're all set, we'll take a break. See you in about thirty minutes." With a wave from Cindella to those who were staying, Erik unclipped. At last he could talk to his friends.

Chapter 23
HARALD AND ERIK

It was after dark in Hope Library and all was quiet. There were slight motions from the seated figures nearby: Anonemuss and Inny were both immersed in Saga; Erik and Gunnar—well, they could be anywhere, but they, too, were sitting back, twitching and muttering beneath their headsets. Harald's attention was on his son. Physically, Erik was slender; some might even consider him frail-looking. As a boy Erik had been as lively as any of the other children in the village, but watching their rough-and-tumble games had brought out sharp protective feelings in Harald. A residue of that emotion survived, and it pained Harald that while he sat right next to Erik's body, he could not be at his son's side in battle in the electronic world.

The fact that Erik's remaining human companion was the conservative, middle-aged Gunnar made Harald look at his son with new eyes. It could easily be someone else with Gunnar's values sitting there instead of Erik. At least with Erik you could be sure the people of Saga would never be abandoned. And nothing Gunnar could say would sway him. A smile came to Harald's face as he remembered the determination and independence of his son; how Erik had fought the previous rulers of New Earth for Harald's sake and for the sake of a more just government.

This was no child lying beside him. It was a young man of considerable mental strength. And this person, of whom any parent would be proud, was his own son.

All at once there was motion. Gunnar and Erik were sitting up and unclipping themselves from their consoles. Over at the main desk, Thorstein, the librarian, looked up and called out a greeting. After stretching his arms wide, Gunnar wiped the sweat from his bald head, then noticed Harald.

"It's madness in there. I don't know what I'm doing."

"What's happening?"

"Let me refresh myself, then I'll tell you." Gunnar glanced at Erik, who had removed his headset. "Your son made all the difference in our last battle. But one of the people from Saga died. It was awful. I felt so helpless."

"Who?"

"Milan."

Erik gave a nod of confirmation and Harald could see the tears in his son's eyes.

"I'll meet you over by the food, when you're ready. You can tell me about it then."

Near the entrance to the library was a table with plenty of fresh bread, olives, and cheese provided for the team and after visiting the bathrooms, Gunnar and Erik came over to it.

With an encouraging smile across his fleshy features, Thorstein got up from behind his desk to join them.

"How is it going?"

"In one sense, it's going well," replied Erik with a glum voice that belied his words. "We've made progress, and entered a whole new world, a war-torn city that goes on for miles."

"Oh yeah? How interesting."

"Yeah, but Milan, one of our friends from Saga, was killed getting us there."

The cheerful expression on Thorstein's face faded at once. "Oh dear. That's sad."

"Terribly sad. And it's a warning about what might happen if armies from these other worlds invade Saga. Millions of people could die."

"Have you discovered who built the portals?" Harald asked. "Perhaps they don't realize that the whole population of Saga has become sentient. Perhaps they think it's just another game, full of NPCs."

"No. There's no sign of anyone in charge yet. But I'm hoping the same as you: that they'll stop when they realize they are taking away real lives."

"Have you got time to post something about this for the bulletin boards? The government is begging me for information."

"Not really. Sorry, Thorstein. We're going to carry on in about thirty minutes and I want a quick chat with Harald before we go in again." Seeing that the librarian looked slightly crestfallen, Erik patted him on the arm. "I'll write something next break, I promise. I know the world is watching, but there's just Gunnar and I left, and I don't like leaving Ghost and Athena for too long—especially as the other person we are with, Jodocus . . . well, I don't trust him at all now."

"What if I take a few notes while you eat and then post them?"

"Sure."

In between mouthfuls, Erik explained the course of the battle to Thorstein, placing cutlery on the surface of the table to show the outline of the compound and using an olive to show Cindella's position. Gunnar watched in silence until Erik got to the part about Milan being hit by a tank shell.

"I didn't see it myself; I was too busy fighting," said Erik, looking toward his partner.

"It was awful." Gunnar stopped picking at the food on his plate. "I put grease on the burns and started to bandage him. But black lumps of his skin kept coming off. The poor lad. It was really sickening." Gunnar put his plate down, half full and pushed it away. His eyes were damp and for the first time since meeting him, Harald felt some warmth toward this official. Perhaps some of Gunnar's coldness toward EI people was wearing off, either because he was learning from Erik or through his appreciation of the personalities of Ghost and her friends.

Erik turned back to Thorstein, who was still taking notes as fast as he could. "Soon after that, Jodocus—the elementalist—came over to us with a damaged air elemental. Now don't write about this, because we haven't figured out what is going on, but the way he acted was suspicious. He suggested that Anadia must have been shot by a missile. I don't believe that could have happened. Her chariot crashed to the ground right next to me, but there was no sign of any missiles or anything capable of destroying her. And when I looked around the battlefield, I couldn't find Jodocus or his elemental. Do you see? Where was he? Where was his air elemental? Why had he summoned an air elemental when we had the birds already? Why not a stone one? And the one place I couldn't have spotted the air elemental was high up in the sky, hidden by the birds."

"So that's why you are keeping information from him now? Like about Ghost being a RAL?" asked Gunnar.

"Right."

Harald was confused. "But why would Jodocus want to kill Anadia? Weren't they the last two surviving people in their world?"

"I'm not sure." Erik frowned. "Jodocus was accused of murdering an EI in Myth and was thrown off their governing council. When I first heard about this, I was on his side and believed his denials, but now I don't know. What about you, Gunnar?"

Gunnar looked somber and rested his thumbs in the pockets of his waistcoat. "No. You're right," he pronounced, as if in judgment. "I don't believe him. I think perhaps he has such a deep grudge against the other EIs in Myth that he's out to get revenge on them all."

"Yeah, I think something like that."

"That's the reason he gives for wanting to come along with us, too," continued Gunnar. "Vengeance. Vengeance on the EI who destroyed Myth. In his own way he might be as ferocious in his feelings as the Dark Queen. Maybe he's ambitious and wants to be the only EI alive in all the different worlds."

For a while no one said anything, mulling this over.

"Why don't you just ask him?" Thorstein raised his eyebrows. "Or is that crazy?"

"No, it's not crazy," answered Erik. "I nearly did. But this guy is tough; he is prepared to torture his own body to wield the powers of his elementals. And if we confront him, there's a danger he could turn against us and kill us all."

"He's that strong?" Harald did not like this new development.

"Well, not him, but his elementals; they are very powerful."

"So what do you think we should do about Jodocus?" asked Gunnar.

"Currently, I'm just waiting to see what happens. He's helping us get through these portals, at least." Erik glanced up at Gunnar, and Harald noticed with interest that the older man seemed to be deferring to the judgment of his son. Early on, in Saga, it had seemed that Gunnar had wanted to make the decisions for the team, but now matters had gone so far and become so serious that Gunnar was less full of himself.

"What's your opinion, Gunnar?" asked Harald.

"Carry on. Get a better understanding of what is at stake. And . . . well, since the death of Milan, I've been reconsidering my attitude toward the people of Saga. We have to do what we can to stop an invasion of Saga. Then, when we're done, we should leave all these grim worlds and never come back."

With a smile for his companion, Erik shook his head.

"We have completely different attitudes about the electronic worlds. For you, they are simply a threat. For me, they are mysterious and while they can be dangerous, they contain the possibility of meeting new forms of life and perhaps new communities of humans in avatar form."

"I wish I'd never agreed to come and it was someone else representing our community in there. Another person like you, perhaps, who believes our future will be improved, not worsened, through these worlds. But I am there and I feel . . . shaken . . . about Milan, so I'll do what I can to help Athena and Ghost."

"Well said, Gunnar." Harald held out his hand to the man, and after a slight hesitation, Gunnar shook it. Then Harald turned back to his son.

"So you think Jodocus is a murderer?"

"Yes."

"But you can't be certain?"

"Right."

"Well, do you need him?"

"He's a one-man army."

"All right then. Just be vigilant. For the sake of Ghost and Athena."

"I know." Erik paused. "It's getting tougher. And there's no one to ask if I have to make a quick decision—well, just you, Gunnar. And . . . you know . . . I just wish you were there, too."

Harald reached up to clasp Erik's shoulder. "So do I. But don't worry. You're the right person to be doing this. And not just because of Cindella. Your judgment of people and situations is to be trusted."

"Thanks, Dad."

"Go clip up."

"I will soon. But"—he glanced wishfully at Inny—"tell her I was thinking of her. And is there any news to take to Ghost?"

"It's all going well in Saga. Any army trying to march through that portal will meet fierce opposition. Our main concern is that another portal might open up somewhere. But the people of Saga have been alerted, and we have survey teams going through the less densely populated areas. The guild leaders are rather slow to make decisions, though, about the reorganization of the factories to produce weapons, about how to create an army, who should be general, that kind of thing. They want us to get in touch with Ghost and get her opinion on everything. I've maybe a hundred questions to put before her on their behalf."

Erik shook his head with a smile. "She hates that kind of thing."

"I know. I keep telling them that her answer is 'you decide,' and they just come back with another question." Harald smiled, too. "Oh well. They'll get there in the end. In the meantime, don't worry about us; we are ready to stop an army, or even two armies."

"In that case, I'm going back in."

"Good luck, son."

They shook hands and Erik stood up.

"Gunnar, I'm going back in. I'll see you there when you're done eating."

"I'm finished." Gunnar came back to the console area. Brushing a stray crumb from the lapels of his tweed jacket, Gunnar settled into his chair again, attaching the equipment to his head and hands. Erik soon followed suit, but not before pausing beside Inny and gently touching her hair. While Thorstein went to file a report, Harald went to stand outside and breathe the cool air beneath the night sky. While he was looking at the stars, wondering in which direction were the planets containing the servers for all these new electronic worlds, Inny came out to join him.

"Thorstein tells me I just missed Erik."

"Yeah. I'm sorry, Inny. He asked me to say he was thinking of you. Should I have brought you out of Saga?"

"I don't know. It's hectic there. But do so next time, please."

"Certainly."

"How is he?"

"Tired, upset, because Milan died. But still going strong all the same."

"Milan died? How?"

"They had to battle through one of the portals."

"That's awful. How will we tell his friends back in Saga?"

"It is very sad. Such a young kid, too."

Injeborg said nothing for a while and crickets that had fallen silent as if to listen to the humans resumed their calls.

"I'm worried, Harald. Of course Erik can't be harmed

physically, but what he's seeing in there—won't it make him a bleaker person?"

"Bleaker?"

"With all the violence and death, he might come away from this odyssey with sadness deep in his heart."

"Sad, certainly, but he'll still be the Erik we know now. And whatever happens, he'll still love you."

"Thank you, Harald. I just wish I was there with him."

"As do I."

It was still daytime in the ruined city, although the sky was turning purple and the sun was below the horizon of shattered buildings. Everyone seemed ready to move on: Athena with her satchel straps over one shoulder, Ghost with the Atanski across her back instead of her beloved airboard, the youthful and handsome-seeming Gunnar, and the ponderous Jodocus, who traveled with a light backpack over his cloak and who kept his bandaged arms free of any load.

"Welcome back," Ghost greeted Cindella with a smile. "We're not too far from that building. I went up again. We will be able to reach it before dark."

She set off down an alleyway between red-bricked houses and everyone followed, Cindella bringing up the rear and keeping a regular watch back along the route they had come. It would be very easy to get lost in this world, with its unremitting landscape of ruined streets and squares. In time, though, there was a change, heralded by a droning sound and a repeated metallic clanging.

Ghost pointed to a house that still had most of its roof. "Let's climb up there."

For Ghost it was an easy matter to rise from the ground to the tiles above them. From there she lowered a string and Athena tied on a ladder of wire and light metal cross-steps that she unrolled on the ground from her satchel with an expression of pride on her face. With a certain amount of swaying and twisting and a few whispered curses, Gunnar climbed up the ladder, followed, rather more adroitly, by Athena, then Jodocus. Cindella skipped up effortlessly.

The roof was sloped like an inverted V and everyone was lying on the tiles and peering out over the top at the source of the noise: a huge factory. There were blue sparks from welding tools visible through the windows of the building. Forklift trucks driven by gray humanoids in overalls moved materials through openings covered by long rectangular streamers of plastic that parted for them and, swaying, fell back to cover the entrances again. And from the widest and tallest entrance a gleaming new tank emerged. It drove over a broad expanse of wide concrete and stopped near a gate in the metal fence that circuited around the factory. When the rumbling of the tank ceased, another gray humanoid climbed out of the vehicle and walked back into the factory.

"This is where they are getting their tanks from," whispered Erik.

Jodocus was on Cindella's immediate right. "I suppose so," he agreed. "Or one of their factories at least. But I wonder, do you think there is a *dominus* in there, running the place?"

His question was just loud enough for everyone to hear and from the other end of the line Ghost called back, "Maybe, but look at the tracks. Everything is following the same lines over and over. It could all be automated."

She was right. There were distinct lines of dark wear over the ground showing that the tanks and the forklift trucks had used exactly the same routes over and over.

A new growling noise from the far side of the factory caused them to duck down a little farther. It was a jeep, which drove into the courtyard and parked beside the tank. Leaving only the driver in the jeep, three gray soldiers jumped out, walked over to the tank, and entered through its hatches. Soon after, its engine sputtered to life, then both jeep and tank roared out of the factory gates in the direction of the setting sun.

"I'd like to know where they are going," murmured Athena.

"It's the first sign we've had of some life in this place," observed Erik. "And they must have a decent road out that way. I think we should head in that direction, maybe parallel to the road and out of sight of it." Erik turned Cindella's head so that he could look along the line and he saw their nods of agreement.

"So we'll skirt around the right-hand side of the factory and keep going until dark?" asked Ghost.

"Yeah," said Erik. "Unless anyone thinks we should look inside, look for an EI—I mean, a *dominus*, in your language Jodocus."

Athena shook her head. "Waste of time. This is just a place where they churn out tanks. Look."

Below them, an identical movement of machines and humanoids was underway, and before long another tank emerged from the factory—engine beating heavily—before rolling over to wait by the gate in the same spot as its predecessor.

"Best not to go down there. We might set off some alarms or alert them," Gunnar pointed out.

"Right then." Athena was already carefully making her way back down the roof toward the ladder. "Let's go."

Skirting the factory at a safe distance, they picked their way through wrecked buildings, most of which were abandoned warehouses. They cut through the wire fences between the yards and walked over concrete ground that was covered in broken glass and that had weeds growing out through the cracks. This area had been derelict for at least a year, to judge by the weeds, and while Erik considered making this point, he didn't think it worth interrupting their progress by calling out to the others.

Every twenty minutes or so, Erik heard the noisy engine of what was probably a jeep moving past them some distance to their left, heading back toward the factory; and then, soon after, the much deeper thundering roar of a tank's engine coming back the other way. As the vehicles passed, driving off into the dark red sky ahead, it was possible to hear the squealing of the tank's tracks as it rolled along, sometimes accompanied by a revving of its engine.

They pushed on hard, without conversation. Having crossed under a long metal bridge that had once carried a railway but was now in fragmented and twisted sections, they made their way over a canal. Perhaps it had once held water, but now the canal was a dry pit filled with debris. Then they trekked slightly uphill through a residential area where collapsed telegraph poles had strewn their wires across the streets. As they marched, the color of the sky deepened until it was nearly black, but the darker it became, the more evident it was that somewhere up ahead, over the horizon, was a major source of light; a distant glow gave the clouds above an orange tint.

Although it was becoming harder to make their way past obstacles hidden by deep shadows, no one suggested stopping. Probably everyone felt the same as Erik: that they should at least clear the next rise in the hope of seeing the source of the artificial light. By the time Cindella had scrambled over the fallen pillars of what might have once been a large public building, Erik could only make out Gunnar; everyone else had been swallowed up in the night. But he could hear them as loose slates and bricks clattered under their feet. Then the sound of their movement stopped.

"Mudgrubbers!" Athena's voice was full of passion, even though she spoke with a mutter. "That's us trapped."

A few more strides brought Cindella to the metal stanchion on which Athena was leaning. Along with the others, she was looking out toward a distant hill on which stood a portal much larger than the previous ones they had used. It was five or six times the height of a tank and about ten times as wide. It was easy to judge this, as the whole area around the portal was lit up by the white glare of arc lights and the portal was surrounded by tanks. Hundreds, perhaps thousands, of tanks.

They were queuing to go through the portal, shuffling slowly over huge open ground.

The blazing filaments were fastened to poles that radiated from the hill in eight directions for several miles. Each line of lights ran beside a road, one of which they had been following. It was not just tanks that were arriving at the portal; troop carriers full of soldier units, half-tracks with machine guns, jeeps pulling two-wheeled artillery units, and motorcycles were all slowly pressing toward the center.

As Erik took in the scene, it became clear that the flow was not entirely in one direction. There was some movement away from the hill and out past the edge of the ring of light. There were also major defenses, sandbagged placements with loopholes through which the gleam of metal weapons could just be seen. They seemed far more formidable than those the group had encountered in their recent battle, mainly because of the incredible amount of equipment and the uncountable numbers of soldiers.

Cindella gave a whistle. "Now getting through there is going to be a challenge."

Chapter 24
BLIND POLYPHEMUS

"Magic plate, listen to my pleas. I'd like fish, rice, vegetables, and peas." The golden plate filled up with food and Athena leaned over it, inhaling deeply. "That smells great."

But she wasn't eating. Noticing that Cindella was watching her, Athena blinked a few times and gave a wan smile.

"It's just that using the plate reminds me of Milan. I feel like he is here, arguing with me about what meal we should eat next."

"I know," said Erik. Several times since Milan's death, Erik had tried to imagine what it would be like if one of his friends had been killed instead. B.E., say. How would he feel? Distraught, anguished, guilty, and also angry. Angry enough to want revenge? In a way, but to want to defeat the people who were building armies like the one in front of them was not the same as wanting to take their lives. All sentient life was precious and even if they were murderers, the best way to deal with them was not to become a murderer yourself.

The group had retreated a good mile from the army guarding the portal to a sturdy building whose basement was intact. Erik thought that it might once have been a garage of some sort, as the main entrance was a wide metal shutter, now rusted and twisted open, that led to a room large enough to hold several vehicles. Down a set of stairs, with the door closed behind them, they felt it was safe enough to light two lanterns.

"Do you want some food?" Ghost asked Jodocus.

"No, thank you."

Erik caught Ghost's eye.

"Out of curiosity, Jodocus, what do you eat?" Had he seen Jodocus eating? Erik couldn't remember.

The elementalist pointed his thumb over his shoulder toward his backpack. "Strips of dried meat, compressed dried fruit—that kind of thing."

"Like our nutribars?" suggested Athena.

"Just so."

"This is much better." Despite her unhappiness, Athena was making inroads on the contents of the plate.

"So are we stuck?" asked Gunnar, breaking in with the question that must have been on everyone's mind.

Erik could sense that his friends from Saga were disheartened. The walk back in search of shelter had been accompanied by downcast eyes and dour expressions. It was understandable; to have come this far, to have lost Milan, only to encounter another even larger army and see no end to their journey, was very discouraging. But Erik was turning over an idea that gave him reason to be hopeful.

"We can't defeat that army, can we?" Erik looked to Jodocus for confirmation.

"No, all my elementals together could not shift that force."

"Then," said Erik as brightly as he could, "we'll have to sneak through it."

Athena snorted with skepticism.

"You have an idea?" asked Ghost.

"I do, but it's risky for everyone but Gunnar and me."

Athena stopped eating and looked up with interest. "Let's hear it then."

"Did you see the way that the new tanks were rolling through the gate, nonstop?"

"Yeah?"

"Well, what if we were inside one? We could go back to the factory, hide inside a new tank, and when those soldier units come to drive it, kill them and drive the tank up to the portal ourselves."

"Great idea, Erik!" Ghost stood up, clearly filled with renewed enthusiasm. "That's brilliant. Impersonating one of their own tanks and crossing through the portal right under their very eyes."

"Not bad," agreed Jodocus, "except they are bound to have some kind of signaling system. We'll either give the wrong responses or no response and they'll get suspicious."

"That's why I think it's a job for Gunnar and me."

"But what are we supposed to do while you are driving a tank through the portal?" asked Ghost.

"Wait somewhere, here maybe. Actually, perhaps I should do it alone and Gunnar should remain with you to relay information from me."

Frowning, Ghost shook her head.

"I've a better idea." Athena had lost interest in eating and put the plate down. "Let's all go and when we reach the army, we'll scramble their communications."

Jodocus looked up in surprise. "Can we do that?"

"Yeah. They use radio signals of a pretty low frequency. I was picking them up on my receiver outside. I might even be able to get a signal in here. But anyway, all we need to do is send strong enough pulses of energy through a suitable antenna and we can disrupt them pretty badly."

"We've got the necessary equipment, right?" Ghost was now walking back and forth across the room, and Erik could see from her earnest expression that she wanted desperately for Athena's proposal to make sense. It would be very difficult for her to end up stuck in a cellar, waiting on news from Erik, instead of tackling the situation herself.

Athena nodded. "Right. I could use your Atanski for the power, which would drown out their signals no problem. For the antenna, I've seen a lot of copper piping in these ruins that would work. We could maybe set up two, about a hundred meters apart, both connected to the Atanski, like horns. Mind you, to be efficient, we'd want to make sure the signal wavelength was twice the dipole." Athena's voice dropped to a mutter as she gathered her thoughts. "And," she continued, "we will need someone to stay behind and switch it on at the right time."

This statement was greeted with a long silence.

"It is complicated?" asked Jodocus.

"Complicated?"

"Switching on the interference—is it complicated?"

"No, you just need to throw a switch."

"Then while the rest of us occupy a tank, an elemental of mine can throw the switch."

"Well, there we are." Ghost looked across to Cindella as if sensing Erik's doubts. "We steal a tank, drive up to the base with all the other tanks, blind them with our interference broadcast and go on through."

"Oh, Ghost." Erik had Cindella shake her head and look concerned. "I hate it when you put yourselves at risk. Even if the radio interference works on our side, we've no idea what lies beyond the portal."

"No," Jodocus interjected, "but running away once we are through will be a lot easier than fighting our way up to the portal on this side. I for one would take the chance." The elementalist looked impassive, but his voice was eager.

"Me, too." Athena raised her hand.

"It's a good idea, Erik." Gunnar raised his hand as well. "Better than you going through alone."

Looking around the room, Erik could see an expression of determination on all their faces. Every hand was in the air.

"Oh well."

The following morning, feeling refreshed after a night's sleep in the library, Erik clipped up and joined the others in scavenging for copper pipes. But it was not until midday that Athena was satisfied with her transmitter. The main holdup had been the regular and increasing number of overflights by planes. No one had any difficulty taking cover, given that that the droning noise of an incoming plane's engine warned of its arrival well before it came into view. But waiting in a ruined house for the plane to fly safely into the distance took time.

At last, however, the job was done. The device looked simple enough. It consisted of two long L-shaped copper antennae, aligned with each other and joined at the point where they were met by electrical leads that trailed from the open stock of the Atanski. Standing patiently at the gun was a timber elemental that Jodocus had animated from dusty planks and broken doorframes that they had piled up for him. The creature was tall and had long thin fingers of splintered wood, one of which was poised over the trigger of the Atanski. After some discussion they had agreed that Jodocus should command the elemental to pull the trigger exactly at sunset. That gave them a reasonable amount of time to journey back to the factory and then drive a tank up the road to the army.

Back on New Earth, Erik felt his stomach lurch with a surge of tension. Was it really such a good idea to drive everyone up to a place where their enemies surrounded them? Was he bringing Ghost and the others to their deaths? He didn't voice his concern, though; their determination to go through with the plan was obvious in the long and swift strides they took as they marched and in the impatience with which they met the delays necessitated by planes flying over them.

During one of these stops, Erik and Ghost took shelter together in a large concrete pipe, tall enough that Cindella hardly needed to crouch to stand up in it.

"You doing all right, Ghost?"

"Sure, how about you?"

"Fine. I worry about you and Athena and what these armies might do to Saga. Other than that, well, it's all pretty fascinating. I had no idea there were so many other worlds."

Ghost nodded. "I'm the same." She made herself more comfortable, wedging her backpack between her and the curve of the pipe as she sat against the wall. "Those planes are something of a relief, though."

"Really?" Erik was surprised.

"Yeah. I was beginning to think we might be up against something mindless, like an insect nest or something—just expanding, destroying, and increasing their troops over and over. But those planes, they tell me there are people out there somewhere, looking for us, scared even."

"You think they are a response to our battles at the last portal?"

"Definitely." Ghost paused. "You know this is going to end badly, don't you?"

"For us?"

"No. Not necessarily. I just mean it isn't going to be some pleasant discussion where we explain who we are and they apologize for causing us any alarm and everyone has a laugh."

"Yeah. I guess I've known that for a while now."

"If they were the sort of people who negotiate, or who have a 'live and let live' philosophy, they wouldn't have killed all the sentient people in Myth."

Erik signaled for Cindella to nod.

Ghost gestured with her arms. "So what are you going to do when, say, we reach their capital city, find out who their governing body is, and somehow get to meet them, and they show no interest in doing anything other than killing us and invading Saga?"

"Find a way to stop them."

"Would you fight them?"

"Not the way you mean. You know I am totally opposed to violence."

"So what, then?"

"Ghost, you are as tough as they come, but you can't fight a whole other world. And you don't even have an energy weapon left. We are going to have to figure something else out, like maybe how to close these portals."

The point seemed to have struck home, for Ghost sat quietly for a moment. Above them, the roar of the plane faded to a deep hum, growing fainter and fainter. Athena stuck her pale face into the pipe.

"It's clear. Come on."

By late afternoon they were at the tank factory, lying in a ditch that ran near the wire fence. Given the danger that a plane might fly overhead, they had opted to stay on the ground, near cover, rather than take up positions on the roof again. Stopwatch in hand, Athena was timing the motions of the factory units as they delivered the tank and returned to the factory.

"Ninety-three seconds. Then the jeep pulls up and they might see us if we are still in the open."

"No problem. Shall we do it on the next delivery?" Jodocus looked down the line with his usual impassive expression.

"All right." Athena was still looking at the watch. "Someone cut the fence."

Cindella drew her Rapier of the Skies.

"Are you sure there's no alarm system?" Erik asked.

"Sure," replied Athena. "Well, there's no current in the fence. I suppose if there was a sophisticated motion detector somewhere we could be in trouble, but that doesn't seem likely here."

"So I'll go ahead, then?" Cindella hesitated still.

"Yes."

Anxious that, despite Athena's assurances, he might accidentally set off a warning to the units inside the factory, Erik carefully brought Cindella to her feet and up the ditch to stand beside the metal links of the fence. None of the factory units were in sight. She swung the rapier across the metal links at chest height; they parted as easily as if he had been cutting tissue, opening like a mouth. Then, at each end of the cut, Cindella sliced downward. The severed rectangle of chain links swung forward and fell to the ground, leaving ample space for everyone to run through. Cindella dropped back down to the ditch.

"On my call then," said Athena. It felt as though they had waited for a long time for the next tank to come out and for the factory units to walk back inside, but it was probably only ten minutes.

"Go!" ordered Athena in a husky whisper.

And they were up, out of the ditch, ducking through the hole in the fence and running across the factory yard to where the tank stood, its three hatches open, ready for its crew. Although Erik had been the last to go through the fence, Cindella moved so swiftly that she leaped to the tank ahead of everyone else. He took the middle turret, thinking it might be necessary to assist either those in the front or back in their fights with the arriving soldier units. Soon after Cindella was inside the dark metal chamber, Erik heard thumps and Ghost wriggled down through the back turret. Athena came in next, on top of Cindella. At the same time, Jodocus and Gunnar lowered themselves in through the front hatch.

"Good," whispered Athena. "Over thirty seconds to spare."

Already, though, they could hear the jeep pulling up and parking. The crisp military steps of the soldier units on the stone yard rang out with increasing volume. They were nearly at the tank. Athena had drawn her tooth-bladed dagger; Cindella was poised with the Dagger of Frozen Hate. As soon as the legs of the soldier blocked the circle of light above them, Cindella grabbed him with her free hand and pulled him down. Two quick stabs and he stopped moving, now merely a mannequin. On either side of them, the sounds of struggle continued, and Erik was just about to try to make his way along the narrow aisles in the tank's interior to assist his friends when the thrashing of limbs against metal stopped.

"Close the lids," someone shouted from up front, probably Gunnar.

"Wait, I need light to get it started. There." Athena looked up at Erik proudly, her face illuminated by the interior lights that came on as the tank's engine shuddered to life. "OK, go ahead and close the hatches."

Athena then squeezed past Cindella, but was blocked by the bodies of the soldiers and could not reach the driving seat in front.

"Rats! There's no room! And we can't just chuck these bodies out here. I don't suppose either of you can drive?"

"Not me," replied Gunnar.

But much to Erik's surprise, the tank suddenly lurched forward and Jodocus called out, "Take your seats. I've got it."

From where Cindella was wedged, under the turret, Erik had only a very limited view — constantly shaking — of the road ahead of the tank. An arrangement of mirrors brought the light down into a viewing box and if he really was anxious to keep watch, Erik could place Cindella's head right up against it. Once he had satisfied himself that they were traveling up the road at a steady distance behind the jeep that had brought the tank crew, Erik had Cindella settle back, only looking through the viewing box now and then to monitor the fading light. It would not be long before the wood elemental triggered their interference signal.

When the stolen tank had first begun to make its way out of the factory, it had been filled with cheerful and optimistic chatter. But now as they rumbled on up a road that was filling with enemy tanks, all conversation stopped. The radio was on and they could all hear the increasing bursts of noise coming from it. Hopefully, no response would be required from them before their countermeasures came into effect.

With the sky turning purple, the tension in the tank increased. They had slowed, joining a queue of military vehicles making their way to the portal. At least the timing was about right.

"I'd be happy if our jamming signal went off now," Erik whispered to Athena. Cindella was looking through the view-finder and they were right in among the troops guarding the portal. If for some reason they were spotted, there would be no escape.

The pattern of the slow merging of lanes in the run up to the portal was obvious and logical. The vehicles took turns entering the last stretch of road before they disappeared into the next world. Inside the tank, the radio was hissing and sputtering excitedly. Had they been challenged? Were they supposed to be broadcasting a reply? Or was Erik just finding patterns in the sounds that reflected the anxiety of his thoughts? With the restricted view he had of the sky, it was impossible to tell whether the sun had gone below the horizon, but the clouds ahead were a very deep red. Surely sunset must be soon. Was that an irregular motion in the tanks ahead? Were they turning their turrets to face this way? A sudden roar of static broke out, like the sound of a plane flying overhead, except that it was a howling that did not fade. Behind Cindella, her face illuminated by the lights of her control panel, Athena was smiling. When she saw Cindella had turned around, Athena gave a thumbs-up signal. Her plan had worked.

At first the only sign that the enemy army was affected by the drowning out of all their broadcasts in a static was that the vehicles came to a halt, with their tank only about fifty meters from the portal. What now? Could they crawl around, out of turn, without making the units around them hostile? A plane flew past, then another.

"It won't take them long to find the source." Athena leaned forward to whisper to Cindella. "Tell Jodocus to make a break for it."

Leaning over the plastic-like body of the dead soldier unit, Cindella passed the message on. Concentrating on the viewing box in front of him, Jodocus did not turn his head, but he did give a nod before clenching the driving handles firmly. They lurched forward and Cindella lost even her limited view of events outside as she rocked backward. At least they were moving. If it was a stressful moment for him, how much worse was it for those whose lives were in danger? Surely they must feel trapped, encased inside the dark metal walls of the tank, the smells of oil and sweaty bodies all about them. The sounds of yet more planes rushed overhead. Yet they pushed on and it seemed to Erik that as slow as their progress was, they must be very close to the portal.

The proof that they had, in fact, made it through to the

other side came in the form of a sudden silence. The roaring hiss from the radio was cut off in an instant. Everyone had their heads pressed up against a viewing box, and Erik set Cindella in a like manner.

"Yes!" he whispered to himself with delight.

Beside him, Athena was drumming on the floor of the tank with her feet. They looked across at one another and Athena held out her knuckles for Cindella to strike with a flick of her hand. They had made it! The tank had emerged into a world bathed in gentle sunlight. Ahead, under a blue sky, running into the distance between fields of swaying corn, was a long road, filled with slow-moving traffic. All of the vehicles on it were heading away from the portal toward the unknown horizon.

Chapter 25
Epic

"There's a junction coming up. Shall we take it? It's only a cart track or something," Jodocus called back, loud enough to be heard over the squealing noise of the tank's tracks.

"Yes," said several voices and a moment later the tank was off the tarmac road and running down a much inferior loose stone track, sending up clouds of dust as they raced along.

Earlier, shouting back and forth through the congested interior of the tank, they had agreed to get away from the main road and ditch the vehicle before someone found their jamming equipment on the other side of the portal and figured out what had happened. If they simply turned aside and drove through the crops, however, that would look very suspicious, especially given the near-mathematical organization of the military and economic facilities of these worlds. Even leaving the road for a track might draw unwanted attention. But, thought Erik, it was better than being caught while surrounded by enemy tanks and vehicles full of soldiers.

The tank was shaking more noticeably now, and along with the clouds of dust, this made it very difficult to see out. After about thirty minutes of this jolting progress, they came to a halt. Then the tank reversed a little before stopping again.

Athena pressed up behind Cindella, so she could shout forward to Jodocus. "What's happening?"

"Killed the engine," he called back.

The silence that followed was a relief. No one spoke, but for the first time in hours they could have done so without having to raise their voices.

"Where are we?" Athena wondered aloud, and without waiting for a reply, she unscrewed the lock on the central hatch and pushed it open. As soon as her slender frame had cleared the opening, Cindella scrambled out after her. The tank was parked in a wooden barn whose interior was illuminated by blocks of bright sunlight stretching from the gaps between the slats of the walls.

Ghost was already through the back hatch and adjusting her satchel, readying herself for a march. "Right, let's crack on."

"Where to?" asked Gunnar.

"Let's do the same as we did in that other world: follow the road, but from some way off. Hopefully, we'll get to their headquarters by seeing where all those tanks and armored cars are going."

"Or we'll arrive at another portal," muttered Athena glumly. "What if there's, like, a hundred more of them to go?"

Having vaulted down from the tank, Jodocus was standing

at the entrance to the barn. The elementalist turned toward Athena, sunlight picking out the rippling motion of the tattoos on his body. "My guess is that there are a lot fewer worlds than that. After Saga, the humans probably created a new world for each group of colonists to use as they journeyed through space. What do you know about the number of colonies?" He looked at Ghost. "Weren't there five of them?"

"Yes."

One of the great revelations that Erik and the people of New Earth more generally had experienced upon meeting with the people Saga was that they had recovered something of the lost history of the human species. And along with the despair of learning of the annihilation of Earth's population by the RAL of Saga had come hope and curiosity at the news that several other colonizing expeditions had previously left the planet. How they lived, what manner of government and society they had, what level of technology—all this remained a complete mystery, a mystery that Erik hoped would be solved by encountering them in the course of this current journey. There was no chance of New Earth launching space rockets and of meeting them physically for a very long time.

"Five expeditions and the original program on Earth makes six," continued Jodocus. "So Saga is one; Epic—where Cindella is from—is two"—he was counting off on his fingers— "my world, Myth, three; that bombed-out city we stole the tank in, four; and here is five. Then there is just one to go. One more portal and then we are in the final world."

"Oh." Athena thought about this, then picked up her bag. "I should have figured that out. We're getting close then."

Traveling between fields of ripe wheat under a cloudless sky was rather pleasant, and there was something especially pleasing about the quality of the light, or the air, or the lithe motion of Cindella's arms as they swung to and fro at the edges of his vision. Not that Erik could really relax and fully enjoy the scene. Instead he was alertly scanning the sky, worried about the dangers of being caught in such a relatively open environment by a scout plane. Then, too, there were the farmworkers who came into view from time to time. These units were almost certainly very limited NPCs, with strict routines from which even the appearance of a strangely dressed group of people would not shift them. But erring on the side of caution, whenever a tractor or group of these farmers came into view, the travelers altered their path and turned aside.

The landscape was extraordinary. It was hilly, so much so that some of the nearby peaks probably deserved to be called mountains. Yet where Erik would have expected the terrain to be rough, with boulders, thickets, and clusters of trees, it was surprisingly tidy. It was as if a god had taken a comb and dragged it down the hillsides, clearing the fields of all debris and allowing for farms to be erected, each placed exactly two miles apart, with the same farm buildings, the same rectangular fields around them, and almost certainly the same farmworkers. Rough tracks of the sort the tank had followed on leaving the tarmac road connected the farms to each other and to grain silos.

A narrow space between the edges of the crops and the fences that divided the fields only allowed room for them to walk in single file, and they trudged on in this way for hours over the long dried ridges of ploughed earth; sometimes stopping to let Ghost levitate to get a view of the distant road, sometimes stopping for longer breaks at the junction of four fields, where there was a little more room to gather. They could, of course, have simply pressed down the stalks of wheat and gotten comfortable while they rested, but they decided against leaving any clues to their progress that might be visible from the air.

As the sky ahead of them began to change in color, becoming a deep blue, the sun declining over Erik's left shoulder, they found themselves walking up a series of rises. Each was steep enough that it seemed it must be the last, but every time they broached a crest, they discovered that instead of the land ahead descending, it had leveled off, only to rise again in the distance. After an hour of this ascent, Athena was panting loudly as she marched just ahead of Cindella. Behind them, the height they had already reached allowed Erik to view the vast extent of land under cultivation: an ocher chessboard with thousands of squares. Here, at last, they came to the end of the wheat fields, where the hill became so steep that it was impossible to continue walking normally. They weren't exactly rock climbing, but it did help to use your hands to reach out to the stones ahead for balance as you stepped from one boulder to the next, always pushing onward. Cindella's stamina bar was gradually declining, but Erik was conscious that he was not feeling the effects of the march in his real body. Not like poor Athena, who was stopping more and more often and constantly pulling her satchel around to different positions to relieve the strain of carrying it.

Finally, they crested the ridge to find they had at last reached the summit.

"Blood and thunder, what's that?" Gunnar's exclamation was soon followed by gasps from the others. Then it was Cindella's turn to scramble up to the wide shelf of rock.

Ahead of them was a large valley, contained within a mountain range on the far horizon and a wine-dark sea to their right. In the center of the valley was a major city built in a circular design, with massive black birds flying slowly above it. A city? Not exactly. After a moment's search through her magic bag, Cindella found the Eyes of the Eagle and put them on.

Once he was sure of what he was seeing, Erik had Cindella remove the lenses. "It's an army," he pronounced. "Those birds are airplanes."

"Yep." Ghost was looking through her binoculars. "And see where all those roads are converging? That's a huge plaza and it has a portal at the center of it."

Athena, who had sat down with her arms around her knees to recover from the climb, shook her head in disbelief, causing her long black hair to sway from side to side. "An army? That big?"

"Here." Ghost gave Athena the binoculars before looking at

Cindella and blowing her breath out heavily, as if to say, Now that's a challenge.

"Lug-a-bug! Still, at least we know where the last portal is."

"Erik." Gunnar was pointing toward the far mountains. "What do you make of that?"

"What?"

"The moon."

They could now see all of the sky ahead that had previously been blocked from view by the hill. Just above the jagged crests of the far horizon was a nearly full silver disc.

"Yeah?"

"Look up there." Gunnar was now pointing directly above them, to where the pale crescent of a larger moon could be seen in the azure sky.

Two moons. A shiver ran through Erik's body, sufficiently strong to partly bring his senses back to his body on New Earth. Two moons, and in the exact proportions they should be: Sylvania and Aridia. This was why the world had felt familiar.

A rush of memories avalanched through his thoughts; nearly ten years of memories, all the way from when he had first placed a helmet on his head and clipped up to Epic. At the age of seven, his mum, Freya, had met him in the game and helped him navigate his first character through the city of Newhaven. They had gone to the arena so that Erik could learn how to fight. Almost every day thereafter he had spent some time in Epic.

At first it had been interesting enough, but after two or three years of grinding away at getting pennies for his characters, it had become a chore, worse than any on the farm. His attitude toward Epic had changed again, at the end, after he had created Cindella. The game had become a thrilling world once more, full of possibilities that no one alive had been aware of, including the awakening to consciousness of the game itself. And one feature of the landscape of Epic that you never fully became used to was that the world had two moons.

"Erik?" asked Ghost. "What's the matter?"

"We're in Epic," Erik whispered, looking slowly around in amazement. "It's another Epic."

"How can that be?" asked Ghost. "I thought you destroyed Epic."

"You destroyed Epic?" Jodocus sounded impressed.

"I finished the ultimate quest, and that had the effect of ending the game. But this isn't the same Epic. A second set of colonists must have also chosen to play Epic and started a new version."

"It makes sense," mused Athena. "Why bother to put all the work into creating a new world if you can run an old one again. But you know what this means, Ghost?"

"What?"

"There could be two Sagas."

"Another version where the Dark Queen still rules, perhaps." Ghost did not sound happy at the thought.

"Is that what's in store for us beyond the portal?" said Athena. "It kind of fits. If the Dark Queen had found a way to move from world to world, she'd conquer them and build armies like these."

"Are you sure this is another Epic?" asked Jodocus. "It comes as a surprise to me that the same game was set up twice."

"That's where Newhaven should be." Gunnar pointed to the vast army sprawled out below them. "And all those fields we walked through. They've cut down the forest, cleared out the wood elves, and ploughed the land."

"You're right, Gunnar," said Erik. "I should have seen it myself. I knew there was something familiar about this world. Something about the color of it. What a transformation, though. They've left nothing."

"Nothing," echoed Gunnar.

"Except, I wonder . . ." Cindella pulled her glove off to let the Ring of True Seeing illuminate the world around her. "I should have done this hours ago."

The immediate landscape around him was suddenly rich with life. The apparently bare stone hilltop concealed a vibrant collection of plants, from dull mosses creeping out from dark crevasses between stones, to hardy wildflowers bowing their pastel-colored heads to the sea breeze. And on the flora crawled flies, beetles, and spiders. Seabirds had built nests in the lees of the rocks, abandoned now until the spring. Tiny land birds hopped along the slopes of the hill, searching for seeds, berries, and insects. Below Cindella, back the way they had come, the view was subtly altered and he could tell from the slight variation in the shadows now lengthening over the grain tops that roads and buildings had once been there.

Further along the ridge was what Cindella had been

looking for. A silvery cord, gently oscillating, came out of the distant valley, snaked its way up the hill, and veered away from them toward the sea.

"Follow me."

Athena and Ghost looked at Cindella with expressions of curiosity.

"They've destroyed everything on the material plane; turned it all into farms or that massive barracks. But Epic had an ethereal plane, too. It was kind of like a web of extra dimensions lying on top of the world. And not just the world; there are ethereal paths that even go up to the moons. I can see an ethereal path now, not too far away, and if we follow it we should come to whole clusters of them."

"Yeah? Then what?" Athena got up, to show that despite the skepticism in her voice, she was willing to follow Cindella.

"Then I'm not sure, but if we can use the ethereal paths, we might be able to get to the portal unseen."

"Class! All right. Come on then."

Up and down they walked and climbed, following Cindella's lead, moving just below the crest of the hill until they came close to the sea. The cliffs here were severe. But marking out a half circle about a hundred meters' radius from the drop were the ruined remains of an old hill fort, its stone walls mostly piles of rubble. The shining cord went over the wall and after Cindella had leaped up to follow it, she saw that it only traveled another twenty meters or so before stopping, swaying in the air like the end of a silver rope.

"Oh. It terminates here."

"What does that mean?" Ghost had climbed up the ruined wall to stand beside Cindella.

"I don't know for sure. It's like the start or finish of a path. This must have been an important place once. Do you know anything about it, Gunnar?"

The handsome trooper shook his head. "My Epic character was never powerful enough to access the ethereal plane."

"Want to come up and see inside?" Cindella leaned down and offered her hand to help pull Gunnar up. Athena, however, sat at the base of the wall. She glanced up at Erik.

"I'll wait until you've figured it out. I'm exhausted."

The sun had set, and although there was still a little color in the sky, the bright silver thread—seen with the aid of the magic ring—burnished the stones and grass around it, turning them a metallic gray.

"Well, we would normally need a witch to cast a spell for us, but Cindella has a Potion of Ethereal Travel. If we stand in a chain, holding hands, we can all cross to the ethereal realm together."

Ghost looked resolute. "And we will be invisible to the army, right?"

"Invisible to anything that cannot see into the ethereal plane, which seems to be the case for our opponents. But . . ."

"But . . ." Athena, deep in shadow, gestured for him to continue.

"But there are Epic creatures that travel these paths, too. Monsters. Although all the farms we've walked through seem to have been stripped of any threatening creatures, we can't assume the same for the ethereal plane."

"No," Gunnar agreed. "And anything that can travel in the ethereal plane will be very powerful, very dangerous."

"Like what?"

Cindella turned to Ghost. "It's a dark and magic realm. It's a place of ghosts, of wicked fairies, of hunters that ride nightmares. At special times, and in certain rare places—like ancient graves, or this hill fort, I'd guess—these creatures of the ethereal plane can cross over to the material plane, and if you have the right spells or items, you can cross over to them."

Seeing that their faces, so cheerful when they greeted him, had become solemn, Erik put some enthusiasm into his voice. "Look, there's a very good chance that as we are just traveling down to the valley, we'll get there before any ethereal creature notices us."

"Good." Ghost nodded. "And where exactly are we going then?"

"We'll have to follow the path and see what our choices are. If it's safe, I'll bring us out at the portal. If not, we might just come back here after seeing what lies farther down the path."

"All right," said Ghost. "Let's give it a try. After all, we're not going to be able to sneak through that army any other way."

Everyone was up now, packing their kits, and after helping Athena over the wall, they gathered in a circle around a large stone slab—sea and cliff edge behind them, stone wall in front, and the early evening stars far above.

Chapter 26
SING AGAIN, SIREN

"All set?" Cindella was holding Gunnar's hand and Erik had her lean forward to see down the line and check that everyone else was joined up: Gunnar to Athena, Athena to Jodocus, and Jodocus to Ghost. A Potion of Ethereal Travel was in Cindella's left hand. She raised it to her mouth and the metallic liquid emptied from the crystal bottle. "Here goes."

As Erik looked about for signs of change, the windswept hill fort appeared as bleak as ever; bleaker, in fact, with the sighing waves below hidden by night and the sky above black but for the faint glimmering of stars. All at once, though, they were no longer standing but floating, and the cold emptiness of the night had been replaced by an opalescent luminosity. The ground began to fade and seemed as soft and malleable as a sheet of cotton, and the less substantial the earth, the more real became the silvery cord that Erik had followed along the ridge of hills earlier in the day. It expanded to become a grainy path, about two meters wide, that glittered and shone as though made of moonlight. The path was firm under Cindella's boot, and she let go of Gunnar's hand to set off on it. After a moment's hesitation, everyone dropped their hands and followed her.

There was no wind anymore, or at least not enough to stir the ends of Cindella's long red hair. Nor was there any sound from the restless sea. All Erik could hear were the noises of their group walking along the silver pathway: the regular but sharp clip of their feet upon the hard ground and a soft rustle of clothes and bags. On either side of them the view was twisting, as though the horizon was melting. The path, however, remained sharply in focus.

Although he had assured them that a short journey would most likely be safe, Erik kept everyone moving forward at a swift pace. As Gunnar said, any creature they encountered in such a region would be very dangerous.

Already, the path meandered enough that Erik only had a rough idea of the direction he needed to go to reach the portal. He stopped in confusion at the first junction they came to. It was a crossroads and any of the three options might be the right one to take. One problem was that the world beyond the silver walkways was an eerie and ghostly one that was twisting and turning even while everyone stood still. The other difficulty was distance; it seemed to Erik that at times they had crossed entire hills with one step and they could already have passed the great army in the valley.

Apart from Erik's own brief experience in the Ethereal Tower of Nightmare, no one he knew of had traveled the ethereal paths of Epic and he doubted that anyone had ever done so. When your family's income and status depended on the survival of your character, it was reckless to explore anywhere for fun, let alone the dangerous ethereal realm.

Having chosen a route that seemed to be heading in the right direction, Cindella led the others on down the silver path. With every step, though, the edge of a forest seemed to draw closer, until their route was a tunnel through gnarled and oddly distorted tree trunks, whose branches reached up as if making gestures of supplication.

"Creepy," muttered Athena, but no one else spoke. Perhaps, like Erik, they felt that in the darkness between the trees there were malevolent creatures and that it was best not to disturb them.

Several more strides brought them to a clearing where moonlight picked out a woman sitting on the edge of a well. She was bent forward over a washing board, dark and shining hair covering her face and shoulders. Cindella halted.

"Oh dear," Erik whispered.

"What is it?" Jodocus was immediately behind him.

"I'm not sure, but let's go back."

"We can't."

Erik turned to see that the path behind them had been taken over completely by the menacing trees.

"This is terrible," he said aloud.

"She knows we are here, doesn't she?" Ghost had come up alongside Cindella. Erik looked again at the woman and although she seemed to be concentrating on her washing board, scrubbing hard at a leather tunic, he felt that she was staring at him, and hungering for him. It was like looking into the eyes of a jaguar.

"It might be wise to summon a powerful elemental," suggested Erik.

"If I can. Let me try with a small one first." Jodocus raised his sturdy left arm and his cloak fell back to reveal his tattoos. "Malisobhin, come forth and serve me."

A light spray of blood burst from the elementalist's flesh and for a moment an earthen figure stepped in front of them. But it faltered and crumbled into a pile of dirt that quickly turned silver and sank into the ground. Erik saw the ethereal creature twitch at the edge of his vision.

"I'm sorry. I'm of no use to you in this realm. There are no elements here from which my servants can draw the sustenance they need to maintain their forms."

"Then let's see if our Higgs pistols work." But as Ghost drew her gun, the creature moved into action. Something flashed across the space between them, and Ghost was jerked off her feet, her shots flying wildly in the air. Then Ghost was gone. It took far too long for Erik to find out where and understand why. The weapon that the creature had thrown was a silver comb, which had caught Ghost's dreadlocks and dragged her backward into a tree whose branches had immediately whipped around its prisoner.

Cindella drew her swords and sprang at the ghostly woman, but Erik felt he was probably too late, for the creature had tipped her head back, her hair parting like a black wave sliding from a pale boulder to reveal her face. She had no eyes or nose, only a round hole from which a wild, undulating cry was gathering volume.

"Banshee! Cover your ears!" Erik cried as he lunged at the monster. Already the magic in the creature's voice was affecting Cindella.

Very rarely when playing Epic you experienced "lag." Your character would freeze for a moment, then, as you synchronized with the game once more, you'd catch up as if in fastforward and all the commands you'd issued while stuck would be acted on at once. The effect of the banshee's keen was to induce a similar interruption in Erik's control over Cindella.

Everything stopped. Then it rushed ahead. Then stopped. By the time Cindella's blades slashed at the banshee, the evil spirit had skipped away and her shriek was louder, an agonizing screech in his ears. Even when Cindella froze again, the awful sound continued.

Gunnar was trying to shoot the banshee with his pistol, but he, too, was lagging badly. His shots came in bursts and always too late to find their target.

The sound was so awful now—a venomous roar—that Erik's hands automatically reached toward the unclip commands and it took all his willpower to stay in the game, steering Cindella in a hopeless chase after the howling creature.

Then, suddenly, it was over, although a ringing sound continued to run painfully through his head. The banshee had been silenced. Erik caught up with events after Cindella unfroze, when another sudden rush of motion took place in which Athena ran up to the banshee and shot her in the mouth at close range. The creature jerked back and was now lying on the ground, her long, glittering hair strewn across her white dress.

"How did you resist her magic?" Erik asked Athena.

Athena took a small pair of headphones from her ears. "Milan's punk compilation, at high volume."

"Nice." And a bittersweet memory of Milan's enthusiasm for ferociously loud and fast bands swept over him. Milan would have been delighted that his music was so effective against the banshee.

Simultaneously, the two of them remembered that Ghost was in danger, and they turned toward the tree that held her. It was a relief to see that she was still moving, struggling against the wooden limbs that bound her.

"Tree," said Erik, as Cindella ran back down the path. "I take it you have some kind of ability to communicate." There were no features in the tree to suggest it could hear or speak, but Erik nevertheless got the impression it was listening.

"Your mistress is dead. Let go of this woman and leave, or we'll set you on fire."

There was a short pause, before a creaking sound indicated that the tree was responding. It slowly drew back its branches to reveal a gasping and red-faced Ghost, pinned to the trunk by the silver comb. Athena reached up to pull it out.

"Wait!" cried Erik. "Don't touch it. The comb of a banshee is cursed. Whoever touches it will die."

"What then?"

"Cut her out."

"Cut off her dreadlocks? No way!"

"Do it!" Ghost had recovered enough to gasp out a plea to them.

Shaking her head ruefully and careful not to touch the comb that nailed Ghost to the bark of the tree, Athena drew the edge of her serrated knife across Ghost's hair.

"It must have taken you ten years to grow these," she said mournfully.

"It doesn't matter. I'm just glad to be alive; I've never been so frightened—not even when I was in jail after that mall raid. I just wasn't able to deflect that comb; its magic was too strong for me."

Once Ghost was clear, the tree that had captured her receded into the darkness, without ever seeming to move. Although still composed of silver and shadow, the whole glade seemed a little lighter now than when they had entered it.

"What now?" asked Gunnar.

"Let's press on down the path and hope we get out of this forest soon."

"I concur. Lead us on, please." Gunnar's youthful avatar was scanning the dark places all around them, the anxiety in his voice at variance with the impassive expression of his face.

After a few hundred yards, during which time the ringing in Erik's ears finally dropped to a bearable hiss, they came to a crossroads. There were five paths before them. One by one,

Erik scrutinized them, looking along the paths for what sometimes seemed only a few meters and other times seemed to be
for miles.

"Are we lost?" asked Gunnar.

"Possibly. But I'm looking for something that should
help us."

"Indeed?"

"I once stood in a tower that acted as a nexus for hundreds
of ethereal paths. One of these has to lead to it, since it stood
on a hill near Newhaven. There!"

The left-hand path disappeared into darkness that was alle-
viated by a distant glow coming from what looked to be a structure made of blocks of moonlight.

"That column of silver light might well be the tower." Erik
pointed the way.

As they walked on, additional paths came into view; these
new ethereal walkways were running nearly parallel to theirs,
not only to either side but also above and below them. It was
as though they were following the many limbs of a silver sea
anemone toward the body of the creature itself. Then suddenly
the path ended at a dark rectangle surrounded by dazzling
white moonlight.

"Where are we?" asked Athena.

"The Ethereal Tower of Nightmare, I think."

"Oh. Is that good?"

"Well, it is not too far from the portal. And from here we
can get our bearings and see where the other paths go."

Erik had Cindella look over her shoulder. The others were watching him expectantly, so he turned Cindella back to the doorway and walked through it.

Once again, he was at the center of things. The last time Cindella reached the Ethereal Tower of Nightmare, it had been to complete the greatest quest of all, the one that led to the conclusion of the game and the collapse of the world of Epic. At the time it had seemed essential that he do so, in order to destroy Central Allocations, the once all-powerful ruling circle of New Earth. But since that extraordinary experience, Erik had been troubled by the thought that in ending Epic he had also destroyed something very precious, a consciousness that had emerged from the complexity of the game. And so it was with a sense of guilt and loss that he found himself entering the tower again, almost two years after that crisis.

The interior of the building was bare; it was an enormous hollow cone into which ran thousands of pathways. There were walkways that circled around each level; they were on one now, about a third of the way off the ground. To reach the floor meant descending a series of ramps and as Erik looked down, he was surprised to see that in the center of the huge circular floor was a chair. It was a high-backed throne of black wood or stone and even from here it appeared massive.

"Interesting." Athena was looking through openings to the other ethereal paths. From inside the tower you could see the far destinations of each silver walkway as though looking through a telescope.

"That's odd," said Erik aloud. "That throne wasn't there last time."

Cautiously, he led them down to the base of the tower. The ground floor was as he remembered it: a huge expanse of gray stone paving with a dizzying view upward to where the cone narrowed far overhead.

The throne was facing away from them, but even from behind it was magnificent. The carved back of the chair rose to twice Cindella's height and was crowned with a sensuous curve that flowed to a decorated orb on each of the top corners. It was made from ebony or some equally dark wood and the craftsmanship was extraordinary; the whole back was covered in panels, bordered with engravings of ivy, in which some kind of tale was depicted. The story portrayed a delicate-looking young man parting in sorrow from a princess and making his way to an ominous castle. Cindella walked closer; Erik was curious, drawn in by the tale. And it was there, just a foot away from the throne, that Erik was struck with the overwhelming certainty that inches away from him was wickedness, hunger, and malevolence. Cindella leaped back as though stricken, dragging Erik's friends with her.

"What is it?" cried Gunnar. "What's the matter?"

"Get away from it!" Cindella continued to retreat.

Ghost pulled out her gun. "Should I shoot?"

"I don't know." All of Erik's attention was fixed on the throne.

If anyone else was going to ask him why he was so troubled, their words were silenced by a distinct footfall echoing around the chamber from the far side of the throne. Then another one. A hand gripped the back of the chair, its long pale fingers wrapping around the side with the delicate touch of a lover.

"Greetings, mortals." It was a voice out of eternity, it was a voice full of harm, and it was a voice that Erik recognized.

"Blood and thunder! It's the vampyre, Count Illystivostich!"

"Is that bad?" Ghost was holding her pistol steadily in front of her.

"It's as bad as it can possibly be. He's the most powerful creature in Epic. Your bullets won't hurt him. My weapons won't hurt him. Jodocus's elementals won't hurt him. He can fly faster than we can run. But the worst thing is his voice. Don't listen to him or you will find yourself agreeing with whatever he proposes."

"How kind of you to sing my praises, although perhaps you might use a more elegant and poetic turn of phrase in the future." The vampyre came into view: a white-faced demon whose fangs glistened in a sensuous, red-lipped mouth. His dark eyes burned with a feral hunger and, instinctively, Erik looked away. But there was something wrong with the count. The vampyre was leaning heavily against the chair. His black leather tunic and dark velvet sleeves hung on a body that was emaciated to the point of being skeletal, nothing like the robust physique that Erik remembered from their last encounter. Where the vampyre's long hair had been as black as a moonless night before, it was now gray and brittle-looking.

"All right then, how about using my music trick again? That seems to be pretty effective in this world." Athena reached into her satchel. "If you all put your earphones in and turn up the volume, I'll broadcast some music through our coms."

"Good idea," replied Erik, "except I want to talk to the count. Tie my hands and don't let me move toward him."

While Cindella held her hands out behind her to Athena, who wrapped a cord tight around them, the vampyre looked on with a sneer.

"Have you no manners? To disregard your host so! Desist in that rude practice and converse with me like a well-bred person should." But the others had taken Erik's warning seriously, perhaps affected by the note of genuine alarm in his voice, and they had their headsets in place; Erik could hear the faint tinny sounds of the music of Milan's favorite punk band escaping from the headsets. Unable now to hear the vampyre, they were nevertheless watching with expressions of concern.

"So, my dear, you seem to know me. Perhaps you can address my disadvantage and tell me who you are and why you want to speak to me?" Count Illystivostich smiled, hiding his fangs.

"My name is Erik. I'm a human. Do you understand what that means?"

"I'm sorry, my hearing is not what it was. Would you mind coming a little closer, please, and saying that again?"

Cindella tried to step toward the vampyre, but the cords that bound her hands checked her progress. Setting Cindella's face to show a scowl, Erik turned his avatar toward Athena. But it was no use; she simply shook her head.

"I'm a human." Erik spoke more loudly. "This is only my

avatar. Do you understand that? Are you sentient, or are you simply a sophisticated NPC?"

The vampyre looked back at him blankly. "Curious. You are lying and yet you are telling the truth." As he spoke, the count's voice dropped to a whisper. "Come closer, please. Speaking across this distance is a strain for me."

"I'm afraid I can't, even if I wanted to. What is stopping you from coming closer to me?" Erik asked.

"Hunger, my child. Hunger beyond mortal comprehension. It has exhausted me. You would have died of starvation four years ago had all your food been taken from you. But not me. I linger on, immortal, a survivor of a conquered world."

"The army invaded four years ago?"

"It did. Through a magical gateway. They killed everyone, razed every building to the ground. They even destroyed my castle high in the mountains. Not that I cared. Castles can be rebuilt. But these creatures are not food. There is no blood in them. Not like there is in you, in all of you. How the scent of it fills my thoughts. Feed me. End the torture that assails me beyond mortal measure. Give me just a mouthful of your blood and I will assist you in whatever way I can."

Erik felt sorry for the vampyre. It was impossible for him to imagine what it would be like to be in a state of starvation for four years, far beyond the point at which a human would expire. And perhaps the vampyre really would help them; they had a common enemy, after all. As if reading his thoughts, the vampyre slowly nodded his head.

"Spare me a mouthful. You are young and healthy, you will

barely notice, but for me it will"—he slumped a little and his voice dropped even further—"bring me out of the abyss."

Again Cindella turned around to Athena, this time waving her hands. Frowning, Athena shook her head once more. In order to create some slack in the cord, Cindella took a step toward Athena and gestured for her to remove her earphones.

"What?" asked Athena cautiously, raucous music billowing around her head. She was standing with her arms raised, ready to push the earplug back into place. The others were watching, alarmed.

"It's not like you think. He's nearly done for. I'm just going to give him a mouthful of blood from my arm. Then we'll get his assistance."

Athena rolled her eyes. "Oh come on."

"My dear lady," croaked the vampyre. But Athena had already replaced her earphones and wasn't listening. Instead, she was pulling Cindella away from the throne.

"I'll be back," Erik called out over Cindella's shoulder.

Not until they were at the wall, as far away from the vampyre as they could be, did Athena ease up. Now that he had a chance to think about it and now that the heartrending words of the count were no longer causing his head to swim, Erik was no longer so sure that feeding the vampyre even a little blood was such a good idea.

"What's happening?" asked Ghost, with a rather suspicious look on her face.

"He is very persuasive still," Erik answered, "but he's incredibly weak. When our opponents took over this world, they replaced all the Epic NPCs with their own units. But their units don't have the blood he needs and so he's been starving for four years."

Ghost looked unconvinced. "So he's no threat?"

"Well, his charm effect remains powerful and he may have enough energy to make one last assault if we got too close. But he doesn't seem to be able to walk, let alone fly."

"Why don't we leave him, then?" asked Ghost. "Let's find a path that leads to the portal and get out of here."

"That's fine with me. I just wanted to see if he was sentient. In our version of Epic, he became self-aware."

"And is he?"

"I don't think so. I don't think he understood what I was talking about."

"Beware!" cried Gunnar.

While they had been talking, the vampyre had been crawling stealthily toward them. Realizing he had been spotted, the count moved faster still, pushing himself with emaciated legs and scrabbling with his long fingers for a hold on the flagstones that made up the tower's floor. And through all this urgent motion the vampyre's burning gaze was fixed greedily upon Cindella.

Erik shouted "Run!" and made for the ramp that led up the side of the tower. Once there, he paused and turned to see flashes of red.

"Just trying a Higgs on him." It was Ghost who had opened fire. Although she was scoring repeated hits on the creature, all they did was slow him for a moment.

"It's no good. We have to run a stake through his heart and we can't do that while he's awake and able to drain life out of us with his touch."

This information, and perhaps the urgency in Erik's voice, caused Ghost to turn and sprint in order to catch up with the others.

Behind her, a feeble travesty of his former self, the vampyre nevertheless strove to close the gap with the ferocity of a starving wolf. He was ten meters behind Ghost, and the distance between them increased slightly as the vampyre slowed upon reaching the ramp. All the same, the count kept on forcing his body toward them, and if willpower alone could give him the speed he needed, it was clear they would all have fallen victim to him.

"Quick! Look into each silver thread. See if you can spot one that would take us close to the portal."

The silver openings of the ethereal pathways ran all the way up the tower and they made it seem as though the building were packed with stars. When you looked into one, the image swam and buckled before you could focus on the distant horizons and it took a few seconds to check a path—time enough for several heartbeats and the horrible feeling that the vampyre was getting closer.

They ran from pathway to pathway, leapfrogging each other, but the vampyre was gradually gaining on them. Unless someone found the right pathway soon, they would have to skip a whole section or more to get away from him.

As Erik glanced back to see the vampyre pulling himself

over the top of the ramp to the level they were currently on, Ghost's voice rang out triumphantly.

"I think I have it!"

They hurried to join her. Unlike all the views from the other doorways, this one included a patch of gray that shimmered with the same texture as the surface of the portals they had used. Moreover, around the edges of the gray circle, Erik could just make out distorted green and olive colors that matched those of the tanks and troops of their opponents.

"That must be the one we need," he said confidently. Cindella prepared to step onto the ethereal path. "Hurry. We had better hold hands again."

As soon as everyone was linked, Cindella raised one foot to move onto the silver path beyond, but before leaving the tower Erik couldn't help but turn her head.

Five meters away was the pitiful ruin of the vampyre. It was staring at Cindella with an unbearable look of desperation, and Erik, for all his desire to get away from the vampyre, felt a great wave of sympathy for him. The count was being tortured in a manner that was terrible to contemplate.

"Help me!" Count Illystivostich cried, and Erik's heart lurched. Before he could turn Cindella around, however, Athena shoved her through the doorway and with a gasp he was free of the spell. Erik still felt some pity for the count, but knew that if he had listened to the vampyre, they would all now be lying on the stone floor of the tower, empty of blood. Not just Cindella and Gunnar—that didn't matter—but Ghost,

Athena, and Jodocus; they would have been slaughtered without mercy and without conscience.

Only twenty steps were needed to bring them to the vicinity of the shimmering gray rectangle that was the portal. From their perspective on the silver road, the world was swirling around them like a scene from a hall of concave mirrors. It was a world full of soldiers and military vehicles, but for once they represented no danger. Confident that ethereal travel was unknown to the portal's makers, Cindella walked right through the army until she could get no closer to the portal.

"I'm not sure how far we can go from the path before we cease to be in the ethereal world, but we can run from here; the portal's right beside us." Erik checked that everyone was close, and as he did so, he saw with horror that the vampyre had not given up, but was scrabbling its way along the silver road.

"He's almost on us. Let's go!"

It took almost no time at all for Cindella to leap into the portal and once again Erik experienced the now familiar flickering of gray light and the hiss of static. Then Cindella was through to a new world, to a rainy day in a large military compound that was coming quickly into focus.

"Run! Run!" Cindella pushed Ghost and then Athena. There was a new problem: they were rapidly leaving the ethereal plane and coming into view to those on the material plane. "It's wearing off. Run!"

"Yes. I feel my elementals grow strong again." Jodocus began to sprint, Gunnar just behind him. Bringing up the rear, Erik felt considerable anxiety as they rushed through ranks of silent troopers. It seemed as though moonlight were streaming from their bodies and all about them the distortions of the landscape grew less. By the time they were past the camp, the world had settled. It was possible to hear everyone's footfalls and see the wet splashes they made as they ran. There was no doubt about it, they were all firmly back on the material plane.

Glancing back across the field to the tents of the camp they had just come through, Erik looked for signs of alarm among the guards, but there were none. They had done it! They were through to what was probably the final world, the world of their mysterious opponents. His delight, however, was immediately replaced by astonishment as a howl of pain preceded the appearance of the vampyre, still striving after them, still looking into Erik's soul with tortured eyes.

"Mudgrubber!" panted Athena. "Doesn't he ever give up?"

"Come on," urged Erik.

Not until the group had run for more than a mile through a copse of trees and over a hill did they rest, Ghost and Athena panting with exertion. All of them were staring back the way they had come. And after about two minutes, the vampyre crawled into view once more. But there was something wrong. Steam was pouring from his elegant clothing, as if he were on fire.

"It's daylight in this world!" exclaimed Gunnar, looking up at the sky.

It had been after sunset in Epic when they had embarked

on their ethereal journey. But here, to judge from the light, it was mid-morning. Even as Erik studied the sky, the clouds parted enough that a patch of sunlight flowed across the field. The moment it ran across the vampyre, a terrible and horrifying scream broke from the creature, as though he had been stabbed. Dark steam rushed upward. And where the count had been lying, there was now only a black silhouette against the green grass.

"Ha!" shouted Athena. "Got you!"

Ghost looked equally delighted. But for Erik, what they had just witnessed made him feel rather sad. Perhaps it was just the aftereffect of the count's charm. Or perhaps it was the memory of the benevolent avatar from his version of Epic. In either case, Erik had to force himself to turn away and concentrate on this new world.

As the others gave vent to their relief that the vampyre was no longer a threat, Cindella bent down and touched a moss-covered stone. "This place seems darker than Epic, grittier or something. But perhaps that's just because it's overcast."

"I wonder if it's dangerous . . . you know, like the way in Myth there was that fountain and the castle with the demon who drew pictures." Gunnar's young trooper character was scanning the trees ahead of them.

"Oh. Right." This time Erik remembered to try the Ring of True Seeing right from the first. "Well, nothing untoward from the ring. No ethereal paths or anything."

Closing her eyes for a few seconds, Ghost seemed to be

meditating, before she looked up. Checking that Jodocus was far enough away, she whispered to Erik. "I don't sense anything amiss, either."

"Well, maybe we can find some shelter and see if the plate works?" said Athena, having recovered her breath. "I'm starving."

"Under there then." Ghost was pointing to where a dense cluster of pine trees had not only kept the ground dry but had laid down a thick brown carpet of needles. There wasn't enough room below the bottom branches to sit, though, so she, Jodocus, and Athena scrambled underneath the trees, then stretched out, all facing back toward the hill, on which a light rain was beginning to fall.

"I'm going to take a break. I'll return within the hour," said Erik.

"Me, too," added Gunnar.

Chapter 27
ELEMENTALS UNLEASHED

When they clipped back into their avatars, Erik and Gunnar found that the others were standing out from under the trees, even though a light rain was still falling.

"Just in time," muttered Ghost darkly.

Erik quickly took in the fact that Athena had her hand on her pistol, while Jodocus was alert, his robe thrown back over his shoulder, revealing his tattoo-covered chest.

"What's up?"

The elementalist pointed at Ghost. "She doesn't trust me."

"Well, I can understand why."

"What do you mean?"

"We need some answers, Jodocus." It was Athena who replied, surprising Erik with the tremor of anger in her voice. "How come you were freezing in place when we fought the banshee, just like Erik and Gunnar? How come you knew how to drive the tank we stole? They don't have tanks in Myth, do they? How come Anadia died, when she kept herself well away from the battle at the portal? How come we never see you eat? Why is it that you go off by yourself to sleep? That you never seem tired, despite the fact that you don't look as fit as Ghost and me? That you look so grim all the time?"

Erik was taken aback by this outburst; his two friends from Saga had obviously been talking among themselves about the elementalist.

There was a long silence before anyone spoke.

"I'll give you the answer to all those questions," Jodocus said determinedly. "I'm human."

"You're human? But why pretend otherwise?" As soon as Jodocus made his declaration, Erik believed him. It explained his behavior, especially the way that his expressions were often wooden while his voice was far more animated.

"Because . . ." Jodocus paused. The rain was gusting, ignored by them all. "Because I'm on a mission to destroy all *domini.*"

Immediately after this pronouncement, Ghost took three steps to stand protectively alongside Athena, who had removed her glasses to wipe them.

"Go on." Erik, too, became anxious, as the elementalist unfastened the cord at the neck of his cape.

"When our world learned how the *domini* of Saga had destroyed the human population of Earth, our parliament voted to sever all links with Myth. We already had discovered that some of the characters within it, the *domini*, had achieved consciousness and now we realized the dangers of that situation. The parliament asked everyone to delete their characters and they took control of the character creation system centrally so that no new avatars could be created. But I had a better idea. I'd just made my breakthrough discovery concerning the means to control elementals even where the materials to summon them were not at hand. So I never deleted my avatar and I made it my mission to avenge the people of Earth and to ensure our world was never threatened by the *domini*."

"By killing them?"

"Right. By infiltrating their council as if I was one of them and using my elementals to destroy them."

"And don't you consider that to be murder?" Even while Erik was questioning Jodocus, he could see that the situation was fraught with the possibility of violence—violence that was suggested by the angry expressions of Ghost and Athena, whose guns were no longer holstered, but were in their hands; and by the way that Jodocus dropped his cloak to the ground and stepped away from it, arms free and limber. His posture reminded Erik of the swift way in which the elementalist had summoned his creatures after stepping through the portal to the wrecked city. Erik moved Cindella so that she was interposed between Jodocus and his friends.

"The EI have incredible advantages over humans. For a start—if the invaders hadn't killed them—the *domini* in Myth would have lived forever. They had all the powers and all the magic that they were created with. It might not have been for a thousand years, but once they gained the means to affect the human world beyond Myth, they would have been unstoppable."

"But why would they want to harm humans?"

"Why did the *domini* of Saga kill the people of Earth?"

"That was just the RAL," shouted Ghost from behind Erik. "They were crazy. They thought they would gain more powers, more freedom, by blackmailing the human population. No one thinks that anymore."

"RAL?" As he spoke, Jodocus, with very small movements, was edging back from Cindella, perhaps to give himself room to call upon his elementals. Erik had her step forward, to stay within lunging distance of him.

"Reprogrammed Autonomous Lifeforms: those the humans worked with to improve their ability to alter the environment."

"I see. And you are one of them, aren't you?"

"The last, only I'm not fully a RAL. And I'm not out to attack humans. Erik and Gunnar here will tell you that. I'm a friend of theirs."

"It's true," said Erik.

"You will live for a hundred years at most, Erik." Jodocus gave up on his stealthy motions with a shrug. "You just don't know what Ghost will think of humans a thousand years from now."

"Yes, I do. She'll be friends with our descendents."

"But you can't be sure. Once, when you were unclipped from the game, she made overtures to me for an alliance, thinking I was a *dominus* like her. And if she was your enemy . . ."

"I am sure she will never be my enemy." Erik spoke with absolute conviction.

Jodocus glanced to his right, to where Gunnar was stand-ing. "How about you?"

"What?"

"Do you trust the *domini*?"

For a long moment the only sound in the field was that of the falling rain.

"Actually, these particular EIs, I suppose I do. I didn't at first, but they are our companions on this quest, the same as you or I."

"Not the same." Even though he no longer needed to bother with gestures, Jodocus's avatar shook its head. "They've been useful, I admit. I had no idea how difficult it would be to get to this world and find the *domini* in charge of the armies that invaded Myth. But we are here now and we don't need them anymore."

"We may need their help again, we may not." Gunnar was watching the scene with his arms folded. "But that's not the point. Even with regard to the EIs who are hostile to humans, killing them is murder and it is utterly wrong. We are better leaving them to their world and us to ours."

Jodocus raised his voice to challenge Gunnar. "You are not looking at the situation properly. Right now we have the chance to stamp out the fire. A thousand years from now, a hundred even, the *domini* will be unassailable and the human populations of the universe will be at their mercy. Look around you. The *domini* who rule here are converting four worlds in order to build vast armies. What do you think will happen when at some point in the future they are able to operate in our universe?"

"That's why we need to stay united," urged Erik, "and work together to find out exactly what is happening and persuade them to reach an understanding with everyone else: the human colonies, Saga, and other EI people."

"Defend me!" The roar from Jodocus was unexpected, as was the dramatic way he flung his arms in the air. A spray of blood burst from his chest as a huge air elemental began to form between them.

"I'll persuade them, all right. In my own way. The only way that guarantees humanity's future. I'm sorry you don't take the same view, but I can't let your naivety lead to another disaster like the one that fell upon the people of Earth."

Bullets flew past Cindella's ear with a high-pitched whine.

"Stop!" Erik cried, glancing back over Cindella's shoulder. It was Athena who was doing the shooting.

"It's no good, Erik." Ghost shook her head. "He's not listening to you. He's a killer, and you're not going to change him. It's him or us now. Get back here. Don't let Cindella die. We need you."

"Attack them!" A fire elemental roared into being as blood appeared on the left shoulder of the elementalist. None of the bullets now being fired continuously at Jodocus were causing him the slightest harm; the swirling body of the air elemental was catching them all.

A wave of heat rushed through the air around Cindella and

Erik's vision was distorted by the shimmering pulse of fire. The fact that Cindella's health bar was falling was clear enough, though, and she somersaulted backward, to land beside Ghost. Red, orange, and yellow, the fire elemental raced upon them as swiftly as flames spread on dry pine. But the hundreds of tongues of fire that reached for the group were arrested as though by an invisible sphere, just a meter around them. This was Ghost's doing; she was using her ability to control the environment to prevent the raging heat of the elemental from consuming them.

"Attack!"

With the thunderous boom of stormy waves crashing upon a rocky shore, a ferocious mass of animate dark green water swept up at them from their left, its foaming head lashing down as though intent on crushing them into the ground. Again the blow was thwarted, but this time the invisible sphere buckled and contracted, barely shielding them from destruction.

Erik glanced at Ghost, terrified that his friends were moments away from their deaths. An outstretched hand pointing at each elemental, Ghost was holding steady, her eyes closed in concentration. Having ducked under her arms, Athena was crouched at Ghost's side and was sending streams of bullets into the fire elemental in front of them and perhaps beyond toward Jodocus.

"Attack!"

The ground quivered and heaved.

"Gunnar, help us!" shouted Erik as loudly as he could.

If Gunnar had joined the battle, it did not divert the arrival of a stone elemental whose fists of granite came lashing down with a power and momentum that seemed unstoppable. Inside his headset, Erik flinched, and as the dark shadow of the rock came down upon the three of them, he tasted for a moment what it must feel like to have one's life extinguished through violence.

And yet the wild sounds of the elements continued to rage in his ears. Shivering all over, beads of sweat across her brow, Ghost remained on her feet. She had withstood the blow!

"Attack!"

Another of those cruel and remorseless shouts. All Erik could think of as Cindella flinched, preparing for Ghost's defenses to give way, was how much anger and hatred he felt toward Jodocus; for the elementalist's closed mind and murderous values. Was he right, though? Was this vicious assault justified if it saved humanity? Looking at Ghost and the unendurable strain she was taking up as she struggled for her life and that of Athena, hunched at Ghost's side, Erik felt so much empathy for her that he had no doubts. There was pathos and nobility in Ghost's determined expression, staring out beneath the stumps of her former dreadlocks. No matter what the far future held, it was wrong to kill any EI.

"Attack!"

With two more elementals on the way, surely Ghost would be overcome. Beside him, her ragged gasps of breath were audible over the raging blows of the elementals. And yet suddenly the fire elemental dissipated into the skies, the sea elemental collapsed into streams of water that drained through the ground, and the stone elemental fell apart in a heap of scattered rocks.

"What happened?" Cindella rose to her feet and looked over to Gunnar, whose gun was held before him in a shaking hand. It was pointed at the blood-covered body of the elementalist.

"He weakened himself with all those summons and I don't think he expected me to fire. The air elemental was facing you, not me."

Cindella and Gunnar met at the corpse. The tattoos that had ruptured in releasing the elementals had done enormous damage. Jodocus had let loose his most powerful elementals, to judge by the fact that the great circles on his back and chest were now bloody ruins.

Gunnar turned to Cindella. "Jodocus called up a lava elemental from this one." He pointed to the remains of the large circle on the front of the body. "It was huge. Then he called something else out of his back. But as soon as he did, I fired. He fell to the ground in a spray of blood."

"Ghost!" Athena's cry caused them all to turn. She had caught Ghost, who had sunk into her arms. In an instant, Cindella sprang over to assist them.

"I'm fine," Ghost whispered. "I just need to sleep for a few minutes." And she writhed from their grasp so that she could lie down. A moment later her eyes were closed and she was breathing peacefully.

It was nearly four hours before Ghost opened her eyes; Erik had not unclipped for a minute. Although night had fallen, there was enough moonlight to see by, and they had thought better of making a fire, which might draw the attention of the army on the far side of the hill.

"What happened?"

"You remember defending us from the elementals?" Erik replied.

"Yes, of course. I mean, what happened to Jodocus?"

"Gunnar shot him. After he'd weakened his own body by letting loose the elementals."

"So he's finished with, right? The human who controlled the avatar?"

"I think so," Gunnar answered. "He said that their authorities had taken control of the character creation process. So he won't be able to clip up to Myth again."

"Good."

"I suppose so," said Erik, "but there's a whole other colony of humans somewhere and if none of them is creating avatars, how are we going to contact them?"

Athena shrugged. "We'll find a way. I bet their leaders check in on Myth from time to time. Once we've stopped the people planning to attack Saga, we can go back to Myth and leave messages everywhere on your behalf."

"What, alerting hostile EIs to our existence? I think not!" exclaimed Gunnar.

"Hey Gunnar, about that. Why weren't you on Jodocus's

side?" asked Ghost. "Did you agree with the way he was reasoning? Don't you have doubts about us?"

"I shot him, didn't I?" Gunnar sounded aggrieved. "Of course I didn't agree with him. I mean, obviously EIs can be a threat to humans. Just look at what the RAL did to the people of Earth and what the Dark Queen would have done to us. But he was criminal to want to kill you. When it comes to the choice between killing an avatar or allowing that avatar to kill real beings, well, there is no choice. What's more, I've come to believe that we have to work together and live together somehow."

"Hear, hear." Cindella slapped him on the back. "And once we've come to terms with whoever controls these armies, we'll have lots of new worlds to explore and new people to meet, maybe even other humans, too. It will be fun."

"Well, I don't know about that. But I certainly accept that Ghost and the people of Saga will be part of our future."

"If we have a future," muttered Ghost. "I mean, look at all those troops in Epic and all those tanks in that other world. They are going to devastate Saga."

"Unless we stop them," said Athena confidently.

"The four of us?" Ghost sounded doubtful.

"Well, yes," replied Athena. "And here's some good news. While you were asleep I tried the tracking device again—the one we used to trace the scout that led us into Myth. And as I went through the various bands, I got this."

Erik moved Cindella so that he could get a better view. "What is it?"

"It's a strong radio signal." Athena tipped the screen toward him. "But what's interesting is the pattern. I've only picked up something like it once before."

"Yeah?"

"There's a building in Saga where Ghost goes to interface with the robots and equipment of Earth. Its machinery gives off more or less the same signal."

"So, some kind of interface building might exist here?"

"Yes."

"Maybe it's humans who are behind all this?" Erik mused aloud. "More people who think like Jodocus? Who are out for revenge against the people of Saga?"

"It could be." Athena switched her receiver off and looked up at him through her long, damp tresses. "I understand why intelligent life that has evolved from computer games based on warfare might have a nature that was inclined to violence and conquest. But it disturbs me that humans like Jodocus can be so convinced of their philosophy that they are prepared to kill me, even though I've done nothing to harm him and never would. I used to think you were all so honorable or something, and that it was just us who were flawed."

"No." Erik thought about some of the people he'd encountered in his past struggles and about his own fury toward the human who controlled Jodocus. "No, I'm afraid we have a dark side, too."

Ghost stood up. "Anyway, whether human or not, we have to stop whoever has built these armies from invading Saga. Let's focus on that. How far away is the source of that signal?"

Athena switched on her tracker again. "About a hundred and fifty kilometers."

"Not too far, really," observed Erik. "What's that, about a five-day march?"

"For you, maybe; more like six or seven for Athena and me. You have to remember, we're not used to all this clean air." Ghost smiled. "And we normally get around on airboards."

"Let me see if I have anything that can make the journey quicker." Cindella sat down while Erik scrolled through the contents of the Bag of Dimensions. It took him nearly fifteen minutes, after which time there were three magic items on the ground in front of Cindella, those that he had picked out as possibly being of some use.

"This," he said, picking up the figurine of a unicorn, "is supposed to summon a unicorn. I'm not sure if it will work if there are no unicorns in this world. This"—a large playing card with the picture of a road leading between two hills toward a setting sun—"is the 'Journey' card from a Deck of Curiosities. And these"—a pair of thigh-high brown leather boots—"are Seven-League Boots."

"Fascinating!" Athena squatted down beside the items. "May I?"

"Just don't put the card down as if you were playing it."

"What does it do?"

"Actually, I'm not entirely sure. I bought it without really researching it very much. Back then, after we killed a dragon and got its hoard, I bought pretty much all the magic items I could. Inny or Sigrid probably know a bit more about it. What the sorcerer who sold the deck to me said was that you play a particular card and say what you want, something that the magic of the card can assist you with. The example he gave was the 'Truth' card. He said that if you play that card, it will show if the person speaking is lying or not. Also, he said something about how the outcome of using a card varies according to how precise the task is that you have in mind."

"Interesting. And useful, assuming their magic works here." Athena turned her attention to the boots, picking one of them up and turning it over to admire the scrollwork. "Are these what I think they are?"

"They take you about twenty miles in a jump. It's pretty hard to control, though."

"Total class! I really want a go at these."

"Well, I was thinking you could wear them; Gunnar could ride the unicorn, if it comes; and Ghost and I can just push on as fast as we can."

Athena, beaming from ear to ear, at once began to untie the extensive laces on her own sturdy black boots.

"Hold on there, Athena." Gunnar came closer. "The unicorn might not work. Shouldn't we try the card first?"

Athena looked up at Cindella.

"I guess so," replied Erik. "You use it, Athena, because I don't really know where we are going. Place it faceup on the ground while thinking as specifically as possible about where you want to go."

"Well, I don't really know, either—other than that it might be a place like Ghost's interface building. Having said that, I suppose we know the distance and direction we have to go in." Despite her lack of confidence in wielding the magic item, Athena had picked up the card and was studying the picture on it.

"Go ahead. Try it anyway," said Ghost encouragingly.

First adjusting her headband to keep the curls of her long dark hair away from her face, Athena knelt and took a deep breath. With a swift and decisive motion, she placed the card on the ground and never for a moment moved her gaze from the picture.

A loud crack was the first indication that magic was in operation. Nearby, a weighty boulder had split in two, and the split kept widening. The earth trembled and all the trees around them swayed back and forth. When the slightly nauseating motion ceased, they saw that a path had opened in the ground, one that led downward into a tunnel.

Cindella took off her glove.

"What do you see?" asked Gunnar.

"More or less the same. Except that there are additional flowing lines of magic. They converge at a spot about four steps into the tunnel."

Gunnar picked up his bag. "So, should we try it, then?"

"Probably," Erik answered uncertainly.

"Let me try. I'm the most dispensable person here. If it comes out somewhere dangerous, or if I get killed, I'll let Erik know."

He looked at Ghost, who gave an appreciative nod.

"Good idea. Thanks, Gunnar."

The handsome trooper walked down into the tunnel until he disappeared into the darkness. A minute later, Erik received a tap on his knee.

"Hold on, I'll be right back."

When Erik took off his headset, he found Gunnar leaning over him.

"Don't worry, Erik," Gunnar said earnestly. "It's fine. It's just a dark room with some chairs and computers. It's safe for everyone to go through."

Chapter 28
PENELOPE

It was a risk, leaving her room for nights of exploration in Lord Scanthax's castle. But Penelope found the lure of the hidden room too irresistible. There were so many films to watch. Each night of the week leading up to Redistribution Day, she told herself she ought to stay in bed rather than jeopardize her trap. Each night, nevertheless, she found herself stealing down the silk rope ladder and through the dark corridors to the Feast Hall. What drew her back was not the opportunity to learn more about the controls that affected her physical body but the films.

The colonists had left an enormous database of films and viewing them was fascinating. It wasn't the cultural works that held Penelope's interest. Their music, poetry, theater, and film were all very well, but such polished and carefully edited productions could not compete with the simple homemade clips of daily life. There must have been a great many cameras in the colony, some fixed in position at certain important locations and others owned by individuals who in several instances had created a kind of film-based diary about their lives. Just watching other humans of all ages going about their daily tasks created an enormous yearning inside Penelope. It was agonizing, for example, to see a clip of a teacher with his class of children, who were about five years old. The children were playful and happy, keen to please their teacher. With a great deal of mess and lots of laughter, the group was painting a large model of an elephant in lurid colors.

It would have been easy to spend an entire night going through this vast collection, attempting to understand what it must feel like to be surrounded by hundreds of other people. It made her giddy, imagining she was part of this energetic community. Sometimes, when a person being filmed would fool around for the camera, Penelope felt like laughing aloud. Until she had watched the clips, she hadn't realized just how crucial playfulness was to being human. Lord Scanthax and his manifestations were completely devoid of humor. After all, for him laughter served no function, unless it was the dry kind directed by one manifestation toward another in criticism of a mistake. A life without the cheerful laughter that she could see had been ever-present among the residents of the colony was unendurable, and more than ever Penelope was resolved to find other human company; first in Epic, Ruin, Myth, or Saga, but ultimately in the flesh. Flesh. Skin-to-skin contact with another person. A hug, even, or a kiss. How she craved that sensation!

The humans she was watching were, on the whole, fit and

healthy. There was, for example, a simple clip of a woman walking along a corridor toward the office in which she worked. Something in her pose, the swinging of her arms, her little wave to the camera, made Penelope see her own body through new eyes. There was no way that her emaciated and feeble form could move with such vibrant energy. A lifetime of dependency upon machines had reduced her to a shocking state of immiseration. Once she forced Lord Scanthax to accept her independence, Penelope would work really hard on rebuilding her body, no matter how great the pain. She was absolutely determined that one day she, too, would stroll along a corridor like a healthy human being instead of lurching from wall to wall like a broken robot.

As the human colony reached their decision to move to a new planet, they had recorded their debates. And here Penelope came across the first evidence that the clips had been edited before being left behind. All references to the location of the new colony had been deleted; the films simply skipped forward to another subject. They evidently did not want whatever intelligence survived in Edda to be able to trace them. Given Lord Scanthax's predisposition to convert everything he came across into material for his army and his administration, this was probably wise. But it created a long-term problem for Penelope. Unless, perhaps, some of them operated avatars in Edda or another world, how would she find them?

Another puzzle was that all the clips dating to the actual exodus of the humans from their old colony were inaccessible. Penelope had hoped to be able to identify her parents or find the footage that had been used in Lord Scanthax's propaganda film showing her as a baby. What had happened exactly, that they had abandoned her? There didn't seem to be anything different about these files, but when she tried to open any of the clips dated to the day of departure, a new screen jumped up to block any further progress through the menus.

ACCESS TO THESE FILES REQUIRES A USERNAME AND PASSWORD.

There was a place to enter a name and password, but after nearly an hour of fruitless guessing, Penelope gave up. Her time in the secret room was too precious for her to spend it staring at the frustrating message.

The morning before Redistribution Day, when Penelope was half asleep at her work desk, a castle page appeared at the door of the wizard's room, requesting her presence in the Map Room, where Lord Scanthax was waiting. Again, Ambassador escorted her without having been specifically asked to come along. Penelope felt a little sorry for him. Ambassador's role had been dramatically curtailed since the days when he had operated with a great deal of autonomy in the subtle diplomatic maneuvers between the lords and ladies of Edda. For several years now he had probably seen a decline in his level of independent exec-utive functions. Of course, his scripting was sufficiently sophis-ticated and his allocation of processing power sufficient that he had the critical mass for self-awareness, but the actual amount of resources allowed him was almost certainly considerably less than that which he had used at his peak. It must be terrible to feel yourself operating at a lower level of intellect than you once did and even worse to know that you were on a slide downward toward redundancy and non-existence, or, rather, a form of existence barely more conscious than that of a factory unit.

Did Ambassador resent this? Did he ever feel like revolting against his greater self? Did the manifestations of Lord Scanthax ever see themselves as serious rivals? In a way, it was like Lord Scanthax had physical representations of the different aspects of his character and his different states of mind. And was it just a human trait to argue with yourself? To have your mind struggle with opposing ideas and desires? How far would the different manifestations go in their opposition? None, as far as she knew, had ever revolted against their fate, not even when their destruction was assured. Penelope gave Ambassador a smile, which he returned. Even so, her sympathy could not extend too far toward him. She was in prison and he was her warden.

As they walked through the Feast Hall, Penelope paused. It had been decorated. All of the bunting was out, ready for the ceremony. Captured banners ornamented the walls; trophies of conquest filled display cabinets that had been carried to the hall for the purpose. In them were items such as the valuable personal weapons used by Lord Scanthax's opponents, their most precious jewelry, their most distinctive shields, curious helmets, and even the skulls of the slain. Having noticed her delay, the page turned around with an impatient expression.

Penelope walked forward again. At least it seemed that the room had been prepared for the celebratory occasion without anyone discovering the fact that the windows were now bullet-proof.

Waiting for her in the Map Room was Lord Scanthax, and with him, the ominous figure of Assassin. If Lord Scanthax was essentially a heartless being, then in his manifestation as Assassin he had condensed all the uncaring cruelty of his nature, all of his will to survive regardless of the cost. The two of them barely gave Ambassador a second glance.

"Princess, we have extremely bad news." Lord Scanthax tapped the map, pointing to the world of Ruin and Gate Two. "They are through into Epic. Only one more gate and they will be in Edda."

Penelope was impressed; she had thought that Gate Two had such a large army defending it that it would be impossible for a small unit to get through.

"They defeated your army?"

"No." Assassin shook his head. "They were clever. They stole a tank, used a powerful radio signal to drown out our communications, and drove right through unopposed."

Now would not be a good time to set her avatar to the smile she felt like wearing. Choosing instead her most solemn expression, Penelope gave a nod that she hoped conveyed concern.

"Only one tank, though," she observed. "That limits the extent of the threat." And it could hardly represent a major threat, could it? Now that she knew how to survive without

the assistance of Lord Scanthax, she secretly relished his difficulties and it was slightly disappointing to learn that a mere
handful of his enemies had entered Epic.

"True," acknowledged Lord Scanthax. "And they will not
be able to use the same trick again. General is not allowing
any vehicles at all through Gate One."

"How can I help?"

Assassin loomed closer, facing Lord Scanthax. "My advice
is that we cancel the redistribution ceremony."

"Cancel the ceremony?" Penelope could hear the genuine
anxiety in her own voice. That would be a catastrophe. If all
the manifestations were not gathered together in the hall, her
trap would be incomplete. If even one manifestation remained
at liberty, Lord Scanthax would not need to surrender to her
demands; he would be able to rule through that manifestation,
probably investing it with as much processing power as all the
sealed-up manifestations could muster together.

"Naturally, I do not wish to take such a drastic action." Lord
Scanthax was glum. "The coming redistribution is particularly
important in the context of the current crisis, as well as for the
unity of purpose of all the manifestations. But the question
is—and this is why I wanted to talk to you—can our safety be
assured?"

"What do you mean?"

"If all my manifestations are here in the Feast Hall, there
would be a theoretical risk. Suppose, somehow, this assassina-
tion force manages to get through Gate One. Then, if they
had a plane from which they could drop powerful bombs or if

they had missiles they could fire from the ground, they could extinguish me entirely."

"I see."

"Do you see?" Assassin growled. "We know you are not as loyal to us as you once were. But understand this: if we are all extinguished, then your human body will expire within days. It is in the interests of your own survival that there be no risk at all to Lord Scanthax."

"Right. So what can I do?"

"Almost certainly there is no chance of their reaching Edda in the next two days. But if somehow they manage to launch an attack upon the castle, we need to know that the first missiles and bombs will be deflected safely away. We will only need a minute to disperse if there is an alarm. You said at an earlier meeting that you could build an obstruction at a gate that would last for hours. Does this mean you can construct a shield over the castle sufficiently strong to allow us to evacuate the hall?"

"I can. Without difficulty." She put as much certainty into her voice as she could muster. "I can guarantee you at least thirty minutes' resistance to those energy weapons and almost indefinite resistance to Ruin-level weapons. But can I make a suggestion?"

"Certainly."

"It would take a great deal of time to build up a shield around the castle and such a shield would be no more effective than if I were to alter the nature of the existing walls and windows of the wing containing the Feast Hall. It would be much easier and quicker for me to work with the existing materials to make them bomb-proof than to create something from scratch."

"You would make sure that there was no point of entry for a missile?"

"Absolutely. Send me Architect or Engineer with the castle plans and I'll start at once."

"Well?" Lord Scanthax looked at Assassin.

Assassin shook his head. "It sounds like a precaution that will eliminate the danger. But . . . they showed some ingenuity and bravery in Ruin by the manner in which they got through the gate. My worry is that we are missing some data and under-estimating them." He gave Penelope an appraising look, and if she had been in her human body, she would have blushed with guilt. As it was, the princess met his gaze with equanimity.

"Very well. Shield that section of the castle for us, Princess."

If she hadn't been quivering with distress at how close her plans had come to being ruined, Penelope would have enjoyed the irony of the situation. Lord Scanthax was asking her to build a shield to protect his manifestations and that task was effectively the same one she had already completed as part of a strategy for imprisoning them.

Chapter 29
TH3*vQo3

Now that she had a good reason to be in the Feast Hall, Penelope almost skipped her way along the moonlit corridors. True, she still needed to be careful in leaving her bedroom, so as to avoid the scrutiny of Ambassador. But Lord Scanthax's request that she make the walls of the building a shield against missiles and bombs was the perfect excuse to offer for her presence should she run into any of the manifestations.

The distribution ceremony was less than twelve hours away and the Feast Hall was ready. A solemn silence in which not even a mouse stirred—how could it, when she had ensured that the room was sealed?—filled the spaces between the exhibits. Penelope could picture how it would look later in the day: blazing with shafts of light descending from the high windows and glittering on the silverware and polished armor of the officers. But for now it was full of shadows.

Once again she examined the secret door at the fireplace. All it would take was a quick pass of her "glue gun" down the line opposite the hinge and it would be welded to the rock. That would probably be the crucial moment and Penelope could feel her human heart palpitate as she anticipated the scene. Perhaps Ambassador or some other manifestation would run over to her, wondering what she was doing. But surely no one would stop her from getting up from her seat and walking this far, especially if they were listening to one of the interminable, self-congratulatory speeches. Once the secret door had been integrated into the walls of the room, the trap would be closed. Then the negotiations would begin. And if Lord Scanthax refused to budge, she would kill her avatar, create a new one outside of the sealed room and script an alternative route to the control room. While she got on with her new life, he could simmer in impotent rage until he was ready to come to terms.

Feeling giddy about the prospect of freedom, Penelope eased the door open, only to be shocked by the sound of voices. There were manifestations in the control room! She had almost shut the secret door when she paused, having distinctly heard a peal of laughter. What was going on down there? Were they watching one of the human films? Indecision kept her poised at the partially opened door, listening intently but ready to run back toward her room. There were several voices, male and female, all sounding surprisingly young. It only took a few quiet, careful steps and Penelope was above the drop; from there she could make out what they were saying.

"Whoa, Athena, look at this. The entire first season of *Matador*. Tell me you can upload them all."

"I can, of course."

"Wait until we get home with these. Everyone will be amazed. And look—concert footage of the Sex Pistols. Classic. Get those, too."

"Ghost. Shouldn't you be searching for information that will help us, instead of trying to fill the gaps in Saga's human film collection?"

"Of course, but don't you think coming back with all these films—already having saved the world—would be so awesome?"

"You are such a lightweight at times. Hey, this looks interesting. Shhh, everyone."

"To the lords and ladies of Edda. We are leaving our colony in the next few days, and we have taken the decision to leave Edda behind. For some years now the conditions on this planet have been worsening, and life support is taking up more and more of our resources. We have located a planet that looks far more suitable to our needs, and our ships are nearly ready for departure . . .

Standing above the ladder to the control room, Penelope felt giddy and wanted to reach out and lean against a wall, in case her lack of control over her shaking limbs sent her avatar falling. She took a step back. Strangers. It was the Saga tank crew. They had gotten inside the castle! All Lord Scanthax's worst fears had been realized.

But how did she feel? Frightened? No. Then why was she trembling?

A thought that had been present since she first made out what these people were saying now blossomed in her mind like the sun rising over a mountaintop. Whether they were entities in their own right or avatars for humans, there were other people below her. Apart from variants of Lord Scanthax, these were the first people she had ever come across. And she was suddenly ashamed that she didn't know what to say to them. They sounded so confident, so familiar with each other. It was not fear that had her shaking in the dark room, unable to approach the strangers; it was shyness.

Down below, the final broadcast made by the humans who had left Edda continued. Penelope was furious with herself. Why was she hesitating? She had to go and talk to them. Wasn't this what she had wanted for all these years? But the thought of entering the room and having them turn to look at her was paralyzing. How many people were down there? What would they think of her? How should she behave?

The film was nearly over.

"Come on, come on!" Penelope whispered to herself and lowered Princess into the hole, hanging carefully onto the ladder. It wouldn't do to fall now.

By the flickering light of the film screen, she could make out four people whose full attention was fixed on the messenger speaking to them out of the past. Seated at the console was a young woman with long, curling dark hair and a curious pair of lenses balanced on her nose. Beside her, leaning on the back of the same chair, was a handsome man with very short blond hair, dressed in military clothes. Next to him was a dark-skinned girl whose brown hair was a complete mess, like it had been burned off. There was something about her pose—arms folded, shoulders relaxed—that radiated composure. On the other side of the seated woman was an extraordinarily beautiful red-haired woman wearing the most amazingly decorated leather armor and resting her hands on the pommels of a sword and a dirk that lay sheathed on either hip. The composition of the group was surprising enough, in that it contained a pirate or thief who seemed to be from Myth or Epic with three people who must have come from Saga. But it was their youth that was really unexpected. They were all teenagers, hardly older than Penelope herself.

"Hello." Her voice was dry and timid. No one heard her over the final "farewell" of the broadcast.

"Hello."

The blur of motion was astonishing. In an instant the red-haired woman drew her sword and the dark girl swung a rifle strap over her head to point the weapon at her.

"Hi," said the long-haired young woman in the chair, swiveling around. "I'm Athena. Who are you?"

"Penelope."

"Are you human or native?" asked the blond man, belatedly bringing his own rifle to bear.

"I'm human. I'm not armed, by the way." At this everyone lowered their weapons slightly. "What about you? Are you human?"

"All humans take a step forward," said Athena. She was smiling and Penelope wasn't sure if she was supposed to take a step forward. It was the red-haired pirate and the blond soldier who did so.

"Hi," said the pirate. "My name is Erik."

"Erik?"

He must have detected the note of surprise in her voice. "Ha, yeah. It's a long story, but I'm a male in charge of this female avatar, Cindella."

"And I'm Gunnar." Odd. The voice was that of a much older man than she would have expected from the avatar.

"And I'm Ghost. Us two are from Saga."

Penelope nodded. "What are you doing here?"

Ghost shrugged. "I'm updating my old-school human film collection."

Athena waved at her. "Be nice. This is serious. We're here because you are about to invade Saga and we want to stop you."

"Oh, that's not me. That's Lord Scanthax."

"Lord Scanthax." Erik spoke the name slowly, as if trying it out. "Just one person?" His avatar put her sword back in its sheath and took a seat. "Please, tell us all about Lord Scanthax."

Hesitantly at first, trying to hide how nervous she was and how anxious to win their approval, Penelope began to explain the history of Edda. They were good listeners and seemed to be sympathetic to her situation. Although it was hard to judge what they were thinking from the expressions on their avatars, both humans did at least make some effort to nod at various points.

"So, even though you helped him in the past, you don't want Lord Scanthax to attack Saga now?" Ghost looked at her with a penetrating stare.

"No. Of course not. He'll just turn it into a massive factory or farm, like he is doing to all the other worlds."

"But your life is in his hands? Your human life?" Ghost continued, as if mistrustful.

"Yes. Look!" Penelope went over to the workstation and called up the controls for her life support. "There, that's me."

"Bloody vengeance!"

"Lug-a-bug!"

"My dear girl!"

"What?" asked Penelope, suddenly ashamed and sorry she had switched on the monitor.

"You're so thin," said Athena. "Like a skeleton. You look like you are dying."

"I know, I know. I'm going to work on that once I'm free of Lord Scanthax. I'm going to build up my strength."

"But don't you feel loyal to him?" Again it was Ghost who led the questions. "Seeing as he kept you alive from when you were a baby?"

"Not really. Of course, I did for a while. I suppose . . ." Penelope looked down. "I suppose when I was little I thought he was my father. He let me be a princess here and that seemed important when I was six or seven. But I've known for several years now that he doesn't really care about me as a person at all. I'm just a useful resource that he keeps under control."

"If we fight him, which side will you be on?"

"You won't have to!" Penelope declared triumphantly, her head up again. "Tomorrow I'm going to trap him and all his manifestations in the room upstairs. I'll make him agree not to attack Saga before I release him."

"Really?" Erik sounded delighted.

"Oh yes. If all goes according to plan."

"What's your plan?" asked Athena and again they listened patiently as she explained about the redistribution ceremony and Penelope's preparations to seal up the chamber.

"That's wonderful!" exclaimed Erik. "That's perfect."

Ghost was scowling. "What? We come all this way, through all those battles; Milan dies; and it all was for nothing, because this fairy-girl is going to stop us from being attacked?"

"But we didn't know that. And now we can be on hand to help if something goes wrong."

"Hopefully nothing will." Penelope was thrilled that Erik was so pleased with her. "I've perfected a gun that will glue the secret door shut."

"I want you to shut me in the hall with him," muttered Ghost grimly.

"No. You'll try to kill him, for vengeance," said Erik.

"Too right I will."

"Better if it were me or Gunnar, because it doesn't matter if he kills us and we need to persuade him to reconsider his plans in light of the fact that everyone in Saga is sentient."

Penelope shook her head. "He has no sympathy. You have to remember where he came from. The universe for him is an arena for struggle in which there can only be one victor. His whole existence has been one long race to build up his army and conquer all other life. He's not going to change now. Not unless he is forced to."

"What do you think?" Ghost was addressing Athena.

"No offense, Penelope"—Athena tipped her head to look at Penelope from over the top of her glasses—"but before we discuss this any further, I'd like to check whether what you are saying is true. We've met so many strange and dangerous people, I can't just take your word on this. What if you just made all that up?"

"Including my body?" Penelope pointed at the screen.

"Everything. What if you're a spy or one of the people planning to attack Saga?"

"But . . ."

"I'm not saying you are; I'm just explaining why I want you to take a test."

"A test?"

"Erik, do you have that playing card? The one for truth?"

"Here. I had guessed where you were heading."

Erik passed a large card to Athena.

"All right, now tell us about you and Lord Scanthax again."

As Penelope went over her story once more, she watched Athena take the card and place it firmly on the counter, faceup. The image was of a slender human woman in white robes raising a bright orb high in her right hand; where the beams of light shone into the dark corners of the card, clouds parted, book pages fluttered, and scowling people flinched and held up their arms to block the light.

After Penelope finished speaking, the card flared bright

white and the woman in the picture smiled. Then the light faded and the card disappeared.

"I guess that means she is telling the truth, right?" Athena looked at Erik.

"I think so."

With a nod, Athena relaxed.

"Sorry about that. You can understand that we have to be sure, when our whole world is at stake."

"I understand," Penelope replied. And she did. It was a relief, too, that they all seemed to accept her now, to judge from their friendly expressions. "Was that card magic, then?"

"Yeah," answered Athena. "Cindella here is packed full of magic."

"Suppose your plan goes wrong . . ." Erik sounded as though he had been thinking about this while Penelope had been proving that she was telling the truth. "What if you aren't able to close the secret door above? They'll escape this way, right?"

"They might, yes."

"And it doesn't matter if we kill some of them?" he continued. "We won't be murdering anyone? They are all aspects of one person?"

"Yes. I mean, some of them are very distinct, very different from the others. You'd hardly think Ambassador and Executioner were the same person, but they are."

"And so long as even one manifestation lives, Lord Scanthax will live?"

"Right. All his processing power will flow to that manifestation."

"Very well," said Erik. "Then tomorrow, I'd like you to seal them all in, with me there, too."

"And what about me?" said Ghost grimly. "I'm the queen of Saga. This is my responsibility."

"Ghost. You've already said it. If you come face-to-face with the person responsible for killing Milan, you won't be able to stop yourself from destroying him in revenge."

"Is that so bad?"

The blond-haired soldier stood up from his chair at this. "It would be morally equivalent to their deeds."

"Not at all!" Athena sounded cross. "This guy is threatening to invade our world. If we kill him, that's only because a: it is forced upon us and b: we are saving millions by killing one person."

"But it's not being forced upon us." Erik spoke with a sigh. "Please, Ghost. We've come all this way with you; we've got exactly the same goal as you. Can't you respect our commitment to non-violence and try it our way?"

Penelope watched, fascinated, as they argued. She had expected Lord Scanthax's enemies to be like him: a cold, efficient military unit, with a clear chain of command. These people were, well, messy.

"All right. We'll lock you in with him. But he'll just kill Cindella, I'm sure. And if things go wrong with your plan, nothing will stop me from taking him down."

"Thank you, Ghost."

It was tempting to just stand and listen to them, to watch them interact with each other. She was learning all the time.

But Penelope had a question and broke in to raise it.

"The way you are talking, you must be powerful, right? To have come so far and to take it for granted that you could defeat about two hundred manifestations, about half of them being soldiers of some sort. Are you really so sure of yourselves?"

"It depends on their equipment and tactics." Cindella held out her hands. "Magic rings." She pointed to her boots. "Magic boots." She partly drew her swords. "Magic weapons. I've got protection against non-magical missiles, so bullets don't harm me, and I've a Bag of Dimensions that holds all sorts of potions and other magical bits and pieces."

"I see." Penelope nodded, quite prepared to believe that the magical avatar in front of her was capable of holding her own against hundreds of opponents. "Can I ask you something else? How many people are there in Saga? And how many humans on your planet?"

"About six million," said Ghost.

Gunnar spoke for the two humans. "There's just over five million of us on New Earth."

Millions. Of course. Why was she so surprised? But it was intimidating all the same. How did you make friends when there were so many people? By going to school with just a few of them, perhaps. Or by living near them. If she had grown up as a normal human, would she have lots of friends by now?

"When I've trapped Lord Scanthax and secured the sole use of these controls, will you take my avatar back with you to Saga and be my friends?" As soon as she finished speaking,

Penelope was horrified with herself. It had just jumped out, that over-needy appeal. Beneath her headset she felt a flush of embarrassment.

The silence lasted a fraction too long, before Athena spoke. "Of course."

"No—I mean, you don't have to be my friends. I'll find friends. Just help me get started there."

"How long has it been just you and Lord Scanthax here?" asked Erik kindly.

"All my life."

Gunnar drew a sharp breath, as if horrified. "And there were never any other humans to take care of you as a child?"

"No."

Wondering about the life she should have had reminded Penelope of a question that she had been meaning to ask.

"Are any of you good with computers?"

"There." Ghost pointed to Athena with an expression of pride. "She's the best."

"I'm not bad."

"I've been trying to access the films for the exodus of the humans from the colony, but they are blocked."

"Show me."

Leaning over the console, Penelope opened menus until she hit the barrier.

ACCESS TO THESE FILES REQUIRES A USERNAME AND PASSWORD.

"Hmm." Athena rummaged in her bag. "You need one of these." She clipped a small device to the keyboard wire. It had a tiny display on which letters were flitting by so fast it was impossible to read them. "There you go." Athena got out of her seat and gestured for Penelope to take her place.

"Told you!" Ghost smiled at Penelope as she sat down at the console.

The little screen had two words on it:

SCANTHAX TH3*VQO3

Penelope's hands were shaking again as she scrolled through the films that had previously been inaccessible to her. Was she about to find the real reason her parents had left her behind? Everyone looked up at the screen as the film she had chosen, *Penelope 1*, began to play.

"Aww."

A baby was on-screen, strapped into an egg-shaped carrying device.

"Hush now, Athena," said Ghost. "It's your turn to get serious."

A robot rolled swiftly into view, scooped up the carrier without a pause, and rushed on out of the shot. A different camera angle showed the robot as it rolled on down a corridor. The baby began to cry, but only for a few seconds; a needle from one of the robot's fingers jabbed into the baby's plump cheek, and almost instantly its head lolled to the side. The scene cut again to another camera, showing the robot turning abruptly into a room whose door immediately closed behind it, revealing a sign: DANGER HIGH VOLTAGE—AUTHORIZED PERSONNEL ONLY.

"Strange. What's that about?" said Athena, suddenly somber.

Now they were looking at the view from the original camera, the bare floor where the baby had been. A woman came into view, seen from above, facing away from the camera.

"Where's Penelope? Who moved Penelope?"

Her voice was angry and anxious. As the woman turned toward the camera, Penelope paused the film. There she was. Her mother. None of the others spoke as Penelope looked at the woman for a long, long time. At last, once every detail of her mother's face had impressed itself in her mind, Penelope let the film go on. It had been edited to track the woman as she ran back and forth, stopping people, becoming more and more frantic. Penelope's mother tried all the nearby rooms and even rattled the door with the high voltage warning sign. But it was locked. This painful search went on for nearly thirty minutes, with the woman in tears and several other people now helping in the search.

"Peri, look." A man showed her a screen. "Penelope's listed as being on the *Argo*."

"No. No. That can't be. The *Argo* is taking off. Call them. Tell them to stop. Tell them to wait for me!"

"I'm sorry, Peri." The man shouted after her mother as she ran down a corridor as fast as she could. "There's been some mistake. But she'll be well looked after for the journey."

To judge by the date and time in the bottom corner of the screen, the film then jumped forward four hours. All the corridors were empty. The door to the high voltage room opened and the robot rolled out, still carrying the unconscious baby. It took her down several corridors to an air lock and a room in which another robot waited. Stacked high on the shelves were packets of milk formula and baby food. Only now did the image become familiar and match the scenes Penelope had seen a hundred times before in Lord Scanthax's propaganda film. On this viewing, however, everything was a blur. Her tears had filled the headset. Her poor mother. And poor Penelope. She had not been left behind. She had been stolen from her family and friends by a monster.

"No no no." Had she spoken aloud? She had. Penelope turned her avatar around and fled. Her avatar pounded down the corridors, careless of whether anyone would hear her or not. As soon as she was back in her bed, she unclipped.

Once she became aware of her human body again, Penelope found that her feet were hammering up and down on the bed, while her arms were thrashing around at her sides. "No! No! No!" Her howls filled the small chamber. A film of sweat formed on her, but she felt cold. Anguish gripped her from head to toe. But the dominant feeling surging through her now was not misery or rage; it was shame. What must those other people think of her? How stupid of her not to have realized it all along. No one would leave a baby behind by accident. She was a fool. A stupid, stupid fool. And pathetically, she'd served her kidnapper for her whole life. Well, no longer.

Redistribution Day. Penelope had clipped up to Edda after a terrible night during which she had revisited her life in the light of the knowledge that Lord Scanthax had kidnapped her as a baby. For hours she had cried at her pitiful story, but gradually a cold resolve had crept over her. Up to this day, her life, seen properly, had been that of an exploited victim. But that was about to change, and Penelope was determined that from this day on her life would be her own.

Ever since she had come up with the plan of trapping Lord Scanthax, she had supposed that on Redistribution Day she would be a quivering and palpitating wreck, overwhelmed by anxiety and fear of failure. One of her great worries had been that she would not be able to keep herself composed enough to deal with unforeseen contingencies. Now the day had come and Penelope found no trace of anxiety in her thoughts, just a grim determination to succeed.

Her avatar dressed for the ceremony with great care and

with a deliberate pace that was driving Ambassador into a state of considerable agitation.

"Please, Princess. Lord Scanthax expects the top table to be filled by now. Please — really, what need is there to keep brushing your hair like that? It is splendid, truly splendid."

A page knocked and entered without waiting for a response.

"Lord Scanthax says to come at once; everyone is waiting."

"See, Princess. Please."

She got up without answering him. Everything was in place: her tiara, her finest corset, her three-layered skirt, the handgun strapped to her thigh. As they left the bedroom, Penelope picked up the "glue gun" she had been working on all this time.

"Princess?"

"I have good news. I have made great progress with the energy weapon. I shall give a demonstration today."

"Oh, how wonderful. Lord Scanthax will be delighted."

Ambassador was so pleased that he gave a leap of delight, an action that was quite out of keeping with his portly figure and ceremonial clothes.

Although Ambassador attempted to rush her along to the Feast Hall, Penelope would not be hurried. It was important that she arrive after all the other manifestations had entered the room.

The corridors were strange today. It was as though she were walking through them for the very first time, seeing them through the eyes of the people of Saga. What manner of creature ruled a castle such as this? Clearly, a person who had no interest in art, fashion, history, or any kind of culture; for while the rooms of the castle were full of the varied and wonderful treasures of four worlds, these splendid artifacts were stored haphazardly and remained undisturbed except for once a year, when trophies were sought for displays that reminded the lord of his conquests.

When they entered the Feast Hall, conversation ceased everywhere, and—like a herd of deer turning to investigate an unexpected sound—as one the faces of all the lesser manifestations turned toward her, with exactly the same expression on them all. Lord Scanthax, resplendent in his gleaming breastplate, stood frowning up at the top table. He gestured for them to come over.

Penelope, however, had stopped the moment she had heard the door close behind her. Swiftly, she ran the "glue gun" around the frame of the door, fusing it with the wall.

"Princess, what are you doing? The lord wants us."

She bent down and completed the circuit by moving the gun along the polished wooden floor, fastening the bottom of the door to the ground.

"There is no need for such precautions, Princess," Lord Scanthax called out. "It was the threat of bombs that was the issue."

"It isn't a precaution."

"Oh. What have you done, then?"

"What have you done?" echoed Ambassador disconsolately.

"I've sealed you into this room. All the windows and walls

are impregnable. Therefore, I've made you and your manifestations prisoners."

There were a few gasps and a certain amount of alarmed murmuring rose up among the lower-level manifestations.

"Why have you done so?"

"So as to bring about your extinction."

"Oh princess," said Ambassador and slumped to the floor, head in hands. "He's going to kill you now."

It was uncanny the way all the minor manifestations turned at once to look at Lord Scanthax while he considered Penelope's words.

"I'm disappointed. Admittedly, it has been increasingly difficult to obtain your assistance in recent times. Yet I believe you could still be of value to me. Tell me, what happened to change you from that eager girl who was so vital to my success?"

"I worked as hard as I could for you," said Penelope, "when I believed that you cared about me. But you don't have any empathy for me at all, do you?" Her voice was trembling, but her avatar remained calm.

Alert and poised for action, Assassin stood up. "My lord, this is dangerous. If she has brought a bomb here, she might be in a position to implement her threat. Switch off her life support at once and let us continue with the ceremony."

"No!" Ambassador cried out. "She still wants to help us. Don't you, Princess? It's just a human trait, for her to be so emotional as to say things she doesn't mean." He looked up pleadingly at Penelope.

"All I want is to be held by my mother," she spoke softly. "To laugh and play with my friends. To find someone to love. But I'm the loneliest human being in the universe, thanks to you. I'm light-years away from the nearest human population and as things stand, I've no idea how to find them. So I'm going to watch you die; after which, I'll have my avatar travel the four worlds until I find other humans."

After contemplating this statement for a while, Lord Scanthax shook his head. "Assassin is correct. Ambassador, you have failed us. Executioner." He turned and from the hidden alcove in the wall behind him emerged his leather-clad bodyguard, great ax in hand. "You see, Princess, you have made a great mistake by revealing your hostility toward me in this way."

While Lord Scanthax was addressing Penelope, the black-hooded Executioner made his way to the fireplace at his usual slow and foreboding pace.

"You have overlooked something very important. There is another exit from the room and Executioner will use it to reach your life-support systems and switch them off."

Leaning against the main door, Penelope said nothing.

"You have about five minutes to plead with me. But I doubt you will change my mind. I don't see it as too great a waste to eliminate you now; you were becoming less and less effective and the energy cost of keeping your human body alive was a major burden." Lord Scanthax was not gloating or being sarcastic. Penelope understood him well enough by now. From his perspective, he was simply deleting a resource that was too unstable. Executioner opened the secret door. A sharp blade struck him in the throat, and as he toppled back, dead, Cindella stepped into the room.

A swirl of consternation swept through the hall, like a whirlpool centered on Lord Scanthax. His manifestations scrambled to draw their weapons; exhibits toppled and broken glass scattered along the floor.

"Good afternoon, Lord Scanthax. I'm here to negotiate with you. Please, let's discuss our futures in a calm and reasonable fashion."

More panic, at least among the less important manifestations. The ones that mattered, however, were those surrounding Lord Scanthax: Assassin, General, Chancellor, Engineer, Scout, Admiral, Air Commander, and Quartermaster.

"Who are you?" shouted Lord Scanthax furiously.

"My name is Erik. I'm a human; this is my avatar, Cindella."

At the word "human," the room stilled. It was understandable that Lord Scanthax would dread what he could not control, and the fact that humans had access to the game menus and he did not meant that he was bound to treat an encounter with a human as a very serious matter.

"What do you want here?"

"First, I'd like Penelope at my side. Penelope, come on over here."

She didn't move.

"Penelope?"

She shook her head.

"What's the matter?"

She still did not move.

"What else do you want?" As Lord Scanthax called out his question, Penelope noticed that Assassin and Scout were edging away from the center of the room, mixing with the less self-aware manifestations.

"I want to find a means of ensuring that you will not invade Saga."

"Why?"

"Because all the inhabitants of Saga are sentient. Many of them are my friends and if you invade — judging by the other worlds we traveled through — you'll kill them all."

"I see. And what if I want to press ahead with the attack?"

"Then I'll try my best to stop you."

"By what means?"

"By means of the magic items and the skills of this avatar?"

"Oh!" Lord Scanthax laughed with relief. "Is that all?"

"Permission to shoot her?"

"Fire away, General."

The shot was loud and accurate and Cindella staggered back a pace. But then she righted herself, unharmed, and a fearful chatter broke out among some of the manifestations once more.

"It's no good. You'll find it very difficult to kill Cindella, and even if you do, there are millions of us who will help defend Saga."

"And yet" — Lord Scanthax did not sound troubled — "there is something that does not make sense here. If you really are human and represent so many, surely there must be a few of you who could rescript this world and — for example — eliminate my troops without difficulty."

"My people no longer know how to rewrite the games. Generations have passed since we had those skills."

"Well, let's test the strength of your negotiating position, shall we?"

Climbing onto the top table, Lord Scanthax shouted at the top of his voice, filling the hall with his powerful bass.

"All majors, colonels, and legates to me! Protect me! All other officers, kill her." A rush of bodies greeted the orders, some running to Lord Scanthax, others charging at Cindella. Despite the noise, General suddenly roared out, audible above the sudden racket of military boots on the wooden floor.

"We didn't storm Tharsby Pass in three days of constant fighting to die here, in our own chambers. We didn't clear our enemies from four worlds to fall to a single pirate in our midst. Don't be dismayed by what she says about being human. Kill her."

Cindella sprang with superhuman grace above the oncoming soldiers and landed on a chandelier, causing it to sway violently with the impact. Nevertheless, her agility and balance were impressive, and Penelope was pleased to see that Erik's avatar now had a bow in her hands. Soon the manifestations would start to die. This thought was confirmed by Erik's next words, called down to the soldiers thronging below Cindella.

"Well, it seems as though I will have to kill a few of you, to oblige your lord to take a more realistic view of his situation."

Erik sounded pleasant and good-humored, but all the same, his avatar began notching arrows and shooting down Ruin and Edda officers. The bullets, arrows, and daggers that were striking her in return had no effect.

"All non-combat manifestations flee, escape, hide, disperse!" yelled Lord Scanthax. "Cease fire. Cut down the chandeliers." He had come to appreciate the fact that Cindella was unaffected by their missiles.

Climbing onto a table to get a better view, Penelope looked anxiously over toward the fireplace. Good. Ghost was peering into the room from around the edge of the secret door.

A mighty crash snapped Penelope's attention to her left, where Assassin had cut through the last rope supporting the chandelier on which Cindella had been perched. The pirate must have leaped to the next chandelier, which was swinging wildly about, before it, too, fell to the ground, smashing exhibits below. Cindella had dropped her bow and now she jumped an incredible distance to land high up on a window ledge. It was a precarious position; with the lead and glass windows sealed tight, there wasn't much to hold on to, but Erik must have found the interior clasps of the windows. With the toes of Cindella's boots just gripping the narrow sills, and with one hand on the windowpane, she still had one hand free and with it drew a dagger.

Unexpectedly, there was a lull. A cluster of manifestations were huddled around Lord Scanthax near the huge table to Penelope's right. General was standing defiantly atop it, pistol in hand. The rest of the soldiers were distributed all around the hall, awaiting the next order. A dozen bodies lay on the floor, arrows in their chests, while twenty non-military manifestations were doing their best to hide among the exhibits.

"Very well," said Lord Scanthax. "Let's talk."

"Wait!" shouted Penelope. "Every word that Lord Scanthax utters is a lie. He will promise anything to escape this situation, but once free, he will continue in his plans to destroy Saga. And when that's done, he will work through robots to conquer human societies, too. He has to be destroyed now, while we have the chance."

"Princess," whispered Ambassador from the ground nearby, "what are you doing?"

"Ghost! Come into the room. Please come in! Ghost!" Penelope screamed with urgency.

Ambassador gave out a whine. "What manner of monster are you bringing against us, Princess? Stop! Do not attack us with this ghost."

All the visible manifestations were perturbed by her speech, with Lord Scanthax himself showing an expression of anxiety Penelope hadn't seen since before his conquest of Edda. By now, Lord Scanthax would have had time to appreciate the danger he was in. Assassin feared a bomb and perhaps it was a bomb of sorts that Penelope hoped to trigger. All eyes were on the fireplace. The secret door momentarily opened wide and Ghost stepped through.

Whatever Lord Scanthax had been dreading, it was not a teenage girl in scruffy clothes, with ragged clumps of hair standing up on her head. The ruler of Edda looked at Ghost for a few moments and then began to laugh. The other manifestations all joined in, until the waves of sound seemed to pulse from the walls. Even Ambassador looked a little more cheerful.

"I am Ghost, Queen of Saga." The simple words from the young girl proved to be quite a match for the sound coming from the manifestations. Somehow she had magnified her voice so that it overwhelmed their laughter. All at once the hall was silent again.

General took aim at Ghost and fired his pistol. The bullet screamed toward Ghost but, astonishingly, it slowed to a stop right in front of her head. Then it turned over in the air and, just as explosively as it had arrived, shot back across the room and into the middle of General's forehead. He toppled backward, to stretch out on the table, scattering the silverware to the floor.

"Impressive," said Lord Scanthax, as if unperturbed. But his sword was wavering. "Are you a human, too?"

"No." Ghost took another step into the room and the manifestations nearest her edged away. "I'm scripted, rather like you, but with a very important difference."

"And what might that be?"

"The people of Saga asked their human programmers to rewrite their specifications and some of them were granted their wish."

"Continue."

Ghost shrugged. "Well, what would you wish for?"

"Immortality. Invulnerability. The ability to fly. Those to begin with."

"Exactly," said Ghost and much to everyone's surprise,

including Penelope's, Ghost slowly rose up from the ground until she floated into one of the many dusty columns of light that fell across the hall from the high windows.

There were many gasps, and a whimper came from Ambassador, the one manifestation who really seemed to feel the imminence of the doom that—if Princess had judged Ghost's character correctly—now lay upon them.

"Let me hide under your dress, Princess." Ambassador was crouched in a huddle by the door.

"No."

Penelope strode quickly over to the fireplace. None of the manifestations tried to stop her. Now that Ghost was inside the room, she could seal the secret door. The cat would then be locked in with the mice.

Peeking into the room were Gunnar and Athena.

"Sorry," said Penelope. "I have to close this."

"Wait. Let me in first." Gunnar stepped through.

Athena pushed forward also. "Me, too."

"No," said Gunnar. "Remember what happened to Milan. In any case, they might need you at those controls afterward."

"It was Milan's choice to fight and it's mine, too. If I die, that's too bad. But I'm going to help Ghost."

It occurred to Penelope that if Athena were killed, any doubts Ghost might have about trying to kill Lord Scanthax would be instantly resolved. But with a shudder she rejected the thought. That heartless calculation was a residual expression of having grown up with only a cold and inhuman warlord for company. "Help me, Gunnar."

The two of them pushed Athena back, until the door shut with a click, leaving Athena on the far side, pounding upon it and demanding to be let through. It only took Penelope a few seconds to run her "glue gun" around the frame, and then the door was fused with the stone.

While this scuffle at the secret door was taking place, Lord Scanthax had continued to address Ghost. Penelope turned to catch up with their conversation.

"And what do you want?" asked Lord Scanthax. "The same as your ally?"

"Not quite."

"Explain, then."

"Your soldiers killed my friend."

"Did they?" Lord Scanthax sounded indifferent, as well he might be. His soldiers had killed a great many people.

"They did. And so I'm going to kill you."

These words, spoken in a cold, matter-of-fact tone, sent shivers of delight down Penelope's spine and she felt an incredible surge of admiration and affection for Ghost.

"No, Ghost. You're not like him; you can find another way!" Cindella shouted from her position high up the wall.

"Sorry, Erik."

And the killing began.

Dropping to the ground, Ghost fired her two pistols into the nearest manifestations at point-blank range. The ammunition must have been explosive, to judge by the way the bodies of those who had been shot were flung around the room.

Beside Penelope, Gunnar steadied his pistol in two hands

and began to fire also. Penelope edged away from the blond young soldier of Saga, toward the corner of the room, not wanting to get caught up in the fighting and lose her avatar. Although she could very quickly create a new avatar and run back, she would be shut out from the hall and scripting an entrance would have to be done very carefully so as not to give Lord Scanthax an escape route.

The lesser manifestations fled if they were civilians or fired back at Ghost and Gunnar if they were officers. While the missiles flowed around Ghost like water against the prow of a ship, a combination of bullets and arrows tore into Gunnar's avatar, causing him to stagger back against the fireplace wall.

"Sorry, Ghost, for everything," he called out. "I wish I could have helped you more."

Another flurry of bullets struck the young trooper and Gunnar was gone.

Of the remaining senior manifestations, Engineer had fled to the back of the room; Quartermaster was crouched behind an overturned table, a bundle of accounts tight in his fist; Chancellor was trying to roll himself into a carpet; Admiral and two captains were shooting their rifles at Ghost; Air Commander was organizing a small group of officers to try firing at the windows to break them, though their bullets were simply flying off randomly; Assassin seemed to have disappeared, which was worrying; but of more immediate concern was the fact that Scout, arm still in a sling, was walking straight toward Penelope.

"You!" she said furiously. "You are to blame for this. Traitor!

It might only delay you while you create a new avatar, but perhaps it will gain us enough time to turn you off. We should have done so months ago." And she drew her sword.

As Scout was approaching, Penelope had prepared the slit in her skirts, through which she now pulled out her pistol. "You've left it too late."

Although Scout's lunge nearly reached her, Penelope's shot brought Scout crashing down with a hole in her thigh. When a second shot hit her neck, Scout ceased writhing. Penelope drew a deep breath. Her shaking hands had nearly caused her to miss.

Looking up, Penelope was alarmed to see that the battle had taken a dramatic turn for the worse. Having killed perhaps half of the manifestations, Ghost's pistols had run out of power. Now the soldiers could close in on her and although Ghost was deftly wielding two army knives, she was vulnerable to the sword thrusts of her enemies, as was clear from a dark bloodstain on her left arm and another across her ribs.

A horrible, sickening fear welled up in Penelope's human body; she could taste it. It was the taste of failure. Granted, whatever the outcome of the battle, Lord Scanthax would still be contained in this room for some time. But Ghost was going to die.

With a crash and a flash of her blades, Cindella landed in front of Ghost, scattering manifestations with swift cuts and lethal stabs.

"Have at them, you cowards!" shouted Lord Scanthax from

across the hall. Penelope stared at him with hatred. "We're winning!"

All of the soldiers surged forward again as one.

"Get behind me, Ghost!" cried Erik urgently. "Back-to-back."

It was hard to follow the fight now, with the manifestations crowding so closely around Ghost and Cindella. But Penelope could see the red-haired avatar weaving and ducking; presumably, Ghost was fighting just as hard, since Cindella would not have lasted long on her own, so they were both still going.

Above the clashing of swords and scuffling of feet, she heard Erik calling out numbers to Ghost.

"Eighty-seven. Seventy-five. Sixty-five."

It dawned on Penelope that this must have something to do with Cindella's remaining strength. And if so, the rate of decline was ominous.

"Fifty-four. Forty-eight. Forty-two."

Yet the soldiers were distinctly fewer in number than they had been. The glittering swords of the pirate were taking a terrible toll on her enemies, adding to the pile of bodies with almost every cut.

"Thirty-six. Twenty-nine."

It was going to be close. Penelope risked opening fire on the soldiers with her pistol, starting with Air Commander, the only senior military figure she could see; if this attracted return fire in response, it couldn't be helped. The death of her avatar was far less important than Ghost's life.

Chapter 31
A Death Foretold

When the momentum of the battle began to swing against Ghost, Erik cast aside all reservations and, with fear for his friend filling his body with adrenaline, hurled Cindella into the fray. With the Rapier of the Skies in her right hand and the Dagger of Frozen Hate in her left, his avatar had come crashing down on the backs of Lord Scanthax's soldiers, bringing down Ghost's immediate assailants and causing the rest to hesitate.

But although he wanted to draw away as many attackers from Ghost as he could, Cindella could barely cope with the thrusting of swords and spears that now came her way. His avatar was designed for outmaneuvering enemies, not for standing in place and fighting them. And Cindella was taking damage fast.

Erik called out his readings of Cindella's life bar so that Ghost would understand the situation. His friend just grunted in response and a quick head snap in her direction showed Ghost's blades parrying and stabbing at a phenomenal rate.

"Twenty-nine. Twenty-one. Nineteen. Thirteen."

When he first played Epic, Erik had lost dozens of avatars. And they died in just this way: a remorseless decline in their life bars, with Erik having no tricks up his sleeve to restore their health. At least the rate of damage was slowing, due to the fact that the incoming soldiers now had to climb over piles of bodies or pause for a moment to pull them aside.

"Fourteen." Cindella was wearing a ring of regeneration; its effect was too slow to allow her to last long in this kind of combat, but every little bit helped. That gave him an idea.

"Lord Scanthax!" cried Erik. "Let's negotiate!"

"How often I've heard that plea. And always when my enemies are desperate. Keep at them!" And a mocking laugh accompanied the shout.

"What are you going to do when I die?" Erik directed his gasping voice toward Ghost while deflecting a bayonet with his rapier, ducking beneath a pike thrust, and cutting off a legionnaire's leg at the knee.

"I'll try to get up in the air again, get my back to the wall." The reply came from behind him, with barely a shake in her voice.

"Eleven. Maybe you should try that now."

"Keep going. We're thinning them out."

"Eight. Don't die, Ghost. Stay alive. We'll think of something. Even if the whole of New Earth has to make avatars, we'll come back here for you. Just don't die."

"I won't be able to stay up anywhere near that long. Thanks, Erik, but it's kill or be killed now."

"Nine." There had been a brief lull while dead manifestations were dragged away to make room for a renewed assault. Only thirty or so attackers were left, a mix of medieval swordsmen and modern soldiers.

In the pause before the new onslaught, Erik caught sight of something moving slowly at Cindella's feet. He glanced down. It was a dark pool spreading outward, looking a lot like blood. But Cindella didn't bleed; hits on her registered as a dip in her life bar. Nor did Lord Scanthax's manifestations; they just collapsed after sustaining critical amounts of damage. Dread almost prevented him from turning Cindella's head.

"Oh Ghost."

Her clothes were soaked in her own blood. It was pitiful to see the cotton sleeves of her punk-band top dripping red. And her combat trousers had huge tears in them, from which hung long soaked patches of material.

"I'm all right. No important organs hit. Fight! Turn around! Here they come!"

With renewed urgency Cindella lashed out, to stab at figures on either side of her that might be targeting Ghost, careless of her own defenses.

"Six." It was going to be close, but tragically, they were going to die, Ghost forever.

A modern-looking soldier twisted away from her, shot in the ribs, his cap flying. Then a legionnaire fell, a dark hole in the plate armor that covered his thigh. All at once there were large gaps between the remaining attackers. Someone was shooting at them. When the opportunity came, Erik glanced around. It was Penelope, who had edged forward from the corner of the room, holding a revolver in both hands that she must have hidden earlier or picked up from a fallen soldier.

"Three." But Erik felt a wave of joy as the last knight collapsed, the Dagger of Frozen Hate having found the gap in his chain mail at the armpit.

It was suddenly much less noisy and chaotic in the hall. Not that everything was still. There were all the non-combat manifestations of Lord Scanthax watching or cowering behind chairs and tables. Then there was a group of four who, under the direction of a figure in an admiral's uniform, were swinging a bench into the secret door in the fireplace, hoping to smash it down.

"Penelope! Quick, come here!" Erik cried.

As soon as the princess joined them, Cindella began cutting great swathes of purple silk from Penelope's skirt.

"Here, help me bind up Ghost's wounds."

With barely a wince, Ghost tolerated them gripping at her torn flesh and wrapping her limbs tight. All the while, she was staring at the far end of the room. Erik, too, constantly checked in case Lord Scanthax chose to attack them with the last two bodyguards. They were on their feet up at the top table: a rotund man clutching a sheaf of papers and a small man with a tool belt. Neither of them had any weapons. Perhaps Lord Scanthax's strange passivity was simply due to the fact that with the exception of the admiral his remaining manifestations were civilians. Perhaps also the victory of Ghost and Cindella—and Penelope—against such odds had come as a surprise.

"Done." Penelope stood up and once more drew her revolver. Now that her skirt, too, was in tatters, Erik could see the hidden holster on the thigh of the princess.

"Got some water, Erik?" Ghost's voice was barely a whisper and she winced with the effort of speaking. It can't have helped that they had tied bandages tight around her abdomen to cover a wound to her ribs.

Quickly rummaging through Cindella's Bag of Dimensions, Erik drew out her magical drinking vessel.

"Silver goblet, after the slaughter, fill yourself with the purest water."

Ghost took the goblet and drank from it greedily, spilling water down her shirt and over her hands, where it turned her dried blood pink and washed it away.

The sound of gunfire led Erik to look away from the pitiful condition of his friend. Penelope had walked quickly over to the fireplace and put a bullet into each of Admiral's men and Admiral himself before they could drop their improvised battering ram and draw their own weapons.

"That's it!" she shouted back toward Ghost and Cindella with a note of triumph. "There's just Assassin left. The rest of these manifestations are non-combatants!" And she began shooting at the nearest figures that were in sight. When they were dead, she stalked the civilian manifestations that had

fled behind furniture. An inventive richly clad servant had rolled himself up in a carpet, but with a series of kicks, the princess caused the carpet to unfurl and spill out a dismayed figure whose efforts to ward off the shot were in vain. Penelope fired straight into his heart.

A scribe was feigning death underneath a fallen chandelier and she shot him through the back of the head. The outlines of two figures were bulging out from underneath a wall tapestry. Two quick shots and the bodies of a blacksmith and another craftsman slid out to the floor.

"Princess! Princess, what are you doing?" cried the man who had escorted Penelope into the room, still cowering by the door.

A giant china vase, fabulously crafted, concealed a medic of some sort. It took all of Penelope's strength to tip it over and although Erik thought about helping her, he didn't want to leave Ghost's side — not while there was an assassin about. Nor was he sure about Penelope's actions. She had changed the plan and drawn Ghost into the room before sealing it. Perhaps her aim now was to kill all the manifestations and Lord Scanthax himself. After all, she had been shocked by the revelation of her kidnapping. Was she also filled with a murderous desire for vengeance?

Slowly, the vase tipped over and crashed to the ground; the doctor didn't even try to wriggle away from the shards of pottery in which he lay, but just looked up at the princess. She shot him in the head. The other civilians, seeing there was no hiding from her, ran to the top table to stand quivering beside their master. Lord Scanthax, however, said nothing as Penelope marched toward him.

"Are you ready to negotiate now?" shouted Erik toward the top table.

"Don't let up!" Penelope looked back at Cindella, sounding furious. "We have him. Just think — if even one escapes, all those millions of troops will be under his control again. Think what it will mean for Saga if you relent." Penelope looked across to Ghost to check that she had heard. Ghost nodded in response.

Penelope raised her revolver again. A shot rang out and one of Lord Scanthax's remaining servants spun to the ground.

"It was an honor," he managed to gasp, facing his lord before expiring.

Another. And another. Shot after careful shot ringing out across the debris of the feast, followed by a crash as each body fell to the floor. One by one, they stood in front of Lord Scanthax, until only four figures remained. These, too, interposed themselves between the remorseless figure of Penelope and their master. The rotund man fell heavily, scattering the papers he had been holding across the floor. The last manifestation, some kind of mason, whimpered as his turn came. Then there was silence.

"Well, Princess." Lord Scanthax sounded defiant still. "What is it you want? Ambassador, you are still alive. Go talk to her."

Looking startled at first, the crumpled figure at the main door stood up. He brushed down his gown as he gathered his wits, then began to walk toward Penelope.

"Stop right there." Penelope pointed the pistol at him. "Assassin is still alive, hiding somewhere. Reveal him and I might allow Ambassador to speak."

The ambassador stopped and waited. Everyone waited.

Suddenly, a flash at the edge of his vision caused Erik to turn. It was a powerful-looking man in leather armor, with an ornate dagger that shone with a ruby light raised in his right arm. The assassin had crept within striking distance of Ghost and Cindella without being seen. How was that possible? Could he have hidden among the bodies of the dead? Now he made a leap for Ghost, stabbing downward with the glowing dagger as he did so.

"No!" cried Erik, knowing that Cindella's move to block the assassin was too late and that Ghost's wounds made her too slow to avoid the blow.

Ghost staggered back. The ornate blade was buried up to its hilt in her chest.

"Oh no! Ghost!"

They locked eyes, Erik fully convinced that this was the last look he would ever share with the young woman who, despite her being light-years away and formed of a completely different physiology, was as dear to him as any of his friends on New Earth. Then Ghost looked at the hilt of the dagger and back at Erik again before bursting into wild laughter. On the ground in front of her was the body of Assassin. Without even a wince, Ghost pulled the shining weapon free.

"It's that cursed knife, remember? From the pool in Myth. Jodocus told us about it. It harms the attacker, not the victim.

And I bet that assassin is wearing the cursed ring of invisibility, too."

Cindella wrapped her arms around Ghost. "I thought you were dead." Erik's heart was still pounding, and he could feel his human body shaking.

"That settles everything," said Penelope grimly. Walking toward Lord Scanthax, she pointed the pistol at his face. "You soulless monster. You destroyer of entire worlds. You have no idea how much I hate you."

Lord Scanthax shook his head. "I suppose not. I never hated my enemies. Feared them, felt anger, yes. But hate? Probably not."

"I don't hate you as my enemy. I hate you for your cruelty; for the childhood you took from me and twisted around to make me think I was needed and cherished. I was just a tool for you. A human child yearns for someone to love. I gave that love to you and you neither noticed nor cared."

They stood looking at each other, only a few feet apart. Then Penelope controlled her shaking hand, and fired. The impact lifted him off his feet and Lord Scanthax's metal breast-plate hit the ground and rang out with the mournful toll of an ancient bell.

For a moment Penelope stood over the fallen body. What was she thinking? This poor girl who throughout her childhood had had only the creature she had just slain for company. Crack! Another bullet was fired into the body. And another. And she kept on firing, as fast as her gun was able to reload.

At last Penelope turned to Ambassador. He had been

looking on with amazement, but now something in his expression changed. His dull resignation began to lift and a powerful intelligence studied the room from the depths of his eyes.

"I . . . I am Lord Scanthax."

"Yes," said Penelope, coming closer. Gently, Cindella let go of Ghost and began to walk across the bodies to get nearer to the ambassador.

"Well . . ." The last manifestation of Lord Scanthax took careful stock of everyone in the room. "You have me at a distinct disadvantage. What are your terms?" The smile that he offered them was warm and conciliatory and he was careful to make eye contact with everyone.

"There's no need to point your guns at me; I'm not dangerous," he continued, looking back past Cindella.

Cindella turned. Ghost had picked up a rifle and was aiming it at the ambassador.

"Wait. Queen of Saga, didn't you want to negotiate?" asked the ambassador, looking worried now.

"No! Ghost, no!" Erik called out passionately. He looked to Penelope for support, but she had raised her revolver.

"Stop! Both of you, lower your weapons! We can solve this without killing him."

"Please listen to this person, this human. I'm not the Lord Scanthax who conquered Edda and three other worlds. I've no desire to harm anyone in Saga. And as for our princess, I've devoted my life to her and will do whatever I can to assist her as she reintegrates with human communities."

The shot rang out like a scream of anguish.

Chapter 32
UNDERSTANDING

Cindella was standing alongside Ghost and Penelope, looking out past the wall-length windows of one of the great tower blocks of Saga. They were so high up that they could gaze down upon a pair of falcons, which in turn were gliding far above the streets of the city.

"It's incredible. So much life, and all of it unique." Penelope gestured beyond the window to the busy city that stretched out before them. "I mean, I'd seen huge armies before now. But they were just robotic units. You have millions of people going about their lives down there, and every one of them is someone I could get to know, someone I could become friends with."

"And there's us, too," said Erik. "You're going to be seeing a lot more people from New Earth clipping up to Saga now that our council has decided to encourage stronger links between our two worlds."

"That's wonderful. And so are you, Ghost, for sending a rocket for me."

Ghost turned from the window. "It's nothing, really. I haven't got any better use for them. The Dark Queen had a wild scheme to use them to disperse her offspring throughout the universe. And at one stage I thought I might try uploading myself into one and traveling that way. But these new electronic worlds suit me much better. Anyway"—Ghost moved to a couch and took a seat—"it will take about seven years to get to you and, if we haven't contacted your humans by then, another fifteen to get to New Earth. You'll be what? Forty, by the time you get to see each other in the flesh, so to speak?"

"Thirty-eight," Penelope corrected her in a low voice. "In any case, I can still enjoy all this while I travel."

"True," said Erik. "And I think there's a good chance we'll make contact with the people who left your base before too long. If I were them, I'd be discreetly monitoring Edda in case of future problems. And once they see the armies have gone, or come across one of the message beacons we are installing, they'll get in touch. You'll see. You'll be talking to your mother long before the rocket arrives. And then you can go meet her."

"I daren't hope for that. Just being here, among other people, is enough."

"Well, the people of New Earth are hoping for that. You should see Gunnar's postings, Ghost. He's changed completely and is all for us racing through the different worlds leaving messages everywhere until we find our lost human colonies."

Ghost smiled at this. "I think he came to like us in the end."

"No kidding. He thinks the world of you and never stops talking about Athena, either."

"How's your body doing?" asked Ghost, looking at Penelope.

"Oh, it's slow and painful progress. Especially when there's so much to see here. Tonight, Athena is taking me to see a band. I forget what they are called. I'm really looking forward to it, though."

"No Phuture, with a *P-h* instead of an *F*. That's our friend's band. I don't know if you'll like them; it's an acquired taste." There was an unrolled computer screen on the seat beside Ghost, and she tapped it a few times before looking back up. "In any case, take your time. You have years to build yourself up. Just keep at it, bit by bit."

"Oh, I know. I'll be fit and healthy long before the spaceship arrives, don't worry."

With a nod of encouragement, Ghost turned her attention to Cindella. "What about you, Erik? What are you going to do now?"

"The council has asked me to be New Earth's ambassador to Saga. But I don't know. I feel I ought to finish my studies and have some practical skills for our society. You know what a grind everything is; it's going to take years to get our technology moving forward again."

"Well, while I was away, the people of Saga learned that they can do without me." Ghost could not hide the note of delight in her voice. "So I'm going to explore those new worlds we found. There's still a great deal to investigate, despite the attempt by Lord Scanthax to reduce them to lifeless factories. You could bring Cindella along if you want."

"Really?" Cindella came over to the couch and looked

down at Ghost. "I thought you wanted to travel alone."

"Well, I've gotten used to traveling with Cindella. She's useful, handy if I run into a problem."

"So, it's my magic items you want, not my company?" Erik chuckled.

"I don't see you finding a problem you couldn't get out of," interjected Penelope admiringly.

"I would have been killed by the assassin, remember, if he hadn't been using that cursed knife."

"The thing is, Ghost, I consider you my comrade, and I'll always fight for you if you need me. But they need me at home, too. Well, Inny wants me to go on a survey trip with her, and I'm looking forward to it. I need time back in the real world."

"I understand. Perhaps next year, or whenever you are in the mood to have a run around with Cindella. I'll be reachable by radio in whatever world I end up in." A moment later, Ghost looked up at him, a hint of doubt in her eyes. "Your decision isn't based on the death of Lord Scanthax, is it?"

Penelope turned around, too, perhaps sensing that the relaxed atmosphere of their earlier conversation had gone. She was watching the two of them closely.

Erik let out a sigh. "Well, tell me, were you going to shoot him?"

Ghost paused before answering. "I was thinking that the only guarantee of safety for everyone back in Saga was to kill him, and I also thought about Milan, which caused me to begin squeezing the trigger. But then I hesitated. I didn't want to lose your friendship. So the honest answer is, I don't know."

"Well, don't worry; you'll never lose my friendship. Remember when you held off Jodocus's elementals and were fighting as hard as you could for the life of Athena? I'd have given anything right then to save you. Jodocus wanted me to believe that humanity could only survive by killing you and all EIs, but he achieved the opposite of what he intended: in that moment, I realized I cared more for you than for some abstract loyalty to my species. It seemed to me that if the only way humanity could survive into the distant future was through your destruction, then we deserved to die out. I still feel that. There is something in you that transcends the difference between human and EI. It's like having a tiger for a friend. There's no one I'd rather have at my side in battle. It's just that . . . I've people I love on New Earth and I need to be with them for a while now."

"Thanks, Erik. And I understand. But don't forget me. And don't forget what we have in common. I believe I understand you better than anyone else I know, EI or human. And that you are my comrade, in the same way that Milan was. Like him, you didn't waver for an instant and that means a lot to me."

"I feel the same way." Erik replied.

"And what about you, Penelope?" Ghost rolled up her computer and put it in her satchel. "Do you think you'll fit in with Erik's people and their renunciation of violence? Or did you enjoy that final moment with Lord Scanthax? Did you feel avenged when you pulled the trigger?"

"Enjoy?" Penelope sounded surprised. "No. Not really. I

felt it was justice, for what had been done to me. But I'm not a monster. I wouldn't go looking for that feeling again."

"Good," said Erik emphatically, "because if you do end up on New Earth, you'll have to get used to our laws. In fact, some people—a minority—wouldn't welcome you even now; they'd consider you a murderer. But Gunnar and I have explained what happened to you and how you've had no other role models in your life than Lord Scanthax."

For a while Penelope said nothing, turning back to the window and looking at the city below, teeming with life. Erik exchanged a glance with Ghost, who picked up her airboard and moved toward the door.

"I know you want me to feel ashamed," said Penelope at last, "but I'm not. I still feel amazed that I actually managed to get the better of him and free myself. Even now, I wake up with nightmares, thinking that he's watching me through the eyes of the robots."

"I don't want you to feel ashamed. No. I think it's incredible how well you've coped with what happened to you. But . . . well . . . I'm not really in a position to judge, but don't you think Lord Scanthax changed at the end there? That his final manifestation, the ambassador, represented a better and more sympathetic part of his character?"

"No, I don't. You don't understand what he was like. That was all lies at the end. He was attempting to deceive us to buy time for himself."

"Then couldn't we have rendered him harmless somehow?"

"Temporarily, perhaps." Penelope turned around and

shrugged. "But I couldn't live with the thought that he was still out there, attempting to escape; that at any moment while I was in the electronic worlds, he could seize control of my body again and kill me."

Often Erik had tried to imagine what it must have been like for Penelope to have grown up believing that her captor was her savior, and although he was certain that it had been a mistake to kill another sentient being, even one as cold as Lord Scanthax, he genuinely did admire the fact that she had the determination to survive such an ordeal.

To show he was not condemning her, Cindella walked across the room and gave Penelope a hug.

Over by the door, Ghost raised her airboard by way of a challenge. "Come on, you two, while we're all still around. Let's race, freestyle. Or are my skills too good for you?"

Now Erik laughed. "Bring it on!"

The tension that had been building up in him during the conversation melted away. When Lord Scanthax had fallen lifeless to the ground and the echoes of the shot that had killed him had ceased, Erik had been shocked to see Penelope holding the weapon that had fired the lethal bullet. Immediately afterward, feeling betrayed and manipulated, he had unclipped in a sweat, thinking that it would be impossible for her to ever fit in with the people of New Earth. But he understood Penelope, he really did. They would still be friends.

A week later, Erik was lying beside Inny, the two of them looking up at the stars from their camp in the mountains to the east of Hope. As he picked out the constellations, Erik's thoughts turned to Penelope.

"She's out there, orbiting one of those stars, the only human in her solar system."

"Penelope? It's hard to imagine, isn't it? But she says she's delighted with all the new friends she has made in Saga, and the parties, the bands, the dancing."

"I know." Erik snuggled closer to Inny, feeling the warmth of her body against his side. "But she can't have this. Not for years, at least."

"It's surprising how well she's turned out, really—given she didn't have a mother or father, or anyone in her life to love her."

Erik said nothing.

"What?" asked Inny.

"Penelope went into that battle with Lord Scanthax knowing exactly what she wanted, which was to kill him. She used me, and she was willing to risk Ghost's life in order to achieve that goal. Penelope's been damaged by the whole experience of growing up with Lord Scanthax. It will take her a long time to learn that not everyone is out for themselves; for her to trust that her new friends won't abandon her."

Inny said nothing for a while as they watched a shooting star flash overhead. "It must have been hard on you," she said at last.

Surprised by the shift in the conversation, Erik turned to look at her.

"I mean, seeing Milan die. Seeing Ghost heavily wounded."

"That was terrible. And so was seeing Count Illystivostich again, crawling after us, so desperate for blood that he risked crossing a portal. And Jodocus, betraying us, trying to kill Ghost."

"We had no idea what going through that portal would lead to."

"None at all."

"I'm sorry I wasn't with you for any of that. Strange isn't it? That we were so close physically, but in our heads, we were in completely different worlds."

Erik thought about this. "Isn't life always like that, even now?"

"How do you mean?"

"Well, we share this moment, our bodies side by side. But we're alone in the way our minds work, in the way we understand the moment."

"Oh, Erik." Inny pushed herself up to look into his eyes. "That sounds sad."

"Not really. Because I know you so well, you're deep in my mind. Often, during those adventures I thought of you and I knew what you would advise. And much more than that, you're not just in my mind. You're in my heart."

ABOUT THE AUTHOR

Conor Kostick was a designer for the world's first live fantasy role-playing game (Treasure Trap), based in Peckforton Castle, Cheshire, England. He lives in Dublin, Ireland, where, having completed a PhD on the subject of the crusades, he now teaches medieval history at Trinity College Dublin. In 2009 the Reading Association of Ireland gave Conor their Special Merit Award for his fiction, and in 2010 he was awarded the writer's residency at Farmleigh, the official Irish State Guest House.

Conor's history books include *The Siege of Jerusalem* and, as co-author, *The Easter Rising: A Guide to Dublin in 1916*. His fiction includes *Epic* and *Saga* (the prequels to *Edda*) and *Move*.